DEATH AT THE DUOMO

ALSO BY ANN REAVIS

Italian Food Rules

Italian Life Rules

Cats of Italy

Murder at Mountain Vista

The Case of the Pilfered Pills

DEATH AT THE DUOMO

A Caterina Falcone Mystery

By
Ann Reavis

DEATH AT THE DUOMO

Published by: Caldera Books

This is a work of fiction, Names, characters, organizations, places, events, and incidents are either product's of the author's imagination or are used fictitiously.

ISBN-13: 978-1530842902
ISBN-10: 1530842905

Cover by Kelly Crimi
Interior book design by Bob Houston eBook Formatting

Email: calderabooks@gmail.com

Secon Edition (January 2, 2017)

For Pauline Kenny and Steve Cohen
for their unwavering support and care.

PROLOGUE

He may have been killed when the force of the blast threw his body against the marble façade of the cathedral. He was certainly dead seconds later when the marble statue of San Antoninus crashed down from twenty feet above; its landing cushioned only by his corpse.

Bill Barton was thinking of sex just moments before the towering Florentine Easter cart, *Carro di Pasqua*, exploded in front of him.

An hour earlier in bed, he was dreaming that his face was pillowed between two firm breasts, when the woman of that bosom woke him by yanking the silky royal blue duvet off his naked body. At the same time the bronze bell of the cathedral struck the hour of ten. The woman flung open the window, seemingly transporting them directly into Giotto's bell tower.

"*Amore, siamo troppo in ritardo. Alzati!*" she yelled over the clamor.

Bill grabbed her arm, pulling her, dressed in a black satin pushup bra and matching panties, to sprawl across his body. He murmured in her ear, "Sweetie, we won't be late. It's only ten. Come back to bed. I have a surprise for you."

"I got your *sorpresa* many times last night. Even if it is one of my favorite things, I want to see the *festa* now." She pushed off his chest, scrambling to stand by the bed, clenched fists on curvaceous hips. "You promised."

"I know, I know, but we have at least thirty minutes." He levered up to sit on the side of the bed, pulling her between his bare legs into the circle of his tanned arms. Standing, she only topped him by an inch, her dark eyes even with his blond-lashed blue ones. He took her earlobe between his teeth. "Come on, Irene. I'm ready."

"*Beel, amore,* you are ready always." She feathered a kiss across his cheek to his mouth, while pulling his hand up to cup her left breast.

He shifted to get better access with both hands, freeing her. She straight-armed him, stepping back out of reach.

"*Festa* first, then lovemaking," she said, picking up a crumpled pair of artfully distressed Dolce & Gabbana jeans off the floor. With much tugging and twisting they created a second skin from her narrow ankles to just below her gold-pierced navel.

Bill watched her gyrations. "Those jeans were certainly worth the price." He stood on the cold, terracotta floor, coming up behind her to slide his hands around her bare waist, pulling her back against him.

She turned in his arms and placed another tiny kiss at the corner of his mouth. "They are my gift most favorite from you."

"There will be more. My father says, 'Gifts for beautiful women are always a good investment.' Honey, you certainly paid out double dividends last night." He traced the arch of her left eyebrow with his tongue while squeezing her hips with both hands before stepping into the bathroom, leaving the door open. "To think just a year ago I was a pudgy frosh who couldn't get a date."

"What is a frosh?" Irene asked, buttoning up a shimmery red rayon blouse.

He came back into the room, rubbing a towel over the blond stubble on his cheeks. "What was that? I couldn't hear you over the water." He threw the damp terrycloth on the bed, ran both hands through his short flaxen curls; then, plucked a pair of briefs off the top of the dresser, sniffed them and put them on.

"Frosh – I don't know that word." She handed him a pair of chinos she picked off the floor beside the window.

"A freshman – a first year student at a university."

"You were a fat frosh?" she giggled.

"Clever girl," he said, shaking out the slacks to remove some of the wrinkles. "Yeah, it's amazing what a late growth spurt and a year in the gym will do. I was one of those kids only a mother could love."

"Your mother – she is beautiful?" She dug in her knock-off Louis Vuitton bag, pulling out a hair-matted brush.

Bill paused in the act of zipping up. "To me, always. My mom's the best. I'll be calling her in California tonight. She'll like the fact that I did something cultural this morning."

"And your father. I thought he lived in Boston."

"He does. They've been divorced for most of my life. To my father, my mother was his surfer girl – his first wife. He's since moved on to a proper Bostonian, whom he didn't marry, and then a Parisian artist. He married her and had two more kids. The last wife was a Japanese girl from New York, who divorced him a couple of months ago." He opened the middle dresser drawer and took out a folded, chocolate-brown cashmere sweater encased in a dry cleaner's plastic bag.

Irene turned, the brush mid-stroke through her long brown hair, "That many wives?"

"My father has a short attention span. He travels a lot for business and he picks up new women along the way. He seems to have the need to marry them. I expect the next one will be Italian or Jamaican."

"Why?"

"Because he's developing resorts in both countries. Where are my shoes?"

"Under the bed," she said, sliding her crimson-nailed toes into a scuffed pair of stilettos.

He squatted near the bedside nightstand and pulled out a pair of kidskin loafers. He slipped them on his bare feet and scooped up his Rolex and wallet.

"Is that why you are in Firenze – the business of your father?"

"Sort of. I came on the semester abroad program at UCLA. My father wants me to pick up the lingo, so I can work with him this summer in Forte de Marmi and Sardinia."

"What is 'lingo'?"

"You know, lingo, language, like, *dove é la mia giacca?*"

"Okay, I'll pick it up on our way out. You ready?"

"Yes, I just need my purse." She plucked the bag off the bed, replaced the hairbrush and searched inside, pulling out a red cell phone. "Have you seen my other *telefonino?*"

"The silver one is in the bathroom on the shelf," he said. He picked up a BlackBerry from the dresser and clipped it to his belt loop. "Why do you need two cell phones?"

She came out of the bathroom, walked up to him and slid her arms around his neck. "The silver one is just to call you. The red one is for everybody else."

He kissed her hard. "Hey, like, I've never had anyone dedicate a phone to me." Keeping his arm around her shoulders, he propelled her to the door. "Let's go. The sooner we get there, the sooner we can come back to bed."

They descended a stairway into the large living room furnished with a mix of authentic eighteenth-century furniture (an ornate dining room table and chairs and an inlaid wood desk), a smattering of Renaissance reproductions (a wedding chest painted with a scene of the Arno and the Ponte Vecchio, a stiff high-back divan and matching chair covered in heavy emerald silk embossed with the Medici coat of arms), and portraits of someone's ancestors framed in baroque, gold-leafed splendor.

Bill found his black leather jacket and sunglasses on the dinner table. As he rummaged through the pockets for his apartment keys, he said, "I still love this jacket. I thought I was just buying it because it was the most expensive and you would get a good commission, but you were right – I look *bello* in it. It makes me look Italian."

His girlfriend laughed as she walked through the door he held open. "Yes, you look *bello*, but with that blond hair and blue eyes you will never look …"

Irene broke off when she saw that they were not alone. An elderly lady, dressed in a pastel, blue and yellow knit, Chanel suit, with a beige handbag on her left arm and matching leather pumps, stood in front of the elevator door.

"*Buongiorno, Contessa*," Bill said, holding out his hand.

"Good morning, William." The woman extended her fingers so that he could only clasp the tips. Her accent was British, but her profile was proof of centuries of Italian forbearers, some of whom could be seen on the walls in Bill's apartment. The slight smile she bestowed on Bill faded as she turned to the woman beside him, scanning her from head to toe with sharp brown eyes.

The younger woman glowered back and pulled him toward the stairs. "Let's take the *scale*," she said.

"Okay." He followed her. "Have a good day, Contessa," he called over his shoulder.

"Thank you, William."

"Is there some problem between you and the contessa?" Bill asked on the way down.

"*É una stronza*. She pays too much time to us."

He chuckled. "You mean she's nosy?"

"Yes, she has her nose in our lives."

"Well, we do share the top floor."

She stopped and turned on the first floor landing, lit by a dim bulb – the bud in a leafy iron wall sconce. "But she asks me many questions yesterday that are not her business." Without waiting for a response she ran down the last two flights of gray stone stairs.

He caught up with her on the last step and slipped his arm around her shoulders. They entered the vaulted entry hall. The elevator, cut into the original stairwell, was rattling down. He pulled open the metal-studded wood palazzo door and they turned left toward the front of Florence's Duomo.

"What'd she want to know?" Bill asked, sliding his sunglasses on against the glare of the sun bouncing off the marble walls of the cathedral.

"About where I was from and where I worked."

Bill let go of her shoulder to dodge around a street artist setting up his easel. The area between the palazzo and the cathedral was a river of humanity banked by portrait artists seated on metal stools, ready to sketch the child of a doting mother or the girlfriend of an enamored swain: the sketchers vying for space with tiny-wheeled trailers unfolded to display Botticelli emblazoned t-shirts, David-endowed aprons, and plastic Ponte Vecchio snow globes.

"So she knows you're from Rome and you sell leather coats, so what?" he queried, catching up to Irene as she wove through the crowd.

"It is not polite to ask."

He stopped for a moment, but she grabbed his hand to urge him on. Her stilettos clattered on the cobblestones. Bill wondered for the hundredth time how she was able to move so fast without twisting an ankle.

"What's not polite about it? She was just making conversation. It's nothing." He tightened his grip on her hand.

"It is nothing to you. Americans, they ask everything; they tell everything. In Italy, it is different." She pulled through to the other side of a slow-moving group of German tourists

"So don't answer. Ignore her, but be polite. She's my landlady after all."

"I do not answer. I don't tell her nothing."

"Anything."

"What?"

"You did not tell her *anything*." Seeing her frown, he said, "Never mind." He looked ahead to where the crowds were coalescing into a tight mass. "Where do you want to stand?"

"Over there." She pushed through the stationary knot of tourists, already attired in shorts and sandals despite the April breezes. The lemming-like masses of Florentines, bundled in long jackets and woolen scarves, looking as if they expected snow to fall any minute, walked with speedy purpose to the front of the cathedral. Hundreds were already packed along the side of the cathedral beside the bell tower, as well as around to the front steps. The sound of drums and trumpets could be heard from the far end of the *Piazza del Duomo* behind the Baptistry.

"*Andiamo*, come on! They've started. We'll be late."

"We're almost there," he said, as they pushed into the ever-denser center of the crowd.

"But I want a really good view." Irene was still moving.

He was pressed against her back, trying to guard her face from the elbows, cameras and backpacks that seemed to come from every side.

"If you can't see, you can always sit on my shoulders," he murmured in her ear.

She stopped pushing forward and turned. "I wouldn't trust you not to drop me. Your mind is not on the *festa*."

"Sorry, sweetie. When I see that world-class behind of yours moving in those jeans, what am I to think?"

"Not now – later. Anyway, you can't see my bottom in this crowd."

When they reached the bell tower she turned sideways for him to pass. "Now, I want you to push through the people over there to find a place on the steps on the other side of the *campanile*." She pointed over the heads of the tourists crowding around Giotto's bell tower to a spot behind a group of uniformed schoolgirls standing on the steps of the cathedral.

"Are we allowed to go up there?"

"Yes, any place behind the red rope."

Two crimson cotton ropes, supported by metal traffic barriers, created a pathway, almost twenty feet wide, through the crowd, all the way from the far end of the square, past the octagonal Baptistry, to the cathedral. In front of the Duomo, the boundary marked off a long oval where the flag throwers were now swirling, swooping and sailing their silken banners high in the air, then dipping them down to the ground and soaring up again.

Two trumpeters in traditional white tunics ablaze with the crimson Florentine lily flanked the open doors of the church.

Bill pushed through the press of spectators. He could feel her hand firmly clamped onto the back of his belt. He advanced up one marble step and then another.

"Made it. Is this okay? Can you see everything?" They were backed up against the marble façade of the church.

"Yes, this is perfect." Her eyes swept the piazza and focused on the cleared avenue through which a group of twelve drummers, in four neat rows of three, marched to their own rhythm, a steady beat slightly slower than that of a human heart. From their red caps to their multicolored leather shoes, they stepped as if out of the Renaissance, resplendent in long-sleeved golden vests, which were also worn by the twelve trumpeters who followed them.

Behind the blaring trumpets came four white oxen, their necks draped in fresh flowers, their backs adorned with tasseled purple velvet cloths bearing a shield of white emblazoned with the crimson Florentine lily. They pulled an ancient wooden cart, towering over thirty feet in height. The *carro* rumbled on four granite wheels held in place by two massive wooden axles. Like a giant's four-layer wedding cake, each blue-gray or maroon tier of the cart, decorated with painted heraldry, was slightly smaller than the one below, and was cushioned by a narrow sculpted section of wood painted silver and gold, like scalloped frosting. A gilded crown, balanced on the tails of four carved silver dolphins, topped the edifice.

Bill wrapped his arms around his girlfriend and pulled her to his chest. He leaned down to her ear to be heard over the drums, trumpets, and growing shouts of the crowd. "So are there enough cute boys in panty hose for you?"

"They are wearing traditional costumes, like from the Renaissance."

"They still look pretty girly to me."

"You can just not let yourself to be serious."

"I am serious," Bill said as he elbowed a burly man to his left who had been trying to move up onto the step where they stood. "I'm seriously thinking we could have watched this from the window of my apartment and missed this crush. I'm a bit claustrophobic in crowd scenes."

"Move over toward the door, closer to the rope."

"I can't, I'll step on one of those girls. I think they're speaking Spanish, but it's too noisy to be sure."

"You are such a complainer. The cart is almost here. Look at it."

"It's so big, we could have seen it fine from the window," Bill pointed up toward his apartment. "See, the contessa is watching from her place."

Irene glanced up and then focused on the cart again. "It is not the same. Did you bring your camera?"

"No, dammit, I forgot. I meant to grab it before we left."

"Too bad, you probably will not see something like this again." She pulled his arms back around her waist. "Now look they are going to make the dove go."

A wire had been attached high on the cart. It passed through the massive open bronze doors into the depths of the cathedral.

"What dove? Where does it go?"

"It is a machine bird."

"You mean mechanical?"

"Yes, mechanical. See that metal thing shaped like a bird? They send it along the wire into the church. It is supposed to pick up fire from the candles on the altar and come back to the cart."

"Why?"

"It has something to do with having a good growing season and harvest."

But the dove did not fly. Men climbed up the cart to check the problem. The bells in Giotto's bell tower began to toll eleven times.

"Does that mean a bad harvest?" Bill rested his chin on her head. He could smell the spicy scent of her shampoo and another scent he associated with their time in bed. "You smell like sex."

She jammed her elbow into his stomach.

"Someone will hear you," she hissed.

"So?"

"So, be quiet."

"Well it's taking a long time to do the dove thing."

"I wish it were faster, too. I need to go to the *toilette*."

"Now?"

"Yes, now. You stay here, so I don't lose you or this space."

"But the dove might go any second. Aren't the fireworks supposed to happen next?"

"I'll be right back. I will run to your apartment. Give me your keys. You stay here. Promise me."

"I'll come with you."

"No, then we will lose this space. I'll bring your camera back." She turned to him and kissed him softly on the lips. She ran her hand down his chest to his stomach and below.

"*Sweetie*," he gasped. "We're in front of a church."

"Promise me you will wait for me."

"Don't I always?" He heard her snicker at his wordplay.

"That is what I like best about you." She stepped back. "I better hurry."

He dug his keys out of his jacket pocket and handed them to her. "Go fast, but don't kill yourself on those bad-girl shoes of yours."

He watched her push through the crowd and turn around the corner of the bell tower. At that moment the crowd cheered and he turned to see the bird leave its perch to race along the wire into the church.

"Shit," Bill muttered, "she's going to miss the beginning."

He looked to see if she had turned back. She had. He could see her pull the silver cell phone out of her bag. He put his hand to his BlackBerry, expecting a call. It didn't come. He heard a twang as the bird arrived back at the cart. He looked back at her. Irene wasn't there.

Bill didn't see her walk quickly out of the piazza, dismantling the cell phone as she went, tossing the pieces into separate trash bins. He didn't see her pass the door of the palazzo where his apartment was located.

He did see the glittering spray of the first of four Catherine wheels attached to the bottom corners of the cart and heard the pop of small firecrackers at the crest. Tiny rockets shot high into the air, bursting into red and white sparkling chrysanthemums. Crimson and white smoke billowed from the top tier. The crowd began to cheer as the ground around the cart erupted in geysers of purple sparks.

Bill saw the bright blinding white light, but did not hear the sound of the bomb that killed him.

Chapter One

At ten o'clock Easter morning, lunch preparations began. The cathedral bell rang out the hour, a muffled background noise in chef Cosimo Falcone's apartment on Lungarno Guicciardini overlooking the Arno River.

"Babbo, where did you put the carrots?" Caterina Falcone asked her father in the sibilant Florentine dialect.

"On the counter near the sink," Cosimo said, as he pulled the cork out of a bottle of Brunello. "I think I'll decant this and let it breathe for a couple of hours."

Caterina checked the label. "Poggio Antico – one of my favorites. Unfortunately, I don't seem to be entertaining much these days, so I don't have an excuse to open a good bottle of wine."

"Great wine needs no occasion," opined her father.

"No, it just needs more than my salary from the police department."

Minutes later, she was dicing carrots using two-handled curved *mezzaluna* knife to cut them into smaller and smaller pieces with a brisk rocking motion, when her father's voice boomed from behind her left shoulder.

"Smaller, smaller, you must chop them much finer for my *soffritto*. You always make them too big, lazybones."

He grabbed the handle of a big butcher knife, elbowed her out of the way and commenced mincing the carrots at great speed. He then did the same with the celery and tiny onion bits she had already diced. "A *soffritto* is not to chew on. It is to disappear. Pure flavor, no texture."

Caterina knew her father claimed that his *soffritto* was the secret to his success at Osteria da Guido, the restaurant that he now owned, named for his father, Guido Falcone, who had started the place with a stove top and five tables. The osteria now boasted thirty tables and was rumored to soon receive a Michelin star.

Cosimo fired up a burner, placed a large iron pot on the flame, poured in a generous amount of unfiltered green olive oil to cover the bottom, and tossed in the three ingredients.

"Now stir this and let me know when it turns golden. I'll take part of it then to cook the *pappa al pomodoro* and you'll cook the rest of the *soffritto* until it's light brown for the *sugo all'anatra*."

"I thought you were making the sauce with *lepre*, not duck."

"The duck looked better than the hare at the market yesterday. Both work well for Easter lunch."

They continued to cook and chat, a seasoned kitchen team, until Cosimo looked up at the big kitchen clock.

"Where is Lorenzo? It is almost eleven. Wasn't he supposed to bring over the fresh bread and gelato before he goes to pick up the kids?"

From the dining room, a sardonic voice answered, "*Caro mio,* you know Lorenzo is always late. He has to get Cosimino and Annamaria before their mother goes to work, so that means he will be carrying the bread and gelato all this time."

A statuesque woman with a cap of red hair, and a graceful neck that Caterina had long envied, walked through the kitchen door. "And because he is late he will have to take them to the fireworks before he comes here, and the gelato will be melted."

Margaret Mary Gifford Falcone, descendent of the Boston Giffords, turned to her daughter and switched into English. "Darling Catherine, when are you going to get that mop of yours cut?"

Caterina raised a defensive hand to her wavy auburn hair. "It's easier to manage this way. I braid it or tie it up for work."

"Well then do so now. It's going to catch fire over the stove and you know I hate to find stray hairs around." Margaret Mary picked up a stray carrot slice between two pearly pink polished nails and popped it between slightly more rosy glossed lips. "*Caro mio,* have I told you how happy I am that you closed the restaurant today so we could have Easter lunch as a family," she said, switching back to Italian.

"*Si, cara.* You were the one who put the idea in my head in the first place." He looked up to see where his sous chef had gone. "But don't chase Caterina out of the kitchen. I don't often get a chance to cook with my only daughter."

"Whose fault is that? She could be in your kitchen every day if she hadn't gotten that crazy idea to go to join the *polizia.*"

"Stop it, you two," Caterina said from the doorway. Tortoiseshell clips on each side of her head tamed her hair. She slipped a black velvet elastic band around the rest and bundled it at her neck. "You know I wasn't going to come back to the osteria after university in Boston. That was never part of the plan."

"The *plan* was not for you to get a degree in literature and languages so that you could carry a gun and arrest drug dealers," her mother said, pursing her lips.

Caterina rubbed the tiny pain growing between her eyebrows. "Mother, you know I only carried a gun for two years and never fired it. Now that I'm part of Magistrate Benigni's task force, I don't even have a gun anymore."

"You were very elegant in your uniform," her father said. "Filippo Marconi told me that the Ponte Vecchio had more class when you were patrolling it."

"Babbo, that's the *vigile* patrolling the bridge. I was only over there a couple of times when we were making more of an effort to stop the illegal vendors from actually setting up shop *on* the bridge."

"Filippo still holds dear the memory of your *gambe perfette* in uniform."

"Well, I haven't worn a uniform for a year, and Mr. Marconi shouldn't be talking to my father about my legs."

"Certainly not," her mother interjected. "He shouldn't be talking about your legs at all." She perched on a kitchen stool. "Now, before I forget, Catherine, I want you to promise me that you will take me to Principessa Orsini's Easter Monday lunch at the Hotel San Michele. No excuses that you have to work."

"Don't worry, Mother. The task force gets the holiday off, so I don't have to go into the office until Tuesday."

"Thank goodness for small favors. Your father insists on being open tomorrow."

"*Amore*, we are always overbooked for Easter Monday," Cosimo said as he peered into the oven at the roasting duck. "You know that."

Margaret Mary frowned. "This time of year the osteria is full, lunch or dinner, no matter if it is a holiday or not. I just think… is that the time?" She pointed at the kitchen clock. "Catherine, try to get your brother on his cell phone. He's late, like I said he would be."

"Mother, you know he's taking Annamaria and Cosimino to the *festa* at the Duomo. I'm sure he picked them up from Sofia, like you said and went straight there. I bet if we open the doors to the *terrazza* we can hear the trumpets and drums." Caterina walked to the double glass doors that opened off the living room to a narrow, walled terrace, lined with terracotta tiles.

"I don't know why Sofia couldn't have taken the children to his apartment last night. Then he could have gotten an early start," Margaret Mary said, following her daughter.

Caterina pushed open the doors and walked out on the terrace. "We're lucky to have them join us for lunch at all. It's not his weekend to have the kids. I think she changed shifts with one of the other nurses, too, so they could have the holiday off."

Caterina heard the sound of drums in the distance. She went to the wrought iron railing and looked out over the murky Arno River. "Remember how Babbo used to take Lorenzo and me to the *Scoppio del Carro* every Easter? We used to walk with the oxen and the cart all the way from Porta al Prato to the Duomo," Caterina said, knowing that the change of subject probably would not work.

"He should never have married her," her mother said, proving her right.

"Lorenzo and Sofia were together for eight years. That's not short." She turned back to look at the cathedral dome, huge even viewed from their spot across the river. "They should be here soon. I think the dove was supposed to fly at eleven," Caterina said, as the bells in Giotto's tower began to ring.

"Lorenzo is better off without her, Catherine."

She turned back to her mother. "No, he's lonely without her, but now he doesn't feel guilty about spending all his time in the kitchen with Babbo."

Her father filled the doorway, ducking his head under the doorframe to join them on the terrace. "Enough, you two. This is a never-ending argument with no answer. Caterina, can you find the heavy cream in the refrigerator? I want to put the finishing touches on the *dolce* before I start the lamb chops. Margherita, *amore*, why don't you check to see if the table setting and glassware meet with your approval, and maybe see if you can find that special spoon Annamaria likes to use."

Caterina turned to go in, but her mother leaned over the railing. "Cosimo, I think I can hear the trumpets. Maybe we will be able to hear the fireworks. What a glorious morning. Spring has certainly arrived. Look at the bell tower sparkling in the sun."

As they admired the view, a roar like thunder on the cloudless day caused them to look to the sky for a cause – a jet, perhaps.

"What was that?" Caterina and her mother said in unison.

Cosimo shook his head. "Maybe a plane – or remember when the water heater exploded in an apartment on Piazza Santo Spirito last winter? It sounded like that."

"*Mio dio*, look!" Caterina pointed at the Duomo, where a cloud of black smoke and gray dust billowed upward, obscuring the bell tower.

Chapter Two

I've got to find Lorenzo and the children." Caterina yanked off her apron, running past her parents and out the front door to her own apartment across the landing. She grabbed up a jacket and purse and plucked her scooter key from one of the small hooks by the door.

"Catherine, call us immediately when you find them," Margaret Mary ordered, standing with her husband in their doorway.

Caterina rushed down the six flights of stairs. She tripped on the step outside the huge wooden palazzo door, but caught herself and ran down the side alley to the tiny courtyard where her red *Vespa* scooter was wedged near the end of the line of similar *motorini*. She jerked the scooter off its stand and out of line, then fired up the engine, raising a plume of dust as she raced out the narrow road.

Speeding up the empty street along the Arno River, she turned left at the first bridge. Descending the north end of the *Ponte Santa Trinita*, she saw people running toward her in the road and along the sidewalks past the closed luxury stores of Via de' Tornabuoni. Some were covered in gray dust, some still clean in their Easter best;

all wore expressions of stark terror. She narrowly missed hitting an old man with a bloody face, carrying a screaming toddler when he stepped without looking into the street in front of her.

"*Mio dio, mio dio,*" Caterina murmured to herself as she swerved around them and slowed, looking for her threesome, as the crowds got thicker. *Where were Lorenzo and his children? Surely they would come this way.*

"*Che e' successo?*" she stopped to ask a man standing at the corner of Via Strozzi. He was looking in all directions, seemingly unsure of which way to go. "What happened?" she repeated in English.

"In *Piazza del Duomo,*" he responded in Italian. "They have bombed the cathedral. An inferno. Everyone is dead."

Caterina's scooter jerked forward, almost hitting a dusty, bloodied couple, arms clutching each other as they stumbled across the street. *Everyone is dead,* rang in her head. *No, not Renzo,* she thought, *not Annamaria, not Cosimino.*

She wove slowly through the growing crowd to the end of the street where it met Via de' Pecori, one of the narrow *strade* that led to the cathedral square. People streamed past her in the roadway between the glass wall of the new Tommy Hilfiger store, once the vicarage of the Church of San Gaetano, and the palazzo opposite. She stopped, dismounted and started pushing her *Vespa* through a group of terrified Chinese tourists, whose guide was urging them, in both Mandarin and Italian, to stay together. Sirens of police cars and ambulances sounded from all directions.

"Caterina?" She heard her brother's voice, but could not see him in the crowd. She turned in a circle, looking over the people surrounding her.

"Lorenzo," she called.

"Over here." On the corner at the next cross street, Caterina saw Lorenzo, right arm upraised.

She jerked her *Vespa* onto its kickstand at the curb and left it to push through the crowd. As she got closer she saw blood was running down the side of Lorenzo's face. Annamaria was cradled high on his left arm, her hands clutching his thick curly brown hair. Caterina looked down to find Cosimino standing with his arms locked around Lorenzo's leg. The five-year-old boy was crying and a nasty bruise was blooming on his forehead.

"Oh my god, Renzo, what happened? I thought I would never find you." Caterina wrapped herself around his right side and reached up to touch the blood running into his collar.

"It was an explosion. A bomb. Something big." He shook his head. "My left ear is ringing; my right one, I can't hear anything from it."

"Your face?" Caterina asked.

"That's nothing; just lots of blood, but a tiny cut. A piece of rock, or glass, maybe."

"Zia Caterina, I have a *bua*." Cosimino pulled at her pant leg and pointed at the bruise above his tear-soaked eyes.

Caterina squatted down beside him. "I see your *bua*, *tesoro*. What happened?"

"I fell off of Babbo."

Caterina looked up at her brother. Lorenzo ruffled his son's black hair, "He was sitting on my shoulders to get a better view. I had Annamaria in my arms. When it happened, someone in front of us pushed me off balance. I couldn't catch him and he went down."

"That must have been like flying, Cosimino, or was it scary?" Caterina ran her palms over his scalp and whispered up to her brother, "Did you check his head for other lumps?"

"Kind of scary, but the noise was scarier." Cosimino wiped the tears off his cheeks with chubby hands, leaving gray streaks. Caterina rubbed the dirt off with her thumbs.

"Do you have ringy ears, too?" she asked the small boy.

He cocked his head. "Yeah, that's weird. Will it stop?"

"Soon, probably by the time you get to Nonna's house," she said as she stood up. "Nonna will help you put a Band-Aid on your *bua* and on your Babbo's cut, too."

"We'll be matching," Cosimino said, taking his father's hand.

"I want to be matching, too," said three-year-old Annamaria.

"Then it's Band-Aids for everyone." Caterina kissed her niece's plump cheek and turned to her brother. "I would give you the *Vespa*, but you will never get through the crowd and it's not safe with three. Go now – and call Mother on your way. She's probably in hysterics."

"You're not coming with us?" Lorenzo asked.

"No. I don't know what happened here, but I'm sure every police officer in the city will be called in. I should stay." She put one hand on her brother's back and the other on Cosimino's head and started moving them toward Via de' Tornabuoni. At the corner, she put her nephew's small hand into his father's large one and urged them to "take it slow and remember to call Mother."

Even with this admonishment, she pulled out her phone and pushed speed-dial for her father's cell phone. "Babbo, don't talk. I found Renzo and the kids. They're fine, just shaken up. They're walking your way. It would help Renzo if you meet them at *Ponte Santa Trinita*."

"I'll be there in five minutes. What happened?"

"I don't know. Some sort of explosion. It's big. I may have to stay. Don't hold lunch for me."

"Be careful Caterina. Call us when you can."

"I will, Babbo."

"I'll go now. Your mother already has her coat on. No, there's her phone ringing."

"That must be Renzo. I told him to call her. Don't run over the bridge. They're fine. We don't want you to have a stroke."

"*Bacioni, tesoro.*"

"*A presto,* Babbo."

Caterina pocketed her cell phone and walked to her scooter. She sat on it, but didn't immediately start the engine. Taking long breaths, she was convinced that she wasn't ready for what was ahead. To delay the inevitable she reached in her purse, pulled out her badge and beeper and clipped them to her belt. She used the speed-dial on her phone again. Her boss, Magistrate Paolo Benigni, answered immediately.

"Sir, Caterina Falcone here. You may not have heard yet, but there has been an explosion at the Duomo."

"What kind of explosion?" he asked. She could hear him turn down the volume of some lively music, maybe Gershwin or Cole Porter.

"Maybe an accident, but probably not. It's big. People are injured. I just arrived. I heard it and saw the smoke from my parents' place. I haven't gotten close enough yet to see the actual size of it."

"Was the *piazza* crowded?"

"It's Easter, sir. The *Scoppio del Carro* was taking place."

"*Mio dio*. I'm on my way."

"Should I send a car for you?" The magistrate lived in the hills overlooking the city.

"No, I'll take mine. I'll park as close as I can and walk in."

"What should I do before you get here?" Caterina hated asking, but she had no idea what her role would be in something so serious.

"Find out who is in charge from the *polizia* and the *carabinieri*. Let them know you are there. If they need you to do something, do it. Try to assess the impact on foreign visitors. And call Marco and get him down there." With that the magistrate rang off.

Caterina scrolled through her contacts and found the cell phone number for Marco Capponi. Marco was the magistrate's other investigator. He dealt mostly with

Spanish-speaking tourists and visitors from Eastern Europe.

"I'm already in the *piazza*, Caterina. Where are you?" Marco's voice boomed in her ear. No greeting, just business, that was Marco.

"I'm walking up Via de' Pecori."

"I'll meet you in front of the Misericordia chapel, on the steps. First, I must telephone the magistrate with my initial assessment."

"He's probably in his car," Caterina said. "I just called him. He's on his way in."

"So he was notified."

"No, he didn't know anything about the explosion until I called."

"*Cazzo*, I thought he would want a briefing before he arrived."

"He needs to see the impact of the explosion first hand, not hear about it on the phone. This is going to be the first major test of the task force."

"I know that. Why do you think I'm here so soon?"

Caterina knew Marco lived a block from the cathedral. She didn't wait to hear him boast of his promptness. "I'll meet you in a couple of minutes." She slipped her phone into her purse, left her *Vespa* where it was parked, and hurried up the street to the cathedral.

Almost a third of the Duomo's intricate green, pink and white marble façade had been blown away; Caterina could see the dark brown scar of the underlying bricks. Her eyes watered from the dust that created a gray haze. An acrid odor of burnt rubber, charred wood, cordite, and what she thought must be seared flesh, permeated the large *piazza*. The Baptistry appeared undamaged, at least along the southern side. Twisted pieces of metal traffic barriers, some wrapped with red rope, were flung around the steps of the church. The huge wooden crown from the top of the *carro*, still attached to one carved dolphin, lay on the ground halfway between the Baptistry and the entrance to Via del Calzaiuoli.

Previously, Caterina's experience with mass death was through the filter of a television screen – suicide bombers in Jerusalem, car bombs in Baghdad markets. This scene with its haze of dust was almost as unreal to her.

The living made it real to Caterina. Amidst the injured and the dead, scurried emergency medical technicians, nurses in blue or green scrub suits, doctors in white lab coats, uniformed police officers and firemen, and civilians, still dressed in their Easter clothes. Screams for help vied with orders of triage and damage control.

"*Attenti! Aiuto!*" Caterina heard a woman scream. High on the Duomo something moved. She watched in horror as a statue, one of the twelve disciples placed in the highest niches on the façade, toppled off its base and hurtled toward the ground.

Chapter Three

For a millisecond it seemed to Caterina as if there was no movement in the *piazza* except for the falling statue, the size of a man. The explosive sound of the marble crashing against the corner of the cathedral steps resounded off the stone walls of the palaces ringing the *piazza*. It shattered, sending marble shrapnel into a group of firemen who had been cordoning off the four long steps in front of the church. One man howled in pain.

Emergency technicians in vibrant orange uniforms were the first to move, racing to the firemen. Someone yelled through a bullhorn for everyone to get away from the cathedral steps. The frenetic activity started again throughout the square.

A uniformed *vigile* stopped her at a barrier constructed of traffic cones and red crime scene tape. Caterina showed her badge and was allowed to pass. The tide of people leaving the *piazza* had turned and now gawkers were arriving to view the carnage.

She walked with slower and slower steps to the next barrier created from the red rope that just an hour before had separated the parade of trumpeters and drummers from the watching crowd. She knew the *vigile* at the barrier. He had been a schoolmate of Lorenzo's.

"*Mio dio*, Lapo," she said. "Are they saying what happened?"

"*Porca miseria*, I don't know. It must have been a bomb. Too strong for an accident with the fireworks on the cart. Not only did it blow the *carro* to bits, it brought down part of the façade and tore a chunk out of the bell tower." He shook his head. "Caterina, I haven't seen anything like this since the Uffizi car bomb in '93. That one made a crater in the street and blew down the wall of an apartment building."

"I was in America when that happened. Didn't it implode some of the museum's walls, destroying the paintings, too? It was mafia, right? Could this be the same?"

"I wouldn't think they would do the Duomo. A museum is one thing – the cathedral something completely different. They'd fear for their immortal souls, assuming they have souls. It's got to be the Arabs, if you ask me."

Caterina didn't respond. She knew she was just delaying. The scene in front of her was so chaotic. The smell, now with the addition of the coppery odor of fresh blood, was making her nauseous. She forced herself to move past the barrier. Remembering the magistrate's instructions, she turned back.

"Who's in charge?"

"That would be Captain DeLuca. See him over there?" Lapo gestured to the covered stone porch of the the *Loggia del Bigallo*, a small medieval building in front of

the bell tower. Captain Filippo DeLuca dwarfed the
officers around him. His broad uniformed chest was
beribboned with past honors and his padded shoulders
bedecked with gold braid. Caterina assumed from the
dress uniform that he had taken part in the Easter
festivities. *He was probably inside the cathedral attending Easter
mass with the mayor and other dignitaries when the cart exploded*,
she thought.

Caterina wished she wasn't wearing thin-soled
designer shoes as she tried to avoid the broken glass,
chunks of stone, discarded clothes, shoes and backpacks.
She passed a nurse in green scrubs, kneeling next to a
bloodied, gray-haired woman, who was cradling a
screaming child.

Huge sheets of colored marble – the cathedral's
façade – lay in rubble. The explosion had blown off both
sections of the marble cladding and the underlying brick
of the bell tower. Caterina was so focused on the damage
to the Duomo that she almost stepped on the foot of a
policeman standing near three overlapping bodies.
Caterina's quick glance down registered the face of one as
a Japanese woman. She glanced away only to see a
drummer in historic costume, dead, his drum still
strapped to his chest, one arm half severed at the elbow.
Bile rose in her throat. She pressed her hand to her
mouth and swallowed hard and rushed, eyes averted,
from the scene to where Captain DeLuca stood, directing
his supervisory staff.

"Make sure they don't move the fatalities. The
medical personnel are to check each body for signs of life
and leaving an orange plastic ribbon tied to the dead. I

want the crime scene investigators to examine them undisturbed. I need photographs and written descriptions of each victim. If you can get to the injured before they're taken to the hospital, take photos and get names, local address or hotel and phone number. If they are foreign, get a home address and phone number. But don't delay treatment if it looks serious."

The captain scanned the group and pointed to two uniformed policemen. "Rossi and Baroni, I want you at the emergency room. Take three or four *vigili* with you." He poked a tall thin officer in the chest. "Innocenti, get a couple of officers and join Nutti at the Savoy. He's already rounded up as many of the spectators as possible and taken them to the hotel conference center to get witness statements. First, though, make sure the *vigili* at the barriers direct every remaining civilian who tries to leave the *piazza* to go to the Savoy for debriefing. If people refuse, then get their names, addresses, and phone numbers so we can contact them later. Finally, Fulvio, get a couple of your smartest to go door to door in the buildings that have windows on the *piazza*. Have them check those apartments for injured – there are a lot of blown out windows – and for witnesses. Get moving. I want reports every thirty minutes."

Caterina waited for the group to disperse and for Captain DeLuca to turn to her.

"Inspector Falcone, do you need something?"

"Sir, Magistrate Benigni is on his way. Is there anything I can do to help?"

He nodded. "You should determine how many *stranieri* are among the dead and injured tourists. That's

going to end up being Benigni's responsibility, anyway.
Help with the gathering of names and contact
information for the injured and from any surviving
friends and family of the dead. If the dead or injured are
Italian or Florentine, leave them to my staff. But if they
are foreign, get the information and help with any
translation or language needs."

"Yes, sir. Marco Capponi, from the magistrate's task
force, is also here."

"Good. If you see the magistrate before he finds me,
send him in my direction."

"Yes, sir."

Caterina turned and crossed to the front of the
Misericordia chapel where Marco, dressed, as always, in a
navy blue suit, white shirt, and Hermes tie – this one
yellow with a tiny blue print – was flipping back and forth
through a small leather-bound notebook, seemingly
oblivious of the emergency personnel streaming around
him. He underlined something on one page and then
looked up at her.

"Where have you been? I thought you said you were
in the *piazza*. I've been waiting." He leaned down to wipe
some dust off his handmade loafers.

Caterina checked to see if the bald spot on the back
of his head had gotten any bigger. In light of his
Napoleonic ego and transparent need to one day be the
youngest *commissario* of the Florentine police force, the
bald spot was the only small joy she experienced in their
collaboration on the magistrate's task force.

"I was talking to Captain DeLuca," she responded.

"What?" Marco whirled in a circle, search the clusters of uniformed personnel in the piazza. "Where is he?"

"I don't know now, but I think he's set up a command post at the Loggia del Bigallo."

"I should go talk to him." Marco started to walk off.

Caterina grabbed his arm. "He said we were to gather info about the dead and injured foreigners."

"I've already started doing that, of course," Marco said, smoothing the cloth of his jacket where her hand had been. "I have some ideas already about the cause of the bombing that I should share with the Captain."

"I don't think he's asking us to determine the cause, just to gather information and evaluate the impact on foreigners." Caterina opened her purse to get out her notebook and a pen.

"But the foreigners are the target of the bombers."

She paused in her search to look at him. "You've already determined this is a terrorist bombing?"

He nodded, stepping out of the way as a gurney was pushed past him to an ambulance. "What else could it be?"

"And you've determined who did it?"

"Well, no, but it must be Islamic extremists." He didn't wait for a response. Slipping a small silver pen into a loop on the notebook, placing it in his right pocket, he walked off, saying over his shoulder, "Tell me immediately when the magistrate arrives."

"Sure thing," Caterina said under her breath, wondering for the umpteenth time why her boss had hired such a supercilious ass.

She walked over to the epicenter of the explosion, midway between the Baptistry's Doors of Paradise and the open front doors of the cathedral. Red plastic crime scene tape encircled the once-mammoth cart, which was splintered and still smoldering. One heavy stone wheel had catapulted into the cathedral doorway. The other was still attached to the cart by a charred piece of axle.

Caterina looked up the steps to the front of the Duomo. To one side of the main doors lay the body of a *sbandieratoro,* an historical flag-waver, partially covered by his purple and white banner, a plastic orange ribbon tied to his arm. Beside him, a blond man lay face down, crushed by a statue. The orange ribbon was tied to his ankle. In front of the two men, scattered on the steps of the cathedral were the small bodies of four uniformed schoolgirls. One, still wearing a small yellow backpack, was missing her lower leg; another had lost her left arm and a portion of her forehead. Two appeared unscathed, but their faces wore the pallor of death. A sketchpad with its unfinished drawing of the Baptistry, smeared with blood, lay under the leg of one victim. A policeman was covering them with a sheet.

Caterina moved quickly to put a hand on his arm. "I just heard Captain DeLuca say that the fatalities were not to be touched until the investigators photograph and examine them," she said, swallowing hard, her voice coming out in a husky croak. "These don't have the orange markers attached yet to show that medical personnel have seen them."

The young police officer turned his red blotchy face to her. "I can't leave them this way. I asked the captain.

He says to cover them. The newspaper and TV people are already getting to the roofs." He waved a hand to the terrace of an old *pensione* near the square. Caterina followed his gesture to see a man with a telephoto lens perched on the balcony rail, one hand gripping the trellis above his head. "There's another bunch of vultures." He pointed to the intersection of Via Calzaiuoli where a Rai 3 news crew was setting up cameras as the reporter combed her blond curls with her fingers and straightened her low cut neckline to a more serious level. "They were here to do a holiday piece on the Easter festivities and now they have a front row seat for this inferno."

Caterina helped him cover the girls. "Are they from here?" she asked.

"No, I think someone said they were with a school group from Madrid."

"Are you going to stay with them?"

He nodded, bit his lip, and responded, "Until the investigators say they can be moved."

Caterina touched his arm, not knowing what else to say. She turned and started back to the Misericordia, pulling out her phone to check on the magistrate's arrival. Before she could dial, a man called out to her. "*Scusi.*" He was dressed in a plaid shirt, shorts, black socks and brown sandals. He sat beside the body of a long, thin woman, holding her hand. A pink sweater stained with bright red blood covered her head and chest. Curly gray hair poked out from under the top edge. A camera still hung from her wrist by a black strap.

Chapter Four

Caterina squatted down beside the stocky old man and tried German first. "Can I help you?"

Relief flooded his face as he answered in the same language. "I just don't know what to do. A doctor was here, but he just shook his head and left. Then the police came and I think they told me that they would send someone, but I don't know when."

"Is she your wife?"

"Yes, Margot."

"My name is Caterina Falcone. What is yours?"

"Gregor Vogler," he said shaking his head. "I should have stayed with her. She told me I shouldn't have gelato before lunch. But me, I said it will only take a minute, I will be right back before the parade."

Caterina felt her throat tighten. "Herr Vogler, I am so sorry for your loss." She put a hand on his shoulder. "It would not have made a difference if you had stayed. Margot was so close to the front."

He started to cry. "That's my fault, too. I wanted to see the fireworks on the cart. I made sure we got here early to get a good place. Margot stayed to hold the space for us. It should have been me. If I had been here, I would have shielded her."

Caterina shook her head. "It happened so fast. You would not have known it was coming. You couldn't have done anything to save Margot." She looked around and waved over a *vigile*, who was talking on his cell phone while leaning against the Baptistry wall. She glanced at his nametag.

"Herr Vogler, I'm going to leave you for a few minutes. This is Officer Sotti. He will stay with you until I can bring an investigator to authorize an ambulance to take you and Margot to the hospital." Then she turned and spoke to the *vigile* in Italian, "Sotti, do not move from here, do not make phone calls and do not smoke. Just stand here until the crime scene investigators come."

"But..."

"Don't argue. Just do as I say." She turned back to Gregor Vogler and switched back to German. "I will be back soon."

Caterina scanned the *piazza* and recognized one of the crime scene investigators moving among the dead. She walked quickly to his side and waited until he finished photographing a severed leg and foot still wearing a Teva sandal. "*Ispettore* Veneziano, could I ask for a favor?"

"I'm busy as you can see, *Ispettore* Falcone. What is it?"

"I was wondering if you could clear a deceased victim whose husband probably needs to be checked out immediately at the hospital." *It is only a small exaggeration*, she thought

"Of course. The pieces can wait." He gestured at the leg. "Where is this man?"

"Over here." She led him back to the German couple. Her cell phone started ringing. She saw the magistrate's name on the screen and answered with "Hold on just a minute, sir, please." She turned back to Gregor Vogler. "They will be finished soon. Officer Sotti will stay with you until an ambulance comes." She said the same to Sotti in Italian.

She turned, took a few steps away, and spoke into the phone, "Yes, sir, sorry sir."

"No problem Caterina, I can see you from here. I know you're busy."

"Where are you, sir?"

"Over by the Loggia di Bigallo with Captain DeLuca. I've just gotten a briefing. Come over when you are finished. Marco is already here."

"I'm coming," she said and closed her phone.

She had only taken a couple of more steps when she heard her name being called.

"Caterina, *stop!*"

"Sofia?" Caterina turned to see a plump woman with a long black braid down her back, wearing blue surgical scrub clothes, weaving through the emergency workers. "What are you doing here?"

Sofia ignored her question and grabbed her arm, tight. "Caterina, where are Lorenzo and the children? Have you seen them? I can't find them anywhere."

Caterina caught her ex-sister-in-law in a hug. "*Tesoro*, they are fine. When the explosion happened, they were on the far edge of the crowd because, of course, Lorenzo was late. Why didn't you just call him? They are at our parents' place."

"*Grazie a dio.*" Sofia burst into tears. "When it happened they sent as many of us here as possible. I left my phone in my purse, and then it got so busy here, and I didn't see them, but some of the ambulances had left already to the other hospital, and…"

"Take a breath, Sofia. It's okay. They're fine. A couple of bruises."

"I was out of my mind. After ten years as a nurse you would have thought I had seen everything, but this is *un incubo*, a nightmare. I will never sleep again."

"Here, I have to go see my boss," Caterina said, shoving her cell phone in Sofia's hand. "I'll be over there." She pointed at the Loggia del Bigallo. "Call Lorenzo and then bring me the *telefonino*."

"*Grazie, grazie,*" Sofia clutched the phone and started to dial. "I will bring it right over." She put the phone to her ear. "*Lorenzo?* Are my children…?" She broke off sobbing.

Caterina gave her another hard hug and left to find the magistrate. She could see him standing among a crowd of black *carabinieri* and navy blue *polizia* uniforms, his tall lanky frame clothed in a sage green corduroy jacket and brown tweed wool slacks. As she approached the group, Marco intercepted her.

"It was a bomb. No group has accepted responsibility. But my money is on ETA."

Caterina wrinkled her forehead. "The Basque group in Spain? I thought you said it was Islamic jihadists."

"Yes, but that was before I learned that one of the deceased schoolgirls is the niece of the Spanish Ambassador to the Vatican, Emanuel Salazar." He pointed to the spot on the cathedral steps. Caterina saw a group of crime scene specialists moving toward where the draped children lay.

"Such speculation doesn't serve any purpose, Marco," Magistrate Benigni said, coming up behind them. "Until there is a proven claim of responsibility or the evidence points to a perpetrator, we shouldn't guess. Stories like that spread faster than fire."

"But, sir," Marco started.

"This is what we do know," the magistrate interrupted. "Captain DeLuca is in overall charge of the investigation. Our task force is not – and I repeat, *not*, Marco – responsible for finding out who planted the bomb."

"So it was a bomb and not some other sort of explosion," Caterina said.

"Of course it was a bomb," said Marco. "An explosion with such force is never anything else."

"Wrong, Marco," said the magistrate. "Remember the explosion and fire at the library last year. It was at least as powerful as this."

"But that was a broken gas line," said Marco.

"My point is, until proven, an explosion can be many things. However, here they have already found evidence that it was a bomb. A sophisticated device that was attached to the underside of the *carro*."

"An act of terrorism," said Marco.

"Not proven," said his boss, raising a finger to silence Marco. "Now as I was saying, it is *not* our job to find out who did it or how it was done. We are tasked with handling all issues involving the foreign victims and witnesses. Caterina will take the British and American tourists and visa holders… you know, foreign residents. In fact, Caterina, you take all the English-speakers no matter where they come from. And the French and German tourists, as well." He turned to Marco. "You have the Spanish-speakers from Europe and the Americas. As you apparently already know, dealing with the authorities is going to be sensitive, Marco."

"Yes, I already have worked up some information on that," Marco pulled out his notebook and uncapped his pen.

"Save it for our briefing later," the magistrate said. "I want us to get started interviewing while people are still in the square. Marco, you will also have the Eastern Europeans and Russians."

Caterina looked across the square where the three dead Japanese ladies lay. "What about the Chinese and Japanese? None of us speak Asian languages."

"We're going to bring in interpreters. Caterina, I would like you to coordinate with them and Marco, you will determine if Arabic interpreters are needed. For any other visitors from countries we haven't assigned here, we will handle them as we go along. Perhaps the best place to start is at the Savoy where the police have been sending most of the witnesses."

Caterina hesitated and then said, "Sir, I wonder if we shouldn't check on the fatalities first?"

"What do you mean?"

Caterina felt a hand on her shoulder. She turned to find Sofia slipping the borrowed cell phone into her hand. The tearful woman mouthed "*Grazie*" and turned back to where the ambulances were still being loaded with the injured and the dead.

Caterina turned back to her boss. "Well, I don't know, but it seems to me that we should get some idea about who the people are who died in the square. The ones closest to the blast. At least, the foreigners who were killed."

"That's duplicative of the crime scene investigators' work," said Marco.

"No, Caterina is right," Paolo Benigni said, looking over Marco's shoulder. "I see Dr. Rosselli over there, Caterina. Ask him for a briefing on the foreigners."

Caterina looked where he pointed. "Of course, sir."

The magistrate checked his wristwatch, "Good. Then Marco, you head to the Savoy. Caterina, finish up here. Both of you report back to me by three. I have a briefing with Captain DeLuca and the mayor at four." He turned to leave.

Marco started in the direction of Piazza della Repubblica and the Savoy Hotel. He stopped, turned back and said, "Sir, can Caterina …"

A crash above their heads was all the warning they got before glass showered down in a deadly rain.

Chapter Five

Caterina was crushed to the paving stones by the magistrate's long body. She pushed against his chest without effect. She could hear the fire chief yelling at one of his underlings through a bullhorn.

"*Idiota*, didn't I tell you not to move the windows. If they're open, leave them open. If they're closed, don't open them."

"Sir, are you okay?" Caterina said into her boss's shoulder.

The magistrate levered himself up on straight arms, wincing as a sliver of glass lanced his left palm. "So sorry, Caterina. I didn't mean to flatten you." He reached down with his right hand and helped her stand. "Are you hurt?" he asked.

Although she felt bruised from head to toe, she shook her head, "I'll be fine. Did the glass cut you?"

Marco, who had thrown himself on to the loggia, stood up and started picking glass out of the back of the magistrate's jacket. "Sir, you have glass in your hair," he said.

"I guess I'd better walk over to the Savoy with you, Marco. Need to get a bit cleaned up and check the damage before I see the mayor. Caterina, maybe you should come with us?" Magistrate Benigni raised an enquiring eyebrow.

She shook her head as she brushed the gray dirt from her jacket sleeves and pant legs. "I'm fine. I think I'll get on with it."

Once her nerves had stopped jangling, Caterina found the director of the Crime Scene Investigation Unit, Dr. Teodoro Rosselli, near the destroyed *carro*. She asked to follow his survey team. Dr. Rosselli, a round soft man with a bald head, wearing round black-rimmed eyeglasses, a dusty lab coat and surgical gloves, nodded.

"We are done looking at most of them. We're getting ready to have them moved to the morgue. I'll give you the short story on the foreigners."

He moved quickly from body to body, followed by Caterina, two investigators in white lab coats, one carrying two cameras, and a small blonde woman with a clipboard. They started with the three Japanese ladies.

Dr. Rosselli pointed at them and spoke with the staccato pace of a resident on medical rounds in a hospital ward. "Three Japanese women. Killed immediately. Part of a group of fifteen." He turned and jerked his thumb at a woman with the clipboard. "Gina will give you their names."

He continued, "They were probably killed outright by the force of the explosion, but as you see wood and metal shrapnel from the cart severed an arm and caused massive head trauma to one."

He moved to the steps of the cathedral. "We have six fatalities here. We may have more later – the most critically injured were on this side." He paused and looked back and forth between the Duomo and the Baptistry. "It was almost as if the bomb was aimed toward the cathedral and away from the *Battistero*." He turned to Caterina. "Maybe they knew the Doors of Paradise are copies," he said, grimacing at his small joke.

Dr. Rosselli marched to the center of the top step and lifted the edge of the drape over the schoolgirls whom Caterina helped cover earlier. "These four also died of concussive injuries. I was told they were with a school group from Madrid. This one – I think her name is Dulce – is related to Spain's ambassador to the Vatican." He pointed to a girl with short curly black hair held back with a red satin bow. "There were four other girls in their group and a teacher. All are in critical condition. More will die." He stood silent for a moment as one of his assistants covered the girls again. Then he climbed the two steps to the doorway of the cathedral.

"This gentleman is Florentine," Dr. Rosselli said, pointing at the man in costume stretched out in the entrance. He showed no obvious injury other than a dried trickle of blood from his nose and mouth. His brown eyes stared unseeing at the cloudy sky. An orange ribbon was tied to his left wrist. "I don't need to discuss him with you." He grabbed the arm of a passing *vigile*, pointing at the dead *sbandieratoro* and ordering, "Get that man covered up."

Not waiting to see his demand met, the medical examiner turned toward the south door of the cathedral and continued, "*Ispettore* Falcone, this fatality is either Swedish, German, or American, given his height and his hair. From the clothes, I'm betting American. We haven't examined him even though someone gave him an orange tag earlier. You see the problem."

Two police officers, directed by one of Dr. Rosselli's staff, were lifting the head and torso of the statue of St. Antoninus off a tall blond man. The rest of the statue lay on the paving stones below the cathedral steps.

"Take a couple of photos of him in this position," the doctor said to his assistant. When this was done, he squatted down by the body to check the back pockets of the dead man's tan chinos. He extracted a leather wallet and opened it. "He's got a driver's license and something from a university." He handed Caterina the two plastic-coated cards. "Here you can probably decipher them faster than me. Didn't you go to university in America?"

"Um, yes," Caterina said. She took the cards. "He's from Los Angeles, California. His name is William Bradley Barton." She spelled the name for Gina. "He's eighteen years old and a student with the UCLA's semester abroad program in Florence – that's University of California, the part located in Los Angeles." She looked up. "I know the program. They have classrooms in the Leopardini Palazzo on Via Belle Donne. Does he have his passport on him?"

"No, nothing in his other pockets. He does have a fancy cell phone clipped to his belt." He held up a BlackBerry.

"Can I take his cards and the cell phone?" Caterina asked.

Dr. Rosselli shook his head and stood up. "No, they have to go to the lab for examination. Write down any information you need, then give them to Gina to bag and tag. You can see them again at the lab if you need more time. Also, the phone... they tell me that the current theory is that the device may have been set off by a cell phone or computer, so we are taking special care to examine all *telefonini,* and the like, found inside the blast area."

"You don't suspect an American schoolboy, do you?" Caterina asked.

"Not really, but we always get into trouble when we exclude evidence before we check it out."

"The person detonating the bomb wouldn't be in the blast area, would they?" asked the assistant with the camera.

"It's been known to happen," Dr. Rosselli answered before turning to gesture the two police officers closer to the body.

Caterina jotted down all the information on William Barton's identification cards in her notebook and handed them to Gina, who slipped them into a plastic bag with the BlackBerry and the wallet. They rejoined Dr. Rosselli as he directed the policemen to turn the body over. Except for a long crease on his face, the American student had no visible injuries.

"What's that mark from?" Caterina pointed.

"He was lying on his sunglasses." Dr. Rosselli picked up a broken pair of Prada shades. He slipped them into the bag Gina held open for him, saying, "I'm guessing concussive injuries again, but we won't know until we get him to the morgue. Of course, the statue may have been the *causa della morte.*"

"Was he alone?" Caterina asked. "You've had some information about who was with everyone else. Was anyone with him?"

"I don't know. Some of the injured had already been taken away before we arrived. The most severely injured were in this area, so they were tended to first. No one has been asking about him, as far as I know. Gina?" He raised an eyebrow at his assistant.

Gina ran her chewed fingernail over two sheets of tiny writing. "Nothing here, sorry."

"Nothing to apologize for. Facts are facts. Let's move on. Pierluigi, did you get photos of this side?" Dr. Rosselli asked his investigator, but then marched off without waiting for a response. "Also, get a distance shot so we know where that statue fell from," he shouted over his shoulder.

Caterina hurried to catch up. In front of the bell tower two bodies lay – a middle-aged man and a younger woman dressed in matching black Izod crewneck shirts, khaki pants, and black New Balance running shoes.

"More Americans," Rosselli said. "It's the shoes and the waist packs. Only tourists have them and only Americans dress like twins." He unzipped the waist pack of the man and removed two passports, handing them to Caterina. "He has a hotel key card, too. No name on it, so I can't tell which hotel." He held up a piece of plastic shaped like a credit card.

Caterina opened the passports to the first page. "Fredrick Hansen and Melanie Hansen, both born in Wisconsin, U.S.A." She wrote down the information and then thumbed through the passports, noting only one passport control stamp on each. "Either they recently renewed their passports or this was their first trip outside the U.S." She handed the passports to Gina.

"The woman got hit by flying debris. See the blood trail down her arm and pool near her hip? The husband was turned and got hit in the back of his skull. There may be something stuck there." Dr. Rosselli ran a gloved hand over the back of the dead man's head. "We'll look at that during the autopsy. We'll be able to tell if the bomb was packed with anything – nails, iron pellets, scrap metal. I don't think so at this point. We aren't seeing the horrible injuries associated with that type of bomb."

"Do you have any more information about the bomb?" asked Caterina.

"No, others are dealing with that problem. I hear they put calls out to London and Washington, hoping to use those databases to compare this bomb with others. Spain is also sending someone who is familiar with the train station bombings in Madrid a couple of years ago." He snapped his fingers at his assistant. "Gina, what was the name of the German woman, the one they took away from over by the Baptistry?"

Caterina answered while Gina checked her lists. "That would have been Margot Vogler. I talked with her husband earlier. It seemed that he needed to be checked at the hospital. I was afraid that he might have a heart attack."

"So you know about her. Good." He looked around, rubbing his chin. "Let's see, among the other foreigners who have already been moved was a man from Estonia." *Snap, snap* went his fingers at Gina.

"No, identification on that one," said Gina. "Just a travel agent's card in his pocket and a few euro. The travel agency is in Estonia. We're just assuming he is from there, too.

"Enough talk, Gina. You two can get together later for the details." Dr. Rosselli started to walk away. He stopped, snapped his fingers and pointed at Caterina. "Almost forgot. Two young Russian men were also taken away. I think they may have been gay. They had matching rings on their right hands. Gina, give *Ispettore* Falcone their names."

Caterina looked at Gina's clipboard where she indicated and copied the information, sounding it out, "Ivan Korolev and Boris Taktarov."

"The three lined up over there under the drapes are Italian, so not for you. And there was a trumpet player on the other side of the center doors who died, I think we've identified all the foreigners who died in the piazza... what?" he turned to his assistant. "Gina, speak up."

"The English man, Henry Tomelson, he was over there," she said, pointing toward the Baptistry. "They took him away about thirty minutes ago."

"Oh yes, the one who lost a foot. He must have been very close. I think his daughter was with him. She's probably still in surgery."

"Is she expected to live?" Caterina asked.

"Maybe yes. Maybe no. Internal injuries." Dr. Rosselli surveyed the piazza, which was now clear of civilians and medical personnel. Police, carabinieri, and firemen commanded the space. "That's all, *Ispettore*. I must go to the morgue. It will be a long week for us."

"Thank you, *Dottore*. Magistrate Benigni and I appreciate you taking the time for our area of interest here, the foreigners."

"I just wish that the *polizia* cared as much for our own."

"Well, yes, but their job is much bigger in scope than mine."

"And they have a hundred times the personnel."

"Well…"

Dr. Rosselli waved her off. "Don't worry. No response needed. I must leave you now. Call Gina if you require any further information."

Caterina winked at Gina before turning toward the Savoy Hotel. Her cell phone rang. She thought it would be Marco, impatient at having to do all of the tourist witness interviews himself.

"Pronto," she answered.

"Catherine…" Her mother's voice pierced her ear.

"Mother."

"Are you safe? It looks horrible on the television. You didn't call." Her voice got louder. "It's been hours."

"Mother, calm down. I'm fine. I was too busy to call. They need all of us here." She started walking toward the Savoy Hotel.

"Lorenzo said there was stone and glass falling everywhere. How can you be safe? The television says it was a terrorist bomb. How do you know it won't happen again? The first one didn't bring the cathedral down. Maybe they will try again. Shouldn't you wait until the professionals determine that there are no more bombs? Maybe they will target the police and firemen next."

"It's okay. I'm being careful. I'm sure they've already checked the Duomo for other explosive devices."

"But what about the danger of falling buildings? They are saying that the buildings around the square have been destabilized."

"Mother, I'm safe. I have to do my job."

"But you aren't a doctor or a nurse or a fireman or even a regular police officer. Wait until the area is secure and then do your job."

"The area is secure. I am working under orders from Magistrate Benigni. I'll probably be on the job until late this evening."

"But, darling…"

"Mother, I have to hang up now. I'll come by… if it is not too late." Caterina snapped her cell phone shut and entered the Savoy. She went downstairs to the conference rooms, flashed her badge to the officer monitoring the hallway and asked where the interviews were being conducted. She was just about to enter the room the *vigile* indicated, when Marco flung open the door and trod on her foot in his haste to leave.

"What a waste of time," he whined. "Either they were people looking for a free meal or they refused food, just wanting to get home or to a restaurant for their planned Easter lunch. No one saw anything useful. Don't bother even going in. It'll just give them someone else to focus their ire on." His phone rang. He flipped it open with a curt "*Dimmi,*" talk to me.

Marco listened for a few seconds, his eyes wide. "Yes, sir.… All through, sir.… Yes, she's here. She *just* arrived.… Okay, we'll meet you there."

He snapped the phone shut. "Come on we have to go."

Chapter Six

A black Lancia pulled up just as Caterina and Marco came out of the hotel. Magistrate Benigni opened the back door. "Get in. I'm on my way to the Palazzo Vecchio to meet with the mayor. He just arrived from his country place in Chianti." Marco slid in beside the magistrate. Caterina went around to the seat by Guido Tozzi, the magistrate's driver.

"*Buona Pasqua,* Guido," she murmured. He winked at her and silently put the car into gear.

As they drove through Piazza della Repubblica, the magistrate asked, "So what's the story on tourist fatalities?"

Marco pulled out his notebook. "I have information on the four Madrid school girls."

His boss interrupted, "Hold that thought, Marco. Right now, I only want general numbers – specifics later, if there's time."

Caterina responded, "Sir, of those who died immediately in the piazza, four were from Spain, three from the U.S., one from the U.K., three Japanese ladies, one German woman, two Russians and one man, who may be from Estonia." Caterina rechecked her notes.

"Yes, that's it. *Dottore* Rosselli estimated that about twenty Italian citizens, either Florentine or from out-of-town, died in front of the cathedral. He also told me that from early triage they estimate that eight others will not survive surgery. However, except for one of the Spanish students and their teacher, I don't know if any of the critically injured are foreigners."

The magistrate looked up from the notes he was taking. "Thank you, Caterina. I want both of you to go to the hospital and find out what the situation is there. Now Marco, what did you find out from the witnesses?"

Marco didn't glance at his notebook. "Basically, nobody saw anything of importance. The ceremony with the flag corps and the trumpets and drums was finished. There was some technical problem with the dove."

"What was that?" asked the magistrate.

"Just a glitch. Lasted about five or ten minutes, depending on whom you talk to. Then the dove ran along the wire into the Duomo and came back. The fireworks had just commenced when the bomb ignited. The explosion seems to have been timed to the fireworks, maybe it was set off by the one of the Catherine wheels or a firecracker, but that's just speculation by onlookers, mostly Florentines. I talked to a few tourists whom the *vigili* rounded up and a couple of expats who live here. They had no useful observations. The Italians, who were familiar with the *Scoppio del Carro* and noticed the dove problem, were angry that they were not being allowed to leave the Savoy. The tourists were mostly clueless, and busy munching on the food the hotel supplied."

The car pulled into Piazza Signoria, past the great
bronze statue of Grand Duke Cosimo I. The magistrate
tucked his notes into his jacket pocket. "Okay, thanks
Marco. We're here and I need to get upstairs to the
mayor's office."

Officer Tozzi stopped near the copy of
Michelangelo's David. The front doors of the Palazzo
Vecchio, usually open, were closed, and guarded by two
policemen. Caterina could see three times the regular
police presence in the piazza. There were no tour groups
and only a few tourists.

"Tozzi, take Inspectors Falcone and Capponi to
Ospedale Santa Maria Nuova. Then, park and wait for me in
Piazza del Duomo. I'll walk over with the mayor." The
magistrate turned to Caterina and Marco. "Get as much
information as possible in the next two hours. Meet me at
the Questura at five. I'll call if I'm going to be really late."

"Sir, what about the consular staffs?" Caterina asked.
"Are you going to meet with them?"

"Thank you, I almost forgot them. The consulates
won't be open today, but their emergency protocols will
have kicked in. We don't want them running amok with
no guidance." He thought for a moment. "Caterina, call
Signora Benvenuti and see if she will come into the office
or if she has the consular contact numbers at her place in
Fiesole. Ask her to call all of the consulates and set up a
joint meeting with all representatives in the morning –
say, at eleven."

Caterina knew that Patricia Benvenuti, the
Australian-born widow of one of the richest Florentine
antique dealers, would already be at the office if she had

heard about the cathedral explosion. Signora Benvenuti was devoted to the magistrate and to the task force. She didn't need the administrative assistant job, but she had applied for the post when her eighty-three-year-old husband died.

"The business was sold five years before Pietro died," Signora Benvenuti told Caterina over lunch one day. "The villa runs itself and I didn't know what to do with myself. One day, at the Ladies' International League meeting I was talking to Paolo's mother. You know Marcella Fontana-Benigni, don't you? I'm sure your mother does. Anyway, Marcella told me that her son had been asked to head up the Task Force *Stranieri*. Marcella thought since I was an English mother-tongue and spoke Italian and French with a bit of Russian – from traveling so often with Pietro to St. Petersburg on buying trips – that I might help the magistrate out by organizing the office. And then it turned into a full time job. I couldn't be happier, dear Caterina."

Signora Benvenuti worked for the task force for six months before Caterina was hired. She saved Caterina from novice mistakes more often than the young inspector liked to think.

"No problem, sir. I'll call her, now." Caterina pulled out her cell phone as the magistrate got out of the car. Officer Tozzi pulled away, navigating the small medieval streets of the historic center in the direction of the hospital.

"Yes, dear, I'm on my way," Signora Benvenuti said, her Italian still accented by her Australian roots. "I was out on the terrace and saw the smoke before the sound got to me. I tried to call the Questura switchboard, but ended up getting the news on the television."

"I knew you would want to come and help," said Caterina.

"I didn't wish to get in the way, but my curiosity got the better of me. I'm having Fabio drive me in, but we're caught in traffic. I guess the whole center is closed off so it's backing everything up."

"Don't worry, the magistrate won't be at the office until at least five, but he did ask if you could make some calls."

"There, we're moving now. I should be at the Questura in ten minutes. If not, I'll walk and it will take me thirty. Who does he want me to call?"

Caterina told her.

"No problem, dear. I'll call all of the consulate contacts in Florence and then start on the few most important embassies in Rome."

"Signora, please make sure you get the American, Spanish, German, British, Japanese, and Russian embassies. Those have citizens who were killed outright." Caterina consulted her list. "And does Estonia have a consulate either here or in Rome? Do you need me to repeat that list?"

"I got it all, dear," was the response. "They are going to ask me who did this. Do we know?"

"No, we don't, but you should just say that more information will surely be available at the morning briefing at eleven," Caterina advised.

"Okay, will I be seeing you at the office or just the magistrate?"

"I'll be there in a couple of hours. Marco will be coming in, too."

"Of course he will, dear."

"Signora, we're arriving at the hospital. I'll check in with you in a bit and give you an update on whether any other embassies have to be notified about fatalities."

Officer Tozzi dropped Caterina and Marco in the small parking lot in front of the *Pronto Soccorso*. Four ambulances were pulled up to the door and three police cars were parked haphazardly filling the rest of the lot. A long hallway led to the emergency room. Caterina had walked through the cavernous dark space many times before, either taking tourists or foreign students in for emergency care, or to interview crime victims who had been admitted. The hall was still dark, but gurneys lined the walls. Medical personnel, family and friends milled around in controlled chaos.

"I'll meet you back at the Questura at five," Marco said, hurrying off, ignoring all outstretched hands as he wove through the crowd.

Caterina was left to respond to questions from all sides:

"Officer, can you get someone to see my son? He's in pain."

"Miss, can you speak German?"

"Are you with the police? Do you know what happened?"

"I can't find my father. He didn't come back to the hotel. They said he was here. Can you help me?"

Chapter Seven

NEW YORK

Zdravstvuite? Hello?"

"What the hell is happening in Italy? Did you know what that crazy bastard was going to do?" The voice was his brother's, yelling in a dialect found only in Siberia. Andrei Goncharov tried to focus on the screen of his cell phone to see the time in the dark. One twenty in the afternoon in Moscow; five twenty in the morning in his hotel room in New York City.

"Who? What?" He tried to shake off the fog in his mind induced by the two bottles of Domaine Dugat-Py burgundy he consumed the night before at dinner with his teetotaler attorney.

"Turn on the television, you fool," ordered Oleg Goncharov. "It's everywhere. He blew up the damn cathedral."

"What cathedral?" Andrei fumbled for the remote control, finding it under the pillow beside him in the wide bed. The flat screen burst to life, sending a pain shooting back from his left eye. Euronews, dubbed in Russian, appeared, depicting the rubble in front of the Florence

Duomo. In less than a minute, the scene changed to film caught earlier by the Italian Rai 3 news camera that had been sent to the festival to take a few characteristic shots of the *Scoppio del Carro*, the only professional footage of the actual explosion.

"What the...?" barked Andrei.

"Exactly," his brother interrupted. "I thought this was to be a simple job. Just sending a message. Like before. What did you tell him?"

"This isn't my fault," Andrei protested. "I told him we didn't want anything like that mess in Spain. Just something clean – same as with McDaniel. Are you sure this was his work?"

"Figure the odds. Of course it was him, you idiot," Oleg said. "What did the lawyer say?"

"He took care of the architects weeks ago, but didn't hear back when he sent the message to the head guy. So I told our man in Italy to go ahead. I didn't know he would do it today of all days, or so big."

"He's getting out of hand. We need to do something."

"First we need confirmation that it's done," Andrei said, getting out of bed, pacing in the light of the television. He tried to think. "I'll talk to the lawyer and get a flight back this morning. If this goes to shit, I don't want to be caught here."

"Once you have confirmation, make sure the condolence letter is sent. Don't do it yourself."

"Oleg, do you think I'm an idiot? I know how this is done."

"Have you heard from Yakov?"

"No, he should have called me immediately. Before you. I'm hanging up. Maybe I have a message from him."

An hour later, Andrei Goncharov checked out of the Gramercy Park Hotel and was on his way in a limo to the airport. The Aeroflot jet took off at eight. He hadn't heard from Yakov Petrov.

Chapter Eight

La Task Force Per Gli Stranieri (The Task Force for Foreigners), was created to meet the special needs of Florence, a city that many called "Renaissance Disneyland" because most the time it was populated by more foreigners and Italian tourists than resident Florentines. The new task force, directed by Magistrate Paolo Benigni, focused on crimes involving foreigners, either as perpetrators or victims.

Caterina had been on the team for six months. The mission of the task force was more limited than it sounded, Caterina assured her parents. It was not charged with the responsibility to investigate or respond to crimes involving the enslavement of foreigners to work in the sex trades or to toil in the broiling sun picking tomatoes and artichokes, both common crimes against undocumented immigrants in certain regions of Italy. It did not fight the impossible fight against the imports of illegal imitation merchandise like designer handbags, watches or movie DVDs. It did not run undercover operations to infiltrate Albanian drug trafficking gangs or Al Qaeda terrorist cells. All of these crimes were already under the purview of other *polizia*, *carabinieri*, secret service and prosecutorial investigators.

The decision to form the task force came after a hot summer when a Swedish tourist was molested by a Hungarian graduate student. Then, a week later, a thief on a motor scooter dragged a German grandmother to her death when he grabbed her shoulder bag and she got tangled in the strap. Her two grandchildren witnessed the tragedy. The tipping point occurred when a British movie star, known for his comedic roles, was stabbed during a burglary of his luxurious rented apartment overlooking the Ponte Vecchio.

It was this last crime that brought Caterina to Magistrate Benigni's attention. She was one of the first *polizia* on the scene. It was not only her investigation of the crime itself that was important; it was also her language ability – which allowed her to be used as a liaison with the actor's American wife, his Italian girlfriend, his business agent and the British Consul General – that made Caterina stand out. It was soon determined that the movie star knew his attacker, a boy-for-hire, who felt he had not been compensated properly and broke into the apartment with the idea of taking whatever he could carry away. Caterina learned of the rent boy's existence from a German-speaking Austrian baroness who lived on the same floor as the movie star, and reported meeting the two in the elevator one evening upon her return from the opera. Caterina passed the description of the young man to the vice squad and he was apprehended the same day.

Since joining the Task Force for Foreigners, Caterina had assisted in a case involving the stabbing of a French woman by her Florentine mother-in-law. She helped negotiate a plea agreement for a shoplifting Chicago socialite with a penchant for Gucci bags. She investigated the kidnapping and death of a Belgian/Italian toddler, who had been the subject of a custody dispute between her Belgian father and Italian mother. The dead child's mother had arranged for her abduction in Bruge, but on the highway just north of Florence the kidnappers and the girl had been involved in a fiery traffic accident.

A month before the explosion at the cathedral, Caterina investigated and acted as liaison in a non-criminal case where an American boy had fallen from a balcony during a drunken party. The New York University sophomore had run out to vomit over the low railing, misjudged the width of the balcony, and pitched over. He fell two stories and was in traction in Florence's Careggi Hospital with two broken legs, a cracked vertebrae, and a fractured pelvis. His parents had arrived and were working with the U.S. Consulate and the hospital to arrange for a transfer to a rehabilitation hospital in the U.S. After that accident, Magistrate Benigni asked Caterina to create a working group with the thirty-eight foreign universities with programs in Florence, to address the problems associated with excessive alcohol use by students, who were thrilled to be in a country with no drinking age limit.

"Gregor Vogler finally let them take his wife to the morgue. He is staying at the Brunelleschi Hotel and I've already talked to the German Consul General about assisting with the arrangements to transport her body back to Frankfurt," Caterina said, wrapping up her report to Magistrate Benigni. They were in his office with Patricia Benvenuti and Marco Capponi.

Caterina closed her notebook. "Also, my German professor from the *Universita di Firenze*, Ingrid Neri, is in a coma. She was born in Germany, but she's a citizen, married to an Italian, so she probably doesn't come under our purview. I just saw her for a minute before they took her off to radiology. I wasn't able to find out why she was at the Duomo or where she was standing in the piazza."

"Caterina, dear, I'll put her on my list anyway for daily status updates," said Patricia Benvenuti.

The magistrate, sitting at the end of a small oval cherrywood table, had taken his jacket off, rolled up his sleeves, and loosened his tie. He capped his fountain pen and turned back through a few pages of his notes. "Check me on this, Signora Benvenuti. We now have a death toll among the foreigners of seventeen. That's three Americans, five Spaniards – four young girls and their teacher, who didn't make it through surgery – one Frenchman, who died in the emergency room, two Russians, one probable Estonian – Marco, you are going to follow up on him – three Japanese ladies, one Brit, and Herr Vogler's wife. The mayor gave me a count of twenty-two Italians, five residents of Florence and the rest from other parts of the country."

Sitting slightly away from the table at the magistrate's elbow, Signora Benvenuti flipped back through a spiral-bound secretarial notepad. "I think you are missing one of the Italians who died in surgery – Hiruko Takara-

Peroni. She was Japanese, but with Italian citizenship, married to an Italian. I have here that she was one of the two guides with the Japanese ladies' gardening group." She took off her red-framed reading glasses and let them drop on their beaded chain onto her ample chest.

The magistrate made a note. "So twenty-three citizens and seventeen foreigners. Marco, are any of the hospitalized tourists not expected to live?"

"No, sir. The two dead Russians, Korolev and Taktarov, were part of a day tour from one of the cruise ships docked in Livorno. Others in the group were hospitalized, but not in critical condition." He glanced at his notes again. "One of the Japanese women is in very critical condition, but the doctor said if she makes it through tonight, he expects that she will survive, but will be hospitalized for at least a month."

"Then it's going to be very important for us to have an interpreter to…" The magistrate broke off, seeing a woman standing in the doorway. "Speak of the dev…, uh, excuse me, this is Lucia Lucchesi, our Japanese interpreter. Come in, come in. Please, pull up a chair, Signora."

Lucia shook hands with everyone at the table. She was a small, studious woman with wire-rimmed bifocals and short, salt and pepper curls. Patricia Benvenuti passed her a typed page with a list of the Japanese victims, dead and injured, as well as the name of their tour group company and of the surviving Italian guide.

"We've never had to work with the Japanese embassy or any Japanese tourists in the thirteen months this task force has been in existence," the magistrate noted. "Even though there are over a hundred thousand Japanese visitors to Florence every year, except for a few pickpocket incidents, they don't seem to be the targets of crimes and they don't commit any infractions, small or serious."

Marco straightened his tie. "Is it possible they don't report crimes?"

"It is certainly possible, but I don't think that is the case. It's the reason we never selected anyone for the task force with Japanese language skills. Caterina, I want you to work with Signora Lucchesi, conducting the interviews and assisting the Japanese victims."

"Okay," Caterina said as she passed a business card to the interpreter. "Let's get together after this meeting."

"Also, Caterina, I want you to follow up on a phone message that Signora Benvenuti received." He shuffled through his stack of papers. "Where did I put it?"

His administrative assistant rescued a pink slip of paper off the floor near his right foot.

"*Alora, grazie.*" He peered at the handwritten slip. "Contessa Montalvo-Ligozzi called the mayor's office. They referred her to us. She says... what does this say here?" He pointed at a word.

Patricia Benvenuti put on her glasses and peered at the slip. "Tenant."

"Her tenant, William Barton, did not come back from the cathedral this morning. She wants to know if he is in one of the hospitals."

Caterina checked her notes. "I've got a Barton. William Bradley Barton. He's the young man who was almost buried under the façade. He died."

"Please contact the Contessa and let her know. It might be better if you stop by to see her in person, given that she knows the mayor. I vaguely remember her from somewhere."

"Barton is the one with a student I.D. card from UCLA," added Caterina. "I was going to contact the program director in the morning to get a home address and emergency contact information. Maybe the Contessa has that info."

"Call her tonight – here are both home and cell numbers." He slid the message slip down the table. "Now Marco, what do you suggest that you work on tomorrow?"

Marco is always at attention, Caterina thought, *whether standing or sitting*. He sat even straighter and shot his cuffs. Still wearing his suit jacket, his tie cinched tight, he cleared his throat. "Unless some Islamic or anarchist group claims credit for the bombing, it is my opinion that this is the work of *Euskadi Ta Askatasuna*."

"Why ETA?" asked his boss.

"The Spanish ambassador's niece, Dulce Caron, was one of the group that was positioned closest to the cart. Four students, including little Dulce, and their teacher are dead. Four other girls sustained horrible injuries."

"But, as far as I know, ETA has never operated outside of Spain. This seems to be a stretch."

"The goal of terrorism is intimidation and control. Spaniards are traveling more or, at least, more often to Florence." Marco pulled out a bound report and opened it to a page marked with a green paperclip. "In fact, there has been a sixty percent increase in tourism from Spain to

Florence in the last three years. What better way to protest than to hit Spain's government with a highly visible act where they least expect it? Here, ETA gets international coverage for its message."

"I don't recall any act of terrorism by ETA that was in or near a Catholic church, but be that as it may, we are not going to be investigating the cause or the perpetrator of this tragic event. Is the Spanish ambassador going to be with us for the briefing tomorrow morning, Signora Benvenuti?"

"No, he is sending his second-in-command. The ambassador will travel to Florence with his sister, the girl's mother, tomorrow afternoon."

"Marco, have you shared your hypothesis with anyone from the Spanish Embassy?"

Marco frowned and checked his tie again. "No, I felt it was more appropriate to discuss it here first and with Captain DeLuca before proposing that Spanish Secret Service get involved."

"Very well. I am sure they are already involved and are being briefed by their Italian counterparts," the magistrate said, as he scanned a note passed to him by Signora Benvenuti. "It seems, Marco, that Estonia is replacing both its ambassador in Rome and its Consul General in Florence. I want you to find out who is the proper contact at either the consulate or the embassy and try to figure out who the dead Estonian is, or where he's from if he isn't Estonian. I believe you said earlier that he had no identification on him."

"Yes, I called *Dottore* Rosselli, since Caterina did not see his body before it was moved. The coroner told me that he had nothing but a few euro, a travel agency business card in his pocket."

"He's your mystery to solve, *Ispettore*."

"Will do, sir." Marco made a note with his silver ballpoint pen.

The magistrate turned to the full table. "All right, people, remember our job is not to solve this crime. Our job is to provide information to Captain DeLuca about any of the foreigners who were witnesses or victims today. We are also tasked with the responsibility of providing assistance to our foreign guests and expat residents, especially to the families of the dead." Benigni paused and thought for a moment. "Our most pressing work is going to involve briefing representatives from the consulates and embassies tomorrow at eleven. Captain DeLuca expects that not only will the U.S. Consul General be coming to the briefing, but that the American embassy in Rome will be sending the Legal Affairs Representative – the Legat. He's also an FBI agent. He will meet with Captain DeLuca and me before the briefing and then will join us at eleven."

Marco looked up from his note taking. "How can the FBI be involved? They have no authority outside the U.S."

"They have the authority to receive information regarding how crimes on Italian soil affect Americans. The Legat also is charged with the authority to share intelligence data with the Italian police, *carabinieri*, and secret service, concerning similar crimes, suspects, communications, and the like. I'm sure he'll explain all this when he gets here." The magistrate ended the meeting abruptly, "Okay people, let's get to work."

Caterina followed Patricia Benvenuti out to her desk in a reception room adjoining the magistrate's office. She sat waiting for the older woman to organize the work in front of her, but when Signora Benvenuti started searching the desk a second time. Caterina leaned over and plucked a pen out of her haphazard bun of gray hair, "Is this what you're looking for?"

"Thank you, dear," she laughed. "I lose more things in there." Her face grew serious. "Was it horrible at the cathedral?"

Caterina suddenly felt exhausted, the last of the adrenalin seeping away. "Worse than I could have imagined." Her eyes started to fill. She dashed the tears away with one hand and gave a short laugh. "Look at me. Not a tear all day and now that I'm in a sane, safe place for the first time in nine hours, I cry."

"It's a normal reaction." Patricia pulled a tissue out of a box in her desk drawer. "I just can't imagine why someone would target Florence. It's so out of step with modern times. It has no political or ideological importance."

Caterina nodded, dabbing her eyes.

The older woman continued, "It's really a museum that pretends it's a city."

Caterina choked out a laugh. "Or a city that pretends it's a museum."

"Maybe the Catholic Church was the target, not Florence. The Pope has been critical of Islamic fundamentalists. The Duomo is less well guarded than St.

Peter's. In fact, there are no security measures taken in the cathedral at all."

"Who would have thought it needed protecting?" Caterina asked. "It's stood for six-hundred years without attack."

"Maybe that's exactly the point – that nothing is safe. Remember when the Taliban dynamited the ancient stone Buddhas in Afghanistan?"

Caterina shook her head. "I don't think it was the cathedral. This seemed to be aimed at the crowd – not only Catholics – all sorts of people. Tourists watching the historical re-enactment of a medieval festival. What's the message in that?"

Chapter Nine

Caterina slipped off her new shoes, now scuffed and dusty, the instant she sat down behind her own desk in her small windowless office. She absently rubbed one reddened heel as she wrote William Barton's name at the top of an empty page in her small notebook. She dialed Contessa Montalvo-Ligozzi's home number. There was no answer. She dialed the cell phone number. After five rings it was answered.

"*Pronto,*" a woman said.

"*Pronto, posso parlare con Contessa Montalvo-Ligozzi?*"

"This is she. Who is this?" The strong Milanese accent gave Caterina an instant picture of a slender, elegant, older woman dressed by Armani or Chanel.

Caterina introduced herself and referred to the phone message Magistrate Benigni had received from the mayor's office.

"What? Paolo is too busy to return my call?" the contessa asked. "I know his mother."

"He must have wanted you to get an immediate response," Caterina said, covering for her boss. "He's going to be busy until late tonight."

"Immediate? I telephoned Mayor Moretti hours ago."

"I called your home, but you were not there," Caterina said, omitting to say that she had made that call only minutes earlier.

"Of course I'm not there. All of the windows were blown out of my apartment. I could have been seriously injured. There was glass everywhere."

"So your apartment is near Piazza del Duomo?"

"My dear, you could touch Giotto's *campanile* from my balcony, or so it seems."

"Were you injured?"

"Just a cut or two, nothing of any consequence. That's not why I called Davide Moretti."

"Your message said that William Barton, an American, is your tenant and is missing."

"I don't know if he is missing. I just know that in the two hours I spent at my apartment after the explosion, he didn't come back. I even used my key to see if he was there. He wasn't. I know what you're going to say – how do I know he's even in town? Well, I saw him in the piazza with his trashy girlfriend right before the cart blew up. Maybe he walked away or maybe he's in the hospital. If he went back to the apartment, he's out of luck. There are no windows and no electricity."

"Contessa Montalvo-Ligozzi, I'm sorry to have to inform you, but we believe Mr. Barton was killed today."

"*Dio mio*, are you sure?"

"There was a blond American, who had a driver's license from California and a UCLA student card, both in the name of William Bradley Barton. Would that be your tenant?"

"Yes, that must be him. It never occurred to me... dead. Poor boy... what a horrible..."

Not knowing what to say, Caterina got on with the task at hand. "Contessa, I need your help. I must contact his parents. Do you have any telephone or address information for his family?"

"No, I don't," the contessa responded. "What am I supposed to do now? Should I call the school?"

"It's Easter Monday tomorrow, so the school will be closed. I can't guarantee we will find someone at the school phone and the crime lab has William's cell phone, so I won't be able to get the numbers from it for a day or two." Caterina paused, looking at her notes from the meeting with the magistrate. "Contessa, may I come see you in the morning? I would like to talk to you more about Mr. Barton and perhaps, see his apartment. Maybe we can find a phone number or other contact information inside."

"I can see why you want to see his place, but why do you need to talk to me, *Ispettore* Falcone?" the older woman asked.

"We are interviewing everyone who was in the piazza about what they witnessed." Caterina switched the phone to her other ear, freeing up her right hand. She picked up a pen. "We also need information concerning those who died, especially if they didn't have family or friends with them."

"You think this young man may have had something to do with the bomb? That he was a terrorist? That's absurd."

"No, I don't think that, Contessa, but I am responsible for gathering information concerning any of the Americans involved in this horrible event."

"Well, of course, I will meet with you. I will need assistance with the arrangements concerning the apartment and William's possessions. Also, that poor boy's parents may want to talk to me."

"Where are you staying since your apartment is damaged?"

"I've taken a suite at the Palazzo Magnani Feroni. Do you know it?"

Caterina wrote the name in her notebook. "The hotel on Borgo San Frediano?"

"Yes."

"It's across from my father's osteria."

"So you are Cosimo Falcone's daughter?"

"You know my father?"

"I know almost everyone worth knowing in Florence. Such a provincial little town, don't you think?"

Caterina merely said, "Very well, Contessa. May I meet you at your hotel first thing in the morning?"

"Any time after eight, but I must go out at ten."

"I will be there at eight thirty." She added a note to her calendar.

"That will be acceptable. *Arrividerci.*"

"*Arrividela,* Contessa."

Caterina put her stocking feet up on the edge of her open bottom desk drawer while she jotted a few notes about the call. She looked up at a sound from her doorway. Magistrate Benigni stood there. She slid her feet into her shoes and sat up straight.

"Magistrate, how long…? Why didn't you say something?"

"I did. You were concentrating too hard to hear."

"Not so hard." She smiled and waved a hand to one of the wood visitor chairs in front of the desk. "I made an appointment to meet with Contessa Montalvo-Ligozzi in the morning. She was renting an apartment to the American boy, William Barton, who was killed."

"Maybe you can get some more precise information about him."

"She knows your mother."

"*Mio Dio!* It's a good thing you made the call."

Caterina grinned. "She's a bit miffed that both you and *her friend* the mayor ducked her call."

"She realizes it was a bit busy today?" he asked, running a hand over his forehead and into his gray and black hair.

"Maybe." Caterina noted the dark circles under his eyes and asked, "Any news on the perpetrator, yet?"

The magistrate shook his head. "Hopefully, by morning, the crime scene investigators will have been able to learn something from the cart and the other physical evidence they gathered. I want to be able to give the consular representatives more than just the names of the dead and injured. But the sheer quantity of physical evidence is daunting. They are sending another team up from Rome to help sift through it."

"I saw them emptying out all of the trash receptacles and sweeping up the paving stones in front of the Duomo," Caterina said. "Considering how much garbage the tourists produce, I can't imagine how they tell what is a clue from what is trash."

"I'm surprised someone had the foresight to order it gathered up in the first place, but both Captain DeLuca and Dr. Rosselli are excellent." The magistrate rubbed a hand through his thin, wavy hair again, making it stand on end. "You weren't even born when a bomb blew up in the railroad terminal of Bologna in 1980, killing eighty-five people and injuring over two hundred. Nothing was fully proved; the evidence gathering was abysmal. No one was ever punished. No one will ever know what agenda that atrocity served or whether it achieved anything for the murderers. Then another bomb went off, next to the Uffizi, in 1993. You remember that one."

Caterina nodded. "I remember the aftermath and the rebuilding. I was in the United States visiting my aunt when the actual bombing took place."

"A stolen Fiat van packed with explosives blew up in the middle of the night next to the museum's west wing." Paolo Benigni looked down at his clasped hands. "The fireball and blast killed five people – fewer than the bomb in Milan. But more people remember the Uffizi bomb. Can you guess why?" He looked up and met her eyes.

Caterina just shook her head.

"The Uffizi bomb destroyed three paintings in the *Galleria* and damaged over two-hundred works of art. It destroyed museum archives and a whole library of ancient agronomy stored by the academy in an adjoining building. The blast weakened some of the architectural structure of the Uffizi, seriously damaged the Vassari Corridor, and imploded the walls of the Niobe Room."

"I remember parts of the museum were closed for years for restoration."

The magistrate nodded, rubbing the knots out of the back of his neck. He continued, "Luckily, none of the destroyed or damaged paintings were by Botticelli, Michelangelo, or Caravaggio. But among those shredded by the blast were three, each over three hundred years old, created by followers of Caravaggio. The terrorists, whoever they were, would no doubt have preferred to have destroyed Botticelli's *Birth of Venus*, or Giotto's *Enthroned Madonna*, and perhaps, Di Vinci's *Annuciation*; but the bombing of the Uffizi is an example of a perfect act of terrorism."

"I see what you mean," said Caterina.

"It seems that the damage or destruction of a symbol – the World Trade Center, the Uffizi, and today, the Duomo – is so much more terrifying than the killing of dozens of people, like in Milan. Few remember the Milan bombing, but many remember the others. People will talk about today for decades."

"You mean, like people don't remember the thousands killed in Afghanistan, but they remember the Buddhas dynamited by the Taliban? Signora Benvenuti just referred to those when we were trying to make sense of today."

"Exactly, the Serbs blew up the mosques and torched the ancient archives of the Bosnian Muslims, and the Sunnis and the Shiites destroy each other's mosques because they understand the debilitating, demoralizing effect of the act. It's the destruction of the past; of memory, culture and civilization."

They sat for a minute in silence until the magistrate almost visibly shook himself out of his dour stasis and into action. He stood and headed for the door where, with one eyebrow cocked, he turned back and looked at Caterina.

"What was I saying before I went down this philosophical track?"

"Evidence gathering," Caterina supplied.

"Right. With the Uffizi bomb, once again, the evidence gathering was inadequate. To give them credit, they were dealing with demolished walls and a raging fire. But none of the evidence led to a conviction or even a specific perpetrator."

"I thought it was the mafia."

"That was the most credible theory. My point is that this time Captain DeLuca is determined to rake through every piece of paper, plastic, and soda can to find the perpetrator. He refuses to lead an investigation that will be looked at with scorn and disbelief, like the others. He wants this to be like Madrid, where they had identified suspects within days and apprehended and tried the terrorists before the year was out."

"How can we help?" Caterina asked as he walked toward the door.

He turned. "Our mandate is to add to the mountain of evidence by culling through the information provided by tourists, visiting students, foreign expats, and anyone else who falls under the guidelines for *La Task Force Per*

Gli Stranieri. We also are to keep the foreign embassies in the loop on the investigation. Make sure you have a typed report on each fatality and each of the hospitalized victims. Signora Benvenuti will keep the master files."

"I'll get her the reports." Caterina stood, too. "I'm seeing the contessa in the morning before the briefing."

"Very well." He opened the door and stepped out into the hall. "Good work, Caterina. Go home now. There will be plenty to do tomorrow."

"Are you sure there's nothing more I can help with tonight?"

"No, get some rest." He turned in the direction of Marco Capponi's office.

Arriving on the other side of the river, Caterina parked her *Vespa* and took the telephone booth-sized elevator to the fourth floor of the *palazzo*. She didn't turn right to her parents' door, but left to her own apartment.

Chapter Ten

Caterina and her older brother, Lorenzo, grew up spending half of their time in their grandmother's apartment, just across the landing from their own home. Nonna Maria Luisa died when Caterina was a freshman at college in Boston. The apartment stayed empty. When Caterina graduated, she returned to Florence to find that her mother had redecorated the space for her. Gone were Nonna's jewel-toned fringed throw pillows and overstuffed armchairs. Nary a painting hung on the walls and the icon of Saint Agata had been sold to an antique store on Via Maggio.

The living room had been redecorated in shades of the lightest butter yellow, from the two comfortable, slim-lined, chairs covered with nubby raw silk to the smooth calfskin divan. The dining table of light inlaid wood had been her grandmother's, but the heavy upholstered chairs had been replaced with slender high-backed, blond Danish-style wood chairs.

The small, sixties-styled kitchen had been replaced with a tall, narrow, brushed-chrome, Sub-Zero refrigerator, and a miniature Wolff range with an electric convection oven. New pots, cooking utensils and pans filled the white enameled cabinets and drawers. Margaret Mary had stopped at selecting the table settings and silverware. After eighteen months, the only thing Caterina had done was to buy stainlessware for eight and plain white plates and bowls from Ikea.

"I should have just gone ahead and ordered a full set from Ginori and silver from Igo Pucci, so I wouldn't be eating on these cheap plates and missing my own things," Margaret Mary had complained.

"I like the Ikea stuff," her daughter responded. "It's simple and functional. I don't have time to make big choices. Whom do I have over for dinner, but you and Babbo or Renzo and the kids?"

"Have some respect for us, then," her mother snapped. "Perhaps someday you will take the time to consider a life partner, too. Maybe he will appreciate some refinement."

"Unlikely; look at Babbo and Lorenzo. Until they were in the running for a Michelin star, they never changed the plateware at the Osteria. They still like the old table settings and glassware better."

"It makes no sense for you to not set a proper table. I think your father and I will be giving you silverware for your birthday and Ginori ceramic table settings for Christmas."

"Mother, that's too generous," Caterina had said with a grin. "But your taste is impeccable. If it will make you happy, please go right ahead."

"Remember that when I start shopping for a husband for you. I don't want any more mistakes like your brother made."

Caterina thought about her mother's warning as she entered the apartment and found the Gifford-Falcone china, set for one, on a linen placemat on her dining table. In front of it were covered serving dishes containing most of the Falcone Easter lunch – thick red *pappa al pomodoro*, rich *sugo al'anatra*, fresh green peas, Tuscan bread wrapped in a white linen napkin, and a small carafe of red wine. In the kitchen was a note in Italian from her father. It read: "In the refrigerator is fresh *paperdelle* and two lamb chops. Cook the pasta for four minutes. Heat up the *sugo* and the peas. You can either grill the lamb chops or (as I did) dust them with flour, salt, and pepper, and sauté them in clarified butter."

Caterina placed a small pasta pot on the range and poured herself a glass of wine. It was the Brunello her father had opened hours before, seemingly in another lifetime. By the time the water began to boil, she had placed all of the serving dishes in the refrigerator. She couldn't face Easter dinner tonight. She needed comfort food.

She threw a small handful of *sale grosso*, rock salt, into the boiling water and added a sheaf of dried spaghetti, setting the timer for twelve minutes. When the count was down to four minutes she was back in the kitchen, wearing her blue flannel pajamas and fuzzy ladybug slippers. She covered the bottom of her smallest sauce pan with green extra virgin olive oil, set it over a low flame, husked two cloves of garlic, and added them to the oil with four tiny dried *pepperoncini*, the hottest chili peppers she could find. Before the garlic started to turn golden, she turned off the fire. The timer chimed. She drained the pasta, dumped it into one of her Ikea bowls and poured the olive, garlic and chilies over the top – *spaghetti aliglio, olio e pepperoncino.*

With another glass of Brunello in hand, she sat at the table, concentrating on her food. Only some distant church bell chiming midnight broke the quiet of the night. The Duomo's bells were silent.

Chapter Eleven

Caterina, are you in there?" Her mother was knocking at the apartment door.

"Yes, I'm here," Caterina said as she opened the door and turned to finish buttoning up her blouse. She walked back to the dining table and picked up two pearl studs, which she fastened to her ears.

"Why didn't you wake us when you got home last night? Didn't you know that we would be worried?" Her mother's eyes approved the black-trimmed, white silk blouse and slim black slacks, but a frowned formed at the sight of the googley frog-eyed slippers, poking out below the fine pleated wool.

"It was late. I was all talked-out."

"You would not have been required to talk, except to say goodnight." Her mother saw Caterina's raised eyebrow. "Well, not much talking. It would have been considerate. I woke up at three and stayed awake because I didn't know if you had gotten home or not. Your father, of course, slept through everything."

"Maybe he understands that, at twenty-seven, I can take care of myself."

"I know you can take care of yourself. It doesn't stop me from worrying."

"Worry about Lorenzo and the children. They were actually there in the piazza."

"They don't seem to have any after-effects. The children stayed with us last night, since Sofia had to work a double shift, and they slept fine, no nightmares. She picked them up early this morning. I guess that accountant she married had the day off, so he's watching them while she sleeps. Lorenzo has to be at the osteria for lunch prep, so he can't have them with him. I offered to keep Cosimino and Annamaria this morning, but Sofia insisted in taking them away."

Caterina poured herself some coffee and changed the subject. "Mother, do you know Contessa Montalvo-Ligozzi?"

"Of course I do. Why?"

"Tell me about her."

"Tell me why first." Margaret Mary sat down on the couch and smoothed her navy linen skirt to avoid wrinkles.

"She reported her tenant, an American college kid, missing yesterday. He was killed at the cathedral."

"A dead student? Darling, I know you don't want to hear this, but your work isn't..."

"No Mother, I don't want to hear it. This is my job. It's what I want to do." Caterina turned, picked up her cup and saucer off the table, walked into the kitchen and dropped them with a crash into the metal sink, cracking the saucer. "Shit," she muttered. She took five deep breaths, staring into the sink, and then squared her shoulders and walked back to the living room.

"Now tell me about the contessa," she said, her voice even. "Where do you know her from?"

Her mother looked into her face, started to say something, bit her lip and said instead, "We served on an advisory committee concerning the restoration of the Museo Blackburn – you know, the villa in Fiesole, owned by that railroad tycoon from Chicago. He married one of the Pandolfini cousins in the late 1800s and made Florence – or rather, Fiesole – their summer home. His descendants gave the villa to the city as a museum."

"How long ago was this?" Caterina asked. "That you met her, I mean."

"I met Luciana, the contessa, about four years ago. The museum restoration started soon after."

"Where is she from? Her accent is Milanese."

"You talked to her?"

"Last evening." Caterina kicked off her slippers by the front door next to a pair with Mickey Mouse ears. She slipped her feet into a pair of black woven leather flats. "I'm following up in person with her this morning."

"I always liked Luciana. The last time I saw her was at the opening of the Maggio Musicale's *Tosca* last year. You are correct, she was born in Milan, but I believe her mother was Florentine – an old noble family – maybe a Bardi or a Vecchietti."

"So what is she doing here?"

"She married *Conte* Montalvo-Ligozzi just after the war, maybe in forty-nine or fifty. Before my time. She must have been very young, no more than nineteen or twenty. I think she's in her late seventies now, but you would never guess it to look at her."

"Is the *Conte* dead?"

"He died over ten years ago. He was much older than she. He couldn't leave her the family's *palazzo* on Borgo degli Albizi, it went to a nephew; so just before he died, he bought the top floor of a building on Piazza del Duomo near the bell tower." Her eyes widened. "Oh my gracious, that bomb must have gone off right under her windows. Was this boy, her tenant, in the building? She's not injured is she?"

Caterina slipped on a black jacket with mother-of-pearl buttons. "No, don't worry. He was in the piazza, not in the apartment when the explosion occurred. If I remember correctly, she was at home and lost some windows, but wasn't injured. She didn't seem all that upset, but it must have been frightening."

"Luciana is unshakeable. I've never met a tougher woman, except my own mother. You know these Milanese — ice-water for blood."

"Milanese and Bostonians — not all that different, Mother?" Caterina smiled.

"Probably not." Margaret Mary stood up and walked to the door. She straightened her daughter's collar. "Where is she staying? Surely not in a windowless apartment."

Caterina shook her head. "She's over here, at the Hotel Magnani Feroni on Borgo San Frediano."

"She has the money for it. The Conte provided for her very nicely, and I think she had some family money as well."

"You might want to call her and see if she needs anything or wants to chat."

"Luciana never chats, but you are right, I should call her," Margaret Mary said as she opened the apartment door. "It would be the civilized thing to do."

"And you know that she will tell you the name of her tenant and all about him. Right, Mother?" Without waiting for a reply, Caterina picked up her purse off a small table under a mirror by the door. She checked her reflection for errant curls escaping from her French braid. "I'm sorry, but I have to go." She waited for her mother to step into the landing. Caterina locked the door and walked her mother to the slightly open door ten feet away. The small glassed-in elevator between the apartments was somewhere below. She pushed the call button. "Give Babbo a kiss for me. I assume he's at the market now."

Margaret Mary pushed her own apartment door wider and turned. "Yes, he left at seven. You know he insists on getting first choice."

Caterina kissed her mother's cheek and took the stairs down to the street. The Palazzo Magnani Feroni was a quick walk around the block. She peeked in the front window of Osteria da Guido. She didn't see her father inside, so she crossed the street to the hotel.

"Will you please tell Contessa Montalvo-Ligozzi that Caterina Falcone is here," she told the trim uniformed man at the reception desk.

"Of course, Signorina," he said as he picked up the house phone. Moments later he rang a small silver bell, calling the attendant, who Caterina had passed near the front door watering a flowering camellia bush.

"Carlo, please take Signorina Falcone to the Machiavelli Suite."

With a smile he gestured for Caterina to precede him to the elevator, which had been cut into the original wide marble stairs of the palazzo. He pulled open the two grilled doors of the wood paneled box. The elevator creaked and rattled to the second floor, where he led Caterina down a wide hallway with frescoed ceilings and a floor of rich parquet oak, partially covered by a long running carpet patterned in rose and gold. The hallway opened into a grand *sala* with a gold silk divan, and two deep emerald green velvet chairs under a Murano chandelier of cut green and white glass. Off the elegant room were four doors, each with a hand painted sign. Carlo knocked on the door with 'Machiavelli' written in ornate script and then slipped away leaving Caterina to wait alone.

The contessa was wearing Armani. Caterina smiled, seeing that her imagining hadn't been far wrong, as she took in the pleated, coral pink, silk skirt, topped by a long-waisted black tunic, accessorized with a spiky coral necklace and earrings. What surprised her was that the contessa had allowed her hair to retain its natural white and gray colors instead of following her peers with a blonde or red tint. Her face, however, was smooth and pale, without the need of any surgeon's skill.

"Caterina Falcone," Luciana Montalvo-Ligozzi stated in greeting. She held out a hand that betrayed her age with its tiny blue veins and enlarged arthritic joints. "I know your mother and, as I said last evening, your father, as well. Would you like to have some coffee before we start on that dreadful business? They serve it in the common rooms all day. Very convenient."

They went back to the *sala* and filled fine china cups with coffee and cream. The contessa added a small spoonful of sugar to hers. Once in her suite with the door closed, the contessa sat in the center of the loveseat and placed her coffee cup and saucer on the low glass table in front of her. Caterina took one of the chairs, sinking into the softness. She took a tiny sip of the scalding coffee before picking up her notebook and a pen.

"My mother sends her warm regards. She asks that you call her if you need anything during this difficult time."

"Your mother is most gracious. I see you have her height and eyes, but you didn't inherit her beautiful hair."

Caterina put a hand to her head to check her braid, which was feeling a bit loose. "No, I got my father's curly hair, not that you can tell anymore, since he's gotten quite bald and keeps the rest trimmed close."

"I must go over to the osteria one evening soon, since I'm now living in the neighborhood."

"He will be pleased to serve you. The osteria is open today for lunch and supper, but unless people stay out of the city center because of yesterday's events, I believe he is overbooked. It's Easter Monday, and it seems all the people on this side of the river stay home on Easter Sunday, but eat out the next day."

"It doesn't matter. Today I have to attend Principessa Orsini's luncheon at the Hotel San Michele."

"Oh my goodness, is that today? I completely forgot. I was supposed to take my mother to Fiesole for that event. I'm not usually working on Easter Monday. She didn't even mention it this morning."

"She probably thought you had enough on your plate."

"I need to remember to call her."

"How would it be if I call her and offer to have my driver take both of us?"

"Would you? That would get me out of a jam with both my mother and my boss."

"Paolo Benigni? Is that dear boy married yet?"

"Uh… No, he's not."

"His mother must be tearing her hair out."

"I wouldn't know, Contessa, he doesn't say much about her to us at the Questura." Caterina opened her purse and pulled out her notebook. "Could we talk a bit about yesterday and William Barton?"

The contessa leaned forward, hands clasped together. "That poor boy. You could tell that his mother taught him some manners, but his taste in women was abysmal."

Caterina decided to ignore this and asked only, "When did he start renting your apartment near the Duomo?"

"I have three rental properties. William rented the one next door to my home. The others are on Borgo degli Albizi. He arrived the first week of February. He wanted it for three months." She paused. "Are you sure he is the one who is dead?"

"He was found right up by the façade, near the center doors of the cathedral. We think he died immediately."

"So young. He was so young." She shook her head slowly, looking at the floor. "I met him in the hallway that morning. They must have been on their way to the *Scoppio del Carro*."

"They?"

"William and that trampy girlfriend of his. I was going out to get a copy of *La Reppublica*. I gave my girl the day off for Easter, so I had to get my own paper. William and that woman came out the door as I was waiting for the elevator. Was she found with him?"

"No, there was no woman near him after the explosion. It's possible she is among the injured in the hospital. What can you tell me about her? Was she American? There was only one American woman killed, but there were three injured."

"No, she's not American."

"Italian then? Do you know her name or can you describe her?"

"Hmm," the contessa mused. "I thought I was wrong when I saw her walking away from the *festa* just as the *carro*'s fireworks started."

"What do you mean, walking away? Where were you? In the street, getting your paper?"

"No, I had returned to my apartment, as I said. I was standing at the window watching the first of the fireworks. I thought I saw her and then the phone rang and I went to answer it. That's why I wasn't hurt when the windows blew out."

Caterina scratched her head, pulling loose a long curl that she tucked, without thinking, behind her ear. "I'm sorry, Contessa, I'm getting a bit confused. You saw William and his girlfriend as you were going out *and* from the window?"

"As I said, I saw both of them on the landing before I went to buy my newspaper, and later, while I was at the window..." She was quiet for a moment, taking another sip of her coffee. "I thought I saw them in the crowd, but then I got distracted by the man climbing up on the top of the *carro*."

Caterina felt a tingle run up her back. She stopped writing and stared at the countess. "You saw someone actually on the cart?"

"Yes, they seemed to be having trouble with the mechanical dove and the wire. This was before the dove traveled the line into the cathedral to the altar."

"What did the man look like?" Caterina continued writing, taking down every word.

"I think there were two of them. They looked like the men who lead the oxen – you know the *contadini*, the farmers who take care of the white oxen – they were wearing the white loose shirts, worn leather vests and leather pants. What everyone seems to imagine a medieval peasant looked like."

"You saw them both on top of the cart."

"One was on a ladder and the other was standing on one of the stone wheels."

"Did you see them put anything on or under the cart?"

"No." She paused, throwing a skeptical look at Caterina. "You don't think they had something to do with the bomb? That's absurd. In front of everybody?"

"I don't know. But this is the first I've heard of someone touching the *carro* after it was pulled in front of the Duomo."

"It can't be them. These men live for the *Scoppio del Carro*. It's an honor for them to lead the oxen and bring the cart to the cathedral. You know it's stored down by the Corsini Palazzo, near the Villa Medici Hotel."

Caterina nodded. "I know. I used to walk next to it with my father when they brought it to the Duomo. It's just something – the men climbing on it – I should tell the magistrate."

"There were police around. They would have noticed if the men on the cart were wrong."

"What about William's girlfriend? When did you notice her again?"

"At about the same time. I saw them working on the cart and then I looked for William again to see if he got a good spot to see the fireworks. I thought I saw her walking toward my building. I remember she stopped to use her phone because my phone rang seconds later. I walked across the room to answer and the explosion rocked the building."

"If you don't mind my asking, who was calling you?"

"It certainly wasn't her. It was my brother calling from Milan to wish me '*Buona Pasqua*'. He got out three words and the world seemed to blow up. The phone went dead."

"Were you hurt?"

"No, except I nearly had a heart attack from fear. Pieces of the fresco on the ceiling fell and a portrait of my late husband's father came off the wall. As I told you, all of the windows shattered. An ugly, but very valuable, Murano vase that my husband loved and I hated fell off a side table near the window and broke into a million pieces." The contessa's face lit with a satisfied smile.

Caterina chuckled at her expression and flipped back through her notes. "About the girlfriend …"

The contessa interrupted, "A strumpet. Do you know what that word means? I'm sure she was years older than him."

"His driver's license puts him at eighteen."

"She must have been at least twenty-five."

"She was Italian?"

"No, you keep assuming that. I'm sure he thought so, too. She pretended to be Italian, but her accent was completely wrong. I talked to her one morning when she was leaving his apartment. He wasn't with her. I asked her where she was from. She said 'Rome' and I said 'that is not where you were born.' I knew from her accent, she was foreign. She refused to answer. She just quit talking. Very rude."

"Where do you think she was from?"

"Eastern Europe. Russia, maybe. William introduced her to me as Irene, but he said it as '*i-ree-na*', instead of the Italian '*ee-ray-nay*'. The Italian is similar to the Russian for that name, with a slightly different pronunciation."

"Did you learn her last name?"

"No, he didn't give me her full name. You know Americans. They are so casual, never making a proper introduction. He introduced me by saying ..." The Contessa switched to accented English. "'Irene, meet the Contessa. She owns this place.'" She laughed and switched back to Italian, "Can you imagine?"

Caterina shook her head and smiled, thinking that was exactly what her mother would say about Bill Barton's manners.

"And then he said 'Contessa, you should check out Irene's shop, she sells the best leather coats in Florence. I'm going to get one for my mother.' As if I would ever step inside one of those squalid leather emporiums that clutter this city."

Caterina choked on a laugh, trying to pull up that image. "So you think you saw Irene right before the bomb exploded."

"Again, like I said, she was walking across the piazza using a cell phone," the contessa said with a frown.

Caterina turned back to that page. "Sorry, yes, I have it. Your phone rang and you left the window."

"That's correct."

"Have you seen the apartment William was renting?"

"After about an hour, when he didn't answer my repeated knocking, I went in. No one was there. I turned off the gas at the wall and checked the rooms. Except for the window glass, it didn't seem like there was much damage. That apartment was replastered only five years ago in preparation for renting it. I had it painted again last year, so the plaster isn't very fragile; unlike my fresco."

"Did it appear like anyone had entered after the explosion? Perhaps Irene."

"I didn't hear anyone. It looked like both his and her clothes were lying around. There were some dirty dishes in the kitchen sink. I saw a cheap charm bracelet on the kitchen table. It must have been hers. Also, there was a woman's shearling coat draped over one of the dining room chairs."

Caterina took a sip of her coffee and found it cold. "Do you know if they both had keys to the apartment?"

"He had a set and I had a set. One of the keys is extremely expensive to copy, so unless he never locked the main bolt lock, he wouldn't have made her a set. I never saw her entering on her own any time in the last couple of weeks. The only instances when I saw her alone were when she was leaving the apartment. I never saw her lock up. She just closed the door. It locks automatically."

"When were you last there?"

"As I told you, I had no windows or electricity, so after about two hours I packed two suitcases and came here. Luckily they had a suite for me. I haven't gone back. Actually, I don't think the authorities are letting anyone enter."

"If I can get us in, would you let me see William's apartment?

"If you can wait until after Principessa Orsini's luncheon, I can meet you at my building."

"My guess is that they are not letting people into Piazza del Duomo today, much less the buildings that open on to the square. Why don't you call me when you are coming back from Fiesole. I'll meet you in Piazza San Marco. With my badge they will let your driver park near the cathedral and let us through the barricades."

"That is an excellent idea. I'll call you."

"I don't want to delay you further. I know you said you had someplace to go at ten and I also have a meeting." Caterina flipped back through her notebook. "One last question, do you have contact information for William's parents?"

The contessa shook her head. "No, the rental was completed through the Pelossi Realty Agency. They probably have that information. They handled the contract, the deposit, everything."

Caterina jotted another note. "I know where their office is, over on Via Pucci. I'll drop by tomorrow. They should be open after the holiday."

"I'm sorry I can't help you with that. His parents must have heard about the bombing. Certainly they would try to reach him. When they could not find him surely they would call his school's director, and then the police or the consulate."

"Sometimes it takes a while for those calls to get through the system to our office. Maybe I will have a message when I get in today." Caterina stood and held out her hand. "Thank you for your help, Contessa. I will see you this afternoon."

The elegant older woman offered the polished tips of her fingers. "It's been a pleasure to meet you, my dear. If you will give me her number, I will call your mother immediately. I'm afraid my address book is still in my home."

Caterina wrote the number on the back of one of her business cards. "More thanks for your assistance with

Mother. Here is my number as well, so you can reach me when you come back into town this afternoon."

As Caterina stepped out of the massive front doors of the Palazzo Magnani Feroni into the morning sun, she wondered how she was going to track down Bill Barton's girlfriend, Irene. If the woman was injured or killed, it would be easy, but to find an Eastern European, possible Russian, shopgirl, without knowing her last name, was going to be difficult. Maybe if she could find Barton's college mates, they would know something about Irene.

Chapter Twelve

Bomba Terrorista! Caterina stopped at the newsstand. Usually on Easter Monday there were no newspapers because Easter Sunday was a national holiday and the Italian presses didn't run. But three of Italy's publishers had produced overnight special editions and all of the international papers led with the story. She bought the national papers as well as the *International Herald Tribune*, the *London Times* and the *Wall Street Journal* international edition.

On her way into the Questura, she used her cell phone to call the Japanese interpreter for an update. Lucia Lucchesi reported that she was on her way to interview the injured tour guide at the hospital and would meet with the administrator of the tour agency and the Japanese Consul General that afternoon.

Caterina entered her office, closed the door and skimmed the news reports on the bombing. All speculated that it was a case of Islamic extremism.

Next, she called the Pelossi Realty Agency to get contact information for William Barton. No answer. She tried the UCLA Florence Study Abroad program number. No answer. Easter Monday was going to slow her progress, she realized. She walked down the drab gray hall to the magistrate's office. Patricia Benvenuti was sitting at her desk in the small reception area. The room had the same gray marble floor as the hallway, but the magistrate had provided the funds for a maroon, Turkish kilm carpet and furniture: a small sofa and two chairs covered in gray-striped ruby silk. Over the couch hung a large modern painting that depicted the Duomo, the Ponte Vecchio, Giotto's Tower, the Arno River and the Palazzo Vecchio as if they were all bunched together instead of quite distant from each other.

"Signora, have there been any calls specifically about the American dead or injured victims?"

The administrative assistant, attired in a geometric patterned Missoni knit dress, was peering at her computer's screen, which sat atop an 18th century desk that had once graced her late husband's antique gallery. "Um, just a minute. I'm checking on something for Marco about the Spanish ambassador's niece. Absurd to think she was the target of this thing. Who would use a bomb to kill one girl? How would they know that she would even be close enough to the *carro* to be hurt?" She clicked on the print icon and turned to Caterina. "Calls about Americans?"

"Yes, I'm trying to find contact information for both the Hansen couple and William Barton."

"There have been... where is my list?... almost forty calls from the United States that were referred to this office. Mostly from family members who were trying to find out if their loved ones had been injured. Some calls came in from newspaper and television sources, but I referred those back to the Questura press office." She ran a stubby finger down the list. "No inquiries about Barton or the Hansen couple. There were eight, no nine, calls about the two Americans who are still in the hospital. I returned those calls and provided telephone numbers for the hospital and the U.S. consulate."

Caterina shook her head. "I'm not sure where I'm going to find contact information for those three."

"You *just* asked about phone calls. I *do* have more info about Mr. and Mrs. Hansen. Remember you said they had a hotel key card that went into one of Dr. Rosselli's evidence bags? Only ten hotels in Florence use those, so I called around this morning and found them listed at the Lungarno Hotel. The manager gave me their home address and phone number."

Caterina knew that all of the hotels were required by law to gather passport, address and telephone information from all clients. It was reported daily to the local police. Usually the data was just stockpiled, but Signora Benvenuti told Caterina that there was a push to get the last three days of documents sorted and added to the computer database.

Signora Benvenuti read off the information from the typed document. "They lived in Madison, Wisconsin. It will be the middle of the night there now, but you might be able to get someone by phoning late this afternoon. Do you want me to make the call?"

Caterina took the sheet of paper from the administrative assistant. "No, Signora, I'll do it."

"Child, you don't have to do everything," she protested. "I can help."

"I know Signora, but I feel I must speak directly with the families, especially the parents or children of those who died. The press reporters or others like them – I'm not so interested in speaking directly to them."

"Unlike Marco." Patricia Benvenuti jabbed a thumb in the direction of his office. "I've been making calls for him all morning."

"Signora,…"

"Caterina, I have been begging you for six months to call me Pat, or even Patricia. I may be old, but *Signora* makes me feel ancient. Pretend we are in the States or Australia. Don't stand on ceremony."

"Okay, Patricia, but my mother, who is Bostonian through and through, would not approve," Caterina said, shaking her head. "Not all Americans are so informal."

"We won't tell her," Patricia said with a laugh. "I met her once. Did I tell you? She sold an icon of St. Agata to my husband; a beautiful piece. I was in the shop that day waiting for Pietro to take me to lunch. He gave her a good price for it and then turned around and sold it to one of the *nouveaux riche* Russians for twice that."

"Mother always hated that icon. It was my Nonna's," Caterina said. The magistrate's door opened and she turned. "Sir, I was coming to ask if there is anything I can do before the meeting at eleven."

Magistrate Benigni winked at her. "Bring sharp wits and as much information as you can."

"I was just giving Caterina the British, American, German, and Japanese lists of injured that I got from the hospitals," his assistant said, handing two typed pages to Caterina.

Caterina tucked the papers into her notebook and added, "We were talking about the American fatalities. I met with the Barton boy's landlady, Contessa Montalvo-Ligozzi, this morning. There is a bit of a problem finding contact information for him because of the holiday, but I'm going to see his apartment this afternoon. I'll also find out if his girlfriend knows anything, if I can figure out where she is."

The magistrate nodded. "Okay. Now what about the Japanese ladies?"

"The interpreter is handling most of that. I'm meeting with her before the meeting, hopefully with someone from the consular staff. All of the injured and dead were traveling with the same tour group. The tour company is being very helpful."

"And Herr – what was his name – Vogler?"

"I saw him last evening at the hospital. His children are arriving this morning. He didn't see anything at the *Scoppio del Carro* that could help in the investigation. He's just a very sad old man. The German Consul General has already contacted him and arrangements are being made."

"Sounds like you have things under control. I'll see you in the conference room at eleven." He turned to go back in his office.

Caterina stopped him, saying, "One moment, sir. The contessa told me she saw men climbing on the cart before the bird flew. I thought it might be important."

Paolo Benigni nodded. "Captain DeLuca told me that a number of witnesses reported that fact. It turns out there was a loose wire on the mechanical dove's battery. It had nothing to do with the bomb."

"Sir, is there any more information on the explosive device or the perpetrators?"

"There is, but if you don't mind, Caterina, I have one or two things to do before eleven. The preliminary information will be discussed at the briefing. You'll be there." He closed the door.

Caterina turned to Signora Benvenuti. "Do you know what they found?"

"No, he's been very tight-lipped. Not like himself at all. All I know is that an FBI guy from the U.S. Embassy in Rome was here with the magistrate when I arrived this morning. They went off for an hour or so to meet with Captain DeLuca."

"You say Marco asked you to look up some information…"

"Marco was 'Johnnie on the Spot' this morning, if you know what I mean. He, too, was here before I got in. He kept pacing outside of the boss's door. Without even a '*buongiorno*' or 'how do you do,' he hands me this list of computer searches and phone calls to make." She pointed at the pages still coming out of the printer. "He wants these for the meeting at eleven."

Caterina felt a twinge of envy. "Did he go to the briefing with Captain DeLuca?"

"No, but not because he didn't try. The magistrate told him that he needed to get all the information together on his assignments, you know, the Spanish girls and that Estonian chap, before the meeting with the consular officers."

Caterina said, "I wonder if he came across a woman, maybe injured, maybe Russian, named Irene."

The older woman pulled out another list. "Last name?"

"I don't know it."

"I don't see anyone named Irene on the list Marco gave me or the ones that came from the hospitals. There haven't been any calls about someone with that name. Are you sure she's not Italian? We don't have the list of Italian victims yet."

"I have it on good information that she is Eastern European."

"If calls come in from places like Poland, Estonia or Russia, there is almost always a language problem with the switchboard at the Questura. The routing is slower. Usually the families end up calling the closest Italian consulate in their country or a neighboring country and the inquiry comes to us from there. It may take a couple of days. Who is this Irene?"

"She may be William Barton's girlfriend," Caterina answered.

"She's missing?"

"I don't know."

Chapter Thirteen

Marco pushed past Caterina to enter the conference room before her. Patricia Benvenuti and one of the secretaries were setting a side table with bottled water and glasses.

"Too close to lunch for coffee. Everybody will stop by a bar on the way in for a mid-morning espresso, if they…"

Marco interrupted, "Signora, where is the information I requested two hours ago? I need to be prepared for this meeting."

"I put a folder containing all of the printouts on your desk forty-five minutes ago, Marco," she replied. "Didn't you see it?"

Without saying a word, he placed a pile of documents, including three newspapers, a magazine focusing on political commentary in Spain, two file folders, and some loose papers with handwritten notes and post-its attached, on the table across from Caterina and one seat closer to the head of the table. He then turned and hurried out the door.

"That boy needs to learn that *more* is not necessarily *better*," Signora Benvenuti said, as she took her seat against the wall slightly behind where the magistrate would sit.

Paolo Benigni opened the door and stepped back to allow a tall blonde woman, dressed in a black linen pants suit and a charcoal-gray blouse, to enter.

"Patricia Benvenuti and Catherine Falcone, I would like to introduce Consul General Susan Whitmore to you."

The three women looked at each other and all started laughing. The magistrate looked from one to another, waiting to be made privy to the joke.

The American Consul General spoke first, "Paolo, remember that for three weeks Caterina and I worked on the case of the college boy who fell from the balcony? As for Patricia, she has graciously invited me to her famed lunches: once when she was hosting the British Ambassador and then, for the Anglo-American bridge club. I was trying to learn my way around the expat community in Florence and Patricia was one of my most efficient guides."

"Of course, of course," the magistrate said, leading her to the seat between Caterina and himself. "I'm completely out of the social whirl, but it's troubling that I forgot that poor boy. He's back in New Jersey, isn't he?"

Susan Whitmore shook her head. "He's being flown out next week. He's got about six more months of physical therapy to complete, but his mother says he's much improved." She opened her capacious purse, took out a silver MacBook Air and opened it on the table in front of her seat.

"Good, good." The magistrate placed a thick leather folder on the table and looked up as the door opened. Marco rushed into the room followed by Signorina Lucchesi, and the Consuls General of Japan and Germany. The magistrate nodded to the Japanese interpreter and moved to greet the two men behind her.

Susan Whitmore spoke *sotto voce* to Caterina, "I was hoping we could meet privately today or tomorrow."

"Whenever you wish," Caterina responded.

"I have a luncheon to attend today up in Fiesole that I can't get out of, but I'm free after this meeting, until about twelve thirty. Maybe we can take a few minutes in your office."

"That works for me," Caterina said, glancing down the table as the door flew open, straight-armed by a short man with dark, straight hair, dressed completely in black, who surveyed the room with barely suppressed rage. "Who is he?" she murmured to Susan.

Marco heard the question and looked over his shoulder. He leaped out of his chair, rushed up to shake the red-faced man's hand, and then tap the magistrate's arm to get his attention. "Sir, may I present Enrique Perez, the political attaché to Spain's Embassy in Rome. He will be…"

Perez interrupted, holding out his hand to Paolo Benigni, "I will be representing Ambassador Salazar, who wishes to be with his sister, who lost her youngest daughter in this outrageous attack. Now, Magistrate Benigni, can we get to work?"

The magistrate took the Spaniard's hand. "May I express the city's sorrow at the loss experienced by the ambassador's family? Please convey our sympathies to him and his sister, Señora Caron. Of course, we will bring this meeting to order immediately. I believe almost everyone has arrived." He addressed the rest of the room, "Please be seated and I will start with introductions."

Representatives of the United States, Britain, Germany, Spain, Japan, and Russia, from consular offices located in Florence or from embassies in Rome, and the trade representative from Estonia sat around the table. Various administrative assistants, the Japanese interpreter, and two police lieutenants from Captain DeLuca's staff sat in chairs along the wall.

The magistrate stood at the end of the table. He released a button on his chocolate-brown, tweed jacket and checked if his tie was cinched tight. He introduced each participant, barely looking at the list Signora Benvenuti had prepared for him. At the end of the acknowledgements, he paused and seemed to be collecting his thoughts before speaking slowly in Italian.

"It is difficult to fully describe the horror we feel, as Florentines and Italians, at the travesty perpetrated on the City of Florence, our centuries old cathedral, and, most of all, on our citizens and the esteemed visitors, who have always had a special feeling for this unique place. We are charged with assisting the foreign visitors – both tourists and residents – who were killed or injured by this murderous bomb. We also wish to help the families and loved ones of those victims. The Task Force for Foreigners stands ready to coordinate with the consulates, the embassies, and the individual families to get through this trying time without bureaucratic delays and frustrations.

"I am not good at speeches and so I beg your indulgence if I leave the language of grief and anger behind and move on to the facts. For this first meeting, we have only invited representatives from the countries which lost citizens in the explosion."

He enumerated the dead and injured from each country and then read the names of each fatality and the names and hospital location of each of the seriously injured. Although Caterina already knew the statistics, the naming of the victims caused her throat to tighten and a chill to run up her back.

"Signora Benvenuti," the magistrate said, turning to his administrative assistant, "is going to give each of you a list of your countrymen and women who were either killed or injured. If you have additional names to bring to our attention of people who have been reported missing; please provide us with this information in writing." He spoke for another few minutes about the assistance the embassies could offer before being interrupted.

"Let's get to what is important," shouted Enrique Perez. "Who did this? No one at the Questura or the mayor's office will tell us anything. Dulce Caron was our ambassador's niece. I would think we would get some consideration."

"Thank you   Perez. I know this seems very bureaucratic when you have experienced a personal loss, but…"

The door opened. A tall broad man, with short blond hair and light eyes walked in. "Sorry I'm late," he murmured in Italian. "The mayor…"

"Your timing couldn't be better, Mr. Turner," said the magistrate, standing to greet the newcomer.

The man made a quick scan of the room. He nodded to Consul General Whitmore and advanced to shake hands with the magistrate. Caterina watched Marco eye the man's well-tailored suit. She leaned to her left and whispered, "Susan, who is he?" She got no response.

"Ladies and gentlemen, please may I introduce Maxwell Turner, Legal Attaché to the U.S. Embassy in Rome," Paolo Benigni said. "As many of you may know, the Legal Attaché, or 'Legat' for short, is an employee of the FBI, tasked with the job of providing information and intelligence from U.S. sources to law enforcement agencies in the country where the embassy is located."

"Finally, someone who knows something," said Enrique Perez.

Benigni paused, cleared his throat and continued. "In return, the police and secret service provide the Legat with information concerning crimes, antiterrorism and the like, when they impact American citizens. Mr. Turner has been posted in Italy for a two-year tour of duty and has been in Rome for just over six months. I asked him to join us because of his expertise and his international viewpoint on terrorist acts."

The magistrate moved back to the end of the table, shifting his chair to the left and pulling an empty chair from against the wall to the table. "Mr. Turner, what can you tell us?"

Maxwell Turner thanked the magistrate, put a couple of manila files on the table and set his briefcase on the floor. He remained standing and addressed the group in good, but not perfect, Italian. "Good morning, as Magistrate Benigni said, I'm Max Turner. First, let me clarify a bit what the magistrate has said. The U.S. FBI has no authority to independently investigate crimes and apprehend criminals in countries outside U.S. territory. But I do act as a source of information for the Italian *polizia*, *carabinieri*, and the secret police, as well as others. I gather and analyze intelligence provided by those agencies."

The Russian consular officer began to speak. Turner raised his hand to stop the question. "Excuse me, sir. I must tell you that I arrived in Florence just last evening and we are at the very beginning of this investigation. Since you are all working with Magistrate Benigni's task force regarding crimes committed by or against those who are not citizens of Italy, Captain DeLuca, who is heading up the full investigation of this terrorist act, asked me to speak to you."

The German General Consul spoke, "I thought we were getting the formal briefing tomorrow with the mayor and all of the police agencies. Are you just giving us FBI guesswork?"

Max Turner pulled out the chair and sat down. "Before you all dive in with questions and comments, let me tell you what we know so far. I admit this information may change as we gather more intelligence and analyze the evidence we have gathered. Also, since this information is preliminary, I must ask you to keep it confidential. We cannot have any press leaks before tomorrow's briefing and the press conference that follows. There may be information that I give you that will be withheld from the press."

"Why are you even talking to us then?" asked the Russian representative.

"Because there are one or two discrete tasks that need to be initiated immediately. I will speak to this in a minute. Now, here are the facts. First, this was not an accident."

Down the table, someone muttered, "No surprises here."

Turner did not pause. "Since the blast was so big, this seems to be a no-brainer, but since the *Scoppio del Carro* event includes fireworks, firecrackers, and small explosive devices, it needs to be said that this was not an accident involving the set up of the fireworks.

"Two, the explosive used was C-4. This means that a relatively small amount of explosive material had the capacity to create a large and damaging explosion. C-4 is a plastic substance that can be molded to most any shape. This is also why the device went undetected."

"Where was it?" asked Marco, scribbling a note at the same time.

"It was attached to the underside of the cart on the right side, the side nearest the cathedral."

The Japanese Consul General asked, "Was the cathedral the target?"

"We don't know, sir." Turner responded.

"In this day and time, post 9/11, didn't someone check the cart?" asked the Spanish envoy.

The magistrate answered. "Mr. Perez, the *carro* was inspected for safety since it is so old. I was told that the original medieval cart was replaced in the early 1800s. That makes the cart used yesterday over two hundred years old. The inspection was done two days before the festival. It was inspected *again* after the fireworks were attached on Saturday. We assume the perpetrator attached the bomb last evening before the cart was locked up for the night."

Turner added, "It would have taken about three to five minutes to attach the bomb." He paused and seemed to collect his thoughts. "Since there was no chatter on the known terrorist networks and none of the intelligence services obtained any information from other sources that Florence was targeted, there was no heightened concern about this event. It's taken place for hundreds of years without incident. In fact, most of the attention among the anti-terrorist agencies was focused on Rome, at the Vatican, for the Pope's annual Easter address."

"But with the Twin Towers and the Madrid train station bombing and the tragedy in the London underground, shouldn't someone have checked more closely?" Marco asked. The magistrate walked behind him and placed a restraining hand on his shoulder. Marco looked up in surprise and then slumped down in his seat.

The Legat nodded. "Hindsight is always clearer, but as I said, none of the interagency services had any inkling of a possible incident."

"Maybe this is the work of some crazy person," said the Estonian trade representative in heavily accented English.

Turner responded in Italian, "I was just coming to my next point. This was a sophisticated device. Simple in its operation, but sophisticated in its design. The explosive material was detonated by the use of a cell phone."

"How do you know?" asked Perez.

"The crime scene investigators, along with bomb experts, found not only traces of C-4, but bits and pieces of a cell phone, including a piece of a melted cell phone cover, a burned battery and the data chip, or SIM card. The plastic was buried in the wood of one axle, another piece of plastic was found on autopsy in the head wound of an American tourist, the battery was hurled inside the Duomo and the data chip was found stuck in the leg of the poor *sbandieratoro* standing at the door of the cathedral."

"So you have a cell phone and C-4 explosive. Any fingerprints?" Japanese Consul General sounded impatient.

"No prints, but something almost as good."

"The SIM card?" guessed Susan Whitmore, looking up from typing on her laptop.

"No, the SIM card was no help. The phone was unregistered."

"So what do you have?" asked Marco, despite the continued presence of the magistrate behind him.

"We have a signature," said Turner.

The German representative barked out a laugh. "A signature? Handwritten?"

Max shook his head and smiled. "The way the device was put together is the signature of one particular bomber."

"Who?" asked the Russian consular officer.

"We don't know his exact identity."

There was a general dissatisfied rumble of low voices and someone spoke up from the far end of the table. "But you must know something."

The Legat nodded. "We know that this bomb-maker has created bombs used on at least three previous occasions. Maybe more, but three that we know of."

Chapter Fourteen

Maxwell Turner looked out at a room that was dead silent for a moment. Then a babel in at least four languages flowed around the table. Caterina only heard it as a buzz, distant and incomprehensible. *A serial bomber has attacked Florence?* The question resounded in her head.

Marco's voice broke above the rest. "Did this bastard make the bombs that destroyed the Madrid trains?"

"No, but he or she – the profile of a bomb-maker is usually that of a man, so I will stick to that for our discussions here – did make the bomb that went off in the lobby of the Guggenheim Museum in Bilbao last year, killing five people, including the Spanish Cultural Minister."

"See? That's what I suspected," Marco said, looking down the table at Enrique Perez. "The bomb-maker is either ETA or an ETA sympathizer. Here he and his group targeted the Spanish Ambassador through his niece." Marco started digging through his briefing material on the Basque group and passing it to Perez.

"Just hold on a minute," Turner protested. "It's possible there is an ETA connection, but there was never any formal claim of responsibility at Bilbao, which is unusual for that group. Also, if the bomb-maker worked for ETA, it is because they hired him, not because he is a sympathizer."

"How do you know this?" asked Perez.

"Because the other two bombs didn't target Spain or its government. Before the Bilbao incident, there were two fatal bombings, one in Turkmenistan and the other in Jakarta."

Caterina spoke up, "Did anyone claim credit for any of these bombings?"

Max Turner looked at her for a moment before responding, "Each time there were phone calls and letters from various groups, but none of them ever panned out. They were probably groups grabbing on to the coattails of the real perpetrator.

The magistrate interjected, "In fact, last night Mayor Moretti received a letter purportedly from an Italian pro-Palestinian group, but police informants inside the organization say that there was no evidence of planning or execution by the group's insiders.

"Also," Turner continued, "you may have heard on television early this morning that someone called the Mediaset TV station, speaking in Farsi, and claiming to be from a group called Sword of Allah; but intelligence from the CIA and Mossad leads us to believe that this small, fanatical group is unable to carry out terrorist activities in four different countries."

"Could this be an assassin for hire?" asked Susan Whitmore.

Turner walked over to the sideboard and got himself a glass of water before he answered. "It's possible, but usually an assassin is more surgical. It is hard to use an explosive device in public places to target an individual."

"But if you are saying it's one bomber, then there must be a group or client behind him," Marco insisted.

"The computers at Langley are working overtime on this, trying to make some connections. Tomorrow you will be given more detailed information about the previous bombs and their victims. What we need from this task force and the representatives of the different embassies is for everybody to keep in mind the three other bombings as you talk to your citizens, whether injured or survivors or other witnesses. Captain DeLuca's team will be looking at connections between the people injured or killed at the Florence Duomo and those in Jakarta and Turkmenistan. We're already reexamining the Bilbao incident. If you see any connection, no matter how small, please inform Magistrate Benigni." Turner nodded toward the magistrate.

Paolo Benigni made a short wrap-up speech, ending the briefing. As the room cleared, Caterina waited for the American Legat to finish talking privately to Susan Whitmore and the Japanese Consul General.

"Mr. Turner, I'm Caterina Falcone," she said in English.

He shook her hand. "Call me Max."

She nodded. "I'll be gathering information for Magistrate Benigni on the Americans injured and dead. As you know, you lost three U.S. citizens and at least four more are seriously injured. Do you want me to just pass information regarding these people on to you after the magistrate reviews it? Or would it be more helpful for you to be involved in the actual investigation?"

He poured himself another glass of water and then one for her. "It depends on what you are investigating," he said. He sat on the corner of the table, bringing his head down level with hers.

Tall is good. Caterina, wondering where that random thought came from. She took a sip of water and set down the glass. "For instance, this afternoon I am going to inspect the dead college boy's – William Barton's – apartment. Do you want to be there?"

"I'm going to be up to my eyeballs with briefings. How about if you take the initial look see and then let me know anything seems hinky."

"Okay." Caterina turned to pick up her notebook and pens.

"Thanks for asking," he added with a crooked grin.

She noticed his green eyes for the first time. *Tall with gorgeous eyes,* she mused. While mentally chastising herself, she tried to think of something to ask to prolong the conversation.

"What do you think of my colleague, Marco Capponi's, ETA theory?"

"Capponi seems sharp, but it's easy when you only have a narrow focus or area of investigative interest to think it must be important. It's too early to tell. But I'd rather have him focused, than uninvolved." He walked around to the other side of the table and picked up his briefcase. He came back and held out his hand. "I'm sorry, but I must get to Captain DeLuca's office now."

She shook his hand – a warm, hard grip – then watched as he walked over to the magistrate, who was frowning at something Perez was saying. The three of them left the room together.

Caterina spent the next thirty minutes with Susan Whitmore, briefing her on the American victims. As the American Consul General got on the elevator, she winked at Caterina and opined in an undertone that the Legat from Rome was "sharp, professional, and dishy."

"And tall, too," Caterina whispered back.

Susan smiled. "You must tower over most Italian men," she observed, catching the door as it shut, causing it to slide open again. "That's your mother's fault."

"No, I get it from both sides. It was a blessing in the States, but a curse here." Caterina could hear the American woman's hearty laugh as the door closed again.

On the way back to her office, she stopped to collect Lucia Lucchesi, who was in the magistrate's reception area talking to Signora Benvenuti. The Japanese interpreter briefed Caterina on the status of her assigned list of tourists and tour groups.

Caterina then called the assistant to the German Consul General to discuss Herr Vogler and his wife. After she set up an appointment with the British Consul General for the following morning, she went out and bought a *panino* made of a smear of goat cheese, three slices of salami and a sprig of *radicchio* to eat at her desk for a late lunch. The sandwich churned in her stomach fifteen minutes later when she made an agonizing call to the Hansen family in Wisconsin, waking them up to the news of Fredrick's and Melanie's deaths.

The afternoon shadows were growing long as Caterina scrolled through her cell phone messages while standing at the taxi stand in Piazza San Marco, when a black Mercedes pulled up to the curb. She saw the NCC placard on the dashboard, the permit that allowed the driver to enter the restricted "blue zone" of the historic center. A middle-aged man in a dark suit and an almost-convincing toupee jumped out and started to open the rear door for her.

"It's better that I sit up front," Caterina said.

He nodded and opened the front passenger door for her, "As you wish."

"Good afternoon, my dear," the Contessa said from the back seat.

"*Buona sera*, Contessa. Did you leave my mother in Fiesole?"

"She decided to catch a ride back with Zoe Bascome. Do you know her? She's the British artist who has become very popular with her portraits. She borrows a lot from Caravaggio."

"I don't think I've seen her work."

"Ask your mother. Zoe has a very interesting, almost scandalous, love life. She likes girls, you know…"

To get to the edge of Piazza del Duomo, they had to go through two checkpoints; one limiting access to the city center to residents, and the other further restricting entry to the piazza to official personnel.

"We will have to park at the end here near Via Proconsolo and walk over to your building," said Caterina.

The older woman gave her driver instructions to wait as he held the door open for her.

"About thirty minutes should be sufficient, correct?" she asked as she joined Caterina.

"More than enough time." She matched the contessa's slower pace as they walked along the side of the cathedral.

As they approached the front of the cathedral they could see two construction lifts on tractors raised against the Duomo's façade, supporting building engineers, who were checking for structural damage beneath the cracked and crumbling marble.

"This is my *palazzo*," said the contessa, walking up to a large double wooden entry door, closed and crossed with crime scene tape.

A *vigile* hurried over from the bell tower. "State your business," he demanded. "You can't go in there."

"Contessa Montalvo-Ligozzi is with me." Caterina pulled out her police inspector's identification and her badge. "She owns an apartment here."

"All of the buildings along here have been evacuated. No one can enter until they have had a structural inspection."

"When will that be completed?" asked the contessa.

"They expect to clear all of the buildings by Friday."

"We need to see part of this building today," Caterina said. "It involves one of the victims."

The *vigile* wasn't going to give way. "But it may be dangerous and there isn't any electricity."

"Then it's better that we see it while there is still some afternoon light," the contessa snapped.

"But my orders…"

Caterina intervened. "I will take responsibility."

"I will have to report you."

"Please do," Caterina said over her shoulder as she turned back to the door and removed the crime scene tape.

"Here you go, dear," said the Contessa as she handed over a ring of keys with one selected for Caterina's use. "I guess this means we can't take the elevator."

"I'm afraid not."

"It shouldn't be too bad. There's a skylight over the stairwell."

Dim sunlight filtered down reflecting off dust motes. The stairs were covered with small chunks of plaster. The air smelled of stone and dust with background notes of a humid sewer odor common to buildings in the historic center of Florence, all of which were built over ancient septic tanks. Caterina tried, but could not detect any whiff of leaking gas.

"Do you need to stop at your apartment for anything? This may be your last chance before Friday. I'd be happy to carry anything down for you."

"No, I have enough clothes to last me for a week and the hotel can provide everything else." The contessa was breathing hard as they rounded the fourth flight of stairs.

"Then, let's look at William's apartment before it gets dark. I need to find some contact information for his family."

"What about his school?"

"The school and the rental agency were closed today, but they should be open tomorrow," Caterina replied. "I really don't want to wait that long. It's been twenty-four hours already."

"That's very considerate of you, my dear." They got to the top of the sixth and final set of stone steps. "Here we are. Now where are those keys?" The contessa rummaged around in the bottom of her Louis Vuitton purse. "Here they are." She opened the door by inserting an intricate modern bolt lock key and then using a simple latchkey in the door handle. It was lighter inside than in the hallway. The windows gaped with a few teeth of glass still clinging to the frames.

"Maybe we can figure out how to close the shutters before we go." Caterina touched a shard of glass that fell in and broke on the floor. She looked out the window to the bell tower and downward at an angle to the Duomo's front steps.

The contessa didn't say anything for a minute while she looked around the dining area. She started to say, "Caterina, I think… just a moment…" She moved into the dark windowless kitchen. When she came out, she said, "I think someone has been here."

Chapter Fifteen

MOSCOW

Oleg Goncharov lumbered past the shapely blonde secretary sitting outside the door of his brother's office. Opening the door without knocking, he caught Andrei by surprise as he poured a cut crystal tumbler half-full with an expensive, single-malt scotch. The liquor splashed on the ebony wood of the credenza behind his desk.

Andrei swept the liquid off the surface onto the plush white carpet with his hand. "Damn you, Oleg. Look what you made..."

"Have you heard from Yakov?" Oleg interrupted as he lowered himself into an antique Empire Period chair in front of the desk. Except for the ebony desk and credenza, all of the furniture in the office was covered in black silk accented with tiny gold embroidered fleur-de-lys.

"No, but I got..."

"Why hasn't he called in? He always does by now."

Andrei took a sip of his drink. "I don't know why Yakov hasn't called or, better yet, returned to Moscow. But, more important, I have..."

"What could be more important?" Oleg slapped his beefy palm against his knee.

Andrei, a younger copy of his brother, but four inches taller and twenty pounds lighter, angled over the desk, braced on both hands, said in a low even voice. "The boy. The boy is key. Do you want to hear what I know about him?"

"What? How?"

Andrei held up the thumb on his right hand. "What? He's dead. He extended the first finger to join the thumb. "How? I assume you mean how do I know, right?"

Oleg nodded.

"I had our American lawyer call the consulate in Florence to ask if his 'nephew' was on the list of dead or injured. The assistant to the Consul General expressed his regrets when he confirmed that William Barton was unfortunately among the fatalities."

"Did you tell the lawyer to... ?"

Andrei sat down. "What do you take me for, Oleg? Of course I did. The letter went out this morning, nine o'clock New York time."

Oleg looked horrified. "Not in your name, I hope."

"Certainly not. Jeffers signed it. But the Barton kid's father will know it's from me."

Chapter Sixteen

What do you mean?" asked Caterina, looking around the dim *sala* with its heavy furniture and ancestral paintings.

"I mean someone has been in the apartment since I was here yesterday following the blast."

"How can you tell?" Caterina felt a slight unease. She walked to the kitchen doorway and looked into the darkness, but didn't enter. *Why didn't I think to bring a flashlight?* she thought.

"Remember, I said that there was a woman's coat here on one of the dining room chairs?" She placed her hand on the back of the wooden chair closest to the door. "It was right here – and now it's gone."

"Is it on the floor? Maybe it slid off."

"No, it's gone. And so is the charm bracelet."

"Charm bracelet?"

"I saw a cheap charm bracelet on that counter in the kitchen." She pointed to the corner of the white ceramic counter closest to the doorway. "I remember it distinctly because I thought it was so ugly. It's gone, too."

"What else is missing?" asked Caterina scanning the ornate living room.

"Nothing here that I can recall, at least, not in these two rooms."

"Let's check the bedroom."

"I bet it was *that* woman," the contessa said, straightening a painting of her great-grandmother holding a small pug dog on her lap. "She came back for her things."

"Where's the bedroom?" Caterina asked.

The contessa pointed. "Up these stairs. The bedroom was an addition built at roof level in the sixties, a version of a loft. My husband and I used it as a glassed-in porch."

Caterina started climbing the stairs. She could hear the wind blowing through the windows.

The contessa came up behind her. "When I decided to make this a small rental apartment, separate from my home, I had my contractor take out the glass walls and close it in. A small bathroom was added then, too."

The air smelled of dust, burnt wood, and dirty socks. Glass was blown across the bed; the filmy white curtains had offered no protection. A grey sweatshirt and black running shorts lay in a pile on the seat of the armchair. A blue terrycloth towel was bunched on the bed. Peeking out from under the bed was a pair of black Puma running shoes with athletic socks stuffed in them.

"Not everything is gone then," observed the contessa.

Caterina opened the armoire. Two suit jackets and a number of pressed cotton shirts hung next to a down ski jacket and a black Gortex windbreaker. There were a few empty hangers pushed to one side. A pair of highly polished Bruno Magli men's wing-tipped shoes and a set of rubber beach flip-flops were lined up on the closet floor.

The contessa opened the top drawer of the dresser. It was divided by a wooden slat. One section was empty. The other side contained a black leather folder that contained a class schedule and a legal pad covered with what looked to Caterina like notes Bill Barton had taken in an art history class. Under the folder were some loose brochures about Sardinian resorts and Venetian hotels, a train schedule for the Eurostar trains, a Lumix digital camera, and a plasticized map of Florence.

Caterina pulled everything out and put it on the top of the dresser beside a stack of books, two for Italian language studies and one about post-war European history.

The next drawer down contained briefs, socks and a few white t-shirts. Beneath the underwear was a brown leather travel portfolio. Inside, Caterina found a return airplane ticket from Florence to Los Angeles, dated for the last week of May. The other side of the portfolio had three slots labeled: Currency, Credit Cards, and Passport. The currency slot was empty. The credit card slot held an American Express platinum card and a Citibank ATM card, both in William Barton's name. The passport slot was empty.

Caterina showed the contessa the travel folder. "I might be wrong, but I bet there was cash and a passport in here when William left the apartment yesterday morning. We found ten euro in cash, a driver's license, and a student I.D. in his wallet. Many of the American universities warn their students not to carry their passports, but to always have some sort of identification with them."

The contessa pointed at the empty space in the top drawer. "I think, Caterina, that his girlfriend used half of this *cassetto* for her small things and maybe kept clothes on some of the hangers in the *armadio*. But if she took the money and his passport, why didn't she take the credit cards?"

"Probably too difficult to use, Caterina said. "Almost everybody knows that credit cards can be traced. She may be able to sell the passport. There is a strong black market, especially for American passports." She paused, dropping the portfolio on the top of the dresser, and dug a pair of latex gloves out of her purse. "Just in case this turns out to be a theft," she murmured. She turned to the contessa and said, "Maybe it would be best if I do the the sorting and you just observe, but don't touch."

"Probably a wise idea, my dear,' said the contessa with smile. "I rarely watch those police shows, but the newspapers frequently report 'contaminated crime scenes' as the reason for a botched arrest."

"I never considered this a potential crime scene until the passport turned up missing," Caterina said. "Better safe than sorry. It may be nothing. Maybe the school holds their passports for safety." Caterina picked up the digital camera and looked at the dials on the top and back. "Let's see if I can turn this on." She slid a tiny switch and the screen lit up. "It seems to have a charged battery. Now let's hope there are photos." She studied the dials again and moved one clockwise. A photo of three young men in UCLA logo t-shirts and matching sunglasses appeared on the screen. She turned the camera so the contessa could see the picture.

"The middle one is William," the older woman said.

"The others are probably in his school program here," said Caterina. "I think that's part of the Ponte Vecchio in the background."

She pushed a button of the back of the camera and the picture changed to one with Bill Barton wearing a black leather jacket with his arm draped across the shoulders of a short, slender woman with long wavy brown hair.

"Is this Irene?"

The contessa nodded. "That's her. You see what I mean about her."

"Her blouse is a bit skimpy," Caterina observed, swallowing a grin.

"Almost non-existent. With her it is either not enough on the top or not enough to cover her bottom."

Caterina tried to pull up another photo, but failed. "It seems there are only two shots on the camera's chip."

"Chip?"

"Yes, the photos are saved on the memory until they are downloaded."

The contessa shook her head. "I know nothing about these things."

Caterina pulled and envelope of evidence bags out of her purse. "I'm going to take the camera, the portfolio and the airplane ticket back to the Questura with me."

After filling two plastic bags and labeling them properly, Caterina entered the bathroom. After a couple of minutes she stuck her head out the door. "Have you been in here since Bill moved in?"

"In the bathroom? No, I didn't come up the bedroom stairs yesterday, which was the first time I entered the apartment at all since he moved in."

"I think you said that he had been dating Irene for at least a couple of weeks."

"I don't know how long he's been dating her. But I do know she has been staying overnight on a regular basis for at least three weeks. I heard them in the hallway morning and night."

In the bathroom on a low shelf there was shaving equipment, a tube of Crest toothpaste, a coffee cup with a worn toothbrush in it and a hairbrush with blond hairs woven among the bristles. A bar of soap with a sandalwood scent lay on the edge of the sink. A towel matching the one on the bed hung at an angle on a metal rod near the shower stall. "It seems strange that there is no evidence of her in the bathroom, then. Not even a toothbrush."

She looked under the bed. "There's something over there." She went to the other side and reached under to pull out a pair of orange thong panties and a bunched up athletic sock. "Hers and his, I would guess." She placed them on the bed.

Caterina looked around the room again and then went to the windows, opened the frames, careful to avoid the broken glass. She reached out and closed the shutters. "I'll do this downstairs, too, and then we'll close the ones in your apartment. It will give some protection until the glaziers do their work. I want to get you down to the piazza before we lose the light."

She picked up the orange thong. "I'm going to take this with me. It's the only evidence we've found that the girlfriend was here," she said as she sealed the plastic bag and slipped it with the others in the long side pocket of her purse.

"I hope you find that girl," said the contessa as she descended the stairs into the living room. "Someone has William's keys to this place, including one to the palazzo's front door. I guess I'll have to have the locks changed as soon as I can."

"That would be best," Caterina said, following the older woman out the door and across the landing to the contessa's apartment.

When they were back down on the square, the contessa asked, "Did you find what you were looking for, my dear?"

"Not really. I was trying to find something that would give me a clue about finding his family today. Now I either have to get the crime lab to give up his phone or..."

"Or?"

"Or it may be easier to get the number from his university tomorrow or from the Pelosi Realty Agency."

"What about the girl?" asked the contessa.

"I don't know. This visit to William's apartment has created a whole new mystery. Now, I'm really going to have to try and find Irene. Why, in the midst of all this destruction, would she go back to his apartment? Maybe to look for him? Maybe to steal from him?"

"If she's innocent, why didn't she try to contact the police about William? Or why didn't she contact me by leaving a note on my door?" The contessa was insistent.

"We don't know if she has her own set of keys. You didn't think so yesterday, but as far as I remember no keys were found in William's pockets. Maybe she had them." Caterina paused and rummaged in her pocket for her notebook. "Also, I have to remember to tell the U.S. Consulate that his passport is missing."

The contessa's driver was lounging against his car, talking to the same *vigile* who had confronted the two women earlier. The chauffer came to attention immediately, seated both women, and drove off. He opened the door for Caterina outside the Questura ten minutes later.

Caterina leaned back into the car. "I'll call you later in the week, Contessa. Thank you for your help."

Caterina took the elevator to the third floor. When the doors opened she almost collided with Signora Benvenuti, who was carrying a tray with two small cups of espresso.

Patricia continued on her way, saying over her shoulder, "I'm so glad you are back. I left a note on your desk. There is a message from the Questura switchboard. A woman named Candace Seagraves from Santa Barbara, California, telephoned about that poor boy, William Barton."

Chapter Seventeen

The woman sounded scared and wouldn't let Caterina get a word into the conversation. "I'm his mother. He calls me every Sunday. I've been trying to call him, but he doesn't answer his cell phone and his apartment doesn't even *have* a phone. He's not responding to email. I called the school, but no one answers. This is the first time I've had trouble contacting him. I know I worry too much. He's a grown boy."

"Mrs. Seagraves, can I just verify a bit of information for my records. Would you give me your son's full name?"

"William Bradley Barton III"

"And his father's name?"

"William Bradley Barton, Jr."

"Is his father with you?"

Candace Seagraves was silent for a moment. "Do you mean are we still married?"

"Sorry to be confusing. I'm just writing down the contact info. I wondered if Mr. Barton was either in Santa Barbara with you or in Florence or someplace else."

"No to the first two. We're divorced. Bill's father is, I think, sailing off the coast of Sardinia somewhere – or, at least, that's what Bill told me last week."

Caterina flipped to the page of her notebook for the information she had copied from William Barton's driver's license. "And finally, what is your son's address in the U.S.?"

"Twenty-two Cortez Court, Los Angeles." It matched the license.

Caterina leaned her forehead into her left hand. Her right hand gripped the telephone tightly. She took a deep breath. "Mrs. Seagraves, I'm sorry to tell you this over the telephone, but we believe your son was killed yesterday in the explosion at the cathedral in Florence."

Silence was followed by a whisper. "No, this isn't possible. You must be wrong."

"I am so sorry Mrs. Seagraves, but we are almost certain. We only lack an official identification by a family member or acquaintance. He was carrying his driver's license. The name, photo, and address match."

"No, No, *No!*" The words got louder and louder. Then there was just the sound of sobbing and a man's voice in the background.

"Honey? Darling? What's wrong?" The voice became more distinct over the phone line. "Who is this?"

"This is Caterina Falcone with the police in Florence, Italy. Who am I speaking to, please?"

"John Seagraves, Candy's husband. What did you say to her? Is it Bill? Something's happened to Bill?"

"I'm glad you are there, sir. Your wife's son was killed yesterday."

"What happened? Why didn't somebody call? Was it a car accident or something to do with that damn father of his?"

"No, sir, a bomb went off in Florence yesterday at the cathedral."

"Bill's not Catholic, why would he be at some church? Are you sure you have the right person?"

"Mr. Seagraves, have you seen the reports on the television or in the papers?

"Never watch TV. And it's eight thirty in the morning. I haven't gone out to get our paper out at the box on the road. There wasn't anything in the Sunday paper."

"Sir, yesterday, Easter Sunday, a bomb exploded in the center of Florence. It is on the news in the U.S., I'm sure. It will also be on the front page of your newspaper this morning. It happened near William's apartment building. He was outside in the square. He was killed. I am so sorry." Tears welled up in Caterina's eyes.

John Seagraves paused before saying, in a low measured tone, "I can't talk now. I've got to help Candy. Give me your number. It's Caterina, right? I'll call you back." Caterina gave him her full name and direct telephone number. She expressed her condolences once again before he hung up without a word.

She sat at her desk with her head in her hands. There was a soft knock on her door. It was the Japanese interpreter.

"Uh, yes, uh, come in, Lucia," she said, wiping tears away and sitting up straighter. "What can I do for you?"

"*Sta bene, Signorina Falcone?*" She hovered near the door

"Call me Caterina. Sit down. Sit down, please." She waved her hand at one of the visitor chairs. "I'm okay.

Really. I just will *never* get used to giving family members bad news."

"I know what you mean," Lucia said, perching on the edge of the chair, clutching her files in her arms. "Especially in a case like this. How do we explain it? Particularly when people are on a holiday. Tragedy is the furthest thing from their minds."

"So how are you doing with the Japanese ladies?" Caterina shuffled the paper on her desk. She found the right page. "Has the... what is it?... Kyoto Royal Renaissance Tour Company been of assistance with the families?"

"Very much so. The agency has arranged for airplane tickets and hotel lodging for one or two family members of each of the four slain women, as well as the injured ladies who are still in the hospital. Everyone else was given the choice of returning immediately to Japan or staying for the five days remaining in the tour, two days here and three in Venice. I think at last count, ten people are leaving for Tokyo today and the other nine are going to Venice on Wednesday."

"Will you please give Signora Benvenuti the home addresses of the women who died and of the injured ones? I heard that the mayor may be sending out some sort of condolence letter, but I'm not sure."

"Of course I will. Also, I wanted to tell you the Italian guide with this group died of her injuries this morning."

"*Dio mio*, how many more?" Caterina shook her head. An ache started to grow in her right temple. "It just gets worse. Let's see... I don't know if she is our... does she have family in Florence?"

"Yes, they were with her in the hospital."

Caterina's phone rang as Lucia answered her query.

"*Pronto....* Hello, Mr. Seagraves. Just a moment, please." She put her hand over the receiver. "Lucia, I have to take this. Can you leave the tour guide's address here, too? Let's meet again tomorrow."

Lucia Lucchesi gathered up her files and left with a nod.

"Mr. Seagraves," Caterina repeated.

"I'm sorry, I was an ass. We just didn't know. We're on the coast north of Santa Barbara. It's a bit isolated."

"I understand. We were trying to get information so we could contact William's family, but it's a holiday here, Easter Monday, and we hadn't been successful reaching anyone at the school."

"Hasn't his father contacted you?"

"No," Caterina responded. "You said he was in Italy, right?"

"Sardinia. At least, that's what Candy thinks. On a boat. Knowing Barton, it will have all the bells and whistles, so he should know about the terrorist bomb. I can't think why he didn't try to contact Bill and then us when he didn't reach the boy."

"Before I told you about the explosion, you assumed Bill was killed with his father, or did I misunderstand you? I think you asked, 'Did it have something to do with that father of his?'"

"Like I said, I was acting like an ass. I got scared when Candy started screaming."

"What did you mean?"

"Candy's first husband is something of a thrill-seeker. You know, fast cars, faster boats, sky diving, hang gliding, rock climbing. If you can die doing it, he does it – and now he takes Bill along any time he can. In the last three years, that boy has had more broken bones, stitches, and the like, than any kid I know of. Before he was fourteen or fifteen, Barton ignored him. Now, he's making up for lost time. It was his idea that Bill should attend the UCLA program in Florence. Not that I think that's dangerous… oh, hell… you know what I mean."

"Why did he want his son in Florence?"

"Barton has a lot of international real estate and resort businesses. He builds them, leases them and sells them. He's working on two in Italy, one in Sardinia and the other on the coast somewhere. He wanted Bill to work in the business in Italy this coming summer. So Bill was in Florence to learn Italian."

"What year was Bill in at UCLA?"

"He was a sophomore. You know – spring semester abroad."

"Can you tell me how to contact his father?"

"You could call the company office in Boston and ask them. Candy doesn't have the number, but I bet they have a web site. It's Barton Enterprises. Just Google that and William Bradley Barton and it should come up. You Google in Italy don't you?"

Caterina smiled. "Yes, I know how. Is your wife still in touch with her ex-husband?"

"She hasn't talked to him in four or five years. Everything she knows about him these days comes through Bill – or it did. Now, what can you tell me? You are with the police, right? Was Bill killed immediately or was he in the hospital? Candy wants to know if he suffered."

"He probably didn't know that it happened. He was right in front of the cathedral, very close to the bomb."

"Why was he there? It's not really his kind of thing. I read the articles in the paper. Wasn't it some sort of historical recreation for Easter? Bill's a modern kid. Like I said, ancient history is not one of his interests. He's not a religious type, either."

"I don't know why he was there. The *Scoppio del Carro* is a colorful pageant, and it was happening right outside of the building where his apartment was located, Mr. Seagraves."

"Call me John. What do we do now? Candy wants to fly out immediately. Is that what we should do? She's already called the travel agent."

"We will keep Bill until a family member comes to claim his body. If Mrs. Seagraves feels that it is better that she come here – rather than Mr. Barton coming from Sardinia – she should do that. I want you to contact me when you get here. Also, I should warn you, the coroner probably still needs to complete the autopsy."

"Why an autopsy? You know how he died?"

"This was a crime, we must collect evidence and the dead unfortunately may be able to provide us with information about how it happened."

"Was it terrorists? The newspaper said it probably was part of some Islamic jihad, with the church, the Easter service, and all."

"We don't know. We are gathering as much information as we can." Caterina paused. "Let's see, you've already got my office phone number. I'm also going to give you my cell phone number and that of the U.S. Consulate."

As she put down the phone, she kicked off her shoes, opened her desk drawer, put her feet up on it, and laid her head against the tall back of her chair. She closed her eyes, just letting the tears flow.

There was a knock on her door. It was Max Turner.

Chapter Eighteen

Sorry to disturb you," the American Legat said with a smile.

Her feet thumped to the floor. "Come in, come in." She rubbed both eyes and then put a hand up to check her hair. She was sure her curls were sprouting out of the clips.

His expression grew serious. "What's wrong?"

Caterina wondered if her eye makeup was smeared, but couldn't figure out how to check it. "I, um, I was talking to Bill Barton's mother and stepfather," she said.

"The UCLA student," he clarified, silently handing her a white handkerchief from his back pocket. With a hand on the back of one of the two chairs in front of her desk, he asked "Do you mind if I join you?"

"Of course not. Sit. Sit. Sit." She waved a hand in the direction of the chair, while searching around the floor with her stocking-clad feet in an attempt to find her shoes without actually looking. She dabbed at each eye and was relieved to see no smudges as she handed back the handkerchief.

"So you found his family," he said, as he seemed to be giving her more time by focusing on the long pen and ink drawing of the New York City skyline that hung on the wall behind her desk. "I think you were checking out his apartment earlier."

"Actually, I didn't find his family info there. In fact, that's still a mystery."

"How so?" His green eyes snapped back to her face.

"Someone, probably his girlfriend, entered the place after the blast and took his passport and maybe some cash. She definitely cleared out her own possessions."

"You're sure?" Max crossed his right ankle on his left knee. He wasn't wearing a jacket or a tie anymore. The sleeves of his white shirt were rolled up over tan forearms.

Caterina briefed him about Bill Barton and his missing girlfriend.

"You're convinced Irene isn't among the dead or injured? Maybe someone else had the keys – or perhaps it was just a common thief taking advantage of the empty building."

"She's not on the records of the foreigners or, at least, no 'Irene' is listed. I haven't had a chance to check with Captain DeLuca's staff about the Italians. It seems implausible that someone else would've had an interest in only her things and leave all of the contessa's antiques and silver."

Max was silent for a moment, massaging the back of his neck with one hand. "It might be worth some of your time to find the girlfriend. But don't listen to me. Ask the magistrate. I was just in with him. He updated me on everything he knew about the American fatalities, including the Hansen couple from Wisconsin. I wondered if you had learned anything new."

Caterina flipped through her notebook, pausing to read a page. "There's an injured man from Seattle, Peter Harper, who is here researching a *Da Vinci Code* type of novel he wants to write about Machiavelli. I talked to him at the hospital. He said he was trapped in the crowd and couldn't even see the *carro*."

"How did he get hurt?"

"When the mass of people turned to run, he was trampled underfoot. His ankle was crushed and he got a concussion, probably someone kicked him by accident. He seems all right, but the doctor said he was to stay in for forty-eight hours for observation."

"Anyone else?"

"I don't have anything more on any Americans." Caterina flipped back to the beginning of her notes from the day before. "I believe that Patricia Benvenuti said there were two other injured Americans, an older couple from Florida, but they were treated and released before I got to the emergency room. I could try to track them down today." She added a note to her to-do list.

"Don't bother on my account. We have plenty of witnesses, and this bomb wasn't set by some retirees from Florida."

Caterina crossed through her note. "Anything else?" she asked.

"Who else are you following for the task force?"

"The Japanese, French, and Germans are mine. The Japanese fatalities were all middle-aged ladies on a garden and shopping tour. The shops weren't open on Easter, so their guide thought they would like to get photos of the historic costumes in front of the cathedral."

"The magistrate told me about the German woman and he said there were no French tourists injured. What about the Estonian man?"

"I haven't got any information on him. He's on Marco's list. Still no identification as far as I know. Signora Benvenuti has asked for the hotel info sheets on all of the fatalities, but if he was in a B&B it may take longer. We don't get many Estonian tourists in Florence. As their economy grows, more and more of their citizens come to Italy, but like the Russians, they usually head to the beaches at Rimini or Forte de Marmi or Sardinia." Caterina closed her notebook and looked at him. "Are you tracking all of the dead and injured?"

"I'm working on a profile of the bomber and the group behind the bomber, if there is one. If one of these people was the target... I mean, rather than an anonymous mass of tourists, or the cathedral, alone, as a symbol of some sort... well, I need to figure that out. This bomber seems to sometimes target *places* – the Bilboa Guggenheim and the Duomo – and sometimes *people* – the Russian industrialist in Jakarta, the American Cultural Rep in Turkmenistan."

"Have you talked to Marco? He's gathering information about a Spanish connection, maybe ETA."

"Marco has been very helpful and emphatic," the Legat said with a slight smile. "He's convinced the answer is in Spain."

There was another knock on the door. The magistrate stuck his head around the corner. "Can I join you two?"

"Sure," said Max.

"Of course, sir," said Caterina, standing up. "Would you like to go to your office or the conference room?"

Her boss pulled out the other visitor chair. "Here's fine." Caterina had never seen him look more exhausted. Dark circles were forming around his brown eyes. His white shirt was rumpled, the button at his neck open and the purple and brown tie pulled low.

She turned her attention back to the FBI agent. "Didn't you say this bomb had the same signature as one in Spain last year?"

"Yes, Bilbao. But, I think the fact that the Spanish ambassador's niece was standing so close to the detonation site was a fluke. One of the injured girls told us that their teacher, who died, decided to get a good spot for them to view the fireworks by bringing them early and having them sketch what they could see from the steps of the cathedral to keep them from getting bored. We're checking the teacher's background. I don't expect to find her in league with a terrorist."

The magistrate looked at his watch. "Max, we've got to go. We need to meet with Captain DeLuca and the mayor. Then DeLuca wants to have a working dinner to plan strategy for the coming week. The head of the anti-terrorist squad is going to be there, too."

He turned to Caterina. "Would you follow up with Marco and see if the trade representative has had any luck identifying the fatality from Estonia and finding the family, so we can make some disposition of his body."

"Of course, sir," she responded. "Tomorrow morning I plan to find William Barton's father. Then, I hope to go over to the UCLA program offices to talk to some of his friends. I'm trying to find his missing girlfriend."

"Sounds like a plan. If you can't get back by twelve, call in. I need an update before two. Remember the mayor is briefing everyone at the Palazzo Vecchio."

Before Caterina left the Questura, she stopped by Patricia Benvenuti's desk. "Signora,…" She saw the raised eyebrow. "Okay… *Patricia*. I was just going to say don't wear yourself out here. There will be plenty to do tomorrow."

"I know, dear. I just like to get things in order before I go home."

"And now that I've suggested you get out of here," Caterina said with a grimace. "I'm going to ask one last favor."

"Of course, what is it?" Patricia plucked a pencil out of her bun of hair.

"Can you do some checking – either by phone or internet – to see if you can come up with a phone number for William Barton's father. He's supposed to be on a boat off the coast of Sardinia. The best bet would probably be through the company office in Boston. It's called Barton Enterprises. Here, I wrote it down for you." Caterina put a slip of paper on the desk. "There should be someone there now. They don't take Easter Monday off in the States."

"No problem," Patricia picked up the paper and taped it to the edge of the screen of her computer. "I'll have the number for you in the morning."

Caterina rode her *Vespa* home taking the long route, circling the ring road around Florence, so she wouldn't have to go through the destroyed center again.

She entered her apartment, took off her shoes and slipped on a pair of fuzzy pink bunny slippers with white satin ears – a Christmas present from her brother. Her collection of slippers was vast, accumulated over twenty years. Whenever a friend or family member was stuck for a gift idea, she received slippers. The novelty had worn off, but she was powerless to stop the trend.

Moments later, there was the rat-ta-tat-tat of her mother's heavy gold ring on her door. She opened the door, but wasn't able to get a greeting out of her mouth before her mother started talking.

"Catherine, why am I hearing about your day from Luciana Montalvo-Ligozzi, not from you? Why can't you pick up the phone like a normal daughter?"

"Mother, it's been a stressful couple of days, so…"

"More reason for you to tell us what you are doing. You father has been worried."

"Can I expect him tonight, also?"

"Of course not. You know the osteria is packed for Easter Monday. I don't expect him until after midnight."

"Is that why you are still dressed up?" Margaret Mary was wearing an emerald green silk dress, cinched at her still-slender waist by a wide, cordovan belt. She topped Caterina by two inches because of her green-and-white spectator pumps.

"I just got in," she said, sitting on the couch to remove her shoes and massage one foot. "I thought your father might need help with the first seating. It's a good thing I went. One of the waiters didn't come in, so I was greeting customers and your father was waiting tables."

"Was he sick?"

"Who?"

"The waiter."

"No, he's not sick. His sister was at the cathedral. She had surgery last night and he had to stay with her today. Their mother lives in Calabria."

Caterina was entering the kitchen to get a glass of water. She turned. "You mean Beppe? His sister?"

"Yes, Beppe, the one who keeps dropping plates... he's charming, and the customers love him, but he's clumsy."

"How is his sister?"

"She's fine – just something with her spleen. You know, one can live without a spleen."

"Nevertheless, she was injured bad enough to need surgery," commented Caterina. She decided to get a glass of wine in place of the water. She called from the kitchen, "I haven't met her. Is she older or younger than Beppe?"

"Younger, I think. Ask your father."

Caterina carried a glass of white wine into her bedroom, making conversation through the open door. "So things are busy at the osteria. How are Lorenzo and the kids?"

"Lorenzo is fine. And as I told you this morning the children slept well last night. I am sure Sofia won't be stupid enough to tell them what really happened."

Caterina walked out of her bedroom dressed in red sweat pants and a Boston University fleece pullover. Her mother eyed her flop-eared slippers.

"I saw a beautiful, midnight blue, velvet lounging robe at Loretta Caponi's shop the other day. It would look so nice on you. It matched your eyes. I'm sure I could find some *matching* silk slippers, too."

"Mother, I have to warn you that I might fall asleep standing up, so let's make this a brief visit."

"Excuse me, I thought, considering that I haven't seen you for more than fifteen minutes in the last forty-eight hours, I might have a bit of your time."

"I've got to eat, but then I've got to sleep." Caterina opened the refrigerator. "Would you like a glass of wine?"

"No, nothing. Well, maybe a glass of mineral water, sparkling, cold, if you have it. I ate at the osteria."

Caterina poured a small tumbler full of Pellegrino water as she contemplated the other contents of the refrigerator.

"I suppose Babbo's lamb chops are still good. It's only been a day. It seems much longer."

"You didn't eat them last night?"

"No, I could only face a bowl of pasta. I had no appetite after what I saw."

"What did you have for lunch today?"

"A *panino*."

"No wonder you are exhausted. No lunch yesterday, pasta for supper last night, nothing for breakfast, and a roll with probably two thin slices of prosciutto for lunch."

"The *panino* had *salami, caprino,* and *rucola.*"

"So in the last twenty-four hours you've had a dab of cheese, a slice of salami, and some sprouts.

"And a bowl of pasta last night – and about six coffees."

Margaret Mary swept into the kitchen. She reached around her daughter, pulled out the lamb chops and pushed Caterina toward the stove. "Cook those up somehow – the easiest way." She turned back to the refrigerator. "Have you got any salad? Oh, here are the peas from yesterday. You cook the meat. I'll microwave the peas and toast some of this bread so it won't be too stale."

"This is too much food. I'm not that hungry."

"Nonsense, you need to eat, especially protein and vegetables. We can't have you getting sick."

Caterina laughed. "Margaret Mary Gifford, you're sounding very *La Mamma,* very Italian, right now."

"I am *La Mamma,* so try acting like a good Italian daughter and listen to your mother. *Mangia, mangia.*"

They prepared the simple meal in silence. Caterina broke a couple of sprigs of rosemary off the plant on the windowsill. She placed the two small lamb chops on top of the rosemary on the sizzling hot grill. Soon the aroma of herbs, grilled meat and steamy peas filled the kitchen.

"So was it bad?"

"What?"

"Piazza del Duomo."

"Yes, Mother, it was bad. It's one of those experiences that is so hard to get your mind around, even if you actually see it in person, not just on the television, or hearing about it from others. I can't imagine being there when the bomb went off. Are you sure Renzo and the kids are okay?"

"At lunch yesterday, the children were more excited than scared. Lorenzo must have just gathered them up and run out of the piazza. All they remember is the noise and the light. They seemed to think it was part of the fireworks show. They were even intrigued by the ringing in their ears that lasted until late afternoon."

Caterina pick up a tiny lamb chop and ate the succulent meat in two bites. "But not Renzo. We have to pay attention to him, Mother. In a couple of days it may all come down on him. Sofia, I know, will be suffering. She was working so hard to keep people from dying."

"She never struck me as all that sensitive. She must deal with that kind of thing every day at the hospital."

"Not like this." Caterina shuddered. She forked up two bites of peas and then pushed the rest around her plate.

"And you? Haven't I told you that you need more suitable work. But for your job, you would never have had to see what went on in the *piazza* yesterday. You wouldn't have even been there."

"We all have to deal with this, Mother. It is the world we live in now."

"But, darling." Margaret Mary pursed her lips on what she wanted to say.

"Thank you for checking on me, but I really need to sleep." Caterina swallowed the rest of her wine and carried her plate, still containing one lamb chop, some peas and a slice of toasted bread to the garbage bin under the sink. Her mother followed with an empty water glass, kissed her silently on the forehead and left the apartment.

Sleep did not come. Caterina finally dozed on the couch in front of the television, watching *The Maltese Falcon*, dubbed in Italian. In the middle of the night she reached over to stroke the naked chest of Humphrey Bogart, only to have him morph into Max Turner, who looked down at her with slumber-filled green eyes. She woke just before her hip hit the living room floor.

Chapter Nineteen

A gum-smacking woman, speaking English, answered the phone. "UCLA in Florence."

It was nine when Caterina finally got through to the semester abroad program. She introduced herself and asked to talk to someone, a teacher or an administrator, about William Barton.

"You hafta, like, talk to the director."

"What is the director's name?"

"Leigh."

"May I speak to Director Leigh."

"Her first name is Leigh – Leigh Hopper."

"May I speak to Ms. Hopper?"

"Uh, yeah, just a minute." Gum-smacker put Caterina on hold.

Two minutes later, "I'll, like, pass you, now."

"Thank you."

"No problem." The phone rang through.

"*Pronto*, good morning."

"Director Hopper?"

"Yes."

"This is Caterina Falcone with the Florence police."

"How may I help you, Officer Falcone?"

"I work with a task force charged with investigating and assisting foreigners involved in crimes in Florence, either as perpetrators or as victims."

"Is there a problem with one of my students?"

"William Barton was killed at the Duomo on Sunday."

"Oh my lord, I was trying to check on everyone personally today.... Oh heavens.... What should..." She broke off. Caterina heard her rummaging. The director blew her nose and then started speaking again, "You know almost all of the students take advantage of the long weekend to travel to Spain or Switzerland, some even go to Prague or Istanbul. I somehow assumed if I hadn't been called about any of them yesterday, then they were okay. We weren't open on Easter Monday.... Oh my lord... his parents..."

"I talked to his mother last evening. I expect to talk to his father..."

"He's in Sardinia, I think."

"So I've been told. I may need help finding him."

"No problem. I may have his phone number. What else can I do?"

"I had another issue come up when I inspected Bill's apartment yesterday. His passport seems to be missing. The school doesn't hold the passports for students, does it?"

"We only have a photocopy, not the original."

"We think Bill's girlfriend may have gone back to his apartment. I'd like to talk to her."

"His girlfriend?" Leigh Hopper paused. "I'm sorry, I know very little about his personal life."

"Did he hang out with any of the other students?"

"Yes, two of the boys who took the long weekend to go to Venice, Ralph Harris and Toby Jones. They are... uh... were... friends of Bill."

"Are they in school today?"

"I haven't seen them yet, but let me check the class lists." Caterina could hear paper shuffling and the director breathing. "Here they are. Both Ralph and Toby have an art history class at ten. Oh lord, Bill was supposed to be in that class." She paused and blew her nose again. "They will be out at eleven and then, Toby has a Dante class at two. Ralph is free for the afternoon."

Caterina checked her watch. "Could you ask them to stay after their art history class. I should be able to be there by eleven. The school is on Via delle Belle Donne, right?"

"That's right – number fourteen. I'll leave a note to their teacher now. Please ask for me with the *portiere*, he'll ring me and I'll come down and get you."

As Caterina hung up the phone, Patricia Benvenuti tapped on the door and walked in, saying, "I have everything you need to find that poor boy's father. He's still in Sardinia."

"Great, that's just what I was going to ask you for. What did you find out?"

"I called the Barton Enterprises office in Boston last evening and talked to a *very* executive secretary, if you know what I mean."

Caterina nodded, waiting for more.

Patricia looked at her notes and continued, "The company is developing a resort on Costa Smeralda in

Sardinia. Mr. Barton is presently on a yacht off the island. He's running a 'team building' exercise, his secretary said." Patricia made two air-quotes and dropped the files clamped under her arm. "Bloody hell." She squatted to scoop them up.

Caterina retrieved a folder under the desk. "Did you get a phone number for him?"

"Of course." She dropped the files on a chair and picked up a pink slip of paper from the floor. "Here is his cell phone number. I thought you might want to make the call. I didn't tell his secretary about his son. I just said we had some questions about the business."

"Thanks, Patricia. I'll call him when I get back. I'm going over to the UCLA semester abroad classrooms on Via delle Belle Donne. I'd better leave now if I want to get back in time to brief the magistrate." She was half way out the door when Patricia called her back.

"Before I forget, dear, I have another message for you." She flipped through the phone messages. "It's from Herr Vogler. He didn't want to disturb you, saying he knows you're busy. He just called to thank you. His children are here and the medical examiner has released poor Margot Vogler's body. They are taking her home to Frankfurt tonight."

"I'm glad they were able to make arrangements so quickly. That new German consular officer is a big improvement over the last one. It probably helps that he used to be an executive with Lufthansa. I bet he was the one who was able to pull strings with the airline to help the family."

"I wish the same could be said for the Spanish ambassador. He's had a representative camped out in Marco's office all morning. Not that Marco minds, but he's supposed to find out about the dead Estonian man. We still haven't been able to find out his name or that of a family contact."

Caterina glanced at her watch. She was late. "Patricia, I've got to go. I'm off to the lab to get Bill Barton's camera, and then I'll be interviewing some of Bill's friends. Please tell the magistrate where I am and that I will be back to brief him before one."

After signing out the camera in its evidence bag, Caterina drove her *Vespa* across the Piazza del Duomo, showing her badge to a *vigile* on Via Proconsolo to allow her to pass along the south side of the cathedral. A ten-foot barricade of plywood and pine two-by-fours encircled the bell tower. As she passed in front she could see that a high, temporary fence blocked the view of the bottom half of the façade of the cathedral. Caterina had read in her morning edition of *La Repubblica* that the Doors of Paradise were being dismantled to check for additional damage beyond that visible on the four lower panels.

Across from the bell tower, under the Loggia del Bigallo, a growing mound of flowers, notes, photographs, and a couple a stuffed toys was a mute statement of the loss people felt. A young female *vigile* with long blonde hair guarded the roadblock twenty feet from the Loggia. As Caterina passed on her *Vespa*, she saw a woman with a young boy stop at the barrier. The boy handed a bunch of daffodils wrapped in paper to the police officer, who carried it to the memorial under the loggia.

She cut through Via della Spada to Via delle Belle Donne. At number fourteen, the door was open. She walked through a grand vaulted entryway to the porter's closet-sized office. The old man placed a phone call to Leigh Hopper.

"*Arriva subito*," he said and went back to his pink sports newspaper.

Within three minutes, a short, round woman, wearing black wool leggings and an oversized, knee-length, maroon, turtleneck sweater, accessorized with chunky, black, bakelite jewelry, descended the bottom flight of stairs. She punched the button on the elevator and held her hand out to Caterina.

"Officer Falcone, I'm Leigh Hopper. Toby and Ralph will meet us in my office. Let's take the elevator." She pulled the outer doors open and turned. Her eyes were red and puffy. "I always walk down and ride up. It gives me the illusion of exercise." She pushed open the inner doors and stepped inside.

Caterina joined her in the small metal and wood enclosure. "Thank you for arranging this meeting so quickly."

"I only wish I could do something more. One feels impotent in a catastrophe like this."

"What has been the response of your students?"

"Except for one student, a girl from New York City, who is flying home tomorrow, my thirty students are doing all right – much better than their parents, for the main part. Of course, that was before they heard of Bill's

death. Now there is a real sadness mixed with the horror.
I expect more will decide to leave. I'm holding a meeting
at my apartment for all of them tonight. There's an
American psychotherapist, married to an Italian, who has
a small family practice here, mostly for American expats.
I've asked her to come and talk to the kids."

They got out of the elevator on the third floor.
Caterina asked, "Are you getting a lot of calls from
parents?"

"From about half. Yesterday, in my email, I asked all
of the students to call their parents, if they hadn't already.
Yesterday and today – it's just five in the morning on the
east coast – I've received calls from four sets of parents.
Those of the New York girl, Nora, asking me to make
arrangements for her to cancel her apartment contract
and get to the plane on time. The parents of two of the
students have asked me to terminate the program and
bring all of the students home. The mother of one boy
just had questions about the continued safety of her son.
The rest of the parents either haven't woken up yet and
will call later, or they are dealing with the issue directly
with their children. The chancellor of the university will
be sending out a letter to all of the parents today telling
them that although the safety of their children is
paramount, the program will continue and that they can
contact me with any questions."

They passed a youngish woman sitting at a reception
desk in the hall. She was still chewing on a large wad of
gum. Leigh Hopper didn't say anything to her, so neither
did Caterina. They went through a doorway behind the

woman into a small office. "She is the bane of my existence," whispered the director as she closed the door.

The office contained a metal desk, comfortable desk chair, metal visitor chair, and two file cabinets. The only things on the desk were a blotter-sized calendar and a white Apple Macintosh. Two pictures hung on the walls: One was a collage of Disney cartoons with speech balloons in Italian; the other was a print of a surfer painted on a wave cresting the Ponte Vecchio.

Caterina sat down. "Did you think of ending the program early?"

"Of course it was a consideration, but most of the students want to stay and unless something else happens, God forbid, we're going to finish the semester here. I've asked Consul General Whitmore – I finally got her on the phone after I talked to you – to come and talk to the group later in the week, once her schedule permits."

There was a knock on the door. "Come in," called Leigh. Two boys stood in the doorway. Caterina recognized them as the two from the photo in Bill Barton's camera.

"Right on time, you guys. Let's go to one of the classrooms," said the director, standing up and taking a spiral-bound notepad and a pen out of her desk drawer.

They crossed the hall into a middle-sized room with a small rectangular metal table flanked by eight chairs. Tall windows along the wall opposite the door presented a view of terracotta rooftops and small portion of the upper half of the façade of the church of Santa Maria Novella.

"Officer Falcone, this is Toby Jenkins." The director put her hand on the shoulder of a tall, skinny boy with a wispy goatee and dark blond hair, cut short on the sides and long in back. "And that young man is Ralph Stone." She waved her arm toward a blond, curly-headed boy with pink cheeks. He looked about thirteen, but must have been at least eighteen. Ralph took a chair across the table from Caterina. She reached over and shook his hand and then shook Toby's hand as she pulled out the chair beside her own and said, "Please sit here." The director took a place at the head of the table.

Caterina stood for a minute looking back and forth between the two boys. Then she sat and opened her notebook to a clean page. "First, let me say that I am so sorry that your friend was killed."

Ralph's jaw clenched and his eyes started to fill with tears, but he didn't say anything. Toby stared at her, his face blank.

"Can you tell me why Bill Barton didn't go to Venice with you two this past weekend?"

Ralph slammed his fist on the table. "That was so screwed up. He should have been with us. He wouldn't have been blown to bits."

Caterina decided to back up a bit. "Did you guys know each other in Los Angeles?"

"Naw, we met here," Toby said. "We were in different majors at… "

Ralph interrupted, "He was the best. Always ready for a good time, but he was serious, too. I always thought he would end up being a millionaire or something. Not that he looked like one, but he could talk anybody into anything. We kept trying to call him yesterday, his phone kept rolling to voice mail."

"We never thought… "Toby started and then stopped, biting his lip and staring at the table.

"So why didn't he go to Venice with you two?"

Toby mumbled something. He rubbed both of his eyes, hard.

"What was that, Toby?"

"His girlfriend talked him out of it. He was pussy-whipped."

"Tobias, please," said Leigh Hopper, frowning at the boy. "Let's keep it clean."

"Well he was – and now he's dead."

"Did you meet his girlfriend, Toby?" Caterina asked.

"We both met her. In fact, we were with him at the disco when he first saw her. She came on to him and that was it. He was down for the count."

Ralph laughed without humor. "It was like she was a heat-seeking missile and we were ice-cubes."

Toby added, "B3 was the only one wearing a Rolex."

"B3?"

"It's what we called him. Bill Bradley Barton. B3. Get it? Also, Bill the Third. B3. Get it?"

"Uh, yeah." Caterina jotted a note. "What disco was this?"

"The *Stella Nera*. You know it? The Black Star."

"I do. It's very popular with the American students."

"We used to go there two or three times a week," Ralph interjected.

"Had you ever seen the girlfriend – what is her name? – before."

"Her name is Irene. No, that was the first time." Toby frowned. "What's with the interest in Irene?"

"She seems to have disappeared or, maybe not; we just don't know how to find her."

"But why do you care?" Ralph pulled at thread raveling from the hole at the knee of his jeans.

"It looks like she may have taken some things out of Bill's apartment."

"That's weird." Ralph exchanged a glance with Toby. "I don't think she had a key."

"Why was that?"

Toby responded, "Bill said he had never lived with a girl before – or even had a steady girlfriend. He thought a guy could never know when a relationship might go down the tubes and changing the locks gets expensive."

Caterina managed to turn on the camera in the evidence bag. She pressed the screen against the plastic and showed the picture of Bill Barton with the woman first to Ralph and then to Toby. "Is this Irene?"

Ralph answered, "Yeah that's Irene. I took that shot in Bill's apartment a week ago." His eyes started to water, but he didn't try to wipe the tears away.

"So Toby, you made the Rolex comment. You think she was after his money?"

"Probably not just that. But he wasn't exactly a chick magnet. He was tall enough, but he still looked like a kid. He was shy and didn't have a good track record with the babes."

"So he didn't have a lot of girlfriends?"

"He had lot of girls as friends, if you know what I mean. But, for at least the last three weeks or so, just

Irene. You would have thought he was a virgin or something. Like I said, he was wh... " Toby shot a look at Miss Hopper. "He was *infuckinfatuated*. He said he had never experienced anything, uh, anyone like her before."

"What do you know about her?"

"She looked real good in tight pants."

"I mean," Caterina said as she looked back and forth between the two boys, "where did she live? What kind of work did she do? Was she a student?"

Ralph answered, "Bill didn't let her move her stuff in, so she must have had some place else. She spent most nights with him. He'd hang out with us after class and then meet up with her late in the evening."

"Did she work somewhere?

"Funny you should ask, that's the second place Toby and I saw her. I guess she told B3 that first night at the disco that she could find him the best leather jacket. So the next day, the three of us turned up at this leather store on the *lungarno*, you know, along the Arno, and there she is, working there. Sure enough, Bill buys a black bomber jacket."

"It was a sharp look, with that California surfer dude thing he had going on." Ralph looked at his friend. "Oh man, I can't believe he's gone." He got up and went to stare out one of the windows, his hands stuck in the back pockets of his jeans.

Caterina gave him some space. "Toby, can you remember the name of the shop?"

"No, but it's right by the roast chicken place."

"A *rostiscceria?*"

Toby nodded. "Just about a half a block up the river from the Uffizi."

"Do you know if she was still working there in the past week or two?"

"I walked past there last Thursday afternoon and she was standing outside smoking a cigarette. Slow day, I guess."

Ralph turned back to the table and slumped back down into his chair. "We've told you everything we know. So, tell us, who did this? Who murdered our friend? Arabs? Al Qaeda? Albanians? Who?"

"I wish I could tell you. I wish we knew. There are some leads. We just don't have enough evidence and we haven't had time to understand what we do have."

"It's a g.d. shame Bill got in the middle of this," said Toby, his voice pitching higher. "He wasn't political. He didn't hate anyone. He was smart. His father was paying for him to go on to Stanford, after UCLA, to get his MBA, so he could join the family business."

"Was Bill happy about that?" asked Caterina.

Toby nodded. "Sure, he loved the idea. His father has all of these sexy resorts he puts together all over the world. I think he's in Sardinia right now working on the new beach hotel and spa. What's not to like?"

Ralph pushed back his chair. "When is his father arriving? He must be coming to take Bill back to the states, isn't he?"

"That's a problem we have, Ralph. We're trying to reach his father. You wouldn't know how to do that, would you?"

"Call his secretary." Toby bit off a piece of fingernail with an audible click. "That's what Bill would do."

"I've got someone trying to do just that." Caterina looked over her list of questions. "I almost forgot. Did Bill ever talk about Irene borrowing or taking things?"

"Like what?"

"Bill's passport and the keys to his apartment are missing. Maybe some money, too."

Toby looked at Ralph and shook his head. "Wow, no, Bill never said anything negative about Irene. He gave her things like clothes and stuff, but he never said anything about giving her money or her even asking for cash. He was a generous guy, but I don't think he'd like being hit up for dough by a girlfriend. It's too much like paying for sex. He was kinda insecure about why a hot-looking chick like her wanted to go to bed with him."

Ralph focused on something else. "You don't think she had anything to do with the bomb. She was just a shopgirl."

"It's not that. We just want to find her and ask about the missing items."

"She should be at the store today. She did a Tuesday to Saturday stint – the place is always closed on Sunday and Monday."

"Did either of you know that Bill had plans to go to the *Scoppio del Carro*?"

"The *what*?" they asked in unison.

"The festival at the cathedral on Easter, where the explosion took place."

"He was supposed to be in Venice with us, but Irene made a big deal about it being her birthday on Saturday and she had to work, so she couldn't go with us. Not that we would have invited her. But she insisted that she wanted Bill to take her out to a special birthday dinner, which, of course, he wanted to do anyway."

"Focus on the festival, Caterina urged. "Was he interested in that kind of thing, historical reenactments?"

"Bill? Not at all. History isn't... uh... wasn't... his thing, except for school credit requirements. I mean...," Ralph paused and thought. "He'll go see the David and the Uffizi because you have to see those places, they're famous. But he was here to learn Italian, so he could work with his father for the summer. Maybe he went on Sunday because his apartment was right on the square and the thing was going on under his window."

"Do you know if Irene is Italian?"

Ralph looked surprised. "Of course she is. She speaks Italian. Her English is okay, but not great."

"It's just that Bill's landlady..."

"The contessa," Toby interjected. "We met her. She's a cool lady – kinda like my grandmother, if she was Italian."

"The contessa doesn't think Irene is Italian. She thinks she may be from Russia."

"Russian? No way," Ralph said. "Irene said she was from Rome. She looks Italian, not Russian."

Toby laughed. "Hey dude, what does a Russian chick look like?"

"Not like a babe, like Irene."

"What about the tennis chick – Sharapova – she's hot and she's Russian."

"You're right, but she's blonde. Irene's not. She's Italian. I'd bet on it."

Chapter Twenty

Caterina wrapped up the interview a few minutes later. It was twelve fifteen when she left the school. She road through the back streets to the Santa Trinita Bridge and then made her way east to the *Ponte Alle Grazie* where she crossed back over the river to the one-way street heading west bankside to the Arno. She wanted to get to the leather shop where Irene worked before it closed at one, as did most of the other stores in Florence. She also needed to be back at the Questura to brief the magistrate.

She found the *rotiscceria*; its front window display case full of golden roast chicken, fried polenta balls, and crispy fried artichokes and nuggets of fried rabbit. The aroma made her stomach growl.

Persephone was the name of the long, narrow leather shop, only as wide as the two glass doors, one of which was being propped open by a blonde shopgirl, smoking in the entry. From the sidewalk Caterina could see that jackets covered the walls, some hanging on hooks up high by the twenty-foot ceiling. The odor of cigarette smoke and tanned leather mixed with the aroma of spit-roasted chicken, was an unpleasant combination. A headless mannequin, clothed in a short blue leather dress and black jacket, stood sentry in front of the second door.

Inside the store, a woman with short spiky hair, wearing a pink angora sweater with "Ciao Bella" spelled out in silver sequins, was fingering the lapel of a red ostrich-skin car coat. At the end of the rack inside the shop, a lanky young woman in tight, expensively torn jeans and a black spandex shirt with "Persephone" printed in red at an angle across her left breast, chewed on the cap of a plastic pen. She gave a furtive glance over her shoulder, unclipped the cell phone attached to her belt, and checked the screen.

"*Mi scusi,*" Caterina said. "Are you Irene?"

The girl paused mid-chew, clipped her phone back on her waistband and shook her head. She glanced over her head again at a man at the back of the shop who was looking in their direction.

"Is she here?" Caterina asked the shopgirl.

The pink sparkly woman looked up. "Excuse me, but could you wait your turn. She's helping me now. Or ask the other one." The accent was pure New Jersey. It reminded Caterina of one of her former classmates at Boston University.

"I'm sorry," she murmured in English, as a voice from deeper in the shop said, "May I help you?" in Italian.

Caterina watched the man behind the counter close a ledger and step out into the shop. She switched back to Italian, saying, "I'm looking for Irene. I was told she works here."

"She does, but I'm sorry, she's not in today. Perhaps I can help you find something." His accent was Tuscan, not Florentine, but Caterina's first thought was that Italian wasn't his birth tongue.

She paused before answering, taking in his closely-cropped black hair, dark eyes under heavy brows, and trendy, two-day stubble. He was about three inches shorter than she was, like most Italian men. She watched his gaze change from bored to flirtatious under her perusal.

"You just need to run your fingers over the new deerskin jackets that I got in this morning. So soft. They are my design, made especially for someone like you."

"I'm sorry. I'm not shopping. I just need to find Irene."

"Did she promise to find you something special? Offer you an unbelievable price?"

"No, I'm not a customer. I'm ..."

He interrupted, "Are you a friend of hers?"

"I'm with the police. I would like to ask Irene a couple of questions. Are you her boss?"

He glanced down at the floor. When he raised his eyes, the 'come hither' look was gone. "I suppose so. I'm Omar Pellione. I own this shop and a few more like it. Is Irene in some sort of trouble?"

"Not that I know of. I was told she dated an American college student who was killed by the bomb at the cathedral on Easter."

"Terrible – that bomb, I mean. I was with my family in Pontedera for Easter Sunday, but it must have been horrifying to be in the piazza when it happened."

"Worse than anything you can imagine."

"Who would have had the balls to take on the Catholic Church?"

Caterina frowned and shook her head. Her tone was sharp, "You don't need to be brave; you just need to be a psychopath. Over thirty people died."

"I didn't mean courage," he said, putting up both hands as if to ward her off. "It doesn't take courage to blow up a bunch of people. It's not like the assassination of an important man – the people who died won't be remembered years from now, but the fact that the Duomo of Florence was attacked will be remembered."

"I don't agree. The family and friends of those people will never be the same again." Caterina cut him short. "I need to find Irene. Since it seems she is not among the dead for you to mourn, I want to talk to her."

"Wait a moment. He gave her a small smile and moved to touch her shoulder. His hand dropped. "I see I must apologize. I was being insensitive. Even though I didn't know anyone who was killed in the piazza on Sunday, I feel bad for the people there." He frowned and said, "You say it *seems* that Irene is not among the dead. Are you sure you have the right girl? When I talked to Irene she didn't say anything about being in Florence on Sunday and she didn't tell me her boyfriend was dead. Maybe it's another girl named Irene you are looking for."

"You talked with her this morning?"

"Actually, it was last evening. She asked for the day off. That is why I am here – to take her place."

"Did she say why she needed the time?"

"She told me that she was in Rome over the Easter weekend and had some family business to finish up. So she couldn't have been in the piazza when the bomb went off. She plans to take the train back tonight. I expect her to be here tomorrow morning to open at ten."

"Someone saw her near the cathedral on Sunday. I have some questions to ask her about Bill Barton."

"Barton is her boyfriend? Was he the tall blond one? Maybe you do have the right girl. I think I saw him once. Irene never mentioned his name."

"William Barton, or Bill," said Caterina in a clipped tone. "If she never mentioned his name, why do you think he was the tall blond one?"

"Irene usually dated older Italian men. This one looked unmistakably American. And you said he was a college student, so he must have been young. As I said, I only saw him once. At a distance."

"When do you expect Irene to be back in the shop?"

He he held up a finger and turned toward the door as a dark green, motorized, three-wheeled *Piaggio Ape* pulled to the curb. The logo *Pellione Pelle* was written in red on the side. A dark-haired man wearing a black leather jacket got out, waved a hand at Omar, and went to open the back doors of the tiny vehicle.

"Nadia, help Jamal bring in the merchandise," Omar said to the blonde shopgirl, who tossed her cigarette butt into the street.

"Do you have an address and phone number for her?" asked Caterina.

"What?" asked Omar, keeping watch as the two employees carried piles of jackets, sheathed in plastic, to the back of the shop, through a small door and down a narrow staircase.

"That's what great about these shops along the Arno," said Omar. "They have as much space down in the *cantina* as they do at street level."

Caterina repeated, "Do you have Irene's phone number and address?"

"Yes, of course, but for that information, I will have to see some identification from you."

"I'm sorry. I didn't even tell you my name. I'm Inspector Falcone." Caterina reached in her purse and pulled out her badge. "Here is my identification card and badge."

Omar walked to the counter in the back of the store and picked up a small leather covered agenda near the phone. "Let's see…" He flipped through the pages. "Irene's cell phone number is 333-273-2544 and she lives on Via della Scala. I think she shares an apartment with another girl. Number eight, Via della Scala. I don't think they have a landline phone, or, at least, I don't have the number."

"Do you know her roommate's name?"

"No." He turned toward the doorway where the other shopgirl was standing outside checking her cell phone screen. "Marcia, do you know who Irene rooms with?" Marcia shook her head without looking up. Omar Pellione muttered, "New girl. Started last week in one of my other shops. Probably doesn't know Irene well. It's hard to find good help."

"I almost forgot. Irene? I don't have a last name for her."

"Irene Paloma."

"Is Irene 'good help'?" Caterina said, making an "air-quotes" gesture as she spoke.

"I can't complain. She's lasted longer than most — since December."

"Do you know anything else about her?"

"Like what?"

"I'm not quite sure. I'm just trying to fill in the picture."

"I don't think I can help you much with details about her. But if you are interested in a nice jacket…" He waved a hand back at his merchandise.

Caterina gave him a brief smile. "No thanks. I appreciate your time. May I have one of your business cards?"

"Sure. Here's one." He handed her the card, but held it tightly between his finger and thumb, so she had to look him in the eye. He winked and then let go of the card. "Stop back any time, *bella donna*."

Chapter Twenty-One

Patricia Benvenuti looked up as Caterina rushed in late, heading toward the magistrate's office.

"Did you get to your interview at the school on time?"

"Just barely." Caterina nodded, smiled, looked at her watch and knocked on the door.

"Did you call the Barton boy's father?"

Caterina knocked again as she answered, "Not yet. I'll do it right after I brief the magistrate.

"I believe he just stepped out and went down the hall, probably to the loo. Here he comes." The older woman pointed behind Caterina.

The magistrate, dressed in charcoal-gray corduroy pants, a butter yellow shirt, and a gray-and-yellow bowtie, was walking slowly back to his office, head down. He looked up at the sound of their voices and picked up his pace.

"Sorry, almost forgot. We're supposed to be meeting, aren't we, Caterina?"

"Yes, sir. Do you have time for a quick briefing now?"

"Come on in. I've got to leave… " He looked at his watch. "… in ten minutes. So talk fast."

Caterina briefed him on her morning's activities and then went to her office. She dialed the number for William Barton, Jr.

"Barton."

"Mr. William Barton?"

"Yes, who's this?"

Caterina introduced herself.

"Police? What's up?"

"Mr. Barton, you're in Sardinia, aren't you?"

"About a half mile off the coast on a yacht, but yes, I am."

Caterina wrote Barton's name at the top of the page in her notebook as she thought of how to broach the subject of his son. "Have you been keeping up with the news the last couple of days?"

"News? What kind of news?"

"Do you know there was a terrorist incident in Florence on Sunday?"

"No, why?"

"You haven't heard anything about it?"

"Look Inspector, I've been out of contact with the whole world since Friday. No radio, TV, or telephones. We've been conducting one of those touchy-feely, team-building, idea-generating seminars. And we're doing it at sea. Not one of my better ideas. We just got our cell phones back this morning. I just turned it on ten minutes ago and haven't even gotten through the messages from Friday and Saturday. I haven't been in Florence in a month. What does this have to do with me?"

"Mr. Barton, a bomb exploded during Easter festivities in Florence on Sunday. I'm sorry to inform you that your son was one of the victims."

There was a long silence.

"Mr. Barton?"

"By 'victim' you mean he was injured by this bomb? He's in the hospital?"

"I'm so sorry, but no, he wasn't injured. William was killed. He died immediately. I was told he probably didn't know what happened; that he didn't suffer."

"Dead? Bill is dead? No, I'm sure it must be someone else. Bill wouldn't be at an Easter festival. He isn't religious. This is just a screw-up by someone. That's not my son."

"We feel certain our identification is accurate. He was carrying his driver's license and UCLA identification card."

"Has someone – someone who knows him, I mean – seen this body you have?"

"Not yet. But he hasn't returned to his apartment since he was last seen there Sunday morning. He hasn't called his friends. He didn't attend class today." Caterina paused to let the information sink in. "His mother is arriving tonight."

"Candy is flying to Florence?"

"I talked with her last evening. We weren't able to get contact information for you until this morning."

"I'll be there, too. I should be able to get a chopper out of here in an hour or two. Then it will take a couple more hours to get to Florence. Where should I go, once I'm there?"

"Why don't you reserve a room at a hotel in the historic center and call me when you get there."

"Okay, I'll probably be able to get something at the Savoy. I always stay there. Give me your number."

After she hung up Caterina jotted a note on the conversation and then flipped back in her notebook to the number Omar Pellione had given her for Irene Paloma's cell phone. She dialed and got directed to voice mail. She decided not to leave a message.

"Are you ready for the mayor's briefing?" Paolo Benigni was standing in her doorway, shrugging on a jacket. "I didn't get out of here as fast as I'd hoped, so I thought we might go over together."

"Is it already two?" Caterina looked at her watch. "Just a moment, let me grab my briefcase." She put a hand to her hair, but decided he didn't have the patience for her to check it in a mirror.

As they walked to the elevator, the magistrate told her that Marco had left fifteen minutes before. "Always punctual," he observed. "Now, is there anything more I should know before we get there?"

The magistrate's car and driver were parked at the front steps. Caterina waited until they were under way before responding. "Nothing new that's important. I just got off the phone with the Barton boy's father, so now all of my death notifications have been done. There's still no sign of the boy's girlfriend, but it's probably not so important that we find her immediately. She'll turn up at her job tomorrow. I'll pass the suspected theft report of the passport and keys on to Captain DeLuca's chief of staff. Signora Benvenuti called the U.S. Consulate this morning about the missing passport."

"I think that's the right course of action, but even with that done, keep track of what DeLuca's staff uncovers. The theft still involves a foreigner. So it's still on our plate."

When they got to the conference room in the Palazzo Vecchio, it was full. Caterina took a seat against the wall beside Marco and behind the magistrate, who was seated next to Max Turner. The American turned and gave Caterina a wink. She gave him a quick stiff smile, trying to banish the image of him naked on her couch – *the virtual image, that is* – she reminded herself.

The mayor sat at the end of the table with the deputy mayor, a stocky woman in a dark suit, to his left, and Captain DeLuca in full dress uniform, seated to his right. Down one side of the table were representatives of the foreign consulates and embassies. On the other side were members of various police forces – the *carabinieri, polizia, vigili, guardia di finanza* and the SMI, the Italian intelligence agency.

A casually dressed, curly-haired man stood in one corner with a television camera balanced on his shoulder, the viewing lens angled in front of his face. The Rai 3 microphone was placed among the bouquet of other press microphones in front of the mayor.

"Let's get started," said the mayor, walking to the podium while buttoning a button on the dark gray suit that was perfectly tailored to broaden his narrow shoulders. "I want to thank the representatives of the international community, the local and federal police agencies, and the press for joining me today to discuss our early findings on this terrible crime. I will be holding another briefing in three days, on Friday, to update you on the investigation, so I ask that you be patient today with the little information we can make public.

"To date, forty-two people have been killed – thirty-one were visitors to our city, both Italians and from other countries. Nine of the dead were residents. There are two individuals, a Japanese woman and a young girl from Madrid, Spain, who are in the intensive care unit in critical condition. Otherwise, there were one hundred and fifty-four people injured, thirty-eight of whom are still in the hospital.

"We know now that this terrorist bombing was not, I repeat, *not* carried out by Al Qaeda, as reported in many newspapers and on at least two television stations. We also know that it was not the Red Brigades or any other radical, fundamentalist, or any known religious or political terrorist group. I can't give you any specific information about the perpetrators at this time, because of the need to protect the integrity of the investigation. But I will tell you this. The person or persons who committed this heinous act will be hunted down and held accountable. We will not rest until justice is done." He spoke for ten minutes more on camera, then excused the media, and briefed the other attendees in private.

An hour later, Paolo Benigni, Marco, and Caterina left the Palazzo Vecchio and got into the magistrate's car. Clumps of tourists flowed amoeba-like around Piazza Signoria.

"It didn't take long for them to multiply," observed Marco, waving a hand toward a group of sightseers following a guide holding aloft a sign that said *Carnival Cruises.*

Chapter Twenty-Two

It was just past five at the Questura when Captain DeLuca's secretary took orders for coffee from representatives of the police and intelligence agencies, the magistrate, Marco, Caterina, Max Turner, and a secret service agent from Spain, Eduardo Potero.

Captain DeLuca instructed everyone to sit down. "I asked you here to listen to Mr. Turner and Señor Potero. We seem to be dealing with an individual, not a group, but a person who has struck at least three, maybe four other times, always masking his or her action as a terrorist event; when in reality it is an assassination, a professional hit. Everything that is said here today is confidential. It is to stay among the various investigative services, not to be shared with the press, the diplomatic services, other civilians, or even your closest family or friends."

A wave of low voices washed around the table. *Maybe four previous bombs*, Caterina thought. *Max Turner only told us about three.*

"Is this what we heard yesterday?" Caterina whispered to the magistrate.

He nodded and added in a low tone, "But with details we didn't want to give the press or the consular officers."

"Quiet please," said Captain DeLuca. "I will turn this over to Maxwell Turner."

Max Turner opened a laptop computer on the table in from of him and touched the mouse pad.

"Thank you, Captain DeLuca." He looked around the table. "Evidence from the bomb itself led us to identify the bomb-maker – not to the man himself – and our profilers say that there is a ninety percent chance this it is the work of a man, and a seventy-three percent likelihood that is a man working alone or with maybe one other – a partner, who could be male or female. After his first two bombs, we nicknamed him Cobra – just as a shorthand to keep everyone on the same page."

"So you knew about him before he got to Italy," interjected Marco.

Max frowned. "We do not know who he is or where he lives. We believe that he is hired to do this work. We don't know if he has more than one client. We also don't know if he has input regarding the choice of target or the method of the assassination."

"So you don't know…," started Marco, but stopped when he caught sight of the withering look from the magistrate.

"We have some information about one alleged client, but I will get to that later," Max continued without pause. "He was first identified – or his signature bomb-making style was ID'd – after a small bomb exploded inside a café adjacent to the U.S. Trade Mission Offices in Ashgabat,

Turkmenistan, two years ago. Because it was assumed that the Trade Mission was the target, there was a lot of cooperation between the local government and U.S. agencies. We got access to all of the evidence and noticed similarities in the bomb's construction – again remember, that's the bomb-maker's signature – to a bomb used in Jakarta over three years before. Just yesterday, the CIA discovered one other previous incident in Croatia."

The fourth bomb, Caterina thought, flipping to a clean page in her notebook.

"How did they do that?" asked one of Captain DeLuca's lieutenants.

"An intelligence analyst went back to the database of unsolved bomb attacks where one or more people died and excluded all those occurring in war zones. Then she looked for bombs made with C-4 and/or incorporating cell phones as the triggering device." Max looked down at the screen of his laptop. "She found a report of a bomb set off in a resort in Opatija, Croatia."

He looked up again. "She thought that the combination of a bombing and a resort site might be relevant. The Croatian intelligence agency didn't send us the files two years ago. The Croatian embassy hasn't responded to the request we made yesterday. But we discovered that one of the injured guests was Australian. At the time of the event, the Australian Home Office was marginally involved in the investigation. They received reports from the Opatija police, and sent us the specs on the bomb this morning. It was a Cobra device."

Captain DeLuca spoke up, "So as I see it we have two assassinations of government officials, in Spain and

Turkmenistan. And two resorts with civilians involved. And now the cathedral, a religious site with no political target that we know of. I see the possibility of Jihad targets in Indonesia, and possibly Croatia, but not in the other places, although I don't know much about Turkmenistan."

"Sir, you are thinking just like we did. Indonesia has experienced a great deal of unrest in the Islamic population; the Serbians fought Albanian Muslims in Croatia. Even with the targeting of the American Trade Mission – Turkmenistan is over eighty-five percent Muslim – the theory fits. But you're right, it all falls apart after that, except for the incident here; Al Qaeda and Hezbollah have both verbally threatened the Catholic Church in Italy. At least two credible plots have been diverted in the past year."

"But I thought the mayor said that there wasn't a radical Muslim organization behind the Duomo bomb. Was there any such group responsible for the others?" asked Caterina.

"No, we never got any reliable attribution in the first three cases, either," answered Max. "Of course, we had the usual suspects jumping up and down claiming credit, but it never went anywhere. Our break came when we started to look more closely at the victims. In Jakarta, the bomb destroyed a penthouse hotel room occupied by the CEO of a Russian oil refinery. He was killed while he was having an afternoon fling with a local call girl, a regular, monthly liaison we were given to understand. The bomb had been placed in the girl's cell phone, which she put in a docking station on the nightstand. Most of the C-4 was contained in the docking station. We've always assumed that whoever gave her the cell phone told her it contained a listening device or some other innocuous purpose and instructed her exactly where to position it."

"Did the Russians help identify suspects since it was one of their citizens who died?" asked Marco.

Max shook his head. "We were given general information about the oil executive's business, but the list of potential enemies was too long to be helpful and none of them had ties to Jakarta."

"Did he have business in Turkmenistan?" asked Caterina. "If I am remembering right, there's oil there."

"You are correct, but remember, at the time we were focusing on the American trade mission," said Max. He punched a couple of keys on his computer and reading from the screen: "Six people died and four were injured in Ashgabat, Turkmenistan. Most were in a small cafe next to the building where the U.S. trade mission was located. One was the daughter of an American oil company executive."

Oil again, thought Caterina, almost missing what Max said next.

"… in Ashgabat as a Peace Corps volunteer. She was having lunch with the U.S. trade rep, Art Feeney, and her boyfriend, Owen Mars, another Peace Corps volunteer. They were all killed outright. After the death of his daughter, the CEO ended contract talks with Turkenbat Oil. A Russian oil company got the contract. Witnesses said that a waitress, who died in the blast, made a big deal of seating Trade Representative Feeney and his party at a table by the window. The bomb was in a cell phone attached to the underside of the window table. Since the waitress also died, we don't know if she was being used by the bomber."

"So two oil deals," prompted Magistrate Benigni.

"Yes." Max nodded, closing his laptop.

"What about Croatia?" asked Captain DeLuca.

At the same time Paolo Benigni asked, "Did anyone talk to the American oil CEO whose daughter was killed?"

"First, I'll answer Magistrate Benigni's question," Max said as he looked between the two men. "Of course we talked to him."

"And?"

"He denied any coercion. He said he just couldn't contemplate the idea of doing business in the country where his daughter died. We think he was threatened with further reprisals."

"From whom?" ask Caterina.

"Just a minute Miss Falcone, I promised to respond to Captain DeLuca's question next," said Max. He turned to the man seated beside him.

"At the Croatian resort," asked DeLuca, "was there a victim with connection to the oil business again?"

"Not this time. The guest who was injured in Croatia was an Australian resort developer, Nic McDaniel, whose left leg had to be amputated after the explosion. The month before the bomb went off, he had been in negotiations with a Turkish company to develop a luxury cruise line and resort on the Black Sea. After he got out of the hospital, he abandoned the project. We got that information from an internet search this morning. We are trying to get more details from Mr. McDaniel."

Caterina was still thinking about the oil executive connection – the Russian killed in Jakarta and the daughter of the American CEO killed in Turkmenistan. "Was it the same Russian oil company in the Jakarta and Turkmenistan cases," she asked.

"Astute question, Ms. Falcone," said Max. "Yes, it was a company called Goncharovgaz, owned by Oleg Goncharov."

Marco jumped up, pushing back his chair. "And Goncharov has real estate interests, too, right? All of these new Russian mafia types have their fingers in both commodities and real estate."

"That is a question we still need to answer," said Max. "Once we talk with Nic McDaniel and manage to pry some information out of the Croatian authorities, we may see a connection. All we know is that it was the same bomb-maker. Maybe he hires out to different entities. Croatia may have nothing to do with the Russians or Oleg Goncharov."

"So what is the connection to Florence? Do these Russians have business dealings in the city or Tuscany?" asked one of Captain DeLuca's lieutenants.

"We don't know. Again, perhaps the bomber is acquiring more clients, maybe…"

"Excuse me for interrupting, but do you have a connection with Goncharovgaz and the Bilbao bombings?" asked Marco, sitting down again and opening one of his file folders.

Max pointed down the table to a tall, slender man with short black hair and a large, beaked nose. "That's why Eduardo Potero, deputy assistant director of the Spanish secret service, arrived yesterday with the investigative files on a bomb used six months ago at the museum. He was sent here because of the death of the Spanish ambassador's niece. He was the one to make the connection between Cobra and the Bilbao incident. I'll let him tell you about it."

Potero came to stand at the head of the table and did not refer to any notes. "Five people died at the Bilbao Guggenheim Museum – the Spanish Cultural Minister, a woman from Barcelona and her son, as well as an American woman and her tour guide. The American woman was a tourist passing through the lobby with her guide. The Spanish Cultural Minister was accompanying the two from Barcelona. At the time, we were sure it was an ETA bomb aimed at the Cultural Minister, as the Basque group is known for using bombs. But they denied the act. We thought ETA disclaimed the act because of the bystanders who were killed – the American woman was pregnant. But because of the death of young Dulce Caron here we looked at the construction of the Bilbao bomb again on Sunday. It has the signature of this bomb-maker. So then we started looking at the victims again. The Barcelona woman, Alita Fernandez, accompanying the Cultural Minister, owned an architectural firm. The bomb, again triggered by a cell phone inside a wrapped package the size of a book, was in her son's briefcase when it detonated."

One of the officers from the Italian secret service, SMI, spoke up, "Did the son have business with the Russians or with the Croatian resort or with Florence?"

"We don't know. The young man, Alberto Fernandez, was a student at a university in Barcelona. We looked for ETA ties and found none. He wasn't political or religious. He majored in art history with an emphasis in Renaissance sculpture. That is the thin tie he has to Florence. We don't even know if he was aware of the bomb in his briefcase." Mr. Potero went back to his seat.

"So can you sum up where you think we should go from here, Mr. Turner?" Captain DeLuca asked.

Max started speaking. Caterina wrote quickly to get the entire summary down in her notes. "This is what we know and some of what we don't know: Goncharovgaz benefited from the work of an assassin – the man we call Cobra – to kill or maim two individuals. The killings appear to have a business connection. Another entity with real estate interests, perhaps also owned by Oleg Goncharov, has hired the same bomb-maker to target someone in the Croatian resort. In Bilbao, we know we have the same bomb-maker, but we haven't figured out a business interest that could be served by that incident.

"The bomber does not seem to care if innocent bystanders are killed," Max continued. "Or worse, maybe he wants his target to be in the midst of a group. Why? Is he trying to confuse the situation by having the bombs look like terrorist events? Maybe he thinks we won't bother to sift through the victims to find the target. Perhaps Oleg Goncharov or someone else at

Goncharovgaz instructed him to cover up the identity of the intended victims.

"Each bomb has been detonated by a cell phone. The bomb has been contained in a cell phone or a cell phone has been part of the firing mechanism." Max stopped for a few seconds and then emphasized, "That means the bomber has to know when the intended victim is in range." He shrugged his shoulders. "How does he do this?"

Max closed his laptop. "Finally, we don't know how the bomb-maker is being paid. We don't know how the contract or contact is made. We don't know who the intended victim in Florence was and if he or she was injured, killed or spared."

Paolo Benigni had also been taking notes throughout Turner's summary. He looked at Captain DeLuca and asked, "May I?" With the Captain's nod, the magistrate said, "It seems to me we have these tasks to complete: Determine the intended victim. Find out if Goncharov has any business interests in Italy. Find out if anyone killed or injured at the cathedral has business dealings with Goncharovgaz or any Russian business. We know that two men who were killed have Russian passports. We also need to look for other similar bombings – the American intelligence services are already on this. There is more, but I think our focus has to be the target."

"I agree, Magistrate," said Captain DeLuca. "I want your team to examine the foreign victims, dead and injured, with this new information in mind. I will get my staff on the Italians – both residents and visitors."

Max interjected, "We have to put out the word to all of the intelligence services to review their files for the past ten years, looking for similar bombings. This bomb-maker may have been active before the Jakarta blast, and more active in the intervening years than our analysis shows so far. Also, the CIA is compiling a dossier on Oleg Goncharov. We request that the Italian intelligence services, particularly the *Guardia di Finanza*, look for Goncharov holdings or contracts in Italy."

It was almost seven when the meeting broke up. Caterina waited for Max Turner to finish a conversation with the magistrate and Captain DeLuca.

"Excuse me, Mr. Turner," she said.

"Call me Max."

"Max, then, I have some more information about William Barton that seems to fit your scenario for the previous bombings."

The FBI agent's face looked blank for a moment and then he nodded. "Oh yeah, the one with the missing girlfriend."

"Right. She may have been in the piazza with him, but seems to have left before the bomb went off. Then it appears that she went to his apartment and cleared out her stuff and his passport."

"Anything else?"

"His father is a property developer, specializing in resorts. Two of your bombs happened in resorts."

"Yes, but only one may have targeted a resort owner or developer."

"Yes, but…"

"Are you hungry?"

"Huh?"

"Are you hungry?"

"I guess."

"I'm starved," he said, putting his laptop in his briefcase. "Let's eat and talk. You need to look at this Barton kid closer. We should talk about how you should do it. Since he's American, I can help. Can I take you to dinner?"

"Sure. May I suggest a place?"

"It's your town. Do we need reservations?"

"I think I can get us in."

Chapter Twenty-Three

Caterina was waiting at the curb on her red *Vespa* when Max walked out the front door of the Questura.

"How do we do this?" he asked.

She handed him a helmet. "Here. You have to wear this. Florence has a zero tolerance rule in regard to helmets. Then, unless you have a license, you're on the back."

"I've got a license and a *Vespa* GTV 125 in Rome, but I don't know my way around here and it's your *motorino*. I'm in your hands."

Caterina moved up on the saddle seat. Max swung his leg over and hooked his heels on the passenger footrest. He put one hand on her waist and she accelerated down the street.

She couldn't remember the last time she rode tandem on a scooter. She felt his warm-muscled chest against her back and one large hand on her hip. She stopped at a light and caught a whiff of his aftershave, something with a touch of citrus.

Caterina slowed to a stop in the alley behind her condo. Max dismounted and unsnapped the helmet. She pushed the scooter up on its kickstand, stored their helmets and swung her purse over her shoulder.

"Where are we going?" he asked, looking both directions in the dark ally.

"Osteria da Guido. Have you heard of it?"

"No. Captain DeLuca took me to Cibreo last night."

"A popular choice," she said with a nod. "Did you enjoy your meal?"

"It was okay, except for two things."

"What were they?"

"They don't serve pasta and I ordered something called *collo di pollo*. You will never guess what came on my plate."

She looked at him with a raised eyebrow.

"The chicken's head," they said in unison.

"So you know about that," he said.

She led him through the alley. "Cibreo is famous for their stuffed chicken neck – you know *collo di*, neck of, *pollo*, chicken. I think they use a veal puree for the stuffing. It's one of my favorite dishes."

"I've got to admit it tasted great, but having that bird's beady eyes on me was a bit much."

They turned left at the corner of Borgo San Frediano. A group of tourists was blocking the sidewalk and most of the street outside of Ristorante D'Medici.

"The head is stuffed, too," Caterina added, dodging around a fat British lady, who was describing to anyone who would listen about the deal she had gotten at the outlet mall on an original Prada bag. Caterina continued, "You're supposed to take a fork…"

Max cut her off. "Give me a break."

"No, really. The first time I saw that dish at Cibreo, a friend of my brother ordered it and then he proceeded to dissect the optic nerve of the chicken."

"Gross."

"You won't be surprised to hear he's now a surgeon."

"No kidding. Enough about that. Promise me that I get pasta tonight."

"No problem. I know the chef." She stopped at the door of Osteria da Guido, waiting as a couple chatting in German with their two children entered. "This is the place."

Max accepted the open door from the blond man in front of them and held it for Caterina. She walked into the golden warmth of the entryway. The air was redolent of garlic, tomato sauce, and roasting meat. Two benches lined the wide, short hallway. There wasn't an empty spot.

Caterina looked at her watch. "It opens at seven, thirty, so they've got a five minute wait. It's almost always booked up, but there's always four tables reserved for walk-in customers, so there's usually a line when it opens."

She walked up to the inside door and knocked.

"Shouldn't we wait?" Max asked, catching frowns from all sides.

The door was thrown open and Caterina was enveloped in her father's long arms.

"*Tesoro mio*, it seems like I haven't seen you forever. You didn't tell me you were coming by tonight. Come in. Come in." Caterina and Max stepped past him. Cosimo Falcone turned to the bench-sitters and said "*Torno subito*" to the Italians and "I'll be back in a minute" to the rest. He shut the inner door again and turned to his daughter.

Caterina stood on tiptoe and kissed his cheek. "*Ciao* Babbo, it seems like a long time, but it's only been two days. We were hungry and I told Max that I knew where we could get fed." She turned toward the tall American. "This is Max Turner. He works at the U.S. Embassy in Rome."

"Good to meet you, Max." Cosimo said in Italian, holding out a big blunt-fingered paw.

Max shook his hand, but looked at Caterina. "This is your father's restaurant?"

"It was my grandfather's place first; now my father and brother own it. It's been here over fifty years. It's one of the oldest – and best – in Florence."

Cosimo led them through the tables. "Let's get you seated. I have to let the crowd in now. It's seven, thirty."

"Can we sit at the family table, Babbo? We're going to speak English and I don't want anyone overhearing." The family table was an oval table in an alcove near the kitchen door that could seat up to six people.

"Of course, *tesoro*. You'll have it to yourselves. Your mother is going to a gallery opening this evening – some sculptor from Pietrasanta is showing his stuff at that place on Via Cavour. I'm hoping she doesn't buy anything." He sat them against the wall at the big table. "And Lorenzo's kids are with their mother tonight." He put golden-hued butcher paper placemats in front of them and passed two napkin-wrapped bundles of silverware. "I'll send Renzo out. He'll get you plates and glasses. I've got to seat the others." He stuck his head around the kitchen door and yelled, "Renzo, *vieni qui.*" Not waiting for an answer he ambled to the front entrance, straightening a place setting at one table and lighting an extinguished candle at another as he went.

Max shook his head and smiled. "Not a bad setup – a restaurant in the family."

"It's great for me. I love this place. I always know where to find my father… and a great dish of pasta."

"So it wasn't the job for you or your mother?"

"My mother can only make chocolate chip cookies and peanut butter sandwiches. Every trip stateside she brought back jars of Skippy Chunky in her luggage. I, on the other hand, learned early-on that working in a restaurant kitchen is just plain hard."

"Do you cook?"

"I love to cook – just not for two hundred people every night."

"Any other sibs?"

"Just Lorenzo and me." She looked up as the kitchen door opened and Lorenzo stepped through, wiping his hand on a towel folded into the belt of his apron. "Here he is. He's got two children, Annamaria and Cosimino."

Lorenzo came over and cuffed her gently on the shoulder. "Hey Sis, tired of your own food?" His eyes were red-rimmed as from lack of sleep. A line of sweat ran from his hairline in front of his left ear into the open collar of his chef's coat.

"I'm still eating leftovers from Babbo's Easter lunch, so I haven't been doing much cooking lately."

Max stood up and shook Lorenzo's hand as Caterina made introductions.

"Renzo, Max has only eaten at Cibreo since he's been in town, so I thought he should have the pleasure of Osteria da Guido."

Renzo grinned. "Cibreo, that old standby. They haven't changed their menu in decades."

"Probably because it's worked so well for years," said Caterina.

Max lounged back in his chair, watching the byplay between the two siblings.

"Yeah, right, or they just have an assembly line in the kitchen. I talked to a guy who used to work in a great kitchen in New York. He's been at Cibreo for six months and all he does is chop carrots, celery, and onions for *soffritto*, every day, all day."

"And people love it. You can't say Fabio isn't passionate about his food."

"He's nuts about it," Lorenzo said. His grin faded to be replaced by a dark frown. "So *Ispettore*, any idea who the *stronzi* were who caused the slaughter in Piazza del Duomo? I've never been so scared in my life."

"You were there?" asked Max, shooting Caterina a 'why didn't you tell me' look.

"Hell yes, I was there. With my kids. If anything had happened to them, I don't know what I would have done."

"Did you see anything that could help us with the investigation?"

"Why? How are you involved?"

Caterina lowered her voice as her father brought a group of four to a nearby table. "Max is with the U.S. Embassy in Rome. He's an FBI agent."

Max added, "We're trying to get as many eyewitness accounts as we can."

Lorenzo sat down at the family table. "I wish I could help, but then I probably would have been a lot closer. I'm glad we weren't. If I'd noticed anything, I'd have told Caterina. So who was it?" he asked, focusing all of his attention on Max. "I can keep a secret. Al Qaeda messing with the Catholic Church? Some other jihad group? Maybe out of Kosovo or Albania?"

Max put up a hand, palm out. "We don't think so, but it's too early to speculate."

"Is Caterina going to work with you? Not dangerous for her, is it?"

"Caterina and her knowledge of the tourists and the foreign residents will be of big help, but I don't expect that she will be in the center of the investigation."

"She's the smart one in the family. A decent cook, too, but for food it's best to come to me."

"Enough, Lorenzo," Caterina said. "Tell us what you have for pasta tonight. Max is feeling pasta-deprived."

"After dinner at Cibreo, I'm not surprised," retorted Lorenzo. "Tonight I'm making four pastas: *Pici*, a thick noodle, with a hot and spicy tomato sauce. *Penne*, the short tubes with ridges, with a very garlicky pesto sauce. Next is handmade pumpkin *ravioli* with butter and sage. Last, fresh-made *tagliatelle* with a curry cream sauce and fresh shrimp. The last one is a little atypical, but I've got to say, it works."

"Do you have any asparagus as a *contorno*?" asked Caterina.

"I'm serving some great wild asparagus, dressed with just a little fresh olive oil, lemon, fennel pollen, salt and pepper."

"I'm going to have a plate of those with the pumpkin *ravioli*," said Caterina.

"Asparagus for me, too," said Max. "But, I'm going to have the spicy tomato sauce on... what kind of pasta was that?"

"*Pici*. It's a thick noodle, kind of like a very thick spaghetti. We make it each day. It's different from other pastas because it doesn't have any egg in the dough. It's a bit chewy."

"Sounds good. I'll try it."

"Anything else?" asked Lorenzo.

"What do you suggest?"

"If you're really hungry, I'd go for the grilled veal chop."

"Maybe something lighter," said Max.

"Why don't I send out a selection of *antipasti*, and after your pasta you can decide what you want next."

Caterina nodded. "Good idea, Renzo."

"Should I pick the wine?" asked her brother.

"Okay, but think about that red from Bolgheri that you let me try a couple of weeks ago. With the sangiovese, syrah, and a bit of merlot, I think it will be good with both of our pastas."

Lorenzo winked at Max. "She always tries to second guess me on wine, but this time she may be right."

"I'm in both of your hands."

"It's a good place to be," said Lorenzo with a laugh. He pushed open the kitchen door and disappeared.

There was silence in his wake.

"Do you...?"

"What about...?"

They spoke over each other, stopped, looked at each other, and laughed. Max said, "You first."

"I was just going to ask, what about you? Any sibs? Parents still alive?"

"I'm an only child. My parents are alive. Mom is in Dallas and Dad is in Seattle. They got divorced when I was twelve, but Dad didn't leave Texas until I went off to the Naval Academy at Annapolis."

"So you were in the military before the FBI?"

The osteria was almost full. One waiter and Cosimo were moving in and out of the kitchen door, not with food yet, but with bottles of water and carafes of house wine.

"Yes, I was with the Marines in Desert Storm in 1991."

Lorenzo emerged again with two slender glass flutes and a dark green bottle. He put a glass in front of each of them and poured out a golden bubbly wine.

"I thought you should start with a glass of Proseco with the antipasti."

"Thanks, Renzo," Caterina said.

Max raised his glass in a toast, "To new friends." Caterina clinked her glass lightly against his. Lorenzo slipped back into the kitchen, taking the bottle with him.

"So where'd you get your American accent?" Max asked.

"My mother is from Boston and I went to school at Boston University."

"Did your mom meet your dad in the states?"

"No, she was one of the mud angels. Do you know who they were – after the Arno burst its banks in 1966? She met him then."

"She was here during the flood? Didn't they just have a big anniversary of that event?"

"They celebrated the fortieth anniversary a few years ago."

Lorenzo brought a long oval ceramic platter to their table. It contained two servings of a variety of appetizers – *bruschetta*, *fetunta*, *crostini* with chicken liver purée, marinated artichoke hearts, stuffed mushrooms, and golden fried polenta squares topped with a creamy *taleggio* cheese and sun-dried cherry tomatoes.

"What a feast," Max took a small plate from Lorenzo, filling it from the platter.

"Do you want some *affitati*, sliced meats?" asked Lorenzo.

Caterina looked at Max, who shook his head. "Maybe next time, Renzo," she answered. "But can we get a small radicchio salad after the pasta?"

"No problem. I'll get your wine now."

Max and Caterina ate in silence for a couple minutes until Max put down his fork. "Now tell me about the Barton boy and why you think he's important to this investigation."

"He was a sophomore at UCLA and came to Florence at the end of January to do a semester abroad, mostly for the purpose of learning Italian. When you mentioned the murder of the oil executive's daughter in Turkmenistan, something clicked in my head."

"Why?"

"His father is William Bradley Barton, Jr. He's the owner of Barton Enterprises, based in Boston. He builds condominiums and resorts, mostly in the United States, but also overseas. I don't have all of the information, but he is supposedly developing a resort on Costa Smeralda in Sardinia."

"That's interesting. I wonder if he has any connection with the architect Alita Fernandez in Spain or the resort in Croatia."

"I don't know," Caterina said. "But I found out…" She stopped speaking as Lorenzo put two steaming bowls of pasta in front of them. A waiter behind him carried two smaller empty plates and a small platter of long skinny dark green asparagus. Lorenzo crossed to the wine cabinet on the far side of the dining room and came back with two bulbous long-stemmed wine glasses and a bottle of red wine. He poured a small amount in Caterina's glass. She tasted it and nodded. "Renzo, it's still as good as the first time. I hope you ordered many cases."

"Never fear, little sister. Now you two enjoy this. Not too much shoptalk. Concentrate on my food. I'd stay and watch you eat it, but it's gotten crazy in the kitchen."

"Thanks, Lorenzo," said Max. "It smells fabulous." He picked up his glass and took a moment to enjoy the bouquet. "Mmm, nice. Another toast – to catching these creeps."

"*Salutè*," Caterina said, as she touched her glass to his. She took a bite of one *raviolo* and savored the sweet and salty combination of tastes. "Let's see where was I?"

"You said, you 'found out' and then the food came."

"I remember. I found out from Bill's schoolmates that he was supposed to be in Venice this weekend, but his girlfriend insisted that he stay in Florence."

"Was the girlfriend with him at the cathedral?"

"She apparently wasn't near him when he was killed. She wasn't killed or injured. His landlady – remember she took me through his apartment yesterday – told me that she saw the two of them going toward the *piazza* before the cart arrived. Later, she saw Bill standing against the front of the cathedral in the same place where he died. The contessa also thought that she saw the girlfriend talking on a cell phone, walking toward her *palazzo*, the same building where Bill was renting an apartment."

"Interesting." Max quit eating.

"But the contessa turned away to answer her phone and isn't sure it was the girlfriend she saw."

"What's the girlfriend's name?"

"Sorry, I thought I told you yesterday."

"You probably did, but all I remember is that the girlfriend is missing and the kid's passport is, too."

Caterina took a sip of wine. "Her name is Irene Paloma, but there's something strange about that."

"What? No first tell me – you had a couple of photos. Did they check out?"

"Yes, the woman in the shot was Irene. I'm getting copies made."

"So what is so strange about her name?" He tore a piece of bread in half and used it to sop up the remaining pasta sauce in his bowl.

"First, I must preface it with the observation that American college kids rarely pronounce Italian names correctly. Bill's friends kept referring to her as Irina – pronounced *ee-ree-na*. Irina is a Russian name. But in Italian, Irene is pronounced *ee-ray-nay*. In English, it's *i-reen*."

"Thanks for the trip through international pronunciation," Max said, laughing and dabbing tomato sauce from his lips.

"Laugh if you must, but I'm trying to make a point." Caterina threw him a mock frown.

Max raised an eyebrow. "Which is?"

"Bill's landlady is from an old Italian family with roots in Florence and Milan. She talked to Irene and thought she wasn't Italian, even though Irene said she was from Rome. The contessa claimed her accent was more from Eastern Europe, perhaps Russia. So now we come back to the confusion about pronunciation. Irene told the boys, and presumably Bill, that her name was pronounced in the Russian way. They, of course, couldn't tell the difference."

"Do you think it's important?"

"Maybe. I talked with her boss – she works in a leather shop – and he used the Italian pronunciation." She swiped the last *raviolo* through the last of the butter sauce, popped it in her mouth and swallowed before continuing. "He told me she had called from Rome yesterday evening to ask for the day off so that she could deal with some sort of family business."

"I thought the UCLA guys and the contessa said she was in Florence."

"She was here on Sunday morning, but maybe she left that evening or on Monday. Remember, I told you her possessions – and probably Bill's passport – were removed from Bill's apartment after the explosion. Who would have done that, but Irene?" Caterina scooped some asparagus on to her plate with a serving spoon and then commenced to eat it stalk by stalk with her fingers. She had the fleeting thought that her mother would disapprove. *Max certainly doesn't,* she mused absently noticing that his eyes were focused on her lips as she bit the head off another stalk. She blushed and put the remaining half spear on her plate.

He glanced away, grinned and made a visible effort to recall the topic of conversation, if not her last question. "Let's recap a bit. We've got part of the pattern. A girl, maybe Eastern European, may have lured the son of a resort developer to a position to be killed. A distinctive bomb was used. We know someone, who, in the past, worked on behalf of Oleg Goncharov, made it. But there are a couple of inconsistencies. None of the other girls – the call girl in Jakarta, the waitress in Turkmenistan, or the spa girl in Croatia – had long relationships with the targeted victims. They all seem to have been opportunistic choices."

"Bill's friends said that he and Irene had been dating for about three weeks."

"That means there was advanced planning if the relationship was orchestrated for the sole purpose of killing the Barton boy."

"Or maybe Irene was hired at the last minute because she was already Bill's girlfriend."

"Maybe. But a bigger issue is that we don't have a tie to Goncharov, do we?"

Caterina sighed and shook her head. "I don't know. I just learned about Goncharovgaz this afternoon at the briefing, so I didn't get a chance to ask Bill's father about any dealings he might have with the company. Mr. Barton is on his way here from Sardinia. He was going to lease a helicopter. He should be in Florence in the next hour or two."

"That's strange. Why didn't he take a private plane?" Max nodded his thanks to Lorenzo who took their plates and placed small plates of radicchio salad in front of them.

"He was on a yacht off the coast. A helicopter could land on the yacht, so they didn't have to waste time sailing it in to port." Caterina ate a couple of bites of the lightly seasoned greens and then pushed her plate away.

"Why didn't he come yesterday? News of the bombing must have reached him."

"He's been incommunicado – some sort of team-building exercise – no cell phones, no TV, no radio, no contact with the outside world to distract the participants. My call was one of the first ones he received after they were reconnected."

Max nodded.

"Bill's mother is also arriving tonight. She's got reservations at the Excelsior, across the square from your hotel. Mr. Barton said he would try to get into the Savoy. He's got my cell phone number, so I expect to hear from him immediately when he arrives."

"So you haven't had a positive ID of the body yet."

"No, but we have his driver's license and his school identification card. They match the face."

"Did you get any more information on the girlfriend from her boss?"

"Yes, I got the address for her apartment. I sent someone over there this afternoon to ring the doorbell, but no one answered, not Irene or her roommate. I also have her cell phone number, but she's not picking up. Her boss expects her back at work tomorrow."

"Can you get a warrant to search her apartment if she doesn't turn up?"

"The magistrate can issue it. Will tomorrow be soon enough?"

"Sure. The morning would be best. If she is involved, she's probably not coming back."

Caterina pulled out her notebook and jotted a reminder to herself. "Do you want anything else? Veal chop? Roast chicken? Rabbit? Or will the salad do?"

"Salad and maybe a bit of dessert. I admit I have a sweet tooth."

"My mother has a hand in the desert selection, so they are especially decadent."

"You mother is decadent?"

"Anything but." Caterina laughed. "However, she does know what people like and she's never been a fan of traditional Italian deserts – too bland and creamy, she says. She urged my father to bring in an intern from the Culinary Academy in upstate New York to create something better. Now a girl named Amy is slaving away back there, creating mouthwatering sweets."

Lorenzo brought out the salads and cleared away the rest of the dishes.

"Renzo, what's Amy coming up with today?"

"Let's see. A tart lemon crème brulé, and a small chocolate cake with a melted, dark chocolate center. For the waist-watchers, paper thin slices of pineapple with a sprinkle of red peppercorns."

They ordered one of each.

"Amy is a bit young, but Lorenzo has his eye on her. If he can convince her to stay we may... damn, there goes my phone." Caterina flipped it open, "*Pronto.*" It was William Barton, Jr.

Caterina agreed to meet him at the Savoy in thirty minutes. She closed the phone and turned to Max. "Do you want to come along?"

"Absolutely."

"I'll tell Lorenzo to hold the deserts until next time." She went through the door into the kitchen. When she returned, they made their farewells to her father and were back on her *Vespa*, driving across the river on the Ponte Trinita.

Chapter Twenty-Four

William Barton, Jr. was a lot shorter and darker than Caterina imagined. He stood as she and Max entered the Savoy's small neoclassical lobby.

Barton was wearing trendy Italian labels – Prada shoes, Zegna slacks and sweater and an Armani leather jacket. A Gucci man purse was slung over his shoulder.

"Bill got his height and hair from his mother, thank goodness," he said, reading Caterina's expression. Then he sobered and his eyes filled. "Not that that does him much good now."

"Mr. Barton, I'm Caterina Falcone. I'm so sorry for your loss." She took his outstretched hand and just held it until he regained his composure.

"Sorry, I've been this way ever since I got on the damn helicopter. It just hit me all at once and won't let go." He looked over Caterina's shoulder at Max Turner.

"Let me introduce the Legal Attaché from your embassy in Rome. This is Max Turner."

The two men shook hands.

"Legal attaché? Is that some sort of lawyer?"

Max glanced around the empty lobby. "No, I'm with the FBI, assigned to the embassy."

"Good, so maybe you two can tell me what happened here." He sat down on the couch. "I called the Excelsior. Candy and her husband got in an hour ago. Will I be able to take care of the identification of my son's body tonight? I don't want Candy to have to do that."

Caterina and Max remained standing. Caterina answered, "I'm sorry the identification will have to wait for tomorrow. Mr. Barton, would you mind if we go up to your room? It will give us a bit more privacy. It's possible you may be able to help in the investigation."

"No problem." He got up and led the way to the elevator. Once they were inside he asked, "How am I going to be able to help you? I wasn't here. I didn't see anything. I didn't even know he died. *Damn* that seminar. *Damn me*." He slammed his fist against the metal wall of the elevator.

His suite was one of the hotel's largest, with a bedroom behind closed doors off a large living room. The Savoy management had left a fruit basket, a selection of cheeses, a bottle of champagne, and two flutes on a small dining room table. Caterina sat at one end of the black leather couch. "We think it's possible that Bill may have been the target of the bomb blast."

"Ridiculous," Barton sputtered, his face turning a livid red. "Bill was just in the wrong place at the wrong time. No one had a reason to murder my son. He was just a college kid."

Max put his hand on Barton's arm, pushing him down into a chair. "That's entirely possible, sir. Bill may have been one of many innocent victims, but…"

Barton interrupted. "You think Bill did something to get himself killed. You're just plain wrong. Bill is... was... a good boy. Smart as a whip. Everybody liked him. An all-American kid. He was going to be my right hand in the business."

Max sat in the other armchair across from the distraught father. "Caterina, may I take the lead?"

She nodded.

"Would you mind taking a few notes, so we don't have to bother Mr. Barton again?"

She nodded once more and pulled out her notebook, opening it to a clean page.

Max turned and asked, "Mr. Barton, have you ever heard of a company called Goncharovgaz or it's owner Oleg Goncharov?"

"What? What was that? Why do you ask?"

"Do you know the company or the man who runs it?" asked Caterina.

"I know nothing about Goncharovgaz, but I know a guy named Andrei Goncharov. Does he have anything to do with that company? "

"How do you know Andrei Goncharov?" asked Max.

"He's one of those Moscow mob-types, who has a bunch of construction-related businesses. Andrei's company is called AG Holdings."

Max leaned forward, his face intent. "Have you ever had any dealing with AG Holdings or Andrei Goncharov?"

"What do they have to do with Bill? He's never heard of them. He'd never run up against them here."

"I'm not talking about your son. Yet. Can you answer my question?"

"No direct dealings. He's a crook." He looked back and forth between Caterina and Max.

Max let out a sigh and sat back. "Okay, let's back up a bit. Tell me about your business. What exactly does Barton Enterprises do?"

"We design and build resorts, hotels, and mixed retail/residential projects."

"Are they all in the U.S. or are they overseas?"

"We've got a couple of golf resorts in Florida, a condo project resurrected out of a fabric mill in Georgia, and another mill site residential/retail project north of Boston. That's just the recent stuff. My early work was smaller and all around the Boston area."

"What about overseas?"

"A safari resort in Kenya, an upscale fishing camp in Patagonia, and now I'm working up a project in Sardinia and one south of Livorno on the Italian west coast."

"Was Bill slated to work in Sardinia this summer?" asked Caterina. "His friends at school said something about that."

Barton nodded. "That's why he was in Florence. To work on his Italian. What does my business have to do with some terrorist's bomb? I never had a project in any Islamic country, although I did look at one of those man-made islands in Dubai last year. Decided against it."

"Mr. Barton," interjected Max.

"Call me Bill."

"Bill, you're assuming that this was an Al Qaeda-type of bombing. We don't think it was."

"What else could it be? I looked at the press reports on-line on my way here." He started counting off the fingers of his right hand. "Cathedral, Easter festival, bomb, lot's of innocent people killed or injured – what else could it have been?"

Max didn't answer, but asked another question. "Have you any business interests connected to the oil and gas industry?"

"Except for holding a bunch of stock in Exxon and Chevron, no."

"Have you ever thought of developing a project in the old Soviet Union or in Russia?"

"No.... Well... I did look at something briefly a couple of years ago – a project on the coast of the Black Sea, but it was closer to Turkey than to Georgia. It got too complicated and I dropped out."

A chill ran up Caterina's spine. She stopped writing. *Was this the cruise liner/resort deal the Australian was in before a Cobra bomb blew off his leg?*

Max pressed forward. "Did AG Holdings have anything to do with the Black Sea project?"

"Yeah. How did you know?"

"I didn't. Was Andrei Goncharov angry when you dropped out?"

"Not at all. He wanted a bigger piece of the project. I assume he got it."

"Was Nic McDaniel a partner in the Black Sea deal?"

"You're uncanny. How'd you know that?"

"Have you talked to Mr. McDaniel since the day you dropped out of the project?"

"No. Once I decide to bail, I don't have time to keep looking back over my shoulder. Have to move forward. No regrets."

"Did you hear that Mr. McDaniel was injured in Croatia?"

Barton shook his head and laughed. "Don't tell me – let me guess – paragliding, right? He always said he was going to take off from the sea cliffs in that region. Though he said the cliffs in Albania were more of a challenge."

"Mr. McDaniel lost his leg in a bomb blast set in a sauna in the resort where he was staying in Croatia."

"A bomb? Like here?"

"We think so."

"Oh. My. God." Barton leapt to his feet, pacing around the room as if trying to outrun the very thoughts in his mind.

Max looked at Caterina, looked at her notebook, and raised an eyebrow. She nodded, scribbling down the last information.

Max leaned back in his chair. "Have you been in any other business dealing with Andrei Goncharov, his brother Oleg, or AG Holdings?"

"No." Barton stopped in the doorway to the bedroom to emphasize the point. "Like I said, I've never been in business with the likes of them."

"Let me be a bit more specific. Have you had *any* contact, either personally or through your business, with any of them?"

"On the Sardinian project. Andrei – I've never heard of Oleg – wanted to be a partner in the Costa Smerelda resort, but after the complications on the Black Sea thing, I wasn't going to let him mess this deal up."

"Did he threaten you in any way when you told him he was excluded?"

"Not in the beginning," Barton responded, slumping back into his chair. "First, he got some Italian noble – some marchese or prince – to front for him. My Milan lawyers saw through that. Then he threatened to tie up the project in red tape, saying he would put in a competing bid, but it was too late for that."

"When was this?" asked Max.

"Why do you need to know? Are you saying Andrei Goncharov had something to do with Bill's death? He's no assassin. Goncharov is just a Russian thug who was in the right place at the right time when the wall came down."

Max held up a hand. "I don't know if he had anything to do with the Easter bomb. It's way too early to speculate. But perhaps…"

"Because of a business deal?" Barton interrupted. "No way. You're crazy."

"It's early days in the investigation, Bill." Max leaned forward and put a hand on the agitated man's arm. "Please be a little patient here with my questions. I promise I will lay out what I think when we're through."

"Okay, shoot."

"When did the Italian – what was his name, the middle man?"

"Massimo Brambilla, Marchese di Roccabianca."

Max nodded at Caterina. She wrote it down on a separate page with a couple extra notes as a reminder for follow-up.

"When did he contact you?" asked Max.

"About nine months ago."

"And when was the competing bid submitted?"

"Six months ago, but they were two weeks too late."

"Did you meet with Andrei Goncharov at any time on this project?"

"I ran into him in the Sardinian airport around Christmas time. We talked for maybe five minutes."

"Was he hostile to you or threaten you?"

"We didn't talk business. Just social chitchat. I thought he was looking for another project."

"Was your son with you?"

Barton shook his head. "No."

"Did he know you have a son?" Max pressed further. "Although I guess it wouldn't be difficult to discover, either online or in the press."

"I try to keep my family life private." Barton paused for a moment, looking up at the ceiling and then down at the floor. "I'm trying to… just a sec. I may have mentioned to him that I was flying to Milan to meet Bill's plane. Bill arrived just after spending Christmas with his mother. I took him to Cortina for some skiing over New Year's."

"Have you talked to Andrei Goncharov since December?"

"No. I heard from one of the planning commissioners that AG Holdings didn't have any luck putting another project together on Sardinia."

"Has your project gone smoothly?"

"My architect, G.P. Reiner, pulled out a few weeks ago, but that happens," Barton said. He frowned as he saw a look pass between Max and Caterina. Caterina made another note. "It was a pain, but it wasn't catastrophic. He said he had too many competing projects. I got another architect, a better one, I think. That was the reason for the damn team-building exercise this past week – to get the new architect up to speed faster than if we had done it the normal way with meetings here and there, emails, and phone calls."

"So you haven't had any contact with Andrei Goncharov or anyone at AG Holdings in the last few weeks."

"Not at all. But remember I haven't had any contact with anyone since last Friday, until I got Ms. Falcone's call this morning. It was part of the exercise – no phone calls or email. Four days of isolation at sea. I hated it – too touchy-feely-zen for me – but I've got to say the team came up with some great ideas and we cut weeks off the timeline. We actually came out if it ahead of schedule."

Max stuck his hand in his blazer pocket and pulled out a small leather case. "Bill, if you do hear from the Russians, I want you to contact me immediately. Here's my card."

"So tell me – you promised – what's this got to do with Bill?"

Max sat forward, resting his forearms on his knees, looking at the floor. He looked up. "The investigation is in its early stages and frankly, this may have nothing to do with you or your son, but I'll lay out our initial conclusions. I've got to request that you keep this information confidential, even from your family or friends. The press hasn't been briefed and it would be detrimental to our investigation to have this information out."

"No problem. I can keep a secret."

Max told Bill Barton Jr. about the signature of the bomb-maker called Cobra and the other devices that were made by the same man. He explained the findings of the intelligence agencies about the theory of Goncharovgaz's connection to the assassin.

"You think they contracted for the murder of my son to get at me? I read that there were over thirty people killed. Why would they do that if they were just after Bill?"

"We don't know, but many people have been killed by the other Cobra bombs, and we've determined that the actual target was always one person. Of course, we are looking for connections for all of the people who were killed or injured on Easter Sunday. Not just your son. But Caterina picked up on some similarities in Bill's death that seemed to match the earlier cases. So far none of the other victims have had any connection whatsoever."

"Wouldn't they have to contact me to connect the dots, so to speak?"

"They may have tried without success. Or they may be waiting until the reality of Bill's death sinks in. To make this work, either they needed to threaten you with Bill's death before it happened or they need to have a follow-up threat."

"What do you mean?"

"In the case of the American oil company CEO in Turkmenistan, they killed his daughter and then threatened to kill his son, a ten year-old kid. The only reason we know this is because his lawyer told us in confidence. The girl's father refused to have anything to do with the investigation and told us he would not testify if we ever had a case we could prove. "

"So you have to find the bomber. Who is this Cobra? I insist it can't be Andrei Goncharov."

"We don't know," Max said, rubbing the back of his neck, a habit Caterina was coming to recognize. "We hope that because we identified the bomb signature so quickly that we will get him this time. Right now, you are the only credible connection to the underlying contract."

"But it might not be with Andrei Goncharov or AG Holdings."

"It might not. I'm going to have to go back through the Croatian case to see if there is any connection to Andrei Goncharov. I don't even know if Andrei and Oleg are related. For all we know, Goncharov may be a common name like Smith or Jones, millions of them."

"And even if there is a connection, it might not be my son who was the target. These Russians have lots of real estate interests in Italy – and as for oil and gas contracts, the Italians have a lot invested in Russian oil. There's no oil here."

"You're right. Again, we haven't finished looking at the backgrounds of all of the dead or injured for connections to Oleg Goncharov. And this bomber may have taken a job with someone else."

Bill Barton seemed to relax, until Caterina said, "The only other coincidence we have in this case is that there may be a girl involved."

"A girl?" Barton tensed up again.

"Your son had a girlfriend. We have some information that she was with him on Sunday and she isn't among the dead or injured. In fact, she hasn't been seen since the incident."

Barton nodded slowly. "Bill told me he was seeing someone. What was her name?" He took a moment, looking at the ceiling. "Oh yeah, Irene or Irina or something like that. Bill said it was – how did he put it – probably not a 'forever thing.' He said she was 'hot'." Barton made air-quotes with his fingers as he spoke. "That I'd like her. What makes you think she had something to do with this? Maybe she wasn't in town."

Caterina explained, "Bill told his friends he couldn't go to Venice with them because he had to stay in Florence for her birthday. His landlady saw the two of them together on Sunday morning."

"You're looking for her, right?"

"We are."

Max interjected, "The reason why we're especially concerned about Irene, sir, is that in a couple of the other cases, the bomber used a girl to lure or place the victim into a position to be killed."

"Find her. I want to know if she set up my son." Barton checked his watch and stood. "Are we done for now? It's getting late and I need to go over to the Excelsior to see Candy. I'm going to tell her that she doesn't need to go to the morgue tomorrow. Is that okay?"

Caterina nodded. "That's fine. I'll pick you up here at ten tomorrow morning. I'll also help you to make arrangements to move your son's body to a funeral home that can work with you to transport him back to the U.S. Will you be taking him to Boston?"

"No, probably to California. He grew up there. His mother is there."

Max stood up. "I'll go with you to the Excelsior. I'm staying at the St. Regis Hotel across the square. Maybe it would be best if I talk to your ex-wife first to explain what we know, then you will know what our official position is and you won't have to guess about what to tell her and what to keep to yourself."

"Until it's proven, I don't want her believing it's because of me that Bill is dead."

Caterina put her hand on his shoulder and looked him straight in the face. "Stop thinking that way. This did not happen because of you. You did nothing wrong."

He shrugged her hand off. "Candy's not going to look at it that way. Bill was her life." He shook his head, his jaw clenched. "He was mine, too. My only son."

Chapter Twenty-Five

Caterina was speaking on the phone with Max early the next morning. "I'm picking up the search warrant at eight–thirty, and will meet you at nine. Irene Paloma's apartment is just two blocks from your hotel, near the train station. We could walk, but I need the car for the visit to the morgue at ten."

"I'll be waiting out front," said Max. He took a sip of something. She heard the cup clink against its saucer.

"I want to catch Irene at home before she has a chance to go to the leather shop. If she doesn't know we're looking for her yet, she'll find out there for sure."

"If we nab Irene, Captain DeLuca is going to interview with her at length," Max observed. "I'll want to sit in, if he'll let me."

"I can't see why he wouldn't want you there," she responded. "If Irene is a foreigner, not an Italian citizen, the magistrate will ask to be there, too."

"Seems like Irene's going to be very popular."

Caterina gave a humorless laugh, but merely said, "See you once I've got the warrant."

She rode her *Vespa* to the Questura.

Patricia Benvenuti was hanging up her phone when Caterina walked into the magistrate's reception room. "That was the motor pool. A car will be out front for you in ten minutes."

"Thanks, Patricia. Do we have a warrant?"

"I got your email from last night and I just cut and pasted it into the text of a warrant. The magistrate is reviewing it now. You can go right in, dear."

"Sorry to get you in so early, sir," Caterina said as she approach Paolo Benigni's desk. She knew her boss wasn't a morning person, rarely getting into his office before ten. Since the bombing he never seemed to leave, but his crisp blue shirt with tiny pink stripes belied that notion.

"If we can catch this bastard by finding the girl, it's the least I can do." He signed the warrant and passed it across the desk to her. "So the American Legat thinks there's something to your bits and pieces of information."

"He sees some similarities with the other cases. Also, we learned more from the boy's father last night that makes the hypothesis that Bill Barton was the sole target of the bomb more credible."

Caterina took five minutes to brief the magistrate on what William Barton, Jr. had to say about his dealings with Andrei Goncharov.

As she finished, he said, "You'd better get going. Remember that Mr. Turner does not have police powers here in Italy. He can just observe and advise. Don't let him touch evidence or interview witnesses, unless you are dealing with a U.S. citizen. It will just end up compromising our case."

"I understand, sir. I'll call you before I take Mr. Barton to the morgue for the official identification of his son."

"Do that. And when you find Irene Paloma, call both Captain DeLuca and me. If she's an Italian citizen, she's DeLuca's responsibility and I want you to observe the interrogation. If she's a foreigner, I want to be sitting at the Captain's side."

Caterina knew the two police officers, Moro and Renfro, from Captain DeLuca's staff, waiting in a car in front of the Questura. They would execute the search warrant. On the way to the St. Regis Hotel, she briefed them about the upcoming search. Max Turner was standing outside when they pulled up.

"How was Candy Seagraves?" Caterina asked as he settled into the back seat with her.

"She was exhausted, mentally and physically. I don't think she heard much of what we had to say, but her husband seems like a good guy. She just kept insisting on seeing her son. He understood that wouldn't happen before this evening at the funeral home."

"How was she with her ex-husband?"

"They seem to have a good relationship – one of those friendly divorces. They did a lot of holding each other and crying. Seagraves seemed to handle it pretty well, trying to distract me from them with small talk and a subtle interrogation until they were finished talking."

"So she doesn't blame Barton."

"Not really, except to say that he was the reason her son was in Italy."

The car slowed and pulled to the curb. "Here we are. Via della Scala, number forty-two. Irene and another girl share a studio apartment in the building."

There wasn't an elevator. Officer Moro stayed with the car while Officer Renfro led Max and Caterina up six flights of stairs to the third floor. Renfro rapped on the scratched and pitted wood door. "*Polizia. Aperta la porta.*" No answer.

Caterina said, "There's no *portiere*, so we're going to have to break it down unless you want to wait for the owner or a locksmith."

"I say break it down."

"Easier said than done. Do you know what locks are like in New York City? That's what they are like here. Deadbolts with three or four steel bars."

"She may be dead in there," Max said. "Her roommate, too."

"Okay, we'll…"

Caterina swung around as the locks started to unlatch – one, two, three, four clunking deadbolts. Renfro pulled his gun and motioned Max and Caterina to stay behind him.

The door opened to reveal a scrawny, barefoot young woman, dressed in a polyester Chinese print robe.

"Irene Paloma?" Caterina asked.

"She is not here," the woman answered, looking at Renfro's uniform. "She has a new place."

"What is your name?" Caterina asked, holding up her police badge.

"Dimitra Markov."

"Where are you from?"

"Belarus."

"May I see your residency papers?"

"I'll get them," she said, pulling her robe tighter. She turned back into the room, walked to a couch and picked up a tan leather purse.

"May we come in?" Caterina asked. She peered into the large dim room that smelled of boiled vegetables and a hint of floral perfume.

"Yes, I guess it is okay," she said, handing Caterina her *carta d'identita*, a flimsy folded paper card.

Caterina opened it to find a photograph of a younger, fresher Dimitra and pertinent data, including date and place of birth, and the date of issuance – January 5, 2008. Caterina handed the card to Renfro, asking him to copy the information.

She turned back to Dimitra. "You say that Irene moved out?"

"She started taking her things last Friday."

"She's not finished?" Caterina looked around the room for evidence of two occupants.

Max and Renfro stood just inside the open door. Dimitra Markov looked at them as she slipped her feet into a pair of plastic flip-flops. She turned back to Caterina.

"She left some of her clothes, a few pots and pans and that box of books." Dimitra pointed at a cardboard box sticking out from under a bed.

Two single beds, one unmade and the other covered with a red wool blanket, were pushed headfirst against the wall. On the other side of the room was a small square table with metal legs and a plastic top. Behind the table was a tiny kitchen unit made up of a half-sized refrigerator, with a scraped blue-painted door; a sink, full of dirty mismatched dishes; a metal cabinet; and a hot plate, topped with a pan of brown liquid, the tags of two tea bags hanging over the edge.

"She told me she would be back on Monday or Tuesday to get them."

"Today is Wednesday," said Caterina. "Did she ever come by?"

Dimitra shook her head.

"Do you know where she is?" Caterina noticed Max had pulled out a business card and was writing on the back of it.

Dimitra shrugged. "She has a boyfriend. She stays there many times."

"Does she ever visit her family in Rome?"

"She has no family in Rome. Or if she has, she does not say. She says she has only a brother."

"Where does he live?"

"In Moscow."

"Is he Italian?"

Dimitra frowned. "Why would he be Italian?"

"I was told that Irene is Italian by birth," Caterina explained.

"She is not. She is Russian. Her mother and her father are from the countryside near Moscow."

"Does she have an Italian passport or double citizenship?"

"I do not know. I know she speaks Russian like she was born to it."

"She speaks Italian, too."

"So do I and I am not Italian. Irina is good with languages, better than me. She speaks English and some French, also."

"Did you meet her boyfriend?" asked Caterina.

"She never brought him here. She told me he is American. She said she would marry him."

"Had he proposed?"

"I do not think so, but Irina said she would someday be an American wife."

"You call her Irina."

"That is her name, Irina Golubka."

Caterina saw Max jot a note. Officer Renfro leaned against the open doorway to the hall.

"Miss Markov, what do you do for work?"

"I'm a *badante*. I take care of the old mother of the president of Banco Popolare."

"Why aren't you at work today?"

"Wednesday is my day off."

Caterina looked at Max and Renfro and then back at the young woman. "We need to look at Irina's things."

Without a word, Dimitra waved her hand at the room in general. She walked to the hotplate, poured some tea out of the pan into a chipped green china cup and sat on one of the two wooden chairs by the table, sipping the brew.

Max moved to Irina's bed and pulled a cardboard box out from under it. Caterina directed the Officer Renfro to close the apartment door and go through the pockets of the clothes hanging on a metal rack behind the same bed.

"Are those all of the clothes Irina left?" she asked Dimitra, who nodded.

"Who rented this place, you or Irina?"

"I did," Dimitra said. "Another girl lived here until the middle of January. She went back to Belarus."

"How did you meet Irina?"

"We were introduced by a friend. Irina had just moved to Florence and needed a place to live."

A phone rang. Caterina saw Max pull his cellular out of his jacket pocket and looked at the screen. He mouthed, "Sorry. Gotta take it. Private." Opening the apartment door he stepped out on the landing.

Caterina turned back to Dimitra. "Where did Irina move from to come to Florence?"

"I think she was living in Pisa."

"Did she work in Pisa?"

"I think she worked in a shop in Pisa, the same as in Florence."

"Was it with the same leather company – *Pellione Pelle*?"

"I do not know."

Max came back into the apartment with a distracted look on his face. Caterina saw him shake his head twice, which seemed to her like he was mentally refocusing on the room. He walked over to Irina's bed and bent to pull out the rest of the items stored underneath.

"Excuse me," Caterina said to Dimitra and went to get a closer look at what Max had found. The cardboard box was still closed. He added two pairs of high-heeled shoes, one black pair and the other red and purple, a pair of dirty white flip-flops, and small plastic basket of thong panties and lacy bras to the pile. Renfro finished going through rack of clothes – three blouses, a polyfill red jacket, a green polyester crepe dress and a flowered cotton dress. He looked at Caterina and shook his head.

"Nothing here."

Caterina opened the box. Inside was another pair of shoes, strappy silver ones with four-inch clear plastic heels. There were also some papers, some in Russian and others written in Italian, a Diabolix cartoon book, two Russian picture books for children, and a Ryanair boarding pass for the following Tuesday for a flight from Pisa to Gerona, Spain. Underneath the books there was a plastic photograph album and a small velvet jewelry box with a thin gold ankle bracelet, a long slender silver chain with a teardrop of amber, and a golden charm shaped like the boot of Italy. Lastly, there was a cosmetic case with a small hairbrush, two lipsticks, a mascara wand, and tiny tester vial of Dolce & Gabana scent.

"Let's take the whole box with us," Caterina said. She handed Dimitra a copy of the warrant and her business card. "Please tell Irina, when she comes back, that I have her box. She can call me to get it back."

As they left the building, Caterina told Max that she planned to have a background check done on the roommate and would call her bank president employer to confirm her story.

She added, "I met Irina/Irene's boss. He told me that she said she had family in Rome. Although I didn't ask him directly, I assumed that he thought she was Italian born. But he must have seen some sort of residency papers when he hired her. I need to talk to him again."

"I'll come with you," Max said.

"I've got to go meet Mr. Barton now at the Savoy and take him to the morgue. Do you want to see the body?"

"Yes."

"Maybe we can go over to the leather shop this afternoon. If we're lucky, we'll catch both Irina and her employer and get this all straightened out."

When they got back to the Savoy Hotel, William Barton, Jr. was pacing in the lobby. He rushed up to Max and grabbed his arm.

"You were right. It's the goddamn Russians."

Chapter Twenty-Six

MOSCOW

The aroma of eucalyptus could not hide the odor of garlic and rancid sweat that leached out of Oleg Goncharov's pores as he relaxed in the sauna located next to the spacious gym in his apartment on the twentieth floor of a building in Moscow's ritzy, Ostozhenka district.

"You stink," complained Andrei, as he moved to a cedar bench in the corner across from his brother.

"You don't have to be here," Oleg retorted. "Use your own gym."

"I needed to talk to you. It took forever for your trainer to leave."

"Talk fast. My girl is coming to give me a massage in ten minutes."

"Yakov hasn't called."

"We would have heard if he'd been taken in by the police."

"So he's either dead or hurt bad enough not to be able to send a message."

"Wasn't there a girl? There's always someone."

"Let me think. Put some water on the stones – let's get some steam in here." Oleg waited for the humidity sputtered up from the hot stones in the furnace before he continued, "Yeah, there was a slut from Noginsk. She was working in Pisa. She moved over to Florence to meet the boy about a month ago. Irina something, I think Yakov called her."

"If we can't find Yakov, we've got to find the girl," said Andrei, taking a step toward the door.

"She's probably dead. They usually are."

"I'll get someone at the security company to figure it out. If she's out there and Yakov isn't around to clean up the loose ends…" He opened the door. "…Somebody has to," he finished saying over his shoulder.

"Close the door. You're letting in the cold," yelled Oleg.

"Someone has to take care of the bitch," Andrei reiterated before the door snapped shut behind him.

Chapter Twenty-Seven

Goncharov's lawyer – his frickin' lawyer – sends a letter to my office in Boston. It's a condolence letter that also asks after the health of my daughters, Zoë and Abigale. Look at this." Bill Barton shoved a fax in Max's hands. Caterina pulled one side of the page closer so she could read it at the same time. "And they sure as hell know where the girls are," Barton continued. "See it says that they hope Zoë – she's the fourteen-year-old – is enjoying Paris with her mother. That's Chantelle, my second wife. Then they ask whether Abigale is studying hard at Radcliffe. They even know how we spelled Abigale's name, with g-a-l-e, different from the common spelling."

"Where is the original of the letter?" asked Max.

"On my secretary's desk, I guess. She got the letter in the afternoon mail. That would have been Tuesday's mail. She didn't open it until about five. I hate this six-hour time difference." He grabbed the fax out of Max's hand. "Since it was about Bill, she copied it and faxed it over – got here last evening after eleven. But the hotel staff just slipped it under my door, so I didn't see it until this morning. I left a message on her voicemail to overnight the original to the Savoy."

"Do you think she's sent it yet?" Max asked.

"She won't be in the office for another four hours — eight in the morning, Boston time. So, no, she hasn't sent it yet."

"Good. Do you know where it was sent from?"

Bill shook his head. "No, like I say I haven't talked to her. It's the middle of the night there. But the letterhead is a law firm in New York. Anyway, we'll know soon enough. It's the practice in my office to staple the envelope to any letters until I see them and then I throw the envelope away."

"Caterina, if you don't think the magistrate will mind," Max said, turning to her. "I'd like to have someone from the Boston FBI field office pick it up. We'll run tests on it at Quantico. I'd like to know everything there is to know about the letter."

Caterina was cautious. "The crime took place here, Max. Maybe the letter should come here. I don't know what the proper protocol is."

"Talk to the magistrate. I can rush the tests and get the original over here by Friday evening. If you need it before then I'll have the field office put it in the diplomatic pouch and it will be here Thursday night by nine."

Caterina called Magistrate Benigni. He was quick to decide, "I'll talk to Captain DeLuca, but I say, have the FBI look at it. We send things to Quantico all of the time. Especially, if we want fast results. They get it done in half the time. We've got a copy of it, so we can work with that."

Caterina relayed the message to Max who called the Boston field agent and woke him up. "He'll be at your office at eight."

"I'll let Maggie know." Bill Barton ran his fingers over the face of his iPhone.

When he finished leaving a voice mail message, Caterina asked, "What have you done about your daughters?"

"I've already called Chantelle. She'll keep Zoë home from school today. They are in a building with a doorman, so no one will get up to the Paris apartment."

"We'll talk with the magistrate and get the Paris police involved." She looked at Max, silently asking, *"Is that what I should be doing? Or is it your responsibility?"*

He nodded and said, "I'll called my colleagues at the Paris embassy." He turned to Barton. "Last night we didn't talk about the rest of your family, except for Bill and your ex-wife, Candy. Who else might be vulnerable?"

"I've got three ex-wives, but kids with only two of them, Candy, who you know, and Chantelle, who is Zoë and Abigale's mother. Chantelle's father is a developer in France. He and I partnered on the Kenya deal. Yuka Mori is my third wife. She's an interior decorator and lives in New York. She's Japanese, as you might have guessed. I met her on the Boston mill project."

"I'll have the local FBI office call campus security at Radcliffe," said Max.

"You need to contact Ms. Mori, too," Caterina said to Bill Barton.

"She's not taking my calls," Bill said, not meeting Caterina's eyes. "It may be better coming from you."

Caternia nodded. "I will call her." She jotted a note and put her book away. "We need to get to the coroner's office now, and then I think we should meet with Magistrate Benigni and Captain DeLuca to bring them up to speed on developments."

After they were in the police car driving across town, Caterina turned from her place in the front seat. "Bill, I asked the funeral home director to meet us at the coroner's office, so you can make arrangements. Candy and John Seagraves will go to the funeral home this evening to view Bill's body. He can be on his way to California by tomorrow, if flight arrangements can be made."

"Thanks for helping with all of this, Ms. Falcone."

"Call me Caterina," she said with a sympathetic smile. "You need to check in with the U.S. Consulate later today. It's mostly a formality, but there is some paperwork to be done. Especially because we are still missing Bill's passport."

At the viewing, Caterina's throat ached and her eyes filled when Bill Barton, Jr. broke down and cried. Max took only a moment to look at the boy's face and then pulled Caterina out into the hall.

"We have to find the girlfriend, Irina, and we have to find her soon. She may be a dupe, she may be the unwitting triggerman. Hell, she may even be the bomb-maker, although I can't imagine Cobra living in that dump we saw this morning."

Caterina nodded, "And we have to sit Bill Barton down and get every single detail of his dealings with Andrei Goncharov and AG Holdings, including what he thinks they want from him. The letter was innocuous. There must be a follow-up message coming."

"Could Magistrate Benigni take charge of Barton? I don't want him passed on to DeLuca. Would the magistrate allow me to do the interview? I don't know how good his English is or how good Barton's grasp of Italian is. I know Captain DeLuca's English is almost non-existent." Max started pacing back and forth in front of her. "But since Barton is an American citizen, I'm allowed to be the primary investigator if the agent in charge approves it. DeLuca probably won't let me. But the magistrate probably will, don't you think?"

"The magistrate understands about seventy percent of what is said in English. His speaking ability is much less. That's why he hired me."

"If I can do the interviews with Barton, you can concentrate on finding the girl. Since she either has an Italian passport or a visa, I can't take an active part in that part of the investigation, just an observer role."

"I'll have the officer take you and Mr. Barton back to the magistrate's office after he makes the arrangements for transferring his son's body. If Magistrate Benigni thinks Captain DeLuca should be involved, he will arrange it. You can be frank with the magistrate. He's savvy about the interagency politics that you're describing." She opened the door to the viewing room, saying over her shoulder, "I'll call and brief him before you get to the Questura. Then I'm going to take a taxi to the leather shop and see if Irina turned up today for work."

"You're right. You need to find her soon."

Max followed her back to Bill Barton's side.

Chapter Twenty-Eight

Forty minutes later, Caterina stepped out of the cab at the Persephone leather shop. The pen-chewing girl, Marcia, was inside with a short and fat brunette, aged about thirty. *She's certainly not "B3's" girlfriend who "looked good in tight jeans,"* Caterina decided. She wasn't the woman in the photos. Omar Pellione, the owner, was not in the shop. Caterina asked if the two women had seen Irene.

"Last night," Marcia said, looking at the other woman for confirmation. "Was that Tuesday? The same day you were here, officer."

The plump shopgirl shook her head, "Don't know. I was at the other store."

Caterina wondered why she hadn't gotten a call from Omar Pellione.

"Was your boss still here?" she asked.

"Of course."

"Did Irene come to work her shift, or for some other reason?"

"She came to pick up a leather jacket she had the factory alter to fit someone."

"Why isn't she here today? Isn't Wednesday one of her regular days?"

"She quit." The girl rolled her eyes at the plump woman, turned her back on Caterina, and walked back to the counter.

"When?"

No response.

Caterina frowned, following her into the store. "Your name's Marcia, isn't it?"

No response.

Caterina persisted. "*Marcia*, when did Irene quit?"

"Last night, when she came for the coat." Marcia gave an impatient frown, as if Caterina wasn't catching on fast enough. "She told Signor Pellione that she'd found a better job and that she was giving notice. He told her that if she was going to quit, she could go immediately. I heard it all. They were so loud, the people across at the river wall could hear them."

"So she just left after that?"

"She walked out of here with the jacket, counting some money."

"A lot of money?"

"It didn't look like a lot. Probably her pay – a few twenties and a couple of tens."

"Did she tell you where she was going? Where her new job was?"

"She was in a hurry. She didn't stop to talk." Marcia sorted through a basket of leather coin purses on the counter. "It's not like we're friends or anything."

"Her roommate said she was moving out. She started moving last week. Do you know where her new place is?"

"No." She picked up a plastic sack from the floor and removed a few tiny rainbow-colored zippered leather bags and added them to the basket in front of her.

"Have either of you seen Omar Pellione today?" Caterina looked over at the other saleswoman, who was listening to every word.

Marcia pulled a loose cigarette out of her jacket pocket, shook her head and walked out the door to light up in the street. The plump woman answered, "He hasn't been here. Maybe he's at one of the other shops. Maybe he's at the Pisa store. Maybe he's at the factory."

"Where is the factory?"

"In Pontedera. That's where he lives, too. He could be at home."

"Can you give me his cell phone number?"

"Yes," she said, pulling out her cell phone and checking the directory. She read out the number.

Caterina wrote it in her notebook and then walked out to where Marcia was smoking. "Did you know Irene was Russian?"

"I knew she wasn't Italian. She told those stories about a family in Rome, but she didn't sound like she was from Rome. I'm from Rome. She didn't talk like me. She sounded like she was from the east, maybe Czech or Hungarian. But she always said she was from Rome."

"Her roommate said she had worked in Pisa. Do you know where?"

"She came from *Persephone Uno* in Pisa. There's *Uno* and *Due* in Pisa. See we're *Tre*." She pointed up at the sign where 'Persephone' was spelled out in big red letters and *Tre* was in small dark green letters. "There's also *Quatro* –

that's where Silvia was yesterday – and *Cinque* in Florence. And one in Empoli, but it's called *Inferno*. I don't know why."

Caterina thanked them and stepped out into the street. She walked toward the back of the Uffizi Gallery and found a seat in the small piazza that spread out from the exit door of the museum. She rummaged in her purse for her phone and dialed the number for Omar Pellione's cell phone.

"*Pronto. Chi è?*" he answered on the third ring.

"Signor Pellione, this is Caterina Falcone. Remember me? I'm with the Florence police."

"*Si*, I recall, *bella Ispettore*. What can I help you with?"

"We are still trying to find Irene Paloma. I'm near your shop on the Lungarno. Are you in Florence?"

"No, I am at the factory in Pontedera. I won't be in Florence today."

"Marcia, at your shop said Irene had quit."

"That's right – most inconvenient."

"Did you tell her I wanted to talk to her about Bill Barton?"

"No, I didn't. I had other things on my mind, like being short-staffed without any notice."

"Do you know where her new job is?"

"Not only do I not know, but I do not care to know."

"She was also moving to a new apartment. Do you know where?"

"No."

"Mr. Pellione, I wish you had called me when Irene came into the store on Tuesday."

"I apologize. I forgot. It's not like she is a major criminal, is she?"

Caterina chose not to answer, but instead, said, "I need to know more about Irene. I assume you have employment documents for her."

"Of course. I run a proper business. The files are here in Pontedera."

"Are you coming in to Florence today or tomorrow? Can you bring her file with you?"

"I have no plans to be back in Florence this week. I have things to do at the factory."

"Well, if I can't wait until next week, I will call you back and perhaps send someone down to the factory to get the documents. Would that be all right?"

"Of course."

"Did you know she was Russian?"

"Impossible. She told me she was from Rome."

"Can you recall if she has an Italian *carta d'identita*?"

"I don't know, but I can check. We should have a copy for tax purposes. It will take a while to find it. I am not near that office."

"Mr. Pellione, I want you to find her employment file as soon as possible. I will be back in touch with you this afternoon."

"If you insist." He hung up without saying more.

Caterina called a taxi to take her back to the Questura. She hoped to catch the magistrate and Max Turner before the interview with Bill Barton, Jr. started.

"They are over at Captain DeLuca's office. They're trying to get a handle on the Russian connection." Patricia

Benvenuti said to Caterina, who dropped into the chair beside the assistant's desk.

Caterina sighed. "They didn't ask me to sit in. I thought the magistrate would want some help with translating."

"They brought in a professional translator to do simultaneous translation for both Captain DeLuca and the magistrate. I don't think they expected you to join them." Patricia laughed. "Marco wanted to be there, also. The magistrate denied his request."

"Marco knows less English than Captain DeLuca," Caterina huffed.

"I guess that's why the boss said no," Patricia said and then sobered. "Magistrate Benigni asked you to call him if you discovered where young Bill's girlfriend is."

"I haven't found her yet. It's like she dropped off the planet." She pushed back the curls escaping from the big clip at the back of her head and peered closer at the older woman, who looked tired. Dark circles smudged her eyes and the creases on each side of her mouth were deep.

"Patricia, can't you take some time off this afternoon? You were in here at seven this morning. I bet you left after ten last night."

"I'll take some time soon. What about you?"

"I think I'm more depressed and frustrated, than tired. It's like I've been running on adrenalin for days and have hit a wall. I've got a pounding headache. My mother would tell me I'm not drinking enough water." Caterina grimaced.

They sat in silence for a few moments and then Caterina said, "Since I've found nothing that would help the magistrate I think I'll get out of here for a bit. Would you tell the boss when you see him that I've gone home to lunch and then I'm going to the hospital to check on Ingrid Neri, my professor who was injured by the blast?"

"I'll tell him, dear. Please give my regards to Luciano, Ingrid's husband. I met him a couple of times at my husband's events. You know he's also a professor, like Ingrid, although his field was Flemish artists. He worked with the Uffizi on the restoration of the Flemish tapestries, I think."

Chapter Twenty-Nine

Caterina chose to walk home, hoping the exercise would dissipate some of her frustration. She rode the elevator up to her apartment, kicked off her black pumps at the door and put on a pair of white angora slippers with blue cat's eyes, pointed ears and black whiskers.

There had not been time for grocery shopping, so her perusal of her refrigerator yielded little. She found a wrinkled tomato, a carrot, a small zucchini with a wilted flower attached, four eggs, and a half a loaf of stale, rock hard Tuscan bread.

She tossed the tomato into the trash and stored the bread for making *ribolita* at a later date. She set the carrot, the zucchini, and three of the eggs on the counter. Ten minutes later she plated a *frittata con zucchini* and *pinzimonio di carotte*. She poured a glass of sparkling mineral water and was just sitting down when there was a knock at the door. *Mother, of course*, she thought. She opened the door with a carrot stick in hand.

"Mother, I was just sitting down to eat. I don't have much time."

Margaret Mary, elegant in an emerald green tunic and black slacks, pushed her way in. "I will keep you company then. I heard you come up the stairs. The osteria is closed today. Your father has gone off to visit a farm near Panzano, where a couple of new-agers are making organic goat cheese."

Caterina choked out a laugh. "Part of his never-ending quest to find the best ricotta, right? Why didn't you go with him?"

"I never get along well with goats. He'd worry that I was bored – and I would be – when all he wants to do is spend his time discussing the fine points of whey and retsin." She went to the cupboard and took out a wine glass. "He said something about goat cheese ravioli with a walnut sauce. Catherine, do you have any more wine?" She wiggled the empty glass.

"I think there's a bottle of leftover white in the fridge."

Margaret Mary opened the refrigerator and plucked a half-full bottle topped with an old cork out of the lowest tray on the door. "How long has this been here?" She looked at the label, nodded, and poured herself some. "Can I have a sliver of your *frittata*?"

"Haven't you had lunch?" Caterina got a small plate and cut the remaining half of her eggs in two. "Do you want me to heat it up?"

Her mother shook her head. "This will do, thank you. I just need a bite with the wine."

"Mother, something is wrong. Is it the children… Lorenzo… Babbo?"

"Everyone is fine. I'm just feeling a bit low."

"Is it your health? Here, I've mentioned everyone else, but you. You are never sick, never weak, and never sad. You're our rock."

Margaret Mary smiled. "The rock is crumbling at the edges today."

"Tell me."

"I don't know if I can describe it – even to myself. I woke up shaky, with this feeling of foreboding."

"About your health?"

"No, about all of you – you, your father, Lorenzo, the children. It doesn't seem safe here anymore."

"Is it the cathedral bomb?"

"Probably. How could something like that happen here? Florence is so provincial. It lives in the past."

"Patricia Benvenuti said Florence is a museum pretending to be a town."

"Whatever," said her mother, refusing to be cheered. "It's not a place where things like that happen."

"But things like that *do* happen here. Remember the Uffizi car bomb in ninety-three."

"That was in the middle of the night, not in the middle of a huge crowd."

"Five people died that night."

"I know. It just didn't affect me in the same way."

"Is it because Renzo, Annamaria and Cosimino were there?"

"I guess so, but it is something else. The world just feels unsafe. I want to…" Her voice trailed off.

"What do you want to do?"

"I want to leave Florence – go to the country. I want to move the whole family into a villa… with a wall."

Caterina smothered a smile, standing to take her plate to the sink. "What would we all do there?"

"I don't know. Grow grapes, make wine, run an *agriturismo*. Your father could create a countryside trattoria."

"You've really thought about this."

"The Easter bombing was just the final blow – too close to home. First, the World Trade Center, then the London subway and that double-decker bus, then the Madrid train station…"

"Mother, stop…"

"…and the war in Iraq and the situation in Darfur. The world isn't safe. I have money. I should be able to keep my family safe."

Caterina knelt beside her chair and put a hand on her knee. "Mother, stop yourself… think… this isn't the *Decameron* – you can't take off to the hills and miss the plague. Bad things happen. We're more likely to get hurt on the roadway out in the Chianti hills than in Florence. You can find black vipers and wild boar in the vineyards; and scorpions love Tuscan villas."

"I guess you are right."

Caterina stood and kissed her cheek. "Believe me, you are at a greater risk of dying of boredom in that villa of yours. You hate even spending a long weekend in the wine country when Babbo goes on his tasting trips. You would have bought an idyllic villa long before now if you wanted to live like that."

"You're right, sweetheart. I'm just being a weepy fool today."

"What does Babbo say about your fears?"

"I haven't told him. He has had enough on his mind without this silliness."

"It's not silliness. Why don't you call Aunt Gertrude in New York? She probably felt just the same after 9/11, but she didn't move out of Tribeca. Ask her what she did to get through it."

"I know what she did – she got on the Q.E. II and didn't get off for six months."

"But then she went back to her apartment on Reade Street."

"Yes."

"Maybe you should go visit her – get some shopping done, go to the theater."

"I can't leave now. I would worry too much if I couldn't see all of you. And your father is concerned about the effect of this on the osteria's business. I can't leave him now."

Caterina was running out of ideas. She tried one more. "Then have your sister come here. Aunt Gertrude hasn't been to Italy in a few years. There's that Caravaggio exhibit in Rome and she hasn't seen the David since they cleaned him up for his five-hundredth birthday."

"And she hasn't seen the children. Cosimino wasn't even walking when she was here last."

"I wouldn't use that as your best argument. Aunt Gertrude is not exactly kid-friendly."

"She liked you."

"That's because I had a smart mouth."

"That's true."

"Go call her. I have to get to the hospital to see Professor Neri."

"Neri? Wasn't she your German teacher? She was injured at the cathedral?"

Caterina nodded. "She's still in a coma."

"Oh my darling, how horrible for you. She was always your favorite."

"I haven't allowed myself to deal with it, yet. There's an American FBI agent here. He's teaching me how to compartmentalize things."

"How's that going?"

"Not so good."

"Is the investigation progressing with the Americans involved?"

"You know I can't talk about it, Mother."

"At least you won't be dealing with the monster who did this. I probably never told you how relieved I was that you moved into the magistrate's tourist task force. See, you even get to come home for lunch."

"No," Caterina said, her voice full of laughter. "You haven't told me more than twenty or thirty times. And it's not a tourist task force."

"Whatever. Okay, you go and I will call Gertrude." She looked at her watch. "She should be up in an hour." Margaret Mary reached out and touched Caterina's cheek. "Thank you, Catherine. I'm sorry to go all weak-kneed on you. I'm not usually the weak-knee type."

"The thought never crossed my mind, Mother."

Chapter Thirty

At *Ospedale Santa Maria Nuova*, Caterina showed her police credentials to the nurse to be allowed onto the ward before visiting hours. She was taken to the room Ingrid Neri shared with two other women. Caterina was surprised to see Professor Neri's husband sitting at her side.

"They are short-staffed and I told them I could do everything for her, including blood pressure and temperature. They just have to change the intravenous bag when it gets empty. Actually, I could do that, too, if they would leave an extra one."

Caterina kissed him on both cheeks and walked over to the bed to take her former professor's cool, paper-dry hand in both of hers. "How is she?" she asked, looking back at him.

"About the same. If she doesn't wake up by Monday, they are going to put a feeding tube in and take her off the intravenous drip." He undid his wife's long, graying, blonde braid, combed out her hair and rebraided it as he talked. "I thought she squeezed my hand this morning when I was talking to her, but the doctor thought it was a spasm."

Caterina stayed, talking quietly with the distraught man. She was late getting back to the Questura.

Signora Benvenuti looked up as she rushed passed her desk. "You look worn out. So much for taking a break. Go to your office. I'll bring you a cup of tea with a lot of honey."

"No, thank you, Patricia. I'm late. Did they come back from Captain DeLuca's office? I should get briefed on the meeting with Mr. Barton." She raised her fist to knock on the magistrate's door.

"They're not in there, love. Look in the big conference room. They came in five minutes after you left."

"Damn," Caterina swore under her breath.

Patricia smiled, but only said, "They had me order in lunch. They've been going at it for hours, so I don't think they'll miss you for a few more minutes. You should go through your messages and email. And Marco is looking for you."

"Just what I need now," Caterina said, shrugging off her jacket.

"Should I tell him you're in?" Patricia raised a sympathetic eyebrow.

"No, I'll take you up on the tea. After I'm fortified, I'll go find him."

Caterina sat at her desk, flipping through pink phone slips. The Japanese interpreter had called with information that the last of the injured Japanese tourists had been released from the hospital and would be flying out the next day. The U.S. Consul General's assistant had called for an update. On Caterina's voice mail, there was a message from John Seagraves, saying that he and Candy had arrived back at the Excelsior. Caterina made a note to call the American Consulate and then placed a call to the Excelsior Hotel.

"Candy's sleeping," said John Seagraves. "She's done in with jet lag and the visit with the funeral director. He kindly came to the hotel after meeting with Bill Barton. Candy will be able to see her son tonight at the funeral home."

"I was wondering if I could talk to her for a few minutes late this afternoon. I just want to express my condolences in person. I also want to get a bit more information about Bill – some things only a mother would know. We're still trying to find his girlfriend."

"I want her to sleep at least a couple of hours. Would you mind coming after four? We have to go out at six for the viewing."

"Thank you. I'll see you at the hotel around four." Caterina looked up as someone rapped on the wall beside her door. Marco was standing there. She held up a finger to hold him as she said goodbye to John Seagraves.

"Didn't you get my email?" asked Marco in lieu of a greeting.

"Good afternoon, Marco," Caterina responded. "I just got in and haven't turned on my computer, yet. How are you doing?"

"Fine, if you consider it okay to be ignored in the biggest case this task force has ever had. Are you being left out, too?"

"Not that I know of," she said. "Are you angry because the magistrate has Max Turner interviewing Mr.

Barton? The FBI has a legitimate interest in the activities of Americans. Also, since your English is almost non-existent, you couldn't add much." She inwardly winced at her schoolmarmish tone.

Marco scowled. "Don't preach to me, Caterina," he said. "By the way, didn't you check your email from home last night?"

"No, I hardly ever have any email. Usually people call me or text me on my cell phone."

"You've got to start using email more."

"Hardly anyone in the Questura uses email."

"No excuse."

Caterina was getting a headache. "What is it, Marco? Do you want me to boot up my computer while you're waiting or do you want to tell me what the message is."

"I heard that you were looking for the girlfriend of the Barton kid. Any success?"

"Not yet."

"The email I wrote to you last night was to give you a heads up that a dead woman matching her description was found yesterday at Forte Belvedere."

Chapter Thirty-One

Murdered?" Caterina felt the hair at the back of her neck rise.

Marco assumed a nonchalant pose, leaning against the wall. "Neck broken. Professional job."

"Is it Irene Paloma?"

"Can't tell. No identification."

Caterina, tired of the 'just the facts ma'am' attitude, asked the question she knew he really wanted. "How did you hear about it?"

"It came in on the general incident log around eleven last night. I always read the log before I go to bed. I sent you an email immediately, just after midnight. The report should be in the newspaper tomorrow or on the television news today, if that's how *you* track crime in Florence." He smirked and sat down in her visitor chair.

"How old is this unidentified dead woman?"

"She is described as being in her late twenties. No purse or *carta d'identita*."

"How long has she been dead?" Caterina gave up, exasperated, "Look, Marco, just tell me what you know. Don't make me drag it out of you."

"Interested, right?" He pushed the chair back, and crossed one ankle over the opposite knee, while pulling a notebook out of his pocket and flipping it open with the point of his silver pen. "I took it upon myself to call the coroner. He said she died some time around nine last night. Tuesday. She must have been found not long after she was killed. You know a lot of couples head up there around midnight to screw around. Like I said, it made the incident report at around eleven."

"So what makes you think this has something to do with the woman I'm looking for?"

"I saw a copy of the search warrant you executed this morning on Signora Benvenuti's desk. The name on it was Irene Paloma."

"Yes, so what?"

"The coroner told me about the neck break and the lack of identification. But he also said she had a couple of tattoos."

"Tattoos of what? No one has mentioned that Irene had tattoos."

"Maybe they never saw them. There was one in the small of her back. Just a bunch of squiggles to most everyone, but the coroner had an assistant who said it was Cyrillic script."

"Could he read it? What did it say?"

"It was a name – Irina. Irene, Irina, it's close. There was also a dove with a flower in its beak tattooed above her navel." He spread his hands and shrugged. "Paloma – dove of peace. Get it?"

"Got it. It must be her."

"Was the dead American's girlfriend from Russia?"

Caterina nodded. "We learned that from her roommate this morning. Her real name is Irina Golubka. At least, that's what her roommate said."

"That fits. Golubka means 'dove' in Russian."

"I guess I should have run it past you earlier." Caterina hated admitting this to herself, much less out loud to Marco.

"Did you get some fingerprints this morning?"

"I have a box of her stuff over there in the corner." Caterina pointed at the cardboard box they had found in Dimitra's apartment, enclosed in an extra large evidence bag. She had given Officer Renfro instructions to deliver it to her office when he left her at the Savoy Hotel with Max Turner. "It will likely have her prints and there is a hairbrush in there that is sure to have enough hair follicles for a DNA comparison."

"The coroner must have taken fingerprints from the corpse," said Marco. "He'll send them over."

"Good thinking."

"I asked them to check her hands and clothes for bomb residue."

"*Mio dio*, we've got to tell the magistrate."

Marco grinned. "I slipped him a message an hour ago. The boss sent it back with a note," he said, pulling a slip of paper out of his jacket pocket. "It says, 'Good work, Marco. Ask Caterina to examine the items obtained in the search immediately.'"

"Let me call a print technician," Caterina said, picking up the telephone and placing the call. When she hung up she turned to Marco. "I'm going to move the box to the small conference room. Thanks for catching the incident report. Who knows how long the body would have remained in the morgue before I thought to look for a dead body instead of a live girlfriend."

"No problem. You would have eventually filed a missing person report and someone would have checked."

She picked up the box. "Do you want to help look at these things? It'll go faster with two sets of eyes." She really didn't need him, but she felt she owed him.

"I guess I can spare a few minutes."

They walked down the hall. Caterina was still carrying the box. She stood at the closed door of the conference room until Marco, who was looking at his cell phone screen, caught up and opened it for her. She placed the box on the round table and turned. "I know there are a couple of books and some documents written in Russian. Maybe you can take those and tell me what they are about. You can read the language can't you."

"I double majored in Spanish and Russian."

"Right, I forgot."

"And you?"

"Me?"

"Your major?"

"I did my undergraduate work in the U.S. I have a degree in English literature from Boston University. I got a *laurea* in German and French when I got back to Florence. Then I went to the police academy." She paused as she put on a pair of thin rubber gloves and looked at Marco. "Funny, we've worked together for over six months and we know so little about each other."

Caterina thought he looked genuinely perplexed. "Why should we?"

"No reason, I guess." She put on a pair of gloves before she pulled the box out of the evidence bag after jotting a note on the label to record the action. The magistrate had drilled into her the importance of tracking the chain of custody of all evidence.

The print technician arrived. Caterina opened the box and had each item dusted for fingerprints. As the technician finished, Caterina laid the items along the edge of the table. She slipped the hairbrush into a small evidence bag, labeled it, and handed it to the technician. "Please run the prints as soon as possible. Compare them to a set coming from the coroner on an unidentified woman they brought into the morgue last night from Forte Belvedere. Also, please send the brush on for DNA analysis of the hair."

"You know that will take at least a week," said Marco as the technician left the conference room.

"I know. So we should get the lab working on it as soon as possible. However, if the prints match, the DNA won't be vital." She started around the table, pointing at the documents in Russian and two books. "One of the books looks like a children's book, but do you know what the other is?"

Marco put on a pair of gloves before picking up the small thin book. He read the spine and opened it to title page. "It's a prayer book. Russian Orthodox." He flipped back to the flyleaf. "It's inscribed." He turned the book on an angle. "I think it is to a granddaughter from her grandmother."

"Check the books for anything stuck between the pages."

"Patience," he retorted, fanning the book out by its spine. "Nothing in the prayer book." He did the same with a small ragged picture book. "Here's something. A photo. A man, a blonde woman, and…"

"Not Irina, I bet." Caterina looked over his shoulder.

"…and a child with dark, curly hair. A girl, I think."

"Let me see that." Caterina took the photograph from his fingers. "That's Irina's…"

"Irina's what? Child?"

"No. Her boss. That's her boss, Omar Pellione."

"Is that Irina?"

"No, the pictures of her in Bill Barton's camera show a younger woman with long, wavy, dark-brown hair, skinny, with smaller breasts and shapely hips. This woman is blonde, taller, and older. If this was Irina, I think Bill's friends would have mentioned her age first."

Marco opened the plastic photograph album and pointed to the first page. "Is this Bill Barton?"

Caterina looked at the photo and flipped through the rest. "Yes. These are all of him and Irina, the girl in the photo in his digital camera." She pointed at the woman held tight in the California boy's arms, his chin resting on her head. They were both grinning at the photographer. "And these are his friends, Ralph and Toby." It was a snapshot of the three boys, all wearing UCLA t-shirts and running shorts, sitting on a beach.

"Do you know what these documents are?" Caterina asked, handing Marco three sheets of paper written in Russian.

"Some sort of legal documents. Let me take a few minutes with them and I'll tell you." He sat down on one of the padded rolling chairs and pushed away from the table.

Patricia Benvenuti opened the door and stuck her head in. "I just got a call from downstairs in the lab. Your prints match the prints of that poor murdered woman. Have you found Bill Barton's girlfriend?"

"It seems so, but also hit a roadblock. We really needed to talk to her." Caterina frowned, absently twisting a long curl around her index finger. "Patricia, could you ask the magistrate if he could step in here when they take a break?"

"I'd be happy to, dear."

After she closed the door, Marco said, "I can't believe you call her by her first name. She'd take my head off if I did that."

Caterina wasn't going to get in to that discussion. "Maybe it's because she knows my mother," was all she said.

Marco continued to peruse the Russian documents and Caterina looked at the meager jewelry in the velvet box. Five minutes later, Magistrate Benigni walked in.

"What do you have for me?" His hair stood on end like he had repeatedly run his hands through it. His eyes were bloodshot. His tie was loosened and his shirtsleeves rolled up to his elbows.

Marco started, "The body I told you about at Forte Belvedere gave us prints that matched those off the things Caterina gathered at the girlfriend, Irene Paloma's, apartment. We also have photos of the dead boy and the now dead girlfriend."

He handed the magistrate the photo album.

Caterina held out the photograph of Omar Pellione. "This is her boss. I think we should look into a personal relationship between them."

"Do you think there is one?"

"Not really, or at least, I don't have any evidence of it. Mr. Pellione made it seem like he only knew her vaguely as an employee. But she has this picture. It may only be of his family – Irina's not in it – but why would a simple employee have a picture of him with his wife and child?"

"Didn't you go back over to the leather shop this morning?" The magistrate put the photographs down and looked at the other items on the table.

"Omar Pellione wasn't there this morning. The regular shopgirl said Irina came back from Rome yesterday. She went to the shop at seven that evening and resigned, saying she had another job. She also picked up a leather jacket and her final pay."

"Did she tell them that she had been in Rome?"

"I can't remember if I asked the girl that exact question, but that's where they said she was when I was first at the shop on Tuesday morning. I'm assuming they had the same belief on Tuesday evening. Sorry, sir, I didn't ask the question."

He nodded and moved on. "She died only a few hours later, correct?"

Marco answered, "Correct, sir. The coroner put her death at about nine or ten Tuesday night."

"So she picks up her final pay and resigns at seven and is dead at just after nine. Where did she go after she left the shop and did anyone go with her?"

"I don't know, sir," said Caterina. "She told them she had a better job. She told her roommate she had a new apartment."

"Did you talk to the owner, her ex-boss?"

"I called him. He was at the factory in Pontedera. I told him I wanted her employment documents. This was before I knew she was dead. I was still trying to get a lead on her true identity and country of origin."

"We really don't know who she was, am I right? Italian or Russian, innocent shopgirl, gold-digger, or bomber's pawn." The magistrate massaged the area between his eyebrows. After a moment he looked at Caterina and said, "We're going to need those employment papers from the leather company."

"I'll go to Pontedera and pick them up tomorrow and talk with Mr. Pellione again. I'll take the photograph of him with the blond woman and the young girl that was in Irina's apartment and ask about it, too."

"Do that." The magistrate turned almost knocking into his other investigator.

"What about me?" Marco asked. "I've finished reading these Cyrillic documents. They appear to be a visa application for Irina Golubka to travel from Russia to the EU."

"When were they dated?" asked Caterina.

"Last June."

"Okay. Leave those to Caterina and get back to your own assignments," said Benigni. "Have you finished up all of the reporting requested by the Spanish embassy?"

"Almost."

"Have you made Italian translations of all of the requested reports for our files?"

"I wrote them out in Italian first and then translated them into Spanish. They're all done."

"What about the Estonian victim? Have you identified him yet?"

"No. It's with the trade rep. He's supposed to get back to me."

"I think you should concentrate on him tomorrow. There is clearly a Russian connection to this bombing. I've just spent hours on that issue. I'd hate to miss something by ignoring a dead man from a former Soviet state." He smiled slightly at both of them and started to walk out of the room. Over his shoulder he said, "I'll brief the two of you in an hour in the big conference room. I'll be in my office until then."

Chapter Thirty-Two

MOSCOW

You tell him we are not happy, not happy at all," Andrei Goncharov yelled in English into his telephone. "We never had trouble with the old man. But first with Bilbao and now this mess." He drummed his fingers on the arm of his chair waiting in vain for a response. Finally, he said, "Tell him the package has gone to Lichtenstein, but there won't be another shipment for the girl. She was his problem, not mine. You tell him that." He slammed the receiver down. It bounced out of its cradle on to the rich ebony finish of his desk. He picked it up and pounded it against the desk twice. When the phone didn't break he settled it into place with exaggerated care. *This is not good for my blood pressure,* he thought. He turned to the decanter of scotch on his credenza and poured a double shot into a crystal tumbler.

He picked up the phone again and pushed one number for his brother.

"That girl trouble we talked about is over," he said in Russian.

"Yakov called?" Oleg asked.

"No, I haven't heard from him. This was just a messenger from the contractor. I've had no direct contact."

Andrei could hear the click of a lighter as Oleg lit one of his fat Dominican cigars. He sucked in a long draw and asked, "Did the letter go?"

"It should be delivered in the morning."

"Have you talked to Stefanya?"

Andrei took a sip of his scotch, glad for the change in subject. "No, she's taking her exams this week."

"She should come home."

"Her spring break is starting soon. She'll be on a plane in six days. Wednesday next."

"Good. I don't like the way this is going."

"Why? With the slut silenced, there's no link."

Chapter Thirty-Three

Caterina stuck her head around the corner of the magistrate's door. All she could see was an uneven hedge of black hair shot with gray as he sat in his chair, looking out the window.

"Sir, I'm sorry to disturb you."

He immediately got taller in the chair and twirled around to face her. He looked more rested, despite the fact that she knew he had barely left the Questura in the previous three days.

"What is it, Caterina?" His voice was not unkind.

"I'm supposed to meet with Bill Barton's mother at four. Should I do that or stay for the briefing on the Russian angle of the investigation?"

"Better talk to her. She's probably leaving tomorrow or the next day. Her son may have told her about the Russian girl. That is the aspect of this case we need help on now."

"Okay, I'll be going."

"If you have five minutes, I can quickly bring you up to speed. It might help you in your discussion with the mother."

Caterina came fully into his office and sat down. "I told them I would be there sometime before four thirty. What happened with Mr. Barton?"

"All you need to know is the Russians, Oleg and Andrei Goncharov, are indeed brothers. Max Turner got that information from the U.S. Embassy in Moscow. Oleg is in oil – he was an arms dealer before the Berlin Wall came down. Now he is the majority owner of Goncharovgaz, formerly a state-owned entity under another name. Andrei Goncharov has various interests in real estate development under the name AG Holdings. Andrei tried to muscle his way into Barton's resort development on the Black Sea, three years ago. Barton backed out leaving his partner, Nic McDaniel, with sixty percent of the deal – a Turkish firm held the rest.

"Mr. McDaniel is the man who lost his leg in the resort bomb blast in Croatia."

Paolo Benigni nodded. "After that Andrei Goncharov *convinced* McDaniel to sell his sixty percent share. The Turkish partner melted away, too." The magistrate looked down at his notes. "Mr. Turner is trying to get more information from McDaniel. I don't know if he's made contact yet."

"And now Andrei Goncharov has his sights on Sardinia."

"AG Holdings is working on a number of different resort and beachside condominium projects in Italy. We met with two officers in from the *Guardia di Finanza*. They've been tracking the tax implications of these projects for years. The developments are built to attract the *noveau* rich from the old Soviet Union, both from

Russia and other Eastern European countries. As you've surely read, this new wealthy class and the Russian mafia have entered Italy and our economy over the last ten years."

"I've heard that the area just north of Rome on the coast is of special interest as a place for second homes for the new Russian rich," said Caterina.

"That's because in more desirable areas, like Portofino and the Amalfi, there are very strict zoning policies which prohibit additional growth. In Sardinia, development permits are being issued, but there are very few and the process is very competitive, especially on the Costa Smeralda. If you want to attract the billionaires, that's where you have to build."

"Mr. Barton told Max and me that he got one of the Costa Smeralda allotments."

"When Barton got the permit, AG Holdings tried to convince Barton Enterprises to take it on as a partner in the project. Barton rebuffed Andrei Goncharov and moved ahead. AG Holdings filed a competing bid and a complaint with the zoning authority, but it was too late. Then, Goncharov went after Barton's architect. We talked to the head of the architectural studio this afternoon. He hedged, but it's clear he has become the AG Holdings preferred architect for all their South American projects, a deal far more lucrative than one development for Barton in Sardinia."

"Didn't Mr. Barton find a replacement architect?"

"He did. So now Andrei Goncharov is threatening him directly"

"Is Candy Seagraves at risk?"

"Probably not. But Mr. Barton is going to talk to her later and will tell her about the threats."

"So I just need to talk to her about Irina."

"Yes," her boss said with a small smile. "After you get done with the Seagraves, I want you to go to the morgue and look at this dead girl from the Forte Belvedere. Talk to the coroner. I want you to have every bit of information you can get on the circumstances of her death. Find out who is heading up the investigation."

"Do you really think I need to examine the body?"

"Is that a problem?" The magistrate gave her a sharp look. "You've done it before, haven't you?"

"No, sir. I've just been to the coroner's viewing room, like today with Mr. Barton. There really hasn't been any need for me to attend an autopsy before."

"Really? Is this a problem?" he repeated.

"No, sir," Caterina lied.

"I could send Marco."

"I'll handle it, sir."

Thirty minutes later, John Seagraves opened the hotel room door in response to Caterina's knock. He was a tall, redheaded man with freckles and a runner's physique. He waved her into the room with his left arm and held out his right hand, saying, "Ms. Falcone, we really appreciate your assistance."

"I'm just sorry we are meeting in these circumstances," she said.

Candy Seagraves was sitting on the far side of the bed, her long legs pulled up to her chin. Her face, framed by long, blonde hair, looked old beyond her years. Her tired, bloodshot eyes begged for sleep. She held out a slender, tanned hand to Caterina. "Thank you for coming up. I just couldn't face the people in the lobby."

"Mrs. Seagraves, I am so sorry for your loss," Caterina said, taking her hand and holding it. "Mr. Barton told me that your son was a very special young man."

Tears drowned Candy's blue eyes. "Bill was my life. I can't imagine what I'll do when I really come to terms with the fact that I can't talk to him every day. We didn't, of course, but I always knew that he was there to share a joke – he got my jokes – or to cheer me up. You know it was only him and me for fourteen years. He was sixteen when I met John. Actually, it was because of Bill that I met John. He was the high school swim coach." She smiled up at her husband who had moved a chair out from the desk for Caterina to use.

"I hate to impose on your grief, but I need to get a clearer picture of Bill and his life here," Caterina said, sitting down. "You may know some things that are important, even if they don't seem significant to you."

"I can't imagine how Bill's life would have any influence on the events here."

"Maybe not, but we are talking to all of the families."

"What can I tell you?"

"Talk a little bit about Bill's father and you. How did you meet?"

"Bill was in school when I met him. He was going to the University of Minnesota – he grew up in St. Paul. In his senior year, at Spring Break, he and a friend hitch-hiked to L.A. for the holiday." She stopped. A look of horror crossed her face. "Omigod, I met Bill twenty-two years ago – at Easter time." She started sobbing.

John Seagraves grabbed some tissues and put them in her hand. He moved to sit on the side of the bed. He placed a hand on her foot, talking in an undertone, while keeping his back to Caterina. She waited until Candy regained her composure.

"We met on Venice Beach," Candy said and then blew her nose and crumpled the tissue in her fist. "You know where that is? Just north of the Los Angeles airport."

"I've never been there, but it's in a lot of television shows."

"It's just like what they film." She asked her husband to get her a glass of water. She turned back to Caterina. "I was roller skating on the boardwalk and almost ran him over. What I remember most about Bill was how white he was – no tan at all. But he was the handsome one of the two. His friend Peter was a skinny redhead." She smiled up at John as he passed a glass and poured some sparkling water out of a small bottle from the mini-bar. "My taste certainly has changed for the better."

Caterina jotted notes as Candy recounted the story of her romance, marriage and divorce from Bill Barton. With a sad smile she talked of her son's childhood and his plans to work with his father during the summer as he had done for the past four years.

Eventually Caterina asked, "Did your son talk to you about his love life?"

Candy nodded. "Billy was a bit of a late-bloomer. He was cute and didn't lose his baby fat until his senior year in high school. He wasn't one of John's star swimmers."

She reached out a hand and laid it along her husband's cheek.

She turned back to Caterina after a moment. "Last year he added three inches, started working out, and the girls started to call him."

"Did you know he had a girlfriend in Florence?"

She nodded. "He called me two weeks ago, one of his regular Sunday night calls. He told me he was having a great time and was traveling around Italy on the weekends. He thought it was great living in another country, learning the language. He said it was easier to learn since he had met an Italian girl. Even though she spoke some English, they were trading days."

"Trading days?"

"You know, one day speaking only Italian, the next only English. I guess she wanted to improve her English as much as he wanted to learn Italian."

"Did he tell you her name?"

"Irina, I think."

"What else did he tell you about her?"

"He was quick to tell me that it was just a fling; that he wouldn't be bringing an Italian fiancée home."

"Did he tell you about her job?"

"No, I don't think so. He thought she was very attractive. He said she was talking him into a more Italian style of dressing. She told him his California clothes were too sloppy. I thought that was probably a good thing. He always had sort of a surfer dude look." Her eyes filled with tears again and she began to sob.

"I think that's enough," John Seagraves said.

Caterina nodded. "Just one last question, please. Did Bill mention anything about Irina having friends from Russia or spending time in Russia?"

Candy stopped crying. "No, never," she said, shaking her head. "He said she was Italian. I think he told me she grew up in Rome. Why do you ask about Russia?"

Chapter Thirty-Four

The morgue was in a large building not far from the Questura. Caterina told the driver to wait. She went to the administrative desk to ask for Dr. Silvio DePiero. She had to wait for thirty minutes on a hard plastic chair in a small room with dusky green walls and a stout, surly receptionist, whose mouth never relaxed its puckered pout.

Dr. DePiero finally appeared, wearing a clean white apron and blue paper booties over his shoes. He told Caterina, "I've got ten minutes." He was of average height with curly brown hair, shot with gray at his temples. His bloodshot eyes were chocolate brown. He gestured for her to follow him through a locked door, buzzed open by the dour receptionist. "*Grazie*, Aprile," he said.

"Have you ever been here before?" he asked after Caterina thanked him for interrupting his busy schedule to brief her on the dead woman found at Forte Belvedere.

"First time, sir," Caterina said.

"We've got four examining suites and a holding room. I have her in the holding room. I didn't bring her out to the exam room for two reasons – first, because I'm done with my autopsy and second, there's not much of note to see on her. It's pretty cut and dried."

The coroner pushed through a swinging door with a heavy, scratched plastic window in the top half and a rubbery, black material covering the metal frame. He held the door for Caterina, and they passed through into a cool, humid, dimly lit room. He threw one of the light switches and a small ceiling spot light flared three quarters of the way down a wall of metal doors, ten across and three high, each with a large metal handle. The bank of doors reminded Caterina of the cemetery on the edge of Florence where her grandparents were interred on a high wall behind slabs of white marble much the same size as the stainless steel portals in this disquieting room.

"They were all full by Monday morning. Now we are at about fifty percent capacity. I heard you are investigating the death of the American boy. He left about two hours ago. I expect the Paoli Brothers' Funeral Services will have him back in California by Saturday. The husband and wife from Wisconsin are still here. They will be collected tomorrow, I think."

Caterina swallowed to clear the lump in her throat, asking, "And the woman from last night?"

"She's right here," he said, as he pulled open the middle door and then hauled a sliding drawer out of the row directly under the overhead light.

"Is this the one you were looking for?" the coroner asked as he folded back the grass-green cotton cloth that covered the body. The woman Caterina had come to know as both Irene Paloma and Irina Golubka was exposed to her collarbone. Caterina thought it may have been a reflection of the light off the green cloth, but her facial skin had a strange green, blue, and pink tinge. The dead woman's eyes, under bruised purple lids, were slightly sunken and her dark brown hair was pulled back in clumped strands. Her neck was ringed with reddish purple marks. She only vaguely resembled the smiling young woman standing in Bill Barton's arms with his chin resting on her head.

Caterina nodded. "How was she killed?"

Dr. DePiero pointed at her neck. After slipping on a pair of thin rubber gloves, he turned her head to the left, the right and then with the chin pointing at the ceiling. "See here? The bruising. You can see it better on the right side. See? You can even see the marks of each knuckle where his fist was pressed as he pulled the garrote or rope tight. She was strangled. It was probably a thin rope, not a wire."

He looked at Caterina. She nodded and swallowed. Until the moment he started moving the woman's head, she hadn't really allowed herself to think of this as more than an exhibit, like the type of fake body she saw in the American forensic shows. But now Irina's mouth opened slightly and one eyelid moved, pulled down by sideways gravity. A bit of partially digested *frittata*, coffee-flavored, came to Caterina's mouth. She swallowed again and took a deep breath. The fetid air above the body was almost her downfall, but she turned, looked at the floor and then felt in her pocket for her notebook and pen. She did not look back at the corpse.

"Was there any bomb residue on her skin or clothes?" Caterina asked.

"Not on her skin. I don't know about her clothes. The lab has them. I think maybe they're with Agata Morosi. Do you know her?"

Caterina shook her head and jotted down the name of the technician.

"Was she sexually molested?"

"There was no penetration, but she may have fought off a rape," he said, as he uncovered her right arm. "See here. Two of her fingernails were torn and there was some skin under one of them."

Caterina was careful to just look at the tips of the fingers and not associate them with the rest of the body. "Samples went to the lab?"

"Of course." He tucked the right arm back under the cover. "The fight didn't last long. Her neck was snapped."

"So not just strangled."

"It started out with cutting off her oxygen and ended with breaking her cervical spine – right here." He pointed to a spot low on the back of Caterina's neck.

In reflex she started to cover the place with a hand and then pulled back. "Could you tell if it was a left- or right-handed person?"

"Probably right-handed. The movement was left to right. He was probably behind her."

"He?"

"Yes. I've never seen a case, except with a dead child, where a woman had the strength to snap the spinal cord."

Caterina jotted another note, putting the doctor's words in quotes.

"Can I see the tattoos?"

"So you heard about those? Here, let me lift and turn her a bit." He uncovered the right edge of the body, not leaving the dead girl naked.

Like a polite massage therapist might do to save the modesty of his client and preventing a chill, thought Caterina.

Dr. DePiero motioned for Caterina to come around the table and then he partially rolled Irina to expose the Cyrillic writing at the base of her spine. "Do you need a better look?" he asked.

"No, that's fine, thank you. There's another, isn't there."

"A bird by her navel." He covered the body and repositioned her. He moved the drape at her midsection to expose just her naval. "Maybe a bird of peace, do you think?"

Caterina looked at the black outline of a dove in flight with a red rose in its beak. "Or of love. Is there such a thing as a dove bringing a message of love?"

"Sounds good to me."

"I noticed some dark marks on her right side. Was she hit there?"

"That was lividity," the doctor responded. "Where the blood pools. She was left lying on her right side."

"I assume all of her things were sent to the lab," she said, looking up at him as he looked at his watch. "Do you have a list of her belongings?"

"It's out in a file on Aprile's desk." He started to cover Irina Golubka's face. "Are we done here?"

Caterina nodded, watching as he pushed the body back into the wall and closed the door. She followed him back to reception area where the woman, who in no way resembled a breath of spring despite her name, handed Caterina a brown file folder, saying, "This cannot leave this room."

Caterina thanked Dr. DePiero. He nodded, took off his apron, tossed it in a receptacle by the door, and left, still wearing his baby-blue booties.

Caterina sat down with folder and found the list of what Irina was wearing: a black cashmere sweater (no label, size extra large), blue jeans (Dolce & Gabana), high-heeled shoes (red), thong panties (black), a bra (black), a silver charm bracelet and red glass earrings. The inventory noted at the bottom of the page that there was nothing in her pockets. No purse, wallet, identification documents, or cell phone were found with the body.

She pulled out her cell phone. Despite the frown from Aprile, she called the magistrate. He answered immediately.

"Sir, I'm at the morgue and I had these thoughts," Caterina said. She briefed him, ending with the suggestion, "I think you should ask Captain DeLuca to send a crime team over to Bill Barton's apartment. We delayed doing this, but now we know that the girlfriend, Irina, is the body here in the morgue. We know Contessa Montalvo-Ligozzi saw her at the *Scoppio del Carro* and she probably went back to the apartment after the bomb blast. But what if she took someone with her or someone was there in her place? Maybe she went just to steal from Bill. But maybe she wanted to clear the apartment of all traces of herself, because she had something to do with the bombing. What if there are fingerprints or other evidence of someone with whom she was working?"

"*Buon idea*, Caterina. I'll call the Captain now. Do you have the contessa's phone number? It would be easier to get a key from her, than to break the lock on the door."

Caterina flipped through her notebook until she got to the right page. She gave him the number and location for the contessa. "After the crime scene people finish, perhaps Bill's parents can go in and collect his things."

"I'll try to get the Captain to move on this tonight or tomorrow morning at the latest. I'm leaving the office now. I'll see you in the morning."

Caterina snapped her phone shut. "Signora Aprile, thank you for your patience," she said with a smile as she slipped the brown file into the woman's inbox. The receptionist did not respond, giving Caterina a blank stare.

"Well, um, *buona giornata*." Caterina slipped her phone and notebook into her purse and made her escape from the morgue.

As she stepped into her apartment thirty minutes later, her cell phone rang. It was Max Turner.

"I don't have anything scheduled for tomorrow morning," he said. "Are you still going to pick up Irina's employment documents? Is that right?"

"Yes, but they aren't in Florence. They're at the factory in Pontedera."

"I want to ride along. Irina is the closest tie we've got to the potential target of the bomb."

"And you want to get out of town for half a day."

"Have you ever spent a whole day with Filippo DeLuca? Anyone needs some fresh air after that, and you are a lot better company." He laughed with Caterina and then said, "On the serious side, Irina is connected to the interests of an American. How about if we talk this through on the way to... where was the factory?"

"Pontedera."

"How far is that?"

"About an hour."

"So in half a day, we get the goods on Irina and we get to beat to death all of our ideas and solve this thing."

"If you say so." Caterina rolled her eyes, smiling at the telephone receiver.

"Be an optimist, Caterina."

Chapter Thirty-Five

I've arranged to meet Omar Pellione to look at Irina's employment file. Max Turner wants to be present at this interview, if you'll authorize it."

Paolo Benigni looked across his desk at Caterina. "Of course Mr. Turner can go along with you. Once again, remember he is in an 'observe and advise' capacity only. Don't let him take over and run things." He checked his watch and ran a finger down the open page of his agenda. "I'm going to be in meetings all day. Take my car and driver. But be sure to be back in Florence by four-thirty to pick up Mr. Barton."

Patricia Benvenuti was away from her desk so Caterina left a note, telling her where she would be, that she would be available by cell phone, and that she was using the magistrate's car and driver. When she got into her own office she found Max Turner sitting in the visitor's chair, answering email on his laptop.

"The magistrate has approved you accompanying me to Pontedera. He's even letting us use his driver and car, the Lancia. We're riding in style."

Max snapped his computer shut. "Do you have to do anything else or can we hit the road? I probably should be back for the mayor's briefing at two."

Checking the wall clock while shrugging into a tailored black leather jacket, she said, "We should get going. Remember, in the car, let's speak only in English. Guido Tozzi, the magistrate's driver, doesn't understand any, so what we say won't be spread through the motor pool." She closed her office and followed him down the gray hall to the elevator.

"Is there going to be another press conference this afternoon?" she asked.

"First, the consular and police agency briefing, and then the press conference." Max stopped. "Oh hell, I forgot." He turned toward the stairwell. "I've got to make a quick call. I'll meet you in front at the car." He headed down the stairs without waiting for a reply.

Five minutes later they were settled in the back of the black Lancia. She gave directions to Guido Tozzi and put on her seatbelt. Then she asked, "Did you read in the newspaper this morning that another kabob place and a leather store were vandalized last night?"

"One of Omar Pellione's stores?"

"No, not his. It's just some creeps taking out their frustration on the Islamic community," she answered.

"About the vandalized shops," Caterina continued, "an Iranian man and his Italian wife own the leather store. There is a lot of Iranian and Palestinian ownership of shops that sell leather coats and purses in Florence. A Moroccan man operates the kabob stand. The mayor has to get the word out that there is not any Middle Eastern involvement in the cathedral bombing."

"He's going to make that very clear this afternoon at the press conference," Max said. He looked out the window as they passed the botanical gardens. "Are the products for the Iranian stores imported from Iran?"

"Some, but most of the inventory is brought in by ship from China."

"Are you talking about the knock-off Gucci bags and Prada wallets?"

"No, the Iranians are mainly selling the cheaply-made purses and coats that have 'Made in Italy' labels sown in when they get to the dock, usually in Naples. The knock-off products you're describing are mostly sold on the street by Somali vendors who answer to a murky hierarchy of manufacturers and vendors in the southern part of the country."

"So what do the Italian merchants like Omar Pellione think about the Iranians and Somalians cutting into his business? His product is wholly made in Italy at the Pontedera factory, isn't it?"

"We'll have to ask him, both about the products from China and if his coats are one hundred percent Italian-made. I was thinking about him last night after I set up the time for our meeting this morning. Hearing him on the phone without looking at him reminded me that I heard something off in his accent the first time I met him," Caterina said, wincing as a *Vespa* cut in front of the car. Tozzi cursed under his breath.

Max put on his seat belt. "What do you mean?"

They were in the *vialle*, the ring-road around Florence, a broad street intended for three lanes of traffic, but as usual, was congested with cars, buses and scooters, five abreast.

Caterina sat back and said, "He looks Italian, but his accent has a touch of something else. Usually someone born in Italy has a very distinct accent from the town they were born in or from where their parents were from. Italians don't move around much, usually not until after they get out of school and probably not even then."

"Right, not like me, who moved around five states and three countries before I was twelve. A real Army brat."

"Or me. My English accent is hard for most people to peg. My Italian is pure Florentine, but when I speak English, it is mostly with an American accent as opposed to a British one, and it's tinged with a bit of Italy, a bit of Boston, and a bit of an American movie and television accents. Most Americans tell me it's a continental European accent, whatever that means."

"You think Omar may have grown up speaking two languages; that he may not be Italian? Omar is a Middle Eastern name, isn't it?"

"It's also a common Italian name. Maybe he has a non-Italian parent or he grew up speaking Italian in another country where, when he wasn't at home, he spoke another language."

"Like an army brat."

Caterina nodded. "Even when you were in other countries as a child, you were speaking American English, so you have a pure mid-western accent in English, probably from your parents. But you speak American-accented Italian."

"Can you tell where Omar may be from? Perhaps Russia?"

Caterina frowned, trying to remember Omar's voice from the evening before. "It's not an Eastern European accent. It may be Middle Eastern or Moroccan. Actually, Russians are great language learners. They are some of the best mimics in the world. They can achieve an almost perfect accent in Italian, French, German, or Spanish. They have a bit more trouble with English for some reason, but less trouble with a British accent than an American accent."

"Why is that?" He cocked an inquiring eyebrow.

"I don't know. Ask Marco. He's our Russian linguist."

Max pulled a business card out of his pocket and jotted himself a note. "Listen closely to Omar today. Let's figure out where he is from."

Guido Tozzi cleared his throat and said, "*Mi scusi, Ispettore. Che' strada vole a Pontedera?*"

"Take the *FiPiLi*, Tozzi," Caterina answered in Italian. "It shouldn't be too backed up this time of day."

"*Va bene,*" Tozzi said.

Caterina turned to Max. "The Firenze-Pisa-Livorno highway – FiPiLi for short – is always under construction. Sometimes it's faster, taking the toll road toward Lucca and heading south on a country road near Altopacio. But I think we'll risk it today."

"I'm in your hands," he said, smiling.

"Better to be in Tozzi's than mine."

"I'd vastly prefer yours."

"Uh… okay." She blushed as her dream replayed in her mind and quickly changed the subject. "Uh, so tell me – what did William Barton, Jr. have to say during your lengthy interview yesterday?"

"He told us that he first met Andrei Goncharov on the Black Sea resort project."

"The same project that that Australian developer, Nic McDaniel was working on?"

"Yeah. He and McDaniel were partners with a Turkish company. Anyway, Barton was able to pick Andrei's pictures out of a photo line up. He also met Andrei's sister, Stefanya, once in Istanbul."

"There's another Goncharov? Stefanya?"

"Their little sister. Andrei and Stefanya came to the resort site when it was mid-way to completion. Barton guessed that she was about eighteen and at university somewhere."

"Did Barton know that AG Holdings wrested the Black Sea resort from McDaniel?"

"No, he denies knowing anything about the project after he bowed out."

"Bill's ex-wife told me some things about him last night that led me to believe that if a development project wasn't fun, he'd drop it. His whole life has been about short-term deals and shorter-term relationships. So his statement that he didn't follow the history of the Black Sea deal after he got out of it is probably true."

"That pretty much fits with what he told us. All of his construction or conversion deals have been unique, and he's very enthusiastic about them. He's not the type to churn out cookie-cutter housing developments one after..."

The beep of a cell phone interrupted Max. He unclipped it from his belt. "Sorry, let me see who this is." He glanced at the screen, flipped it open and said, "Turner." The conversation took ten minutes, but all Caterina heard was "Yes," "No," "I don't know," "Check it out," and "That's no surprise." When Max snapped the phone shut, he sat looking at the back of Tozzi's head for a few moments and then turned to Caterina with a raised eyebrow.

She brought him back to the subject by asking, "With so much proof of the Goncharovs' culpability in the other incidents, why can't someone go after them?"

"First, they are careful to hide any links to the bombings. And they have threatened all of the potential witnesses – the Australian, Nic McDaniel, the American oil exec whose daughter died in Turkmenistan – so it would be hard to make a case."

"Have appeals been made to the Russian authorities?"

"We have been talking to our counterparts in the policing agencies since the third bombing, the one in Turkmenistan. But they don't seem to be able to assist us and aren't very interested in taking the lead in the investigation. The Goncharov brothers seem to follow the philosophy that – forgive the crudity – they don't shit where they eat. They are reportedly model citizens or, at least, very discreet in their home country. In fact, that phone call I just got was from my counterpart at the embassy in Moscow. The Russian authorities are stonewalling us. They want irrefutable proof that Andrei Goncharov had something to do with the Duomo bomb. They see no reason to investigate a kind condolence note from his lawyer to Barton about the death of his son."

"So how do you get to them?"

"Through the bomb-maker."

"How so?"

"We are tracing funds from the Goncharov companies and even some of their private bank accounts – don't ask me how, the computer geeks at the CIA handle all of this – through both legal and more covert computer searches. Unfortunately, it may be the case that we don't catch the Goncharovs or the bomber this time, but we add to our evidence and we catch them the next time or the time after. We are both very patient and very impatient."

"That's depressing."

"I'm not saying we'll give up, but it's likely that Cobra doesn't work in his home country for the very same reason that the brothers are clean at home."

Guido Tozzi mumbled something from the front seat. Caterina looked out the window at the rolling hills carpeted with short, spring-green alfalfa.

"Max, we're coming to Pontedera."

"I don't see a town. How big is it?"

"Not that small. It spreads out to the north. This is where many of the leather factories used to be. They used to tan and cut leather here."

"Used to? Not any more?"

"In the eighties the business started drying up. First, Argentina and Brazil had the cows and cheaper labor and then, China and Turkey started undercutting even the South American companies. Now, the leather preparation is done in other countries and the goods are manufactured here. Since Pellione is still around and is still run by an Italian family, my guess is that's how they stay competitive."

"Is *Pellione Pelle* an old company?" asked Max

"I looked it up online. It was started in the sixties by Bruno Pellione. It's kind of fitting because *pellione* means big skin. The present CEO is Daniele Pellione. Omar must be his brother."

Max pointed at a roadside billboard with a picture of Audrey Hepburn on a scooter. "I heard that this is where *Vespas* come from."

Guido's attention was caught by the name of the famous Pontedera scooter. "*La fattoria di Piaggio e' a Pontedera.*"

"Correct," said Caterina. "A company called Piaggio started manufacturing motorcycles just before World War II, and now they make the *Vespa* scooter and the three-wheeled *Ape* delivery cart."

"*Vespa* for wasp and *Ape* for bee – their names have to do with the sound they make, I was told," said Max.

"Right, again," Caterina said, looking out the window to check their progress. "I've had a *Vespa* since I was sixteen."

Caterina told Guido to take the next exit off the FiPiLi highway. Soon they could see a large red brick building with a steel roof some distance off the secondary street. A sign that ran across the front of the edifice said *Pellione Pelle*.

"That is the factory," said Caterina. She released her seatbelt and leaned over Tozzi's shoulder to point out a narrow dirt road that ran between a stand of tall cypress trees off the main street. She turned back to Max. "Omar's in charge of sales. They've got stores in Pisa, Empoli, and Florence."

Guido stopped the car in a small parking lot behind a small square building with golden stucco walls and a terracotta roof.

"I think the business office is probably here." Caterina pointed at an awning stretched out over a concrete slab in front of a doorway at the near end of the small building.

Max rang the buzzer beside the door. A young woman, dressed in a brown suede leather skirt and a tight white t-shirt, answered it.

"Is Omar Pellione available?" asked Caterina.

Chapter Thirty-Six

The woman didn't give Caterina a glance, but kept her gold green eyes on Max's face.

"Omar Pellione?" Caterina repeated.

The woman still didn't look at Caterina, but she said, "He's in his office. I'll see if he's free for you, sir. May I have your name?"

"He's Max Turner and I am *Ispettore* Falcone," Caterina responded.

That got the woman's attention. She mouthed the names as if trying to remember them. After she ushered them into the reception area, she knocked on an inner door, tucked her streaked red hair behind her ears, and entered.

Omar Pellione walked out seconds later, followed by his receptionist. He was rolling down the sleeves of a white cotton shirt and fastening the cuffs. His tie was bright blue. He held out his hand to Caterina.

"Miss Falcone, I've been waiting for you. Good to see you again. May I take your jacket?"

Caterina handed him her black leather jacket trimmed in red.

Omar examined it inside and out. "Good workmanship," he commented as he looked at the label. "Casini. My competitor, I see. I must show you something from our exclusive designs. Not what we have in the shops. The ones I'll show you are only for our most special customers." He turned to Max. "Mr. Turner, I do not believe you are a colleague of Miss Falcone."

Caterina responded, "In a way he is. Mr. Turner works for the U.S. Embassy in Rome."

Max elaborated, "*Ispettore* Falcone kindly offered to let me ride along today, so I could see some of the Tuscan countryside. Also, I have a small interest in the matters she has come to discuss with you."

"How is that possible, Mr. Turner? Miss Falcone wants to see the employment files of an Italian citizen. How does that interest the American government?"

Caterina answered, "Remember, on Tuesday, when I came to your shop on Via dei Neri, I was asking about Irene Paloma because of her connection with a young American student who died in the Duomo bombing?"

"Ah yes, now I remember. Would you both please come into my office and sit down. Can I offer you some coffee?"

"Yes, please," said Caterina.

Max nodded. "Thank you. Mr. Pellione…"

"Call me Omar."

"Omar, the issues Inspector Falcone wishes to discuss are hers alone. I really am only here to enjoy Tuscany and her company."

"I can understand both the attractions of Tuscany and Miss Falcone." Omar straightened from leaning on front of his desk when Marina carried in a tray with three tiny white espresso cups, a small pitcher of milk, a ceramic sugar bowl and three miniature spoons on it. She set the tray on a low table between the two visitor chairs. Omar handed one cup to Caterina, making sure their fingers touched. He waved a hand at the second cup, inviting Max to take it. Then he added three heaping spoonfuls of sugar to the last cup and swallowed the mixture in one gulp.

"About Irene," Caterina started.

"Yes? Have you found her?" Omar walked around the desk and sat down. "I must say I was most surprised when she quit."

"We found her." Caterina watched his face closely. "I'm sorry to tell you that she is dead."

His expression froze. "Dead? Some sort of accident? Drugs?"

"Why do drugs come to mind?" Caterina put her half finished espresso down and pulled her notebook and a pen out of her purse.

"I was always suspicious that she was involved with drugs at the clubs she went to at night."

"Drugs like cocaine or heroin?"

"No, more like that drug at the discos. What is it called? Ecstasy? She would sometimes complain of a hangover from... I think she called it 'E'."

"We didn't find any evidence of drugs. She was strangled. Her body was found yesterday. The murder occurred not long after she was at your shop. You were there, weren't you?"

"At the shop, you mean? Yes, I gave her the final salary owed to her." He was quiet for a moment and then asked, "You're saying Irene was murdered Tuesday night?"

"Yes. You may have read about it in the newspapers. The woman found at Forte Belvedere."

"That was Irene? I thought they said on the television that the woman's identity was unknown."

"We had fingerprints from her apartment. They matched."

"Do you know who killed her?"

"No."

He crossed his arms tight and sat back. "How can I help you? I didn't know who she saw – who she partied with. I didn't even know she was dating that American boy."

Caterina leaned forward. "I thought you met him. I remember you described him as a tall blond man."

Omar shook his head. "I said I saw him at a distance. I didn't know they were romantically involved. You told me they were a couple. Again, how can I help you?"

"I just want to see Irene's personnel file. We have some questions about her that may lead to the people who would know why she died."

"I can't see how that would be."

"If you could get her file, I might be able to explain it."

"Of course," he said as he rose. He walked to the door and spoke to the receptionist. "Marina, bring everything we have on Irene Paloma." He waited for her to bring him a thin file. "Take the cups," he said.

She came in and cleared away the espresso cups, rubbing against Max's shoulder as she leaned over the table.

Omar sat down and spread the file open on his desk. "She was only with the company for four months. We hired her in Pisa in December for the Christmas season. Then, we transferred her to Florence in late January. The Pisa store gets hardly any business in January and February. No tourists."

He passed the file across the desk to Caterina. Max didn't express any interest in looking at the documents. He inspected the fingernails on his left hand and yawned.

Caterina read through each piece of paper. The first sheet was handwritten with a dark marker. It stated that the employment of Irene Paloma had been terminated with a date three days earlier. The next line read "Resigned. Salary paid in full." and had two set of initials.

"Are these your initials and hers?" Caterina held the document up and pointed.

Omar nodded.

Under that in blue ballpoint pen and in different script, it read, "I resign". This was followed by a round sloping signature – *Irene Paloma*.

"Did you see her write the last bit?" Caterina asked.

Omar nodded again. "I always have them sign in front of me when I pay them. It saves problems and disputes later."

"So your bookkeeping is current?"

"Of course."

The next page was a sheet from a ledger of work dates and wage payments. It had fourteen lines, starting with the date of the first week of December of the previous year. The name Irene Paloma was in bold type at the top of the page.

"She was paid weekly?"

"Yes, one hundred and seventy euro per week."

"Did she have a regular contract?"

"No, she was a *co.co.pro* under the new law."

Caterina turned to Max. "That means she was a temporary employee with no benefits, vacation or sick time."

The next page was a photocopy of an Italian *carta d'identita*, dated six months earlier, copied flat so both of the inside pages appeared on one page. Caterina read out, "*Irene Paloma*, born on 16 January 1984 in Rome." She examined the official ink stamp in the corner of the photograph and two postage-style registration stamps at the bottom of the second page. It was the last sheet of paper in the file.

Caterina looked over at Omar. "Do you have a copy of her passport?"

He shook his head. "I don't even know if she had one. Many people do not. She may never have had need of one."

Caterina wondered whether to bring Omar into the loop of people with knowledge of Irene's background. *It couldn't hurt; he might have some helpful information*, she thought.

"We went to the apartment that you told me about. We found some things that led us to believe that Irene Paloma, the Italian girl from Rome, was really Irina Golubka, a Russian national from Moscow."

"What?"

If he has any idea, Caterina thought, *he's doing a good job of hiding it.*

"She has family in Rome," he continued.

"Did you ever meet or talk to any of her family?"

"Why would I?"

"I don't know. Maybe someone calling himself her brother came to the shop in Pisa or Florence."

"I never met anyone she was related to, but she called me from Rome. I told you that when I saw you in the shop."

"Was it from a landline phone or her cell phone?"

"Her cell, I suppose," he said, shaking his head. "You're right. She could have been anywhere."

"Her roommate at the apartment on Via della Scala told us that Irene wasn't Italian. Another person who talked to her said that her Italian didn't have a Roman inflection, but sounded more like she was from Eastern Europe. Did you notice that?"

"No, I'm not so good with accents."

"Maybe that's because you don't have an Italian mother tongue. Your Italian is quite Tuscan, but I can hear a faint accent when you speak."

Omar's face grew red as he stared at Caterina, but then he laughed. "You have a very talented ear, Miss Falcone. May I call you Caterina?"

She nodded.

"Thank you. More friendly don't you think. If you will pardon me a little joke – I do have an Italian *mother's* tongue. My mother was Italian. It's my *father's* tongue that was different. My father was Lebanese. I grew up in

Beirut. My mother worked for the Italian embassy there, where she met and married my father."

"So you have dual citizenship."

He nodded and relaxed back in his chair. "It wasn't formalized until I married my wife, Paola."

"Then you aren't related to the Pelliones by blood. It can't be your birth name. How did you come to use it?"

"I took Paola's name when we married. It was much easier doing business in Italy with an Italian name, especially in the closed community of leather goods. Pontedera is so provincial."

"What is your birth name?"

"Omar – see it's easy because Omar is both an Italian and a Lebanese name – my mother picked it. Jaboor is my father's surname."

"What is you mother's surname?"

"Rossi. Why are you asking all of these questions about me?" Omar sat up straight, a frown crossing his brow.

"I'm just curious. I, too, have parents from two different countries. Are your parents still living in Lebanon?"

"No, they died in a car accident when I was eleven. Again I ask, what does this have to do with Irene?"

"Nothing. It has more to do with why you weren't more suspicious about her nationality." Caterina handed him the photocopy from the employment file. "You see? Her *carta d'identita* is only six months old. If this birthdate is correct, she was twenty-eight. Why wasn't her identity card issued earlier?"

"Maybe she lost the old one. This could be a replacement. It didn't matter to me. I just wanted a good shopgirl with legal papers."

"Caterina," Max put a hand on her arm. "Give the guy a break. He probably only looked at her identity card once, if at all. Right, Omar? Maybe you didn't see it before today? Maybe you asked Irene to give it to your receptionist so the file would be complete."

Omar relaxed and almost smiled. "That's right," he declared. "I don't hire undocumented workers, so each file has to have an Italian *carta d'identita* or a *permesso di lavoro.*"

"See Caterina, as long as she had either proof of Italian citizenship or a work permit, he wouldn't have looked at it again." Max looked her straight in the eye for a second, sending some sort of message.

Caterina wasn't sure why Max was stopping her line of questioning, but she went with it.

"Did you ever have problems with Irene on the job?"

"She was one of my best salesgirls. When she wasn't tired from the night before, she could sell anyone, anything. She had a gift. The only problem I had was when she quit without notice."

"What about off the job?"

"What do you mean?"

"Did you have any trouble with Irene in social settings?"

Omar shook his head. "I wasn't ever with her in social settings. I'm a married man."

"We have a photograph of you found in Irene's belongings."

"A photo?"

Caterina took a folded piece of paper out of her notebook. "This is a photocopy. That's you, right?" She handed the page across the desk. Max stood, went around the desk and looked over Omar's shoulder.

"It's me," Omar said. "Where was it taken?"

"I was going to ask you that."

"Let me think."

"Is the little girl… ?"

"My daughter, Petra."

"The blonde woman is your wife?"

"No," he said slowly, at first frowning, then, his face cleared. He laughed. "I remember now. The celebration for three things – the company's fortieth anniversary, Petra's fifth birthday, and *Befana*, the sixth of January. We invited all of the employees and their families. Irene must have been there. I don't remember. Max, are you familiar with *Befana*? You don't have her in the states, right?"

Max walked back to his chair, chuckling. "No, but my kids know about it now. This past January they thought they had struck the jackpot. Presents at Christmas from Santa Claus, and then again twelve days later from *Befana*, the witch."

Caterina lost track of her questions. *Max has children,* she thought. *He's married? Why didn't I know this?* She gathered herself together, looked at her notebook and then, at Omar.

"The woman in the picture is an employee?"

He shook his head. "She's one of our best customers. We invited a number of our oldest friends and loyal customers to the party."

"So you threw a party for the children?"

"My wife's father did."

"And this woman, your client, did she bring her children?"

"I don't think she has any. She's just an English woman, living in Pisa. She has a lot of money and spends quite a bit on our coats and purses. She brought a gift for my daughter."

"What is her name?"

"My daughter?"

"Well no, I meant your friend. You've mentioned Petra by name."

"Yes, my daughter is Petra," he said slowly, obviously thinking of something else. He pointed at the picture. "This woman is not my friend, as you put it, except that she is a good customer. Her name is Elizabeth Willingham."

"Do you have an address for her?"

"Why? I don't want you to bother her. That would not be good for business."

"She is in a photograph taken by Irene, who took the photo for a reason. I want to know why she kept it."

"I don't know why Irene had it. Lots of people had cameras at the party. It means nothing."

"It means something. It's the only one she kept. So do you have an address for Miss or is it Mrs. Willingham?"

"She's single. Or at least I think so. I don't have her address."

"A phone number?"

"Caterina, give the guy some space. The lady is just a client." Max winked at Omar.

Omar smiled back and gave Caterina a shrug. "I'm sorry I can't give you more help. I would if I had the information. I've only seen her in the Pisa shop once or twice. The manager of the store invited her to the *Befana* party."

Caterina paused and looked up at the ceiling debating about her next move. She made a decision that she knew was a bit risky. "Would you give me a DNA sample?"

"What!" Omar shouted.

"What?" Max asked and then swallowed the question in a cough.

Caterina smiled. "Just to rule you out."

"Rule me out as what?"

"As Irene's killer."

"You think I killed her? That's crazy."

"Not really. I mean, *not* 'not really crazy,' but that I don't *really* think you killed her." Caterina gave him what she hoped was a flirty I-don't-know-what-I'm-doing grin. "It's just my boss, you understand. He will ask me why I didn't get a DNA sample from the last person to see Irene alive. Especially since, as you say, you didn't part on the best of terms."

"I didn't kill her. I haven't seen her since I gave her the cash I owed her in the Via dei Neri shop. I wasn't the last person to see her alive, obviously."

"The money wasn't found on her," Caterina said as she opened her briefcase on her lap. "Are you saying you won't give me a sample?"

"It's unnecessary, but if it will get you out of my office, I'll do it."

Caterina unzipped an internal pocket and pulled out a test tube with a stopper. "It's just a mouth swab." She twisted out the top that was attached to a cotton-tipped stick.

Omar opened his mouth and she ran the end quickly around his palate and inner cheek. She slipped the sample back into the tube and wrote his name and the date on the label.

"Is that...? Omar began. There was a knock at the door. The man, whom Caterina saw delivering inventory at the *Persephone* leather shop in Florence, walked in. She tried to remember his name – Gian or Jamal, or something like that.

"Omar, can I borrow your car?" He was wearing a long-sleeved, heavy white cotton shirt, a black leather vest, and black jeans. Mirrored sunglasses hung from the pocket of his vest.

Omar's face turned an unattractive red, as he said in a quiet controlled tone, "Didn't Marina tell you I was busy?"

"She's not at her desk." He didn't move out of the doorway.

Omar opened his desk drawer, took out a ring with two keys and tossed them across the room. "Make sure you fill the tank." The man left, closing the door.

Max's laugh filled the silence. "Hey, was that your brother? He could have been your photocopy."

Omar shook his head. "He's a distant cousin on my father's side. He's here for a couple of weeks of vacation.

It would be nice to show him the sights, but I have no time."

"He's visiting from Lebanon?" asked Caterina.

"Yes." Omar walked to the door and opened it, looking back at Caterina and Max seated in front of his desk. "So is there anything else?"

Caterina got up, collecting her purse and briefcase. "We've taken up too much of your time already." She held out Irene's personnel file. "Is it all right if I take this? I will send you a copy for your records."

"Do that. We keep accurate files for both tax and pension purposes."

"That's good to know." She looked back at the office to see if she had left anything. A large photograph in burnished leather frame sat on the credenza behind his desk. It showed a small, dark-haired, very pregnant woman clasping Omar's arm. His shirt and her dress were made of colorful, matching, tropical print cloth. Caterina could see behind them was the front corner of a building made of wooden poles, standing on stilts with a thatched roof.

Caterina pointed. "Is that your wife?"

Omar picked up the framed photograph and rubbed some dust off the top edge. "It's from our honeymoon in Bali."

"You both look very happy. Did you enjoy the Far East? I've never been." Caterina started toward the door with Max following.

Omar put the frame down and caught up with them at the door. "We were on our honeymoon and very much in love. We could have been anywhere." He waited for them to pass through the reception area and followed them out to their car. Guido Tozzi was smoking a cigarette that he crushed under his foot when he saw them coming. He held the door for Caterina.

Max stuck his hand out to Omar. "We've probably overstayed our welcome, but if you don't mind I'd like to come back sometime and have you show me how your coats are made. I take it that this is the factory for all your products."

Omar shook his hand, saying, "Everything is made here, but we don't tan our own leather like they used to do in the old days. We'd be happy to show you around. I would get my brother-in-law to do the tour. Or my wife's father. They are more knowledgeable about the production side of things. I'm just in sales."

Caterina reached out of the car window, offering Omar her hand. "Thank you for your patience. I will get you the copied file and keep you informed on Irene's case."

Omar took her hand and held it briefly. "Please let me know who murdered Irene. Even though she was not a Pellione employee anymore, we are still interested, *Ispettore* Falcone."

Chapter Thirty-Seven

As Guido drove out to the main street, Caterina turned to Max.

"I'm sorry...," she started.

"You did a good...," Max said at the same time.

"What?" she said

"What were you going to say?" he said

They both laughed.

"You first," he said.

"I was going to say that I'm sorry I screwed that up. I went after him too hard and he clammed up."

Max put a hand on her arm. "And I was going to say that you did a great job, both getting good information out of him and getting that mouth swab."

Caterina blushed with pleasure. "Do you really mean it? I don't have that much experience questioning suspects – not that I really think he's a suspect. But Irina had skin and blood under her fingernails. I had to start somewhere."

"He's a suspect for something. It may be as simple as carrying on an affair with the tall, blonde English lady, Elizabeth Whatshername. He really didn't like you asking about her. Or maybe he was messing around with Irina and was lying about not knowing her well."

Caterina nodded. "Or maybe his books aren't so clean and he *is* hiring illegals. It wouldn't be so hard to falsify an identity card. Many of the businesses in this area hire undocumented workers for their factories. Not so much for sales people – those documents are checked more often, but with a fake *carta d'identita*, he wouldn't have to worry."

"He's holding out on you for some reason. You got a lot of information without getting him suspicious."

"I learned the technique from my mother. She can lead me all over the place and then always goes in for the kill when I least expect it. Usually after I've been out on a date with a new guy." She laughed with him. "You also helped with your 'good ol' boy' comments. They lulled him, but also let me know when I was going too far. Thanks."

"No problem," Max said. "You kept him focused on Irina. He didn't kill her, so he was happy to give you the DNA sample."

"But, you're right, he's jumpy about something."

"Maybe it was the name-change and the Lebanon connection. Good catch on the Middle Eastern accent. I didn't pick up on that."

Caterina grinned. "Linguistics is my life. But seriously, any Italian would have picked it up. We are constantly pigeonholing people by their accent. We still are a country of city-states. If you are Roman, you think people with Florentine accents are snobs. Everyone thinks those with Milanese accents are rich, soulless, moneygrubbers."

"Except for the Milanese themselves," Max said with a laugh.

"Even within a region, the words and accent you use is important. The Florentines and the Pisans still don't like each other – and they can identify the enemy within five words."

"Like 'Name that Tune'."

"What?"

"Nothing. It was an old radio contest in the States in the sixties. Name the tune after hearing five musical notes."

They rode in silence for a couple of minutes. Max was scribbling notes on a business card.

Caterina waited until he slipped the card in his pocket and then said, "I wonder if Omar's cousin is really on holiday. Omar must have forgotten that I saw – Jamal, I think his name is – at the store in Florence the day before yesterday."

"Maybe he was just helping out. You know, volunteering while on vacation."

"It looked like he was familiar with the job on Tuesday. Also, driving an *Ape* in Florence isn't that easy. You have to know your way around."

"You're going to have to look into Omar's past and family. I can help you with some of that, but you will have quicker access to his passport records and the name change thing. That was strange don't you think?"

"A bit, but his explanation made sense. Pontedera is a small community. He would be a constant irritant to his in-laws if his name was always reminding everyone he was a foreigner. It seems clear that he got his girlfriend pregnant and had to marry her. Maybe the name switch was a request – or, more likely, a demand – by her father."

"Did you catch where Omar was on his honeymoon? I saw the photo when we went in, but I'm glad you asked about it."

"He said Bali."

"How long ago would that have been?"

Caterina's forehead wrinkled as she did the math in her head. "Less than six years ago. He said his daughter turned five this past January. I'm betting he has only one child, like most Italians these days. He hasn't aged much since the picture was taken, either. And his wife was very pregnant in the photo."

"So you think it was in October or November, two or three months before – what was her name – Petra – was born?"

"That should be about right. Why?"

"The Jakarta bomb went off in October that year."

Caterina went white. She whispered, glancing at the back of Guido's head, "You can't possibly think Omar Pellione is the bomb-maker."

Max also lowered his voice, "Not at all, but I hate this type of coincidence."

Caterina switched to Italian, speaking to their driver, "Guido, can you give us some music for the ride."

He nodded. "Of course. Let me know if the volume is right." He stuck a disk of the magistrate's favorite Aaron Copland clarinet concertos into the CD player under the radio and turned up the sound.

"*Grazie*," Caterina said and turned back to Max and switched back to English. "So tell me…"

"Hey," he interrupted. "How far are we from Pisa?"

"What?"

"I see we're almost to the freeway. How far is Pisa?"

"About twenty minutes."

"Do you have to get back to Florence right away?" He pulled the card with his notes out of his pocket and skimmed it.

"No."

He squinted at the tiny print, saying, "I've got until the mayor's meeting at two. Why don't we go to Pisa and try to find – what was her name – here it is, Elizabeth Willingham? We can have lunch there, too."

Caterina thought about the blonde woman in the photograph. "I guess we should talk to her before Omar has a chance to set her up with a story that fits his version of the facts. Of course, he might be on the phone to her right now."

"I think it would be good to see her in person, rather than interview her by telephone."

Caterina nodded. "I'll call Signora Benvenuti, the magistrate's assistant. She can find anybody's address and phone number. If by some happenstance, she can't ferret out the info, I'll call the British Consulate."

Caterina told Guido to head toward Pisa, then called Patricia Benvenuti, who first pulled up *Pagina Bianca*, the online residential phonebook on her computer.

Her chin muffled her voice. "Here she is – E. S. Willingham on Piazza Vittoria. Number eight. Phone number 050-244-7678."

"Thanks Patricia, we'll be back in a few hours." As she hung up, she said, "Guido, please set the GPS for Piazza Vittoria in Pisa."

"I know where it is," he responded. "Do you want me to keep the music on?"

"Yes, please," said Caterina turning back to Max. "What were you saying about Omar... ?"

A cell phone rang. "That's mine again." Max dug into his jacket pocket for the phone. He read the screen. "Excuse me, I have to take this." He flipped open the phone. "Hey, sweetheart, forgot to tell me something earlier?" He listened for an extended length of time, nodding occasionally. "Okay, put him on. Hey Buster, I hear you have the stubborn bulldog face on this morning. What's up?" He looked at Caterina and winked. "But don't all of the boys in your school have to wear a *grembiule*? Even the older boys?"

Caterina chuckled. She could picture a small boy in his long-sleeved blue smock with buttons up the front. Then she sobered, thinking, once again – *All the good men are taken*. She blocked his voice for a minute and tuned back in to hear him end the call.

"So you get ready for school and put the boss back on the phone.... Hey sweetie, tough day, huh? Is he putting it on? He's right, you know, they look sissy.... Yeah, I know. Okay, I have to go. I love you. Hang in there."

"I hated them, too," said Caterina.

"What?"

"The *grembiules*. The smocks the boys have to wear aren't half as bad as the pink ones with ruffles the girls have to wear. I refused to wear pink ever again."

"But Julia is right. She does half the laundry here than she did in the states."

"She's got a point."

"More important, Josh has got to do what she says. With me traveling so much, she's the boss."

"She sounds like a good mother."

"She's the best. We met just before I shipped out to Kuwait and Desert Storm. We got married a couple of years later after I got back and was stationed at Quantico in Virginia."

"I thought Quantico was where the FBI training camp was located."

"Same place. The FBI Academy is located inside the Marine Corps Base." He laughed. "I've spent a lot of time there, it seems, in many lifetimes."

"So you grew up in a military family and decided to repeat the process."

"Not exactly. Julia and I decided that we didn't want to be a career Marine Corps family, so I resigned and went to law school on our savings. She already had a realtor's license, so she supported us. I graduated and got a job with a D.C. firm. We got pregnant with Josh and moved out of the rental apartment and into a house in Alexandria. That's the only place Josh had ever lived until we moved to Rome."

Caterina said slowly, "I was kind of surprised to hear you were married."

"Why?"

"You didn't mention it at dinner the other night."

"I didn't?"

"No."

"Maybe we got sidetracked on something else."

"Or maybe you are such a good lawyer that you get into deposition mode and learned everything about me and gave nothing away." Caterina forced out a laugh.

"Maybe. I do that all of the time, Julia says. I tell her that I'm just a good listener. Women seem to think that men always hog the conversation."

"You certainly don't." Caterina turned to face him. "So it's my turn. How did you get from the big law firm to the FBI?" she asked.

Max looked out the window. They were driving into the outskirts of Pisa, full of small metal-sided warehouses and graffiti-marred three-story apartment buildings dating from the sixties.

He turned back and said, "The work I was doing was boring. I put in four years, but was complaining so much that Julia sat me down and told me to figure out what would make me happy. I decided the Bureau was it."

"And Rome, with the embassy – another change of direction?"

"Actually I got into the State Department through the FBI and my first posting was Berlin. I did six months there and Julia stayed in Virginia. Before Desert Storm I had been assigned as a Marine to Camp Darby near Livorno, so I learned some Italian and got to travel around Italy quite a bit. My focus at the Bureau was anti-terrorism, so first Berlin and then Rome. Rome is a two-year posting, so Julia decided that we would all relocate."

"Do they like living there?"

"Sure thing, except for the *grembiules*." He laughed and then sobered. "What were we talking about before the interruption?" He didn't get a response from Caterina because his phone rang again.

"This is embarrassing. Sorry." He looked at the screen. "At least it's not Julia, again. It's a cell phone, not Italian. I should take it."

Caterina nodded. "Of course."

He answered, "Turner... Señor Potero... Tell me." Max shifted around searching his pockets. Caterina handed him her notebook and pen. He wrote quickly, saying little. "Very interesting. Thank you, sir. Please let me know if you get more details... You say you've given this information to both Magistrate Benigni and Captain DeLuca?... Good. Thank you, again. Goodbye."

"What?" Caterina asked as he closed the cell phone and tore the page out of her notebook.

"Wow," Max said. He handed back her pen and notebook.

"What?"

"The Spanish secret service had already looked at Alberto Fernandez when they first investigated the Bilbao case, because the bomb was in his briefcase. They ended up deciding that he was just an innocent victim who didn't know the device was there. You know – college kid, art major, traveling with his mother to a museum. They thought the museum was the target or the Cultural Minister."

"But?"

"They hadn't plugged the name *Goncharov* into the investigation."

"They found a connection?" asked Caterina. "It's about time. You handed Eduardo Potero the Goncharov brothers as suspects on Monday or Tuesday." She noticed Guido Tozzi looking in his rear view mirror. She lowered her voice. "What's taken him so long?"

"Calm down. I think he found the connection immediately. He's just having a hard time believing the motivation for the killing. He wanted to get all the info he could before he shared it with outside agencies."

"What did he learn?"

"Alita Fernandez – remember she was an architect – competed for a project to be built in Ibiza by AG Holdings… "

Caterina interrupted, "Andrei Goncharov *again.*"

"… but she wasn't awarded the contract," Max finished. "Her son, Alberto, worked with her during the summers. He was twenty-two and by all reports extremely good looking and charming."

"What's the connection? I can't see what Goncharov would want from Mrs. Fernandez or her son."

"It seems during the competition, Alberto started dating Oleg's and Andrei's little sister, Stefanya, who was going to enter the university in Barcelona in the fall, also as an art major. Alberto and Stefanya started turning up in the society pages. There was talk of an engagement. Then poor Alberto and his mother end up dead."

"I wonder if Stefanya knows who killed her fiancé?"

Chapter Thirty-Eight

MOSCOW

Yakov is missing." Andrei Goncharov said as he strode into the blood-red dining room.

"Just a minute," his brother said, holding up a hand and leaning toward the trim, honey blonde woman sitting across the long table from him. "Kiki, sweetheart, will you go ask the cook for another plate for Andrei." He looked up. "It's pork roast today."

Andrei dropped into the chair at the head of the table. "Just a thin slice. And have him find me a good Bordeaux, not the dreck Oleg drinks."

Kiki patted her enhanced puffy lips with her napkin, laid it beside her plate of salad, stood, tugged down her skirt as she disappeared through a door at the end of the room without a word.

Oleg shoved in another piece of meat, talking as he chewed. "A little courtesy would go a long way between you and Kiki."

"Kiki doesn't care about what I say. She's got you and her father giving her enough courtesy for two life times."

"She's big help to me, and could be for you."

Andrei leaned forward and put his hand on his brother's arm, stopping a hunk of pork from joining the rest. "Look, enough about the new wife. We have a problem. Yakov hasn't called in. He hasn't turned up."

"What does the security firm say?" Oleg shook off his brother's restraining hand, swallowed the meat and took a gulp of red wine.

"Nothing. They haven't heard from him since Sunday morning."

"They tried his phone?"

"Of course. It's turned off or the battery is dead."

"Maybe he had to lay low."

"He's always been so reliable. An ass. But a reliable ass."

"I thought you said he called about the girl." Oleg smiled at Kiki when she sauntered back into the room carrying a plate heaped with food and silverware rolled in a linen napkin. She dropped both on the table in front of Andrei.

Andrei grimaced and pushed the food away. Kiki smiled. She walked behind Oleg and kissed the top of his big head. "I'm going to the gym, pumpkin." She turned to Andrei and said, "Cook is looking for your bottle of wine."

The two men watched her walk the length of the room until the door snicked closed behind her tight derrière.

Oleg smirked and picked up his fork. "The girl," he prompted.

Andrei got up and paced. "That was just a messenger who called, not Yakov. I told you that."

"Who was the messenger?" Oleg asked with exaggerated patience.

"He wouldn't say. He just claimed to be passing on the news that the girl wasn't a problem anymore."

Oleg pushed back his own plate. "This is trouble. The letter already went out, right?"

"It was delivered this morning. I expect I'll hear from Barton soon."

"Did you say Stefanya would be back in Moscow by the end of next week?"

Chapter Thirty-Nine

Siamo qui," said Guido, pointing at a mid-Renaissance gray stone building to their left.

"Grazie, Guido," said Caterina, flipping open her phone and finding the page in her notebook with Elizabeth Willingham's phone number on it. A woman answered after three rings.

"Pronto," she said.

"Posso parlare con Signorina Willingham?" Caterina asked.

"Sono Elizabeth Willingham," the woman said. *Her accent could be found in any upper-crust British drawing room,* Caterina thought.

Caterina switched to English. "Miss Willingham, my name is Caterina Falcone. I am an inspector with the Florence police department's task force that deals with foreigners. May I speak with you this morning?"

"I suppose so, Inspector. When would be convenient?"

"I am in Pisa. I could be at your home in five minutes. Is the Piazza Victoria address still your residence?"

"Yes. May I ask what this is in regard to?"

"We are assisting some of the victims of the Easter bombing at the cathedral. You may know one of them?"

"Who would that be, Inspector?"

"We are getting close to your street. Could we continue this conversation in person?"

"Of course. Ring the bell with my name."

Caterina thanked her and closed the phone. "Did you just tell me that the Goncharov brothers are now letting their assassin settle personal scores as well as influence business deals?"

"It seems so," Max answered, releasing his seat belt. "Why didn't you just tell her that we were parked outside?"

"That's so Big Brother. It's already off-putting that you can find someone's address and phone number online."

"But you *are* the police."

"That's no reason not to be polite. Also, I wanted to get a sense of whether Omar Pellione called her. She would have recognized my name if he had. She didn't seem to have any idea why I might be calling."

"Good," he said, opening his door. "Let's get this done."

The apartment was on the second floor. The first thing Caterina noticed as the door opened was the creamy, wall-to-wall carpeting. She could hear her grandmother in her head, saying that only the British and Americans insist on rugs that can't be taken up to be shaken or beaten clean. Nonna declared that all sorts of dirt, vermin, and molds lived in foreigners' carpets.

The tall, striking blonde woman holding the door open smiled at Caterina's distracted expression. She said, "I can see that you share an Italian's suspicion of my floors."

Max looked mystified, but Caterina laughed, "Worse – I'm the *nipote* of a Florentine matriarch who feared floors that she couldn't mop every day. You must have lived here a long time to understand 'the look,'" she said, making air-quotes with her fingers.

"I can't tell you how many maids have lectured me on my choice of carpet. But I like to walk around barefoot and not have icy toes."

"My grandmother never let me be barefoot from the moment my feet hit the floor in the morning until I was tucked in at night," Caterina responded. "You should see my slipper collection."

The British woman chuckled. Her focus moved beyond Caterina to Max, who was leaning against the doorframe, a look of total confusion on his face.

Caterina swallowed a laugh. "Miss Willingham, sorry for the strange start. Please let me introduce Max Turner. Mr. Turner is with the American embassy in Rome."

"Please call me Liz." She was slender with large breasts, wearing a long-sleeved black roll-neck sweater. Her long legs were clad in Black Watch plaid woolen slacks. Her feet were bare, toenails crimson.

"It is a pleasure to meet you, Liz," Max said, shaking her hand. His smile widened as her gaze traveled leisurely from his head to his feet.

"My pleasure entirely, Max."

"And I am Caterina Falcone. I don't think I introduced myself, as I came in."

"No, Inspector, you were distracted." Liz Willingham's hand was firm and cool.

"Caterina, please."

"Max, Caterina, come into the *sala*." Liz Willingham led the way down the wide entry hall to a large room with a long low divan and two overstuffed chairs, all covered in Chinese silks topped with Indonesian batik pillows.

The mix of colors and patterns was a bit overwhelming to Caterina. The room smelled strongly of the unmistakable odor of the famed potpourri from the Farmacia Santa Maria Novella in Florence. She chose a chair because the couch looked so low that once a person sat down there would be no way to get up gracefully. Max seemed to make the same decision and took the second chair.

"May I offer you some refreshment? Water, coffee, scotch?"

"No thanks," Max said. Caterina shook her head.

Liz Willingham stepped up onto the low divan. In one graceful move she sank sideways onto her knees, one arm stretched along the back of couch, the other on her bare left ankle.

"Did you come all this way to talk to me?" she asked. Without waiting for an answer, she turned to Max and said, "It seems that you would have no interest in a Brit. I know a few Americans, but not many."

Max looked at Caterina and said nothing. Caterina opened her notebook and unfolded the photocopy of one of the photographs of Irina and Bill Barton that she had found in the photo album in the box under Irina's bed. She got up and handed it to Liz.

"Do you know either of these two people?"

Liz glanced at the photo, shook her head and handed it back. Then she reached out her arm again. "Just a minute." She looked at the page longer, bringing it closer to her face and then stretching out her arm to its full length and squinting. She handed it back to Caterina.

"Don't have my specs here, but I don't know the young man. Is he British? He looks more like a beach boy. Too tan, unless he lives in Spain most of the year. But the clothes are wrong, too." She handed the page back to Caterina.

"You're correct. He's from California. What about the woman?"

"I've seen her somewhere. You can see she's Italian with that semi-slut style of clothing – Cavalli and Dolce & Gabbana – last year's summer collections or knock-offs of the same. Give me a minute – I have a great memory for faces."

She stared at the ceiling for a full minute. "It was here in Pisa, not too long ago, maybe in a restaurant…" She reached out for the photocopy. Caterina leaned forward holding the page out at the woman's optimal sight distance. Liz reached out and tapped the page with a long red fingernail.

"I've got it. She was a *commessa*, a shopgirl, at Omar's store near the tower. She tried to find me some shoes to match a jacket I bought there last summer."

"You saw her last summer?"

"No, I bought… actually, it was a gift… the coat last summer. I was looking for winter shoes at Christmas to go with it."

"When you say 'Omar's Store' you mean…?"

"*Persephone Pelle*. Omar Jaboor owns it."

"I thought his name was Omar Pellione?"

"Pellione is his married name. He took his wife's family name. But he's Lebanese and he should be proud of his name. His father was a Lebanese Christian. His mother was Italian."

Max said, "You keep saying 'was.' Are his parents dead?"

Liz nodded. "He told me they died in a car smash up when he was young."

Caterina pointed at the picture. "Do you know the identity of the girl in the photo?"

"No, I only saw her the one time. When I went back in February, she wasn't there."

Caterina got up again. "I want to show you another photograph." She handed the Englishwoman the photocopy of the photograph that had been taken at the *Befana* party. "You are in it."

"You have a picture of me? How?" She took the proffered copy.

"Look at it and see if you remember the occasion."

"There's Omar." She pointed at the left side of the page and then looked up at Caterina. "This was taken at the *Befana* party this past January. I've never seen it before. Who took it?"

"I don't know who actually took the shot," Caterina said. "Do you recognize the small girl?"

"It's Omar's daughter, Petra. Does this have anything to do with the California man or the *commessa*?"

"The woman – her name is Irene – was killed this past Tuesday evening. Both photographs were found among her possessions. She worked for a while at the *Persephone Pelle* shop in Florence after she left Pisa."

"So what does this have to do with me? I haven't seen her since December. I don't remember her being at the Befana party."

"We are just trying to tie up a few loose ends. We can't understand why she had a picture of you and Omar Pellione."

"I can think of two reasons."

Caterina felt a tingle of anticipation. "Please tell me."

"Most of the girls who work for Omar have some sort of crush on him. So she may have taken, or kept, the picture because he's in it and I'm just a bystander."

"And the second possible reason."

"Well she looks like a sly boots in the other photo – all cuddled up with the California beach boy. She may have hung on to the photograph in some sort of attempt to blackmail Omar."

"How could she do that?" Caterina sat very still. "Blackmail Mr. Jaboor."

Elizabeth Willingham gave a trilling laugh. "It's silly really, because she wouldn't be successful, but maybe she didn't know that. Or maybe I'm wrong and Omar is more sensitive and cautious than I give him credit for."

"I'm sorry Miss Willingham, but …"

"Call me Liz."

"Liz, I'm sure I'm a little slow here, but what are you talking about?"

"Omar and I have been romantically involved for the last four years or so."

"But he's married."

Elizabeth raised an eyebrow. "Technically, he is separated from his wife, but he keeps it quiet because of the business."

"Does he live here with you?"

The Englishwoman shook her head. "He's still living with her – separate bedrooms, you understand. He started the paperwork last year to get a divorce. It's still very difficult to get a divorce in Italy, especially where a child is involved. Many couples just separate and go on to other partners without bothering to make it legal."

"Does Omar's wife know about your relationship?"

"He told me that he discussed it with her. I, of course, haven't talked to her. She must know he's spending his time somewhere."

"Did the separation bother her?"

"They only got married because she was pregnant and he was working for her father."

"You say you know him as Omar Jaboor. Why did he take his wife's name? It's unusual. In Italy, both the husband and wife usually keep their birth names. I know it's different in England or the U.S., but I've never heard of a husband taking his wife's family name."

"I know. As I said before, I think he should use his birth name and not that of a family he is leaving. But he finds benefits to it."

"What benefits?"

"Well, like… Look shouldn't you be asking Omar these questions? I thought you just wanted to know why the shopgirl had my picture. I told you what I thought and now we're off on a tangent here."

"We did talk to Omar this morning. He said he made the name change for business reasons and because of the prejudice he faces in Italy for being half-Lebanese. I suppose he didn't want his daughter to have a foreign name."

"More likely, his father-in-law didn't want a granddaughter with a foreign name."

"His father-in-law was not in favor of the marriage?"

"You'll have to ask Omar that. But you understand that Italians in general have a very closed society. People here are not open to foreigners, not like America. Especially non-European immigrants. My ex-husband is Moroccan and he had the same problems in Britain. The attitude is so colonial. If anyone doesn't have pasty white skin in England, they are automatically in a different class. I felt I was born into the wrong country, so after my divorce, I tried Spain for a while and then I moved to Pisa. And I find the attitudes are even worse here."

"But Omar is half Italian."

"His mother was from Puglia. But that doesn't make a difference in Pontedera. They think southern Italians are another breed and Middle Eastern people are completely under suspicion, especially after the Twin Towers. They don't make any distinction for the fact that his father was a Christian, not a Muslim. I'm ashamed of the role my country and America are taking in Iraq, and I thought I was well out of it by moving here. Then, Italy goes and joins the coalition, too."

"Does Omar share your ideas?"

"Of course he does. Look at what Israel and its supporters, the Americans, have done to Lebanon. He knows first hand about the folly of armed intervention."

"Would you support violent protest in support of Iraq or Lebanon?"

"You mean like a terrorist act, like the cathedral bombing? Of course not. One kind of violence doesn't beget another."

"Does Omar believe in a violent solution?"

"Of course not. Omar is the gentlest of souls." She looked at her watch. "If you two... well, actually, the Yank here hasn't uttered a peep... don't have any more questions about the shopgirl, I have to get going. I have to get my roots done and my hairdresser is not a patient soul."

"Just one last question. Where were you on Easter morning?"

"You think I saw the girl that day? I was here. I slept in and Omar came over about four."

"Where was he before you saw him?"

"That's more than one question." She stood on the couch and stepped off. "I'll answer, as I escort you to the door." She slipped her bare feet into a pair of soft black loafers that lay near the door of the room and started down the hall. As she took a light Burberry rain jacket off the coat tree by the apartment door, she said, "Omar went to mass with his wife and daughter, and then had dinner with her family."

"How do you know?"

"Because he told me. Why would he lie? Also, what else would an Italian family do on Easter? His father-in-law would have demanded that everyone be at his table for Easter lunch."

"But...," Caterina started as she and Max stepped into the building's hallway with Liz Willingham.

The blonde woman locked her door and turned. "Ask his wife where he was Easter morning. I know he wasn't with me. So where else would he be? Omar always likes to keep up appearances, so mass at St. Jacopo is where he would have been on Easter Sunday."

She took the stairs. They followed her down to the curb in front of the apartment building where she pushed a green scooter off its kickstand and fired up the motor. As she put on a black helmet she turned to Max. "You should try not to talk so much, Mr. Turner." She laughed and sped off.

Max grinned. "More and more interesting. I don't know if it has anything to do with Irina or the cathedral bomb, but people are lying to us and that's always intriguing to me."

Caterina pushed back the curls escaping from their clips. "I don't feel like I got anything of importance from her."

"Not important?" Max choked out a laugh. "You did great. You found out that Omar straight-out lied to us about how well he knew her. They've been having an *affair* for at least four years and he says that he *may* have *seen* her once or twice."

"But that's probably because he's not legally separated from his wife. He wanted us to think Irina was taking a picture of him and his daughter and this unimportant client was a bystander. He's probably lying to his mistress about separating from his wife. He just didn't want us messing up his affair or his marriage."

"My point is that he lied to the police. That gives you more reason to go back and look at him. Look at his citizenship status and history. See what his ties to Lebanon are, past and present. See if he has anything to do with Irina's fake *carta d'identita*, or first – even better – if it is a fake. Maybe she got residency some other way. Maybe Irina was married to an Italian."

"I kept thinking there were other questions that I should have been asking Elizabeth Willingham."

"Of course there are. But it's better to see what you dig up on Omar. Then you'll know the precise questions to ask. She's been with him for at least four years. She knows a lot more about him than she told us today. And she likes to talk about anything and everything. That's a plus."

"Let's get back to Florence," Caterina said. "Or did you want to have lunch here in Pisa?"

"Whatever works for you. I can eat anywhere."

"Let's stop at the Auto Grill on the freeway. It has good sandwiches and is quick. I'd like to get back to the office."

"Fine by me." He beat Guido to the car door and held it for Caterina.

Once on the freeway, Caterina was quiet, jotting notes in her book.

Max pulled out his cell phone and pressed one button. "Hey, Sweet Pea. Did you get Josh to school with all the necessaries?... Great... I'll call him just after dinner and maybe bedtime will be easier... Were you able to find something for my mother's birthday?... You're a star. Thanks for that... Okay, gotta go. Big kiss. Love you."

Caterina looked up. "That's another reason I didn't know you were married until you mentioned it to Omar." She pointed to his ring finger. "No ring."

Wiggling his left third finger, he said, "I've never worn jewelry, except a watch. I'd like to get rid of that, but my internal clock is always about thirty minutes late."

"So how do your wife and Josh like Rome?" Catherine asked.

"They think it's great to be near me and since Maddy made her appearance six months before ..."

"Maddy?"

"Yeah, our daughter, Madeline. She's going to have her first birthday in a couple of weeks."

"Two kids?"

"Yeah. You should see what a hit they are with the ladies in Rome. Even the men seem crazy for kids here."

"That's because you hardly ever see a family with more than one child. Two kids who look like they are related is considered a bit excessive." She smiled, thinking of the looks Lorenzo's children got from other young Florentine couples. "Of course, Italians would like to have bigger families."

Guido pulled into the Auto Grill parking lot, opened Caterina's door and followed the two as they walked up the sidewalk to the entrance.

"Why is that?" Max asked holding the door open to the combination café/diner/store.

"Why, what?"

"Why only one kid per family?"

"It's mostly a factor of economics. Children here often stay home until their late twenties or even thirties, especially the boys."

He laughed. "I might have, too, if my mother had insisted on cooking, cleaning and washing my clothes until I left home. She put an end to that in my teens. The family laundry became my chore. Luckily, since I'm an only child, it wasn't as much as it could have been."

Caterina kept talking as she led the way to the glass display case. "Also, Italians are getting married later, so women are having their first baby in their late thirties and one is enough."

She turned to point out her favorite sandwiches. She decided on a *Rustica* with cheese and proscciutto. Max ordered and went to the *cassa,* the cash register, to pay and bring back the receipt that he handed to the bar man who gave him a *Caprese* filled with fresh tomato, mozzarella and a couple of basil leaves, as well as Caterina's *panino* that had been warmed in the grill. "*Due bottiglie di aqua frizzante,*" Max added, pointing at the receipt. "I figured you would want some water, rather than a soda," he said to Caterina, handing her a small plastic bottle of sparkling mineral water.

"Thanks," she said, leading the way to a table.

"Where's Guido?"

She waved a hand back toward the bar. "He's having a coffee and reading the sports paper. I asked him to join us, but he declined."

Max nodded and bit into his sandwich, "Not bad for road food."

"Damn good for road food," Caterina declared.

They ate in silence for a couple of minutes before he asked, "Do you think Liz Willingham is really as ditzy as she comes across – kind of a bohemian type in an unbohemian world?"

Caterina laughed, "I hate to say it, but yes. She reminds me of one of those British girls in the sixties and seventies, who went off to India to sit at the feet of an unwashed guru or who hung out in a Portuguese beach town, working as a waitress or jewelry maker and having lots of affairs with dark, warm boys. The men at home bored her; the Mediterranean types seemed so much more exotic."

"That's why she tried first a Moroccan and then a Lebanese-Italian?"

"No, I think she's – what did you say – ditzy. She likes semi-exotic guys and, though he doesn't do it for me, Omar seems to be her cup of tea. Or at least for the last four years, he has been, at least on an occasional basis."

"However, we don't know how reliable she is for recounting the truth. Omar seems pretty tame to me. He moves to Italy, knocks up his girlfriend, marries her and settles into her father's business. Then he acquires a mistress …"

"Not unheard of in Italy," Caterina interjected.

"… whom he is very discreet about, as far as we can tell."

"Also, not uncommon here."

"There again we need to know if Liz is naïve or realistic about her prospects with Omar."

"More important we need to know what Omar did before he came to Italy."

"What does Liz Willingham do for money? I can't remember you asking her that."

"I didn't even think of it. She may have family money, although for some reason I don't think so."

"You're always going to have another chance at talking to her. First, you should get that DNA sample of Omar's checked against the skin Irina scratched off her attacker."

"You're probably right. Unfortunately our lab doesn't work as fast as the one you have at the FBI – or the incredible ones we see on American television shows. It's going to be a week or so, depending on the priorities. If other investigators have better leads as to the identity of the Easter bomber, my little murder is going to take a back seat in the crime lab."

"I don't think you'll be very credible arguing that Pellione is connected to the bomb just because he was in Bali five years ago." Max stood up. "Can I bring you a coffee?"

Caterina nodded. "Thanks. A *macchiato*, please."

He returned from the counter carrying two small espresso cups on tiny saucers. As he sat down, Max continued where he left off. "It also doesn't make sense to me that Cobra would take a contract close to his home base. I always pictured him as this itinerant assassin moving from place to place. But maybe he is hiding in plain sight. Lay out for me what we know about Omar."

"He was born in Lebanon. His father was a Lebanese Christian and... "

"We need to check on that."

"... and his mother was an Italian woman."

"We need to find out about her, too. How do we do that?"

"The easiest way is to get Omar's application for citizenship. It would have his birth certificate with it."

"Great idea – easy to do without alerting him. Okay, what else do we know about his parents?"

"They were killed in a car accident."

"We need to check on this. I'll do it through my contacts in Damascus." Max pulled a clean business card and a pen out of his jacket pocket.

"If his mother was still an Italian citizen, I can probably find a record of her death, too."

Max scribbled a note on the card. "What next?"

"I forgot to ask if he had any siblings. We get so used to only children here that I sometimes just assume it. Sorry."

"No problem. I didn't think of it either or I would have asked Omar about sibs when I asked him about his cousin Jamal. It would have been a natural spot to ask about the rest of the family." Max jotted another reminder. "We'll put that on the list to find out. Maybe he still has ties to Lebanon."

"We need to know when he entered Italy – coming from Lebanon he would need a visa unless his mother got him a passport when he was a child, which I doubt, since he said his Italian citizenship came with his marriage."

"Got it – visa check."

"If his daughter is five and he got married after she was conceived, then there should be a record of his marriage just over five years ago. Probably right before the honeymoon, but that's not for certain."

"The impressive Signora Benvenuti can probably find that for you," said Max.

"Now about the honeymoon. Would they need a visa to get into Bali?"

"I don't know. I'll check that."

"Is there any way to check for other visas he may have gotten to travel to other places?"

"I'll call the folks at Langley. They would know. I bet it's changed since 9/11."

"I'm going to have to brief the magistrate."

"And Captain DeLuca, but I'd like to keep this inquiry low key. No need to make a big deal out of what is probably just a case of Irina being in the wrong place at the wrong time."

"Maybe, but I'm obligated to keep my superiors informed. And almost everyone is superior to me. Also, there's sure to be an inspector over in the homicide division that has Irina's case."

"Let's just treat it like a simple murder. I'm just mucking around in it because I'm frustrated that I have no other avenues to follow in the Easter bomb case."

"I almost forgot. We have to check out Omar's alibi. Mass at St. Jacopo in Pontedera."

"Any of his wife's family could give us that information."

"I don't think we should talk to her," Caterina said.

"Maybe his father-in-law. If Omar and his daughter are really separated, he probably isn't Omar's greatest fan. You could play it like part of the investigation into an employee's death."

"Perhaps the magistrate knows someone in Pontedera who can make a discreet query."

Caterina's phone rang. It was Paolo Benigni. "Are you back in Florence yet? All hell is breaking loose here with the American boy's father."

Chapter Forty

There was an earlier communication from Andrei Goncharov to Barton Enterprises, before Monday, but Barton never got the message." Magistrate Benigni was summarizing what had been learned from Bill Barton's interview. "It ended up on the CFO's desk in Boston, but *he* was out of town in the Caribbean for the past two weeks. In the mildest of language the letter expresses regret that Barton had to find another architect and hope that it didn't delay the project. Goncharov offers to assist Barton Enterprises in exchange for a piece of the action. The CFO's assistant didn't think it was important since the company had already retained a new architect."

Caterina, Max, Filippo DeLuca and the magistrate were sitting in Captain DeLuca's private conference room.

"Barton says he wouldn't have acquiesced anyway – he doesn't 'bend over' for blackmailers, is how he put it," interjected Captain DeLuca.

"But Goncharov had put Cobra on notice already," said Max. "If Irina was the bait... Well, she and young Bill had been dating for three weeks. The implementation of this attack was very complex. No one could have put it together on a few days' notice."

Paolo Benigni nodded. "We're sure Andrei Goncharov has been weighing his options since the meeting in the Milan airport in December, if not longer. It's cheaper and cleaner to go the less public and less violent route. But after his earlier negotiations with Barton, Goncharov must have known that chances were slim that he would get a deal the easy way."

"But you said Barton was irate," said Caterina. "I think your words, sir, were that 'all hell was breaking loose.' That doesn't make sense that this benign letter made him lose it. The condolence letter from AG Holding's lawyer was much more inflammatory."

"The communication that ended up in the CFO's inbox wasn't the only contact. Barton got a new message this morning that says they will take out his family one by one, saving him for last." Captain DeLuca slid a photocopy across the table to Max.

Caterina, reading over Max's shoulder, asked, "Did this come from their lawyers in New York like the last one?"

"No, this one is anonymous, as you can see. It doesn't mention Andrei Goncharov or AG Holdings. It just says to get out of Sardinia."

Max asked, "Was it sent to Barton's office, like the condolence letter?"

"No, this was hand-delivered to the Savoy this morning," answered Captain DeLuca.

"Any clues as to its origin?"

"None, said the magistrate. "It wasn't left at the desk. We haven't found anyone who saw it being slipped under the door of his suite."

"So they know where he is," said Caterina. "He's in danger."

The magistrate ran a hand through his hair, leaving it standing on end. "Barton has hired a security firm to guard the Sardinia site, the major company employees, and himself."

"What about his other children?" asked Max.

"He pulled his daughter out of Radcliffe. She's on her way to Paris to stay with her mother until this is sorted out. He's arranged for security for them, too."

"What about Candy Seagraves and her husband?" Caterina asked. She hadn't warned them of the potential danger the night before.

The magistrate frowned, saying, "Mr. Barton decided to discuss the situation fully with them. He's with one of his bodyguards and a lieutenant from Captain DeLuca's staff at his son's apartment right now. I believe he and Mrs. Seagraves are collecting the boy's belongings."

The meeting went on for an hour, during which Max Turner related the substance of his telephone calls with Señor Potero about the Bilbao incident and with the Legat from the U.S. Embassy in Moscow regarding the lack of cooperation from the Russian authorities.

As they were walking back to the task force offices, Max asked Caterina, "Are you going to brief the magistrate on the Irina and Omar situation? That kind of got lost in the revelations from Bill Barton. I wish I had been here for the Barton interview, instead of touring Tuscany."

"Max, if Irina was part of this, then our trip today was important."

"Important, yes, but you could have handled it without me."

"I suppose," she said, doubt sounding in her voice. "I sent Omar's cheek-swab to the lab. Tomorrow morning, I'll be going back to Persephone Pelle to see if Irina's co-workers know what happened to her after she left the shop."

"Good," he said, sounding to Caterina like he hadn't really heard her. "I need to focus on the U.S. citizens in this case. You noticed that DeLuca has the original of the note that was delivered to the Savoy. I wish I had gotten it from Barton, first. It would have been on a plane to Quantico right now."

"Max, snap out of it. We aren't exactly a third world country. If there are prints – which is doubtful, don't you think – or other trace evidence, the lab here or in Rome will find it."

"I suppose …"

"And since it is a document that was delivered to an American in connection to a criminal case, you will get the results and probably even get to examine the original itself."

He laughed and slung an arm around her shoulders. "You can be blunt when you want, can't you, *Ispettore* Falcone?"

Caterina blushed and he removed his arm. "I just think…," she started to say.

"I know what you think," he interrupted. "I've got to find Bill's father now. Good luck with Irina's case."

Caterina wanted to say, *Stay. Work with me. Irina was the lure that set the trap. She should be important to you, too.* But instead she watched him walk off before she climbed the stairs to her office.

For the next few hours she and Patricia Benvenuti searched for the documents needed to piece together the story of Irina's existence and Omar Pellione's past. They discovered that before the previous December there was no trace of Irina in Italy. Omar Jaboor Pellione was easier to find, but the files only went back seven years to a visa application listing a Palestinian-owned leather shop in Florence as his proposed first residence upon arrival. A woman in the Pontedera records office said it would take a day or two to send the full file of the application for citizenship made after his marriage.

It was after nine when Caterina left the Questura. In lieu of dinner she stopped at her favorite gelateria on the way home. The owner, Sandra Nuti, a friend dating back to their days in high school, was behind the counter. After asking about Sandra's husband and daughters, Caterina ordered a triple cone with pistachio, raspberry, and chocolate.

"What's wrong?" asked Sandra. Her dark brown eyes examined Caterina's face with concern.

Caterina's tongue caught a drip of chocolate running down her cone. "What do you mean?"

"Who is he?"

"Who is who?"

"The guy who's let you down."

Caterina looked at her friend and then back at the cone. "I don't know what you are talking about, Sandra."

"*Cara*, you only order triple cones when you've been disappointed in love."

"I do?" Caterina choked half on a laugh and half on the chill of the raspberry sorbet.

"You do." Sandra straightened the flowered cotton cap over her short brown curls. "Of course, you've had such a long dry spell that I'd stopped noticing."

Caterina nodded, her cheeks grew pink. "It's been a while. Probably this new job with the magistrate…"

"Don't change the subject. Who is he?"

"There's no one."

Sandra wiped the marble counter with a damp towel, not looking at Caterina. "No one?"

"It was a miscommunication."

Their eyes met. "Now we're getting somewhere," Sandra crowed. "A miscommunication with whom?"

"I've been working a bit with this American."

"American? Good looking?"

Sandra can be counted on to keep things in perspective, Caterina thought. "Married," she said.

"You are ordering a triple scoop because of a married man?"

"I didn't know he was married, at first."

"You didn't ask?"

"It was his height and the green eyes that distracted me. And I'm sure he was flirting."

"All men flirt." Sandra straightened a tower of cones in danger of tipping.

"All *Italian* men flirt. He's American. It lulled me into a sense of complacency."

"But you know to get the vital statistics out of the way, first. We're not eighteen anymore."

"As you said, I've had a dry spell. I'm out of practice."

"So you're heartbroken."

"Well… he is tall… "

"And Italian men are usually short," Sandra finished. "*Tesoro*, you have to give up that rant. Height isn't everything. Look at Giovanni."

"But there's only one Giovanni and you got him."

Chapter Forty-One

I'm going to talk with the shopgirl at Persephone about Irina's last evening." Caterina finished her morning briefing with Magistrate Benigni, Marco and Patricia Benvenuti. "She wasn't very helpful before, but somebody has to know where Irina went after she told Omar Pellione she was quitting and got paid."

Magistrate Benigni nodded absently and turned to Marco. "Find out about that Estonian today. This bombing has turned into a Russian case. We can't leave his death as a loose end now. It may be that our bomber blew himself up." He laughed without humor. "Now that would be ironic."

"I would be happy to assist Marco," offered Patricia. "If he needs any telephoning done to find out where the man was staying, I can help."

The magistrate nodded. "Good." He turned. "Caterina, concentrate on the murder of Irina Golubka, aka Paloma, but be sure to coordinate with the homicide inspector who was assigned to the case."

"Who is that, sir?"

"I don't know. Call Homicide and find out. Let them do the legwork. Limit your investigation to her relationship to young Bill Barton."

An hour later, Caterina was asking the shopgirl, Marcia, about her recollections of Tuesday evening.

"No, I didn't hear what they were talking about," Marcia said. Instead of the end of her ballpoint pen, she was chewing on a ragged fingernail. "I was helping Jamal unload some purses and shoes from the *Ape*. When we finished, Irene was gone. The bitch didn't even say goodbye. It was like out of sight, out of mind. She had a better job and no time for us."

"Did Jamal say anything to Irene?"

"Jamal doesn't talk to girls. If your life isn't all about soccer, Jamal has no interest in you."

"How long has he been working for the Pellione family."

"I don't know. He just runs errands for Omar. He's been in the country for maybe a month."

Caterina jotted a reminder to check on Jamal's visa status. "Do you know Jamal's last name?"

Marcia shook her head.

Caterina returned to her original line of questions. "So you have no idea where Irene went after she left the shop?"

"The funny thing is, I thought I saw her later. After I closed up."

"Was Omar still here in the shop?"

She shook her head. "He left about thirty minutes earlier to drive back to Pontedera."

"How long after Irene took off, did he leave?"

"About fifteen minutes."

"And how long did you keep the shop open after Omar left?"

Maria laughed. "About five minutes.

Caterina did some quick math in her head. "So you think you saw Irene about an hour after she left the shop."

"Maybe I saw her. I'm not sure."

"Where?"

"I was walking down Via dei Neri toward Santa Croce to go home. I thought I saw her in Café de Benci on the corner."

"Was she with someone?"

"She was at a window table with a really tall woman, very elegant, dressed in red."

"Did you recognize the woman?"

"I may have seen her once before, with Irene. She came by one evening when we were closing a few weeks ago. I thought she was a model, lots of makeup, great clothes, but she wasn't thin enough."

"Did you notice anything else that night when you were outside the café?"

"No, I didn't stop. Though I did think at the time that Irene looked angry – you know, mouth tight, arms crossed, defensive like. And the other one was doing all of the talking, pointing a finger at Irene. I remember how long and red her fingernail was." Marcia shook her head, absently biting a hangnail off her left thumb. "Funny – the things you remember."

Caterina left the shop and walked the length of Via dei Neri to Café de Benci. She showed the bartender, a tall woman with a dark ponytail tied with a purple scarf, a photograph of Irina and described the woman Maria had seen.

"I wasn't here that night. Fausto was on. But that's Irina in the photo and I bet the other one was Veronique. I don't know what her real name is, or, I guess I should say, *his* name. Veronique is a transvestite. She's been around for years. She and Irina come here in the evenings at closing time for the shops to have a Proseco, or two, before Veronique goes off to work."

Caterina nodded as she wrote Veronique's name in her notebook. "Where does Veronique work?"

"I assume that she hangs out with the bunch down at the St. Regis and the Excelsior. She was always one of the most elegant. She kept her looks, so I bet she's held her place in the pecking order."

"Do you know how Veronique and Irina got to be friends?"

"Irina showed up only a couple of months ago, so I don't know her well. Veronique has been around for years, like I said. So I guess that's a 'no' to your question, except they're both Russian, you know."

Caterina held out a business card. "Could you give this to Fausto. If he knows anything more about Irina and Veronique on Tuesday night – whether they were fighting, did they leave together, anything – could you ask him to give me a call?"

Caterina knew about the transvestites who hung out at the St. Regis and Excelsior hotels. They sold sex to a select crowd of mostly married men who would never claim to be gay, but wanted a different experience than a female prostitute offered. Unless there was overt action involving drugs or a fight over a client, the police mostly left these working "ladies" alone.

That evening, on a tip from the doorman at the Excelsior, Caterina tracked Veronique down at the Savoy Hotel.

Draped in a long-sleeved, shimmering, silver-and-black, figure-hugging, thigh-high dress, her long legs clad in black silk stockings and her huge feet shod in black strappy stilettos, Veronique was smoking a slender cigar at one of the Savoy's outside tables. To her left was another transvestite, who introduced herself as Kim. She was of a mixed Italian/Japanese heritage and much more petite. The peach, off-the-shoulder, angora sweater complimented her salon tan. Both Veronique and her friend had decided on a classic chignon to set off dangling crystal earrings. Veronique's nails were ruby and Kim's matched her sweater. Veronique had an empty martini glass in front of her. Kim was sipping on a pale pink Bellini.

"Veronique, may I talk to you," Caterina asked, flashing her badge. This caused the third member of the group, a bulky, beetle-browed man with greased-back hair, in a bad suit and sporting a huge diamond pinky ring, to leave the table without a word. Caterina's first guess was that he was Ukranian. She watched him walk off. "Sorry," she said with a smile.

Veronique grinned back. "Not to worry, *tesoro*." Her voice was low, but not masculine. Her Italian was the bland variety heard from television newscasters. "His hygiene wasn't the best. I'm not sorry to see him go.

What can I do for *you*?" She scanned Caterina from head to toe.

"Probably give me fashion advice," Caterina glanced down at her black slacks and charcoal-gray cashmere sweater.

Veronique looked her up and down, again. "First, your shoes are very nice. Prada?"

Caterina held out her right foot. "Bally. Last season."

"Probably don't come in my size, anyway. Second, you need to cut the hair."

Caterina put a defensive hand to her loose curls. "That's what my mother says."

"Listen to your mother, always." She and Kim exchanged glances and broke into guffaws. Veronique sobered first. "Now, what do you really want? The night is wasting away."

"Irene Paloma, or you may know her as Irina Golubka?

"What about Irina?"

"I was told that you met with her on Tuesday night at Café de Benci."

Veronique frowned, sat straighter and recrossed her legs. "So, what if I did?"

"And I've been told that you met with her a number of times before."

"Yes, and…?"

"You may have been the last person to see her alive."

Veronique swished a red tipped nail back and forth in front of Caterina's face. "Irina's not dead. She just left town."

"Why do you say that?" Caterina asked and then pulled out the chair vacated by the odiferous man. "Do you mind if I sit down?"

"Sit. Sit." Veronique waited for Caterina to get settled and pull out a notebook and pen, before she continued. "Irina told me on Tuesday evening that she was going to be paid a lot of cash and had just quit her job."

"Can you remember what she was wearing?"

"Let's see… I think she had on blue jeans and a big black cashmere sweater. I made a comment about her going bohemian."

"She picked up a leather jacket at *Persephone*. Did she have it with her?"

"It was a gift for me." She turned to Kim. "You know – the red one."

"Fabulous," said Kim. "I loved the zippers."

Veronique looked back at Caterina. "She said it was a goodbye present. Like a stupid, she planned to move to Forte de Marmi on the coast, and try to snag a rich man."

"Where was she getting the money from?"

"She didn't say. I didn't ask."

"Did you try to dissuade her from leaving Florence?"

"Of course I did. She had a good job here. She had friends. She could have invested the money. But *no* – she wouldn't listen to reason." Veronique waved down the waiter and ordered a martini. "Worst of all, like the *stupid* Russian she is, she's going to a resort town when *nobody* of any consequence is there. You can't catch a rich man in Forte de Marmi in March or April. You can *barely* find one under seventy in June. That resort is strictly a July, August scene"

"How did you come to know Irina?"

"We're both from Noginsk, just outside Moscow. We have some friends in common. When she moved here from Pisa, she came looking for me. New girl in town, she needed advice."

"When did you come here from Russia?"

"Ages ago. I've been in Italy for over fifteen years."

"Did you know Irina's boyfriend?"

"The American? I saw him once, but never met him. I find Americans a bit naïve for my taste. But he was good to Irina. That was another thing." Veronique waved the nail again. "Why leave a sweet, rich American boy to go to Forte de Marmi where now you will only find old buzzards in wheel chairs and later, just fat old Italians or vulgar, newly rich, Russian mafia?"

"Irina's boyfriend died in the cathedral bombing."

Veronique clamped her hands to her mouth below shocked false-lashed eyes. "Oh my god. Did she know?"

"I assume so, but I wasn't able to ask her before she was killed."

"You said that before. Why do you say she was killed? I saw her just three evenings ago."

"She was found outside of Forte Belvedere that same night. You probably know the place. Where people go to get some privacy." Veronique and Kim both nodded. "Irina was strangled."

Veronique, her hand on her neck, whispered, "Strangled? Irina was murdered?"

"Sometime after you saw her in the café. Had she ever been to Forte Belvedere with you or had you seen her there anytime in the past?"

"Irina and I never had anything going on. I never do women – only men."

"You misunderstand me. Irina wasn't up there for sex. Someone fought with her, snapped her neck and dumped her there."

"How do you know it was a fight?"

"She had skin and blood under her fingernails," Caterina said. "It happened right after she met with you. Could I see your arms?"

"I'm telling you, I didn't kill Irina." Veronique yanked up her sleeves so hard she tore the fabric. Her arms were hairless, waxed smooth. Old needle scars stood out dark and lumpy inside her elbows. "Those are ancient," she said when she saw where Caterina's eyes went. "I'm clean now."

"Was Irina doing drugs?"

"No, Irina's only interests were money and clothes. She might do some Ecstasy at the clubs, but that was it."

"Was she hiding the fact that she wasn't Italian?"

"Not to me, darling."

"But to others?"

"Maybe. It's not easy being poor and Russian in Italy. Everyone thinks you're a whore."

Caterina raised an eyebrow.

"*Tesoro*, there are whores, and then there are *whores*." She thought a moment. "Actually it's not even easy to be rich and Russian in Italy. Everyone assumes you are Russian mafia."

"Did Irina care for the American boy?"

"He was just a step on the ladder. Look, you said he's dead and you think she knew it, but she didn't mention him on Tuesday. She only talked about going to the resorts on the coast. Does that sound like mourning to you?"

Caterina started to put away her notebook and then stopped. "Veronique, do you know if she has family? We're going to release her body in a few days."

"I'll take care of that. Here's my card." She handed over a small embossed card with just a phone number on it. "Call me when I can make arrangements. She had no one left in Noginsk."

Caterina stood, put her business card on the table and held out her hand. "I'm sorry, Veronique."

Veronique offered the languid tips of her fingers. "It's not a new story for me, but thank you for your concern."

Caterina nodded to Kim and started to leave.

"Miss Falcone." The voice purred. Caterina looked back to see Veronique reading her card. "Remember, always listen to Mamma. Yours probably says a bit of makeup, along with the haircut, wouldn't hurt you, right?" Caterina's hand went immediately back to her riotous curls. She grimaced, turned and strode off followed by gales of laughter.

Caterina was putting on her ladybug slippers when the message signal on her cell phone jangled. The screen told her the text was from Marco. *What now? More nudging?*

The text read: "Got Cobra! Estn is our man. Mtg at 7am. Mgistr says b there."

Chapter Forty-Two

MOSCOW

"Yakov is dead." Andrei's phone call woke his brother near midnight on Friday.

Oleg whispered, "What?" Holding the cell phone to his ear, he padded across the floor, through a mammoth closet, into the bathroom, and closed the door.

Andrei repeated, "He's dead."

"How did that happen?"

"He was killed by the blast."

"Damnation." Oleg put down the toilet seat lid and lowered himself on top of it. "How do you know this?"

"The security firm has a contact inside the *polizia* in Florence. Merkevitch has been trying to track Yakov since Sunday evening and finally got a call back."

Oleg was quiet for a moment. He asked, "How are the Italian police looking at this?"

"Merkevitch says they have Yakov on their records as an Estonian."

"So it will take them a while to get to us."

"Maybe."

"Give Merkevitch a holiday on one of those islands off Dubai and get a new security firm. We need distance and time." Oleg closed the phone. He crawled back into bed beside Kiki. She slept on. He did not.

Chapter Forty-Three

Marco found the suspect's hotel room by good hard work. He called every small *pensione* used by Eastern Europeans and finally found one where a client didn't return on Sunday. The proprietors waited a day, then put his possessions in storage and rented out the room again." *The magistrate is almost jubilant*, Caterina thought. *He's lost the haggard look.*

Marco was wearing his best tie. He unsuccessfully tried to hide the self-important look that Caterina disliked so much. "Of course the cleaning of the room wasn't of the best, so we got prints. They matched those of our dead body."

They were in Marco's office. Paolo Benigni and Max Turner sat in the visitor chairs. Max had offered Caterina his, but she waved him off and leaned against the doorframe. Marco sat straight-backed in his chair, twirling his pen in one hand.

"What's his name?" Caterina asked.

"Yakov Petrov," Marco responded. "Can you believe he used his real name on the *pensione* register?"

"You're assuming his passport is authentic," said Max.

"It's not a fake," Marco blustered. "Of course I had that checked out immediately. It turns out he wasn't from Estonia, despite the travel agent's card in his pocket. He was born there, but his passport and visa were from Russia. The hotel was holding his passport from when he checked in. I got more details from the Italian visa office in Moscow late yesterday afternoon. Of course the lazy *Napolitano* bastard who works there had gone home, but I made him go back into the office to check the files."

"What was left in his room?" asked Max. "Or I should ask: What did they put in storage?"

"He had documents and a suitcase with clothes for about two or three days."

"Any connection to the Goncharov brothers in the documents?" Caterina asked.

"That's what broke it last evening," the magistrate laughed. "You tell them, Marco. This was all due to your legwork."

Caterina thought she saw Marco actually blush as he answered.

"He had a piece of paper with a phone number written on it. It was a Moscow phone. It led to an underling in a private security company. A secretary named Marya. Could have been a girlfriend. I did a bit of online checking and came up with the fact that the security firm supplies bodyguards to many of the new Russian moguls."

"Including the Goncharovs?" Max asked.

Caterina could see that Marco was going to drag the story out as long as possible. He didn't answer the Legat, but said, "After I had as many facts as possible, I called

Marya, who was so broken up by learning Petrov was dead, she told me he'd been assigned to the Goncharovs detail for over nine years; first in Oleg's mansion in Moscow and then, on the road with both Oleg and Andrei."

Caterina flipped back in her notebook to the known Cobra bombing sites. "Was his passport new or did it show his past travels?" she asked.

Marco lost his straight face and grinned. He held up a plastic evidence bag with a Russian passport in it. Then he passed around twelve-page photocopies of the same document. "It's all here. He was in Indonesia, Turkmenistan, Spain, Croatia, a number of other places, and now, here."

"Is that *all?*" Max asked, grinning.

Marco missed the irony. "Isn't that enough. *I've nailed...* I mean, *we've* got the guy. We've got Cobra."

Max leafed through the pages of his copy. "No, I mean are there other places he's been. Maybe there are more bombings we should be looking at."

"He has also been to Mexico, Portugal and South Africa." Marco looked at his briefing notes. "The passport only covers seven years of the nine Marya said he had been assigned to the brothers."

"Do the Goncharovs have business interests in the other countries?" Magistrate Benigni asked.

"I don't know. I'll try to get that information this morning," Marco offered.

Max made a note for himself. "I'll check through my contacts, too."

Marco pulled out another plastic bag, larger this time. "Max, you may want to pass this by your people at Langley. It looks like a bomb-building manual to me." He slid the bag across the table, then leaned back as far as his desk chair would go without tipping.

Max became very still. Caterina watched a frown pass across his face. He did not remove the thin document, which was printed on beige paper and stapled together along the binding. The cover was written in Cyrillic. The back cover was blank. "Can you get this copied for me, Marco? I don't read Russian. Two copies. I'll get it scanned and emailed to both Langley and the Bureau."

Marco took the document back. "I skimmed it," he said. When Max looked at him sharply, he added, "With gloves on, of course." He gave a self-depreciating smile. "It's too technical for me to tell if it matched the construction of our bomb. It did discuss the use of cell phones as part of the construction. It has Petrov's fingerprints on it and those of an unidentified person." He handed the bag to Caterina. "Could you get Signora Benvenuti to make two copies of this?"

Demoted to Marco's assistant already, Caterina thought, but she didn't make a comment. As she walked to the door, she heard him say, "Make sure she uses gloves."

When she came back into his office, having left the document in Patricia Benvenuti's capable hands, Marco was saying, "... only visitor he had at the *pensione* was a transvestite named Veronique. The owner of the place knew her from years ago."

Caterina said, "I interviewed Veronique last evening at the Savoy."

Three pairs of eyes turned in unison to her.

Marco frowned. "I hope you didn't spook him."

"Why were you interviewing this person, Caterina?" the magistrate asked.

"Remember, I was tracking down people who saw Irina Golubka on her last evening."

"So Irina and this Veronique are connected?" Max asked.

"Veronique had drinks with Irina on Tuesday evening around seven. They were friends. You'll recall I told you that Irina picked up her final pay and a new leather jacket at Persephone that evening. The jacket was a gift for Veronique."

Marco burst out, "So we have the bomber, who knows a hooker, who is the friend of the lover of the target, Bill Barton. This is all fitting together."

"And the only one still living is this Veronique," said the magistrate. "She was also the last person to see Irina alive."

Max stood up. Caterina noticed for the first time his only concessions to working on Saturday were his blue jeans and white running shoes. Otherwise, he was wearing a pressed white cotton shirt and a tie. "We were way off-base speculating about Omar, I guess."

Caterina nodded.

The magistrate turned to her. "We need to get Veronique in for questioning. Caterina, do you have a way to contact her?"

"She gave me a card. She seems to frequent high-end hotels in the evening."

"Give Marco the card. He can track her down," Paolo Benigni said, looking down at the list he had been writing throughout the briefing. "Also, get the notes of your interview with Veronique typed up this morning and give them to Marco."

"I'd like a copy, also, if that's okay with you, sir," Max said.

The magistrate nodded. "No problem. Caterina will see to it. In an hour, I have to go brief Captain DeLuca. We will need to determine how to proceed with the Goncharov brothers. First, although I assume Captain DeLuca has already done this, I want to find out whether Andrei Goncharov is in Italy. Perhaps we can detain him on Italian soil. It would make proceeding a lot easier. Now that we have a direct link to the bomb-maker, Yakov Petrov, the Russian authorities should start to be more helpful." He stood. "Marco, after the manual is copied, make sure that all of the original evidence from Petrov's room is ready to take with us when we go to brief Captain DeLuca. I'll want you with me for that meeting."

The rest of the group followed him out of the room. Caterina heard Max say, as she turned to her office, "Marco, can I talk to you while the copies of that manual get made?"

"Of course, Max. I'd be happy to give you a more detailed briefing on the work I did yesterday. I won't be going after the transvestite until Caterina brings me his card and her notes *and* I get back from my meeting with Captain DeLuca."

As the door closed behind her, Caterina thought, *Can you be more of a suck up, Marco?*

Forty-five minutes later, when Caterina knocked on Marco's door she carried two copies of the bomb-making manual, the original in its evidence bag, and two copies of her report of the interview with Veronique. She found Max with his feet up on the front edge of Marco's desk. Marco had rolled up his shirtsleeves, trying to look casual, she guessed, but failing.

"Max, I typed this up in Italian," she said, handing him the report. "Marco doesn't read English well, so I thought I would make it easy for him. I can get you an English translation, if you would prefer."

Max smiled, responding, "I can struggle along with this. But it would be grand of you if you could get me a translation some time for my files. No rush."

"No problem." She turned to find Marco glowering.

"Also, give Max two copies of the bomb construction manual I found. I'll take the rest." He held out his hand. "That will be all, I think."

"Hold on just a minute," Max said. "Let's run all this past Caterina." He turned his head toward her while still keeping his feet on the edge of Marco's desk. "Do you have a minute?"

"Sure." She grinned at him and sat in the other visitor chair, turning it so her profile was to Marco and she was facing Max. She brushed at an errant auburn hair clinging to her long-sleeved black t-shirt.

Max put the copies in his briefcase. "I was just telling Marco, I'm a bit confused about the how-to-make-a-bomb book. I would think Cobra could make them in his sleep by now."

"Maybe it's for the construction of a different type of bomb," Marco said. "Maybe he realized that we could track him through the techniques and materials used, so he wants to change. What did you call it? His signature."

"Maybe, but we shouldn't get too cocky." Max looked right at Marco. Then he turned to Caterina. "The other thing is, I wonder how he came to kill himself. Cobra hasn't been careless in the past. He has been so thorough that we don't have his DNA or fingerprints from the pieces of the bomb found here or at any of the other sites."

Caterina thought about the annual *Scoppio del Carro* festival. "This is the first time he planned to assassinate someone in a crowd outside of a building. The other bombs were more surgical, aimed at the intended victim. In the Easter crowd he could have gotten caught. Right at the time of the fireworks, it's impossible to move in the mass of people. Also, he…"

Marco interrupted, "Maybe he made the bomb too big this time, trying to make sure he killed the Barton boy. He underestimated how far away he had to be from that size of blast."

"Maybe." Max shook his head. "But he must have known that just injuring Bill Barton would have accomplished his mission. Look at the Australian in the Croatia blast. He just lost a leg."

"Maybe he got different orders for this job," Marco said.

Max got up and put on a worn leather jacket. "I've got to take the copy of the passport photo over to show Bill Barton. I want to see if he recognizes Yakov Petrov.

Since he was – or, at least, posed as – a bodyguard for the Goncharov brothers, maybe Yakov was with Andrei in Milan at Christmas when Barton talked to him in the airport, or in Sardinia when the two met."

Caterina stood, too. She put a hand on his arm to stop him at the door. "Max, I know you are focusing on a different issue, now, but I would still like to clear up the connection between Irina and Omar. W made a list yesterday and there were two things you were going to have your contacts in Lebanon check. First, the story about Omar's parents' death and second, about his time in Lebanon before he emigrated to Italy."

"I already sent a message to my counterpart in the Beirut embassy. I should hear back today or tomorrow." He turned back to Marco. "Good work, Marco. I would really appreciate it if you would let me observe when you question Veronique."

Marco nodded. "I will be setting that up today, if Caterina will provide me with the contact number."

"It's in the report, Marco," she said, as she walked past Max, who was holding the door for her.

"Marco's a bit uptight, isn't he?" Max said in a low tone as they walked toward her office. "I thought he was going to take out the dust rag when I took my feet off his desk."

Caterina laughed. "I thought you'd done that to get on his nerves. As they say in the States, I think he's lost a stick where the sun don't shine." She waved him through the open door of her office.

"But he deserves a victory lap for finding Yakov. Solid police work."

"So you've discarded Omar Pellione as a suspect?" Caterina moved a stack of files off of her visitor chair and put them on top of the filing cabinet.

"For which murder – Barton or Irina?"

"Either one."

"I think you should follow up the Omar story, as soon as possible. But I was always bothered by the fact that Cobra would both live and take an assignment in his home country. Reportedly, the Goncharov brothers have always been careful not to commit crimes in Russia. I can't think why their assassin would be less cautious by agreeing to work close to home."

"But that's where they needed the job done. Bill Barton was here."

"The Estonian looks like a better prospect, except for the couple of niggling questions I raised back in Marco's office. Remember, I always said that I pictured Cobra as an itinerant, stateless, assassin for hire, not a homebody with a family, like Omar Pellione. Yakov was always moving around. Also, he was protected back in Moscow."

"I'm sure you're right," Caterina said, straightening her desk. "I'm going to be busy with Irina's case today. I need to close my file on her, even though my only connection to the case is her relationship to Bill Barton. There's a lieutenant over in the homicide division, Leonardo Mondadori, who is charged with solving that murder."

"It's still an interest of mine, too. Don't get me wrong. I think Irina had something to do with the bombing. Not through Omar, but through the Estonian and this transvestite, Veronique."

"You'll see from my report that I certainly didn't get any inkling that Veronique knew much about Bill Barton. Maybe I didn't ask the right questions. I was focusing on Irina's death."

"Don't worry. Marco will cover that when he finds her. You didn't know that Yakov Petrov met with Veronique; so, how would you think to ask those questions? And since Irina is still connected to an American death, I will keep the pressure on my end to come up with the answers you or Lieutenant Mondadori need to help find her killer. But I think it's going to be a matter of wrong place at the wrong time. I don't even think Omar killed her. As I said the other day, he gave you the cheek swab too easily. You told him you found DNA under Irina's fingernails. He would have stalled and gotten out of town if it was going to be a match."

"I guess so, but then, who?"

"Have you thought about this Veronique guy?"

"Of course, but after talking to her... well, you'll see when you read my report. Veronique doesn't strike me as a stone cold killer."

"How about a rage killing?" Without waiting for her response, he observed, "Veronique was the last person to see Irina alive."

"The last person whom we know of so far," amended Caterina.

"It makes a much more plausible scenario that Yakov comes to town, looks up Veronique, who recruits Irina to set up Bill Barton."

Caterina shook her head. "The problem is that Yakov wasn't in Florence before Irina met Bill over three weeks ago."

"So he telephones Veronique and tells her to set up a love interest for Bill a few weeks before the bombing. Cobra has a pattern of using honey-traps to get the mark to the right place for the hit."

Caterina laughed. "You sound like a spy from the movies – honey-trap, mark, hit."

"Sorry, he said, grinning. "The jargon creeps in."

"Caterina," Magistrate Benigni said, walking into her office. He stopped, seeing Max. "Sorry, I thought you were alone."

"No problem, I'll leave," Max said, getting out of the chair.

The magistrate put up a retraining hand. "You should hear this, too. Captain DeLuca has decided to go to the press with the information that Yakov Petrov was the bomber."

Chapter Forty-Four

He can't do that. It's just a theory," Max exclaimed. "It may be a good theory, but it's unconfirmed."

"I know. He thinks, however, it is important to give the people of Florence a sense of security that this is not going to happen again."

"He's right about that. With young Bill Barton dead, there isn't much chance that the Goncharov brothers will aim their bomber at Florence again, unless they go after the father while he's in town."

The magistrate shook his head and waved Max back into his seat. He leaned against the doorjamb, sticking his hands into the pockets of his tan corduroy slacks. "The Captain thinks the security is in the fact that Cobra is dead. You have to understand that while people are speculating about the perpetrator, more Middle Eastern residents and businesses are being targeted for harassment and worse. He and the mayor want Florentines to know this is not the start of a wave of Islamic terrorist bombings."

Max argued, "I understand the mayor's problem, but he should still give us a few days to tie up the loose ends. We don't need a bunch of reporters tracking down

Yakov's past, digging into the Goncharovs' business. It won't take them long to make the connection."

"I agree and I was able to get forty-eight hours and some reinforcements to assist in the – how did you put it – the 'tying up of ends.'"

"Also, if Yakov is not the bomber, the Captain is telling the real assassin that we know that the Goncharovs are implicated," said Max. "Right now Cobra is taking comfort from the fact that we apparently don't know the reason for the bomb."

"I told DeLuca that, too. But he is sold on the theory that Petrov is the bomb-maker. He thinks the two days won't yield anything except the certainty that the bomber is dead."

"So what can I do, sir?" Caterina asked.

"Find Irina Golubka's killer. We need to know why she died and if she was working with the assassin. I want you to work at it independently of the homicide division."

"Without letting Lieutenant Mondadori know?" she asked.

"You give him any pertinent information that you find, but I don't want you to have to go to him for authorization to investigate leads. From what DeLuca told me, the homicide division is considering this a case of attempted rape and murder, unconnected to the Easter bomb."

"But we think Irina had orders to make sure Bill Barton was on the steps."

"Captain DeLuca considers that idea mere speculation. He's not even convinced that the Barton boy was the target. He thinks Petrov wanted to make a statement by killing as many people as possible in front of the cathedral on Easter Sunday."

"For what reason?" Max barked, causing Caterina to jump.

The magistrate stepped in the office and closed the door. "He declines to say."

"What about the Goncharovs and Barton Enterprises?" Caterina asked. "Did you discuss them?"

"Of course," the magistrate said, rubbing his hand over his head, making his hair stand on end. "Remember Captain DeLuca sat in on Mr. Barton's interview. He now believes that the Goncharovs were taking advantage of an isolated incident to get a business advantage."

"But Yakov is their employee," sputtered Max.

"DeLuca thinks Petrov was acting independently. You can see how hard it is to think of this catastrophe as business as usual – Goncharov-style." The magistrate sat on the corner of Caterina's desk, leaning toward Max. "I agree with you, Max. We have forty-eight hours to prove your theory is correct. I want Caterina to discover if there is any connection between Irina's death and Omar Pellione. Marco is going to investigate any connection between the transvestite Veronique and Yakov Petrov as it relates to the bombing."

But I discovered Veronique, Caterina thought as the magistrate turned to look at her. *Why don't I get to follow up with her? I'd get more from her than Marco will.* But she didn't protest. She nodded and pretended to make a note.

Magistrate Benigni continued, "I am going to ask you, Max, to assist Marco in pinning down the facts on

Yakov Petrov's history, his travels and his connections abroad and in Italy. I want to know if the bomb construction manual has anything to do with the Easter bomb. I want to know if Petrov was at all of the other Cobra bombings, and if there were assassinations in the other countries he traveled to while he was there."

"I'll get working it, magistrate," Max said. He picked up his jacket and headed out the door with a nod to them both. Caterina's boss took the seat that Max vacated.

"Caterina, you seem a bit distracted."

"It's not that, sir. I just got my hopes up that Max and I were on to something with the investigation of Irina's boss. I guess I jumped a few steps to assuming he was involved some way in the Duomo bomb because he was her employer and he lied to us."

"But he may have been lying to cover up an affair, as I understand it."

"With Elizabeth Willingham." She doodled Elizabeth's name on her notebook.

"I think you are feeling a little deflated because you think investigating Irina's death is sidelining you from the other, bigger investigation. Marco did some good work there and he deserves to follow up on it."

"No, I know." She shook her head. "I'm just surprised that Max Turner got thrown off on the tangent of Irina, Omar Pellione, and Elizabeth Willingham. I'd expect it from me, not him."

"Remember, it was *your* investigation of young Bill Barton's death that led us to the connection of Barton Enterprises and the Goncharov business interests, and in turn to Irina and Pellione."

"But Irina's day job doesn't seem to have anything to do with her relationship to Bill."

"Max Turner has been following this bomb-maker for a long time. The only common denominators we had in this case were the business deal, the dead boy, and a girl who may have gotten him into position. No wonder Max is going to follow the trail of the girl. Of course, what looked like the easy answer could sidetrack him, but he is able to change course and follow the facts. Remember, Marco hadn't found Petrov before you went off to Pontedera."

"I know," she said, still making curlicues around Elizabeth's name. "I guess I'll follow up with Miss Willingham. She probably knows if Omar had other flirts. Maybe he arranged to meet Irina after her drink with Veronique. We only have speculation from the shopgirl Nadia that he went directly back to Pontedera after he left the Florence store."

The magistrate got up. "You do that. I need to go tell Marco that we have a deadline." He passed Patricia Benvenuti coming in Caterina's door. "Patricia, I'm going to be with Captain DeLuca for the next couple of hours. I have my cell phone," he said.

His administrative assistant nodded, and closed Caterina's office door behind him. "So, I see that Marco is spreading his tail feathers," she said, settling into the visitor chair.

"What?" Caterina looked up from her notes.

"I've got a bunch of peacocks up at the villa – my late husband's idea – noisy, dirty birds, if you ask my opinion. The males can always be counted on to fan those feathers when they think they've done something important – mated with a female, chased another male off, scared the dog, whatever. But it's the females who really get things done. What can I do to help?"

Caterina laughed, saying, "I bet you were the one who found Yakov Petrov's *pensione*. Marco made it sound like he had been on the phone for hours."

Patricia smiled, but didn't admit to anything. "Marco can be like that. So now, what can I do for you?"

Caterina gave her the list of documents she needed to be acquired and copied: Irina's visa and residency papers. "Also, remember, last evening I asked you to find Omar Pellione's citizenship application, name change documents, and his marriage certificate? How's that coming?"

The older woman said, "The woman in the Pontedera office said it would take a day or two for us to get the file. I'll try to get her to fax the more important pages." In a swirl of lavender silk, she turned to leave, but stopped to add, "I almost forgot. I got a call from Professor Neri. His wife, Ingrid, regained consciousness last evening."

"Thank goodness."

"Yes, well he wanted to let you know that even though she will have to stay in the hospital for the next week, the prognosis is good."

"That is the only good news I've had in it seems like ages," said Caterina, booting up her computer. "Thanks, Patricia."

She found an amateurish web site for *Pellione Pelle* and the *Persephone* leather shops, but nothing more online about Omar Pellione. The search for Elizabeth Willingham proved more fruitful. She copied off six pages. On her way back from the printer, she saw Max coming out of the elevator.

"I found out some things about Miss Willingham. Do you want to see?"

"Sure. I've got a few minutes."

"Let's take this into the small conference room." She picked up a large spreadsheet made up of six pieces of typing paper stapled together.

"This is low tech, but I made a chart for myself of all of the bombings attributed to Cobra. I'm jotting in notes of things that may fit with those dates."

"Good idea." Max took his jacket off and sat down in one of the chairs.

"I know they may all be coincidences, but it helps me organize my thoughts."

"So how does Elizabeth Willingham fit in?"

"You know how we were wondering about what she does, if anything."

"Yes."

"She has a web site. She's a location scout for films." Caterina laid a photocopy of Willingham's web site, *www.locationlocationlocation.tv*, on the table.

He skimmed the page. "Never would have guessed that one."

"She works mostly for Exeter Studios in London, scouting their Italian locations."

"Makes sense."

"But in the 1990s she was living in London." Caterina handed him another page. "This is from the Exeter Studios' employee roster from 1996."

"Maybe she was still married to the Moroccan then."

"Then in May 2001, she is listed on a shoot in Bali and East Java. Omar was in Bali on his honeymoon in October 2000, right?"

"I think so."

"And the Jakarta bombing took place the same month. We didn't ask her where she met Omar. What if she met him in Bali, when she was scouting locations for the Exeter film?"

"Interesting thought, but you haven't put her in Indonesia in October 2000, yet."

Patricia Benvenuti came in carrying some loose pages. "The records office in Pontedera faxed me the wedding certificate for Omar Jaboor and Paula Pellione. They were married October 15, 2000."

"A week before the Jakarta bombing."

"Their daughter, Petra Maria Pellione, was born about three months later." She held up another fax. "You didn't ask for it, but I thought I'd get Petra's birth certificate anyway."

"Good idea, Patricia," said Caterina.

Max shook his head. "It doesn't mean Omar is the bomber. He would have had to travel from Bali to Jakarta while on his honeymoon. Yakov Petrov was in Jakarta at the same time."

"How did you find that out?"

"Mr. Ito, the cop from the Jakarta investigation, got me the list of the guests staying at the hotel that was hit.

Yakov was on the list." He reached over to his jacket and pulled a folded piece of paper out of the pocket.

"Also, Elizabeth Willingham?"

He scanned the sheet and shook his head. "Neither she nor Omar were registered."

Patricia Benvenuti laid another piece of paper on the table. "The immigration office in Rome sent me the final disposition of Omar Jaboor's application for citizenship. They are sending a copy of the file up tomorrow. He got his citizenship after his marriage and at the same time that he legally took his wife's name."

"This is after his daughter's birth," said Max, looking over Caterina's shoulder.

"That means he was traveling on a Lebanese passport when they went on their honeymoon. Under the name Omar Jaboor."

Max rubbed his forehead. "I'll check the hotel register again, but I believe Ito would have mentioned anyone named Omar, no matter what last name was used."

"I had them read off the information about his parents from the file." Patricia continued, reading her notes. "His father was Tarriq Jaboor and his mother was Elena Rossi. Omar Jaboor was born in 1972."

"Max, can your contacts in Lebanon confirm the deaths of his parents?"

"With the names it will be much easier. Signora Benvenuti, can you help me fax them to the embassy in Beirut?"

"Of course. Come with me," she said, leading him out of Caterina's office.

Caterina called Elizabeth Willingham. In a nonchalant tone, she asked if the English woman could meet for coffee in Pisa.

"I'm new at this job," Caterina said. "My boss asked me to get back with you on a couple of issues."

Elizabeth was quiet and then said, "I don't know what I can tell you that matters. I already told you I know Omar didn't kill that girl. He hasn't got a mean bone in his body."

"Nevertheless, do you have time tomorrow? I could get to Pisa by nine."

"Actually, I need to be in Florence tomorrow morning to check on a location for a costume drama on the Medici family that Exeter Films is going to shoot in July. Worst time of year for filming, with millions of tourists jamming the streets, but I'm going to try to get permits for night shoots."

"Do you have time for coffee in your day?"

"I'm on for a meeting with the mayor's administrative assistant at the Palazzo Vecchio at ten."

"On Sunday?"

"He works Sundays because the museum in the Palazzo is open and he's the liaison between the museum staff and the mayor's office. Meet me at Rivoire at eleven thirty. You can buy me a drink."

"Thank you, Miss Willingham."

"Liz, remember?"

"Liz," Caterina repeated. "I'll see you at the café."

Chapter Forty-Five

Thinking about her Cobra timeline, Caterina leaned back in her chair, breathing deeply with her eyes closed. She tried to clear her mind of petty thoughts of being sidelined in the investigation and worse, jealousy of Marco.

"Snap out of it, girl," she said out loud a minute later, sitting up straight. *Get some backbone and get to work*, her self-lecture continued. She laughed at how her inner voice sounded exactly like her mother.

Her telephone rang. It was her mother. *Scary,* she thought.

"Catherine, I won't take up your time, but I must insist that you come to dinner tonight at the osteria. No arguments."

"Okay, Mother."

"You father is worried that you aren't eating right and I refuse to have your father worry."

"I said I would be there."

"It's not right that you …"

"Mother," Caterina raised her voice.

"What? You don't need to use that tone."

"Thank you for the invitation. I'll be there at eight."

"Oh, that's better," her mother said, her tone softening slightly. "Well, be sure you go home first and freshen up. Don't come exhausted from the office. That will only worry him more."

"Yes, Mother. Goodbye, Mother. I've got another call." Caterina put down the phone, leaned back, closed her eyes and commenced five cleansing breaths, counting in her head, *One thousand and one, one thousand and two, ...*

She got through the third breath when she heard a sound. She opened her eyes to find Max Turner poking his head around her door.

"Sleeping?"

"Breathing."

"Meditating?"

"Breathing."

"Cleansing breaths?"

"Hopefully."

"Don't feel so bad. We've all done it."

"What?"

"Gotten revved up on an investigative track, mixed in a little 'I'll show them,' and lost sight of the big picture."

"I thought I was doing something useful."

"You were. You are. It's just that Yakov isn't your responsibility."

"But Veronique was."

"Having Marco take on that part of the investigation makes it less confusing. Remember too many cooks... "

"So what do I do now?"

"Keep your head down and keep doing the job. Nothing flashy – just good police work."

"I've set up a meeting with Elizabeth Willingham."

"Good," he said, coming around the back of her desk. "Do you have a speaker on that phone?"

"Err, yes, why?" She twisted her neck around to look up at him.

Max flicked a pink phone slip onto her desk. "My colleague in Beirut called and told Signora Benvenuti that he had some information on Omar Jaboor. Want to call him now?"

"Of course," Caterina said, leaning forward as he reached over her to dial the number.

He got the receptionist at the U.S. Embassy and asked for Robert Mathews. He walked back around to the front of the desk, the receiver stretched on its cord, and nodded at Caterina, who punched the speakerphone button.

"Mathews, here," a bass voice said.

"Bob, it's Max Turner," he said, hanging up the receiver and taking a seat in Caterina's extra chair. "I'm calling you back on the Jaboor issue."

"Hey, Max. How's it hangin'?"

"As always, Bob." He grinned at Caterina. "I'm here on speaker-phone with Inspector Caterina Falcone of the Florence police, foreigner task force. Caterina, let me introduce Robert Matthews, the Legat in Beirut."

"Ms. Falcone, pleased to meet you, so to speak."

"Mr. Mathews, thank you in advance for your assistance."

"Call me Bob. Sorry to hear about the recent mess in your town. Always did like visiting there. Good food. Especially the *bistecca*. Almost as good as ..."

"Bob, let me interrupt before you two start swapping recipes."

"Sure, partner."

"The message I got said you have something on Omar Jaboor."

"Sure do. You asked me to look into his parents' car accident. There wasn't one."

"They're alive."

"No, they're dead all right. They died in '83 when the barracks was bombed."

"The Marine barracks?"

"Yeah. Tariq Jaboor was a translator for the U.N. peacekeeping force. He was at the barracks for a breakfast meeting. It seems his wife came along at the last minute because a contractor with the Italian contingent was participating in the meeting and they couldn't get an Italian translator at the last minute."

"I thought she worked for the Italian Embassy," Caterina said.

"Not in '83. She was last on the embassy payroll as a temp in 1972. In the records of the barracks bombing, she's listed as a housewife."

"Maybe she quit when she got married or when Omar was born," said Max.

"I had someone pull the family's records, you know, like Tariq's birth certificate, their marriage license — dated May 12, 1971 — their kids' birth certificates, and the death certificates."

Caterina leaned toward the telephone. "Did you say 'kids,' plural?"

"Yeah, there were two children born to Tariq Jaboor and Elena Rossi. Omar in November 1972, and Amin in June 1974."

"Did you track Amin down?" asked Max.

Bob answered, "No, do you want me to?"

"Yes, do that for me, would you?"

Caterina thought of something else. "Is there any record of Tariq Jaboor having a family in Beirut – maybe parents or siblings? Maybe Omar and Amin went to them when their parents died."

"I'll check back to Tariq's parents and see if they had other children. Tariq was in his forties when he got married, so I don't think his parents are still alive."

"There's a cousin by the name of Jamal here in Italy for a visit. I don't have a last name, but if you can track down uncles, aunts and cousins, that might help."

"Give me a couple of days."

Max spoke up. "Make it a priority, would you Bob? We gotta know why this guy is lying to us. He said his parents died in a car crash."

"Okay, you got it, partner," he drawled. "Nice talkin' to ya, Caterina."

"Thanks for your help, Bob." Caterina disconnected the call and turned to Max. "So what does that tell us?"

"The important question is why did Omar lie about how his parents died?"

Caterina did some quick calculations beside her notes from the call. "He must have been about eleven when his parents died. His brother Amin was nine. I can think of two possibilities: One, there's something else he's trying to hide that we might find out if we connect the barrack bombing with his family; or, two, he doesn't know how they died and was told that they died in a car wreck."

"If it's the first, it's important. If it's the second, then all he's lied to us about is his relationship to Elizabeth Willingham, and that's something I would expect him to hedge on."

"But he may have also lied to us about Irina's murder."

"If that's the case, he's probably fabricated everything and you should pull him in immediately."

"I'll ask Elizabeth Willingham about his parents tomorrow."

Her door opened. Marco walked in. Ignoring Caterina and addressing only Max, he said, "They just brought in the transvestite. Do you want to observe my interrogation?"

Max stood up, slinging his jacket over his shoulder. "Absolutely, Marco. Thanks for asking."

"The magistrate suggested it," Marco said, stepping into the hall. "I'm starting in two minutes."

"I'm coming." Max walked out without a word or a glance.

Caterina threw her pencil at the the door as it closed behind him. *Go, go,* she thought. *Let's all go watch Marco solve this case.*

Ten minutes later, she slipped in to the dark observation room next to the interrogation room. Through the one-way mirrored window she could see the magistrate and Marco sitting, their backs to her, across a brown metal table from a toned-down Veronique, dressed in black pants and a long-sleeved, black t-shirt. Caterina could see that he had not had time to don the figure-shaping undergarments or make-up of Veronique. Her hair, unstyled, was gathered at her neck.

Max sat with his back against the window. Caterina traced the swirl of dark blond hair on the back of his head with her eyes.

Veronique was shaking her head at something Marco had asked.

Marco raised his voice. "Vladimir Markov, remember this interrogation is being recorded. Answer verbally, as instructed."

Veronique/Vladimir responded, "I didn't."

"You deny introducing your friend, Irina Golubka to William Bradley Barton III on orders of Yakov Petrov?"

The magistrate put his hand on Marco's arm and said, "Break the question down for the witness, why don't you, *Ispettore*."

Marco sat quiet for a minute, staring at his notes.

He began again. "You admit that you knew Yakov Petrov, now deceased. You also admit that you knew Irina Golubka, also dead. Did you introduce Irina Golubka to William Barton, an American, who was killed by the cathedral bomb?"

"No, I did not," responded Veronique/Vladimir.

"Did Yakov Petrov instruct you to introduce the Golubka woman to Barton?"

"I said I did not introduce them."

"That is not what I asked. Did you get instructions from Petrov?"

Caterina watched Max massage a tight muscle in his neck.

"The only instruction that cretin ever gave me was to give him a blow job."

Max's shoulders shook. Caterina clapped a hand over her mouth to stifle her laugh even though she knew they couldn't hear her in the next room.

Marco attempted another question. "You knew William Barton?"

"I knew what he looked like. I was never formally introduced."

Marco slammed his hand on the table. "You are evading my questions. You should be careful, Mr. Markov. You knew three people, all of whom have turned up dead in the last week. And here you sit quibbling with my questions. I want a straight answer."

"Excuse me, *Ispettore* Capponi," Paolo Benigni interjected. "Let me give this a try."

"Of course, magistrate." Caterina could see Marco's neck suffuse with color. He crossed his arms and scowled across the table.

"Mr. Markov, how do you know Irina Golubka?" the magistrate asked.

"She came from my hometown, Noginsk, near Moscow. She called me when she moved to Florence."

"How do you know Yakov Petrov?"

"He called my business phone last Saturday night and requested my services."

"What services are those?"

"Social services."

"He wanted sex?"

"Yes."

"He offered to pay?"

"Not for the sex. I am an escort. I get paid for my time. You understand?"

"I think I do." Magistrate Benigni paused and rephrased the question. "Did he ask for anything else besides your time and social services?"

"No."

"Had you ever talked to Mr. Petrov before last Saturday evening?"

"No."

"When did you first lay eyes on him?"

"At about ten o'clock the same evening."

"At his room in the *pensione?*"

"Yes."

"When did you leave him?"

"At about ten thirty."

"So you talked to him for two minutes on the telephone and saw him for about thirty minutes?"

"Yes, that's right."

"And you never saw or talked to Mr. Petrov at any other time?"

"No." Veronique/Vladimir smiled and batted his eyelashes at the magistrate.

"When did you first meet William Barton?"

The witness pouted. "I *said*, I never *met* him."

"When did you first see him?"

"Two weeks ago. Irina pointed him out on the street. She and I were in a café. He was on the corner waiting for her."

"He didn't come into the café?"

"No."

"You didn't go out to meet him?"

"No, I don't think Irina wanted him to know we were friends. Americans are not as flexible in their opinions, don't you agree?"

"Did you ever see Mr. Barton after that one time?"

"No."

"Mr. Markov, did anyone ever talk to you about Mr. Barton, except Irina, that one time?"

"No. Oh, *excuse me*, your nice *Ispettore* Falcone may have asked me about the boy."

"Did Yakov Petrov mention Mr. Barton to you?"

"No."

"Did Yakov Petrov talk to you about Irina Golubka?"

"No."

"Did Mr. Petrov tell you why he was in Florence?"

"He said he had come to see the Easter festivities."

"Anything else?"

"No, just the Easter festivities. I thought he was a tourist."

"Did Irina say anything to you about the *Scoppio del Carro*?"

"No."

"You saw her after Easter?"

"On Tuesday evening this past week."

"Did she tell you that William Barton had been killed?"

"No, she didn't mention him."

"Did she mention any plans to meet someone after she left you?"

"No, she just said she was leaving Florence for the resorts on the coast."

"You parted at what time?"

"About eight thirty."

"Did she catch a bus or taxi, ride a scooter, or walk?"

"I don't know."

"Why don't you know?"

"I left first. She offered to pay for our drinks and said she had to use the *toilette*. So I assume that she waited for the check and then freshened up. I didn't wait for her. I had an appointment at nine across town."

"An appointment with whom?"

"My Tuesday regular at the Excelsior."

"We will want to talk to him."

"Could you talk to the barman at the Excelsior instead? He saw us there from nine to ten." Veronique/Vladimir reached across the table and put his long-nailed hand on the magistrate's wrist. "You understand? My regular is married."

Caterina wished she could see her boss's expression as he looked silently at Veronique's face. In no time, the transvestite was waving the same hand languidly back and forth. "It's a bit warm in here, isn't it?"

Paolo Benigni didn't comment, asking, "When did you learn that Irina had been killed?"

"Yesterday, when *Ispettore* Falcone told me."

"And William Barton?"

"Same time."

"And Yakov Petrov?"

"Early this morning on the phone. Your rude *Ispettore* Capponi woke me up and grilled me, then dragged me down here."

"Do you have any information about the bombing at the cathedral?"

"None whatsoever. I was asleep when it happened and didn't learn about it until Monday afternoon."

"Why is that?"

"I never work on Easter or Christmas. I stayed home, dying my roots, giving myself a facial mask and a mani/pedi. Then I slept another twelve hours. I heard about that horrible bomb from my friend Kim at lunch on Easter Monday."

Paolo Benigni motioned for Marco and Max to follow him out of the room. They entered the observation post where Caterina stood.

"Anything else?" the magistrate asked.

Max shook his head. "I think you covered it. I have nothing more."

"He's lying," said Marco. "Let's let him sit for a while. He'll break."

"I don't think so, Marco. Caterina?" The magistrate gave her an inquiring look.

"Would it be possible to request a lie detector test?" she asked. "I know it wouldn't be admissible, but it would be interesting to get Veronique's reaction to the idea of taking one."

"Good suggestion." The magistrate went back into the interview room. Vladimir Markov, aka Veronique, readily agreed to the test "if it will get you off my back," but added in a sultry tone, "can that strong, silent American give it to me?"

Magistrate Benigni smiled and said that food would be brought in and that the test would be administered in an hour or so. He met the other three in the hall.

"I don't want to let him go until the test is done. Marco, find the best technician we have. Give him a transcript of my interview to use in the questioning."

Chapter Forty-Six

Caterina walked into Osteria da Guido two minutes before eight, fresh from a shower and a change of wardrobe, as her mother had demanded. *Of course*, she thought, *Mother isn't going to approve of my ancient blue jeans and Boston College sweatshirt and I can't wait for tonight's comment on my hair.* Her only concession to family peace was the new pair of Tod's flats that her mother had recently picked up at the Incisa luxury outlet mall.

The restaurant was packed. It seemed that the cathedral bomb hadn't made a dent in the tourist traffic, at least to dining spots in the Oltrarno.

"Caterina, *vieni qui*," she heard from a corner table. It was the Contessa Montalvo-Ligozzi, resplendent in a cherry-red Chanel suit with white trim and gold buttons.

"Contessa, how are you, and how is your apartment?"

"I'm doing well and the work on the apartment is almost finished. It helps that my late husband's nephew is a building contractor. He sent someone over to replace the windows. The mayor promised me that the building will be cleared structurally this week."

"So this is almost your last night at the Palazzo Magnani Feroni." Caterina smiled.

"I'll miss it," the contessa said, nodding. "The staff has been like family to me. And the evening drinks on the terrace are fabulous. I'm thinking of trying to get a permit to convert my rental apartment back into a roof-top porch." She described a few more of the changes she planned for the apartment.

Caterina waited for her to finish, before asking, "Did you meet Bill Barton's parents, William Barton and Candy Seagraves?"

The contessa's face grew somber. "Yes, the mother is a dear. The father was a bit difficult, but I think he was overcompensating for his son's death. I don't know why. Who could have foreseen that his son would have been in that spot at that time?"

"Contessa, as my grandmother said many times, 'Parents are not supposed to outlive their children.'"

"So true."

Caterina pointed toward the kitchen. "I've got to check in with my father."

"Charming man."

Caterina grinned. "I hope the charming man will feed me tonight."

"Stay and have dinner with me," said the contessa, waving a graceful hand toward the empty chair opposite her.

"I'm expected at the family table. My mother should be ..." Caterina, who didn't see anyone coming up behind her, jumped when a beefy arm fell across her shoulders.

"*Tesoro*, why didn't you let me know you were here?" Cosimo Falcone hugged her tight to his side. "Your mother is tapping her nails with impatience at our table. I think she may have chipped the varnish – on the table, not the nails." He laughed. "Why don't you go give her a kiss before she changes her pasta selection once again." He pulled out the chair. "I'll sit here for a moment with the most beautiful contessa."

Caterina laughed and brushed her lips across his rough cheek. She wished the contessa "*buon appetit*" and hurried off to the table by the kitchen door.

"There you are, Catherine," said her mother offering her cheeks to be kissed before pursing her lips at Caterina's attire. "I've been waiting an hour."

Caterina looked at her wristwatch, protesting, "Mother, it's eight ten and I was right on time. Contessa Montalvo-Ligozzi wanted to chat."

"Luciana's here? Why didn't your father tell me?" She put her folded napkin on the table and pushed back her chair. "I must go and extend my regards." She pointed at Caterina. "You find Lorenzo and tell him that we are ready to eat." Margaret Mary walked off to where her husband sat, laughing at something the contessa was saying.

Caterina met Beppe Carpi in the kitchen doorway. He was balancing three plates of *crostini* and a bowl of *ribolita*. One plate slipped from his arm; saved from breaking only because Caterina's foot cushioned the fall. *Crostini* skittered under the table and through the half open door, back into the kitchen.

"*Porca miseria*," exclaimed the young waiter. "*Mi scusi, Signorina* Caterina." He looked around her at the family table. "*Grazie addio*, it didn't break and your mother wasn't here to see it."

"She'll be back in a minute, Beppe, so deliver those." Caterina waved at the two plates still balanced on his arm. "And come back for a new plate of *crostini*." She scooped up two toasted squares of bread, topped with creamy liver paté that luckily had fallen with the sticky side up.

Beppe was back in less than a minute. Caterina used a napkin to gather up the chopped tomato, basil and bread from the *crostini* under the table. He held the door for her to pass into the kitchen.

"How is your sister?" Caterina asked.

"She's okay. The surgery went well. One week more in the hospital and she'll be home. She's taking it better than me. I should have been at the Duomo with her. I'm a wreck."

"He certainly is," said Lorenzo, standing just inside the kitchen. He held a dustpan. "I don't know if our plate supply is going to last out the week." He pushed the broom in Caterina's direction. "You sweep; and Beppe, get another plate of *crostini* out to table four."

Caterina handed her brother the plate of demolished appetizers and the dirty napkin. She took the broom. "Mother says she's ready to eat."

Lorenzo looked through the window of the closed kitchen door. "She didn't see Beppe's act, did she?"

"No, she's over talking to the contessa."

"Thank goodness. She's pushing me to get rid of him."

"Perhaps you should move Beppe to order-taking, instead of serving, for a week or so."

Lorenzo rubbed his chin. "Maybe. Do you think the fact that he can't speak English or German should be a consideration?"

Caterina shook her head. "He has a sweet face and an endearing manner. The customers will cut him some slack. But Mother won't if he keeps dropping plates."

"You're probably right." He held the dustpan for her to sweep up the last of the *crostini*. "Pumpkin ravioli and a veal chop good for you tonight?"

"How about a chop and a salad?"

"Coming up." He took the broom, dodged around Beppe, who was carrying out a tray with three large glasses of beer on it, and headed back into the kitchen.

Caterina called after him, "I need a really, really good glass of wine." He turned and she explained, "It's been a tough day and dinner with mother doesn't guarantee that it will improve."

"Better you than me. She's got some friend's daughter lined up as a dinner date for my day off."

"I thought you were already slated for the pastry chef," Caterina said, looking around to see if they were being overheard. The pastry station was at the far end of the kitchen.

"Amy? That's my wish, not Mother's."

"Lorenzo, why is there chicken liver on my chair?" Margaret Mary followed the question through the swinging door.

"Sorry, Mother, I was giving Caterina a taste and it slipped."

"Catherine doesn't even like liver." She shot her daughter a frown. "Do you?" She turned back to her son. "Why are you standing there with a broom? Didn't Catherine tell you that we are ready to eat?"

Caterina took her mother's elbow and steered her out of the kitchen. "Lorenzo will be right out with your dinner."

Margaret Mary moved her place setting to the other side of the table. "Your father will be here in a minute. He had to seat a group of ten." She tapped a tapered peach-polished nail on the plate next to hers. "Sit down and explain what's been going on. Luciana was just telling me about that poor boy and his mother."

"The contessa was very helpful, both with the family and in our investigation," Caterina said, taking the designated place beside her mother.

Lorenzo came out of the kitchen, carrying a plate of *ravioli* and a salad. Caterina took the diversion to change the subject. "So, Mother, who is the woman you have in mind for Renzo?"

Her mother took the bait. "It's one of the Strozzi girls."

"The San Gimignano Strozzis or the Florence Strozzis?" Caterina raised an eyebrow in her brother's direction. He gave her a rude finger sign behind his mother's back.

"Actually, this is a cousin who grew up in Rome, but is working at Ferragamo in Florence. She's in the P.R. department."

"So she's skinny as a stick and hates food, but looks great in designer clothes." Caterina nodded as Lorenzo turned his back and pushed his way into the kitchen, past Tonio, a thirty-year veteran waiter, who spun nimbly to avoid spilling a carafe of water over the owner's table.

"She looks very nice in everything she wears," continued Margaret Mary. "Quite slender. Marvelous taste. Elegant manners. Good hair."

"Straight, you mean." Caterina tucked a bunch of curls behind her left ear.

Her mother looked up from her pasta. "Neat, I would say. Blunt cut at the shoulders. Expensive highlighting job."

Cosimo arrived in time to hear the last bit. "Are you talking about, *mio tesoro*? Caterina, promise me that you will never cut your beautiful hair."

"Thank you, Babbo. I'm glad somebody likes it."

"Your curls are like my mother's when she was young. She never cut hers."

"Cosimo, darling." His wife put a hand on his, which was resting on her shoulder. "Your mother had the sense to tame her mane in a chignon. Catherine's hair is always flying in her face."

He sat down in the chair opposite his daughter. He smiled at her and then pointed at the pasta bowl in front of Margaret Mary. "Have you tasted those *ravioli*? I added a bit of cinnamon and nutmeg to the filling. Nice isn't it?"

"Darling, your cooking is why I fell in love with you. Never a misstep."

Caterina took a bite of salad – bitter greens dressed lightly with a bit of oil and vinegar. "So why are you pushing Renzo to date a stick who doesn't eat?"

"She eats. She just doesn't indulge herself indiscriminately."

"Who is this?" asked Cosimo, taking a fork and spearing a square of stuffed pasta.

"Georgiana Grimaldi, a distant cousin of the Strozzi family." Margaret Mary continued as Cosimo waved the *raviolo* under Caterina's nose. "I met her at Principessa Orsini's lunch on Monday. She's just moved to Florence." She frowned at her daughter. "Catherine, just eat it. You know what it smells like."

Caterina placed the buttery *raviolo* on her tongue, savoring the spices. "Sage?" she asked, as her mother said, "I thought she might like to meet some other young people."

Cosimo nodded at his daughter about the sage in the *ravioli* stuffing and responded to his wife's comment, "I thought Lorenzo had his eye on Amy; although, I don't think he's gotten up the courage to ask her out. He keeps plying her with tastes of the new dishes he's concocting."

"Of course he hasn't asked her out. Amy is much too young for him," exclaimed Margaret Mary.

"Caterina, have you tasted my *gnocchi* with walnut sauce?"

She grinned, admiring her father's ability to abandon a losing argument. "No, Babbo."

"Have Lorenzo bring you a couple to try. Fabulous, if I do say so myself. By the way, the contessa had very nice things to say about you."

"She saw me when I was actually working on an important part of the case. Today was different."

"I'm sure you are exaggerating," said her father.

Margaret May interjected, "Surely there are more people than just you working on this horrible thing. I don't want you involved with bombs."

"I'm just on the periphery," said Caterina.

Lorenzo came out of the kitchen and picked up her empty salad plate. "Are you ready for your veal chop?"

"Yes please, Renzo. I'm starved. Can I get some *patate fritte* to go with them?"

"Fried potatoes?" he asked with a grin. "I thought you were giving calories a pass tonight."

"I just needed some inspiration. Babbo says to try his *gnocchi*. Just a bite. And where is my wine?"

"Lorenzo, bring her a glass of the *Vino Nobile di Montepulciano*," directed Cosimo. "You know the one – from my friend Gianpiero's new winery. Bring me a glass, too."

"Do you want a veal chop, also?" Lorenzo asked his father.

Cosimo stabbed another *raviolo* off his wife's plate, ignoring her pained look. "No, I'll eat after the rush dies down. Just a glass of wine with my favorite daughter and then I'm back to work."

When Lorenzo brought three glasses and opened a bottle of berry-red wine, he asked his mother, "Finished with the pasta? Do you want something else since Babbo ate half of it? Grilled *pette di pollo*? *Tagliatta*?"

"No, sweetheart, just some slivered artichokes and parmesan. I'm trying to eat lighter." She eyed the veal chop that Beppe placed in front of Caterina – almost an inch thick, pink and juicy at the center, crusty fat along one side.

"Want a taste?" Caterina waved a small piece at the end of her fork.

"Maybe just one." Her mother took the fork and slid the piece on to her bread plate then picked up her own fork and ate it.

Cosimo got up, leaving a quarter of a glass of wine on the table. "Got to go back to work. *Tesoro,* try to get to bed early tonight. Your eyes are tired and sad."

"It's just a tough patch for me now, Babbo. As Nonna always said, 'This too will pass.'"

"My mother was wise and always right. Isn't that true, darling?" He squeezed his wife's shoulder and winked at Caterina and Lorenzo.

Margaret Mary patted his hand and said, "If you say so, my dear." She took a small sip of wine amid their laughter.

Chapter Forty-Six

On Sunday morning, Caterina sat at a small table outside Café Rivoire, sipping a cappuccino, waiting for Elizabeth Willingham. The sun beat down on the grand piazza filled with tour groups listening with varied attention to guides describing the history of the Palazzo Vecchio, as well as the story of each marble statue in the square, while warning that the David they were viewing was a copy from the late 1800s. Caterina's eye was snagged by a flash of color winding through the clumps of sweaty tourists. Elizabeth Willingham, dressed in a flowing, abstract, Pucci silk dress and ankle-length black leggings, caught sight of her and waved.

Caterina didn't get up, but held out her hand. "I love the dress."

Miss Willingham gave Caterina's white silk blouse, paired with a black jacket and slacks, a quick look, as if to see if she could return the compliment, and decided against it. "It's vintage," she merely said.

"How did your location scouting go this morning?" Caterina asked.

Elizabeth pulled out the chair on the other side of the table and raised a finger to catch the attention of an aging waiter in a cream wool jacket and black trousers. "Very well. The mayor's office is very keen to accommodate films on historical subjects. They're letting me use the Palazzo Strozzi for three days in July to shoot a film on Lorenzo de Medici, entitled *Lorenzo the Magnificent*. Hopefully, we won't get too many Italiophiles writing us after the film's released, complaining that Lorenzo is shown living in the house of his sworn enemy, instead of the Palazzo Medici-Ricardi. Of course, the external shots will be of the correct building."

Caterina waited for the British woman to order a Negroni before she said, "You've been doing this type of work for a while, haven't you?"

"About ten years now. I've formed my own company, although I'm the only employee. I also had a web site designed. It's really come together nicely."

Caterina sipped the last of her coffee. "I have to admit, I did an internet search on you after you mentioned location scouting. I saw your site – *locationlocationlocation.tv*."

"Great name, don't you think? I had to finesse it a bit with the .tv suffix. Someone else had gotten the .com one, as well as the .co.uk suffix, sod them." She smiled her thanks to the waiter as he placed a deep red drink in front of her, a small orange slice balanced on the glass rim. "Would you be a dear and bring us some nuts?" she asked in Italian.

Caterina continued, "I saw in the list of your previous films that you worked on a movie in Bali and Indonesia about six years ago.'

Elizabeth took a small sip of her drink and nodded. "That was *Hot Curry and Papaya*, a coming-of-age film with cooking."

"What do you mean 'with cooking'?"

Elizabeth affected a TV critic's cadence, "Young rebellious Londoner with hardworking Indonesian parents, goes to Bali to meet the ancient grandparents and finds her purpose in life through cooking with Grandmum. Kind of *Eat Drink Man Woman*, but instead of Taiwanese, it's Balinese-Brits."

The waiter placed a small bowl of mixed nuts on the table.

Caterina pushed the bowl towards the British woman. "I guess I missed it at the theater."

"It went straight to video." Elizabeth bit off half a cashew and took a small sip of her Negroni.

"Did you meet Omar Jaboor in Bali?"

Elizabeth choked and put down her glass. "Yes. How did you know that?"

"He mentioned that he was in Bali in October that year and it seemed to fit the time when the film crew was there. Also, you weren't living in Pisa then."

"No, I was still in Ibiza waiting for my divorce to come through."

Caterina thought it would be good to move the conversation away from Omar and ease back into the subject later. "That was your marriage to the Moroccan gentleman – what was his name?"

"Nabil El-Amin. Nice enough and incredibly romantic, but he could never hold a job and had a roving eye. Every time I came back from a scouting a location, I found some item of clothing that wasn't mine under the bed or in a drawer."

"So English men aren't your cup of tea, so to speak?"

"Not at all. All that pasty white skin and stiff upper lip. Or if not the stiff lip, then an unhealthy attachment to some sports team – soccer, rugby, cricket – you name it. Same problem with Italian blokes, right?"

Caterina nodded. "In Italy it's only soccer, but then you add in the attachment to *La Mamma* and, for me, a sad lack of stature."

"So you're looking abroad, too. That Yank, Max, was tall enough, good looking, too."

"Married, with kids."

"Too bad. I take it he's not looking to make a change." She threw Caterina an enquiring look.

Caterina played along and grinned. "Doesn't seem like it, but you never know. You're right, though, I have a yen for American guys. They have ambition and an adventuresome spirit that I don't find in Italian men."

"And inches."

"That, too."

"I don't care if they're tall. I want them dark and hot. American men don't get the romance right."

"So Omar fits the bill."

"Absolutely, if he would just get on with it and leave that little mouse of a wife, Paola."

"He was on his honeymoon when you met him, right?"

Elizabeth nodded. "Which tells you that he was trapped into the marriage by Paola's pregnancy. She must

have been five or six months along before they even got
to the altar."

"How did you meet him?"

"We were staying at the same hotel in Bali. I met him
in the bar. She was always resting and couldn't drink. He
was bored."

"Did you see him in Jakarta, too?" Omar hadn't
mentioned going to Jakarta, so this was a shot in the dark,
Caterina thought. She hoped that Elizabeth wouldn't ask
if Omar revealed this, too.

Elizabeth didn't seem suspicious. She nodded. "He
flew down with me for a couple of days. I needed to get
things set up for the film. He didn't know the city and
wanted to see it. We weren't lovers, yet. It was just a good
way to get to know each other."

"You didn't stay together in Jakarta?"

"No, we ran around together for about half a day
seeing the sights and then I had to go off to the West Java
coast to check on some film locations on the beach. He
went back to Bali by himself."

Caterina was incredulous. "He left his wife on their
honeymoon to go sightseeing with you?"

"Like I said, we weren't romantic then and they
weren't either, it seemed. The marriage was over before it
began. His wife was pregnant and sleeping half of the
time. I don't think the humidity agreed with her. She told
him to go see the sights while she was at the hotel spa,
getting skin treatments."

"But to leave her overnight …"

"He never told me how that was worked out. But,
like I just said, their marriage was essentially over before it

began. By the time Petra was born, he was calling me on Ibiza, trying to talk me into moving to Pisa."

"Did you ever travel with him again?"

Elizabeth's face lit up. "All the time. He goes on buying trips with his brother-in-law, Daniele. Omar says that Paola never wants to leave Petra, so she never flies with him."

"So where have you gone with Daniele and Omar?"

"They take a lot of buying trips for furs, skins and leather hides that they use in the manufacture of Pellione's products. We've been to Argentina for tanned hides a couple of times. The Russia trip, three years ago, for fox and mink fur. Serbia, two years ago, for a special kind of lynx. Australia, once for ostrich skins, but now they get those from an ostrich farm in Puglia. Why all of this interest in Omar's business?"

Caterina thought fast for a cover story that wouldn't implicate Omar in any specific act. "We received some information – it may be from a disgruntled competitor, you understand – that *Pellione Pelle* is making illegal knock-offs of licensed goods: purses, wallets, and the like. It wasn't Omar's name that was mentioned. It was Daniele."

Elizabeth's frown disappeared. "*Pellione* would never deal with illegal leather products, either importing the finished fakes or manufacturing them. Daniele's father is a stickler for the business being legit. Daniele and Omar agree with him."

"Why doesn't Daniele object to you coming along with his sister's husband?"

"I suppose it doesn't matter if you know; you don't live in Pontedera, and no crime is being committed."

Caterina shook her head. "I'm confused. What are you trying to say?"

"Daniele is gay. His lover is one of Pellione's designers, Franco Dequattro."

"I still don't understand why that keeps him quiet about you and Omar."

"Daniele is married and has a son. The only extended periods of time he gets to spend with Frankie is when they travel. Same with Omar and me. So Daniele and Omar are each other's alibi, so to speak."

"You're saying that Daniele was on each of the trips you took with Omar?"

"Every one of them, except for the one from Bali to Jakarta. Daniele wasn't along on Omar's and Paola's honeymoon, needless to say."

"Have you ever been to Spain with Omar?"

"The four of us went to Valencia a couple of times, but that was four years ago, before they found that the Argentinean and Turkish suppliers could get them quality hides for less money."

"So you didn't go to Spain last year."

"No."

"Did you ever go to Croatia with Omar?"

"No."

"Does he ever travel without you?"

"Not that I know of. It's always possible, of course, but I think he would have told me." Elizabeth finished the last sip of her drink.

Frustrated, Caterina was aware that the trips Elizabeth described didn't go to the countries, much less the cities, where the Cobra bombs had been detonated.

But the timing of each trip was eerily familiar. Then she had an idea. "Do you go to the tanning plants – I guess that's what they're called – or the fur suppliers with Daniele and Omar?"

Elizabeth shook her head. "Frankie and I usually stay by the pool or in the hotel spa while those two do their business. Sometimes we go shopping – Frankie's got a great sense for the fashion trends, much better than mine."

"Can you remember when you were in Serbia?"

"Two years ago in September, we…," She broke off, focusing on Caterina's face. "This can't have to do with fake bags. Why do you need to know?"

Caterina change directions again. "Actually, I don't. I was just thinking of going there myself and wondered how it was since the war."

Elizabeth spit a cube of ice she was sucking on back into her glass. "It's gorgeous. We were only there for three days. The hotel was nice, the staff was very helpful and the shopping was so cheap. I can probably find the name of the hotel for you. Or Omar can."

"No rush. My next vacation doesn't come until August. But thanks, you're going to be my resource for traveling. You go to all of these places with Omar, but you must also travel a lot for your own business."

"That's true. I'm probably in Pisa only two weeks out of each month. One of the benefits of living there is that it has a great airport."

"Does Omar travel with you to film scouting locations?"

"No, I wish he would, but he can't get away."

"Did you tell Omar about our conversation the other day?"

Elizabeth shook her head. "You see, I never call him. That's the deal – he does the calling."

"Why is that? It must be frustrating."

"It is. But for obvious reasons, I can't call him at home. At the office, Marina, his secretary, is a friend of Paola's, so he doesn't want me to call him there. If I really need to contact him, I call the Pisa shop and leave a message, but he doesn't want me to do that too often."

"What about his cell phone?"

"Omar hates them. He says a person can never be really alone if he can always be reached on a cell phone. He never carries one. He's a bit old fashioned that way. Not that I disagree, but it can be frustrating."

Caterina decided not to mention the fact that she had Omar's cell phone number and had called him on it. "I thought you said he was separated from his wife. So why the need for secrecy?"

"Sometimes, I wonder about that, too. He always says it's not about Paola, it's about his father-in-law."

"Do you want another drink?" Caterina looked around for their waiter.

"No, I've got to go soon."

"Then I'll get the bill." Caterina made the universal writing signal to the waiter. He nodded and kept on taking the order from a table of German tourists. She turned back to Elizabeth. "On another subject – remember I was asking you about Irene Paloma?"

"The shopgirl with the photo of me and Omar?"

"Yes, did Daniele know her?"

"Probably, but not as well as Omar. Daniele deals with production, Omar with sales. It's a small company, so Daniele probably met Irene a few times. He was at the *Befana* party where she took the photo of me and Omar and Petra."

Caterina took the check from the waiter. "Elizabeth, it's really been fun talking to you. This is the first relaxing day I've had recently."

"It's been good for me, too. I never get to talk to anyone about Omar."

"I'd appreciate it if you don't tell him we've talked. I'm sure the investigation of the fakes is going to wrap up soon and Pellione will be vindicated. You've certainly helped."

"To tell the truth, I'm a bit out of sorts with Omar right now. I haven't seen him in two weeks and he hasn't called since Monday. So I'm not going to tell him anything. If he wants to know who I'm seeing, he can drop by."

"Is this unusual, him not visiting you for a few days?"

"Not at all. Sometimes a week goes by without him calling or coming by. Usually I think it adds spice to the relationship, having a bit of uncertainty. Also, he brings expensive gifts depending on the length of time he stays away. I'm expecting something pretty nice real soon." She picked up her blue, ostrich-leather purse from the ground beside the table. "He gave me this bag after three weeks apart last year." Looking at her wristwatch, she said, "I have to run. I've got a meeting at the Medici Villa at Careggi before I go back to Pisa."

"For your upcoming film?"

Elizabeth Willingham stood, checking the table to see if she had left anything. "You know Lorenzo de Medici died there. His doctor was giving him ground pearls as medicine. After his patient died, the doctor committed suicide by throwing himself into a well. Great drama isn't it?"

"It works for me, Elizabeth. I look forward to seeing the finished product." Caterina stood and held out her hand.

"Call me Liz," she said, shaking the offered hand. "Next time, it's my treat."

Chapter Forty-Seven

When Caterina got back to the office, Patricia Benvenuti whispered, "Watch out for Marco. If smugness was poison, we'd all be dead."

"What's he found out now?"

Marco's voice came from behind her. "Last evening, I had a little chat with the travel agency girl in Tallinn, Estonia. Remember the business card in Yakov's pocket that was the basis for our belief that he was Estonian? It was hers. Good thing my Russian is so good – her accent was really thick."

"I take it from your tone that she knew Yakov Petrov," Caterina said, turning to look at him.

"I guess about ten years ago Petrov worked out of the Tallin office of the same security firm. He got a promotion to Moscow, but kept using the same girl to book his travel. She was sweet on him, like the secretary I talked to yesterday at the Moscow home office." Marco crossed his arms and leaned against the reception room doorway, trying to look relaxed and failing in Caterina's eyes.

"She hadn't heard that he died?" asked Signora Benvenuti.

He shook his head. "I broke it to her. In the midst of all her crying, she faxed me his itineraries for the past ten years."

"Let me guess," said Caterina. "He was at all of the locations of all of the Cobra bombs."

"Ninety percent of them."

"Which ones did he miss?" Caterina crossed the room and took a seat on the small couch.

"He flew in the week before all of them and out on the day after, except for Bilbao. He was in Spain for that one, but we can only place him in Barcelona. Of course, he may have driven north or taken the train to Bilbao, but we don't think so."

"Why is that?"

"He flew into Barcelona with Stefanya Goncharov as head of her security detail the day the bomb exploded at the museum. She didn't leave the city for the next week. The day after the boyfriend's funeral, she and Petrov both flew back to Moscow."

"So he set the bomb off from a distance or someone did it on his instructions," guessed Caterina.

"That's my theory, but the FBI guy isn't buying it."

"Why not?" asked Patricia. She quit pretending to work on the files on her desk and stuck her pencil into the bun on the back of her head.

"There's not the same seven-day advance preparation cycle. Petrov was always on site a week before each of the other bombs exploded."

"Who says the bomber can't change his *modus operandus*?" asked Caterina.

"I do," said a low voice behind her.

Caterina whipped around to meet Max's grin. He was standing in the doorway to the magistrate's office. Paolo Benigni entered the reception area behind the American.

"It's as simple as this," Max continued. "Bombers never, or hardly ever, change their *m.o.* To make, and place, a successful bomb takes incredible precision unless you're driving a suicide car bomb into a building, planning to blow yourself up along with the entire structure."

"You're saying that Cobra's bombs are too precise," the magistrate observed.

"They all use a cell phone as the triggering device. We haven't found evidence that he ever misses. That's precision. He couldn't be on the other side of the country, much less in transit when the bomb goes off. Too many variables. Not enough control. If Stefanya's boyfriend was the target, Cobra had to know that the cell phone was in the briefcase, and that the briefcase was with the boy, before he set off the bomb."

"You've never seen this type of bomber change his plans?"

"Only once, with disastrous results."

"What happened?"

"A bomber in Kuwait, who was trying to move the device when his target changed chairs at a conference table, blew off four of his own fingers and killed an untargeted bystander."

The magistrate opened his office door. "All of you come in here. Marco, bring in an extra chair. Captain DeLuca just called to say that a battery cover of a cell phone was among the trash collected from one of the

Piazza del Duomo trash cans on Easter. It had a fingerprint that matched Irina Golubka."

"*Gotcha*," exclaimed Max.

"She's the bomber?" asked Marco at the same time.

"Did they find the SIM card?" asked Caterina.

"One at a time," said Magistrate Benigni. "They did find the SIM card. It also yielded a partial fingerprint. And, before you ask, it did not lead anywhere. Only one call had been made to an unregistered cell phone, somewhere in Florence. Not the phone on the bomb. Not Yakov's phone, either."

"Which trash can?" asked Max.

"The one in front of the building just east of the Barton boy's apartment building."

Caterina nodded. "That fits with what the contessa saw. She said Irina was using a cell phone as she walked toward the palazzo."

"So Yakov gave Irina the cell phone and told her to call when the kid was in position," said Max.

"Maybe," the magistrate said. "It certainly brings the Russian woman back as a person of interest. Caterina, do you have something to report?"

"I still think we have to do the work to rule Omar Pellione out as Cobra. Like Yakov, he seems to be traveling too much to places of interest. I don't have the exact dates, but I probably have enough for a warrant to search the *Pellione Pelle* files, and perhaps the homes of Omar and Daniele Pellione, on suspicion in the death of Irina Golubka – and maybe for the Cobra bombs."

"I thought Omar was just Irina's boss. Who's Daniele Pellione?" asked Marco. "How would he and Omar have anything to do with the Cobra bombs?"

"I said a *suspicion*, Marco, not proof. They were in or near the countries where the Cobra bombs went off. Daniele is Omar's brother-in-law. Elizabeth Willingham told me that they always travel together."

"That sound pretty far-fetched, said Marco."

"Give me an hour or so to go through my notes to see if there is any credible match to the timing and locations of the bombs," she said, looking at the magistrate. "The trips included ones to Moscow, Argentina, Spain, Istanbul, and Serbia."

"Except for Spain, none of those match up," said Marco.

Caterina focused on Max Turner, ignoring Marco. "Elizabeth Willingham said that Daniele and Omar routinely go away for a day or two during each trip to conduct business. All of their locations are within a two-hour flight of the bomb locations. I didn't want to get too specific in my questions for fear of sending her off to warn Omar."

"What did she think you were asking about?" asked Max.

"I told her *Pellione Pelle* is under investigation for importing or manufacturing knock-off merchandise. She was comfortable believing that that would never be the case, therefore she was very chatty."

"Do you have any dates that are confirmed matches?"

Caterina didn't need to look at her notes. She nodded. "The Jakarta bomb and the Croatia strike. Omar traveled with Elizabeth to Jakarta the day before the hotel explosion."

"With his new bride?" asked Max, shaking his head.

"She stayed at the resort in Bali. Willingham said that Paola Pellione wasn't feeling well."

"A few hours out sight-seeing is one thing. An overnight trip is another. What did he tell Paola?"

"I don't know. We'll have to ask her."

"Did Willingham and Jaboor check into the hotel that was bombed?"

"Elizabeth didn't. She left after half a day of seeing the sights in Jakarta with him to go off to the coast of East Java to scout film locations. She believes Omar traveled back to Bali the following day."

"What was the other confirmed date?" asked the magistrate.

"They were in Serbia the same month as the Croatia bomb in Optija. I'll check the exact dates."

"So you're saying he left her to fly to Croatia and back?" Marco asked, pacing in the back of the room.

"It's only a one-hour flight."

The pitch of Marco's voice went up. "But at the *same* time, I have confirmation that *Yakov Petrov* was *checked in* at the resort hotel in Optija where the bomb went off."

The magistrate frowned. "Marco, we're just listening to what Caterina has to say. We'd feel like idiots if there was a connection and we ignored it." He turned to Caterina. "I have a problem, however, with the fact that

Omar was with his brother-in-law when he's not with the Willingham woman."

Caterina nodded. "Until we talk to Daniele we won't know if he went off on his own to look at lynx pelts and Omar went somewhere else. Omar is really only along on these trips, as far as I can see, to provide cover for his brother-in-law's gay love life and to further his own romance with Elizabeth Willingham. He didn't need to be on these excursions for *Pellione Pelle* business. He works in the sales end, not the manufacturing side. So I want to know exactly what Omar was doing when he wasn't with Elizabeth."

"I think it's a long shot," said the magistrate. "But we have a bit more leeway, given the nature of the Duomo catastrophe, so I'm going to authorize you to follow up on this, Caterina. Get me more support for the warrants – names, dates, and locations – before I issue them."

Caterina nodded, gathered up her briefcase and jacket, and headed to the door.

"Did you get any more info on Irina's murder?" asked Max. "Do we have a viable suspect in the Pellione family?"

Caterina paused and turned back. "Both Daniele and Omar knew her. I think the theory about Irina trying to blackmail Omar is weak. Elizabeth is adamant that only his father-in-law cares about the continuation of the marriage between Omar and his daughter. Now, if Irina knew about Daniele's significant other, that might have been something else. Daniele is trysting with another man, one of their designers. He would have a motive to get rid of her. But was he in Florence at the time of her death? We don't know."

"That reminds me," interjected Paolo Benigni. "I think Signora Benvenuti was making some calls for you, Caterina. Patricia, what did you tell me earlier?"

"It completely flew out of my mind, dear," the older woman said, turning to Caterina. "I called the priest at St. Jacopo. He told me that he saw Omar, Paola, and their daughter at Easter mass that started at noon in Pontedera, like that Miss Willingham claimed."

"So, like Yakov wasn't in Bilbao the day of the Guggenheim bombing, Omar wasn't in Florence when the *Scoppio del Carro* blew up," said Marco.

"It seems so. The cart blew at eleven," said the magistrate. "Though he could have made it to Pontedera in an hour given the usual light traffic on Easter Sunday."

"That's cutting it awfully close, sir," said Caterina.

At the same time, Max said, "I insist this bomber is always within visual range of the bomb."

The magistrate stood up. "We don't know if the priest saw Omar Pellione at the beginning of the mass or the end. I think we have to pull all of them in tomorrow. At least for initial interviews. I'm going to set it up with my counterparts in Pontedera. I want simultaneous searches of the *Pellione Pelle* manufacturing plant and business offices, as well as the homes of Daniele and Omar Pellione. I also need to brief Captain DeLuca. He may want to take the lead in the interrogations and send support for the location searches. These are Italian citizens – not under our remit."

"What about Yakov Petrov?" asked Marco, still standing in the back of the room.

"He's dead and not going anywhere, Marco. You've uncovered enough evidence to link him to the Cobra bombs. I've given that information to Captain DeLuca. Mr. Turner, here, has briefed the Americans. There will be a meeting with the Russian ambassador in Rome to lay out the connection between the Goncharov brothers and Petrov, as well as his presence at each of the Cobra bomb targets. I think our time should be spent clearing up any possible connection between the Pellione brothers, Irina Gulubka's murder – we know Yakov didn't strangle her – and the Duomo bomb. We should be able to do that in a day."

Caterina went back to her office, pulled out the spreadsheet she had made for the Cobra bombs, grabbed her laptop computer, and dug in her purse for her notebook containing the information she had gotten from Elizabeth Willingham. She took all of these to the small conference room. Within an hour, using on-line maps and transit schedules, she had plotted how Omar Jaboor could have logistically been in each of the locations to supply and activate the bombs.

What she didn't have was any connection between Omar and the Goncharov brothers – or between Omar and Yakov Petrov.

Chapter Forty-Eight

What I can't figure out is why Omar hasn't run, if he's the bomb-maker," said Max on Monday morning in the magistrate's car with Tozzi at the wheel. Caterina sat beside him in the back seat. "He knows you've been tracking Irina and suspect him for her murder."

Following them were two blue *polizia* vehicles, one carrying Marco and two of Captain DeLuca's lieutenants, and the other with three more policemen. They were scheduled to rendezvous with police from Pontedera at the exit to the town from the FiPiLi highway. Marco would lead the search of Omar and Paola Pellione's house. The other three officers would search Daniele's house. Max and Caterina, with assistance from the Pontedera police force, would serve the warrant for a search of the Pellione Pelle office and factory.

Caterina thought for a moment. "You never thought we would get him for Irina's murder because the DNA wouldn't match. Maybe he thought that was his alibi. Or maybe he thought I was just a low-level female cop assigned busy work."

"Or maybe he is gone."

"What a pessimist. If he had taken off, the surveillance guys would have called it in."

"You're an extreme optimist if you think someone as smart as Cobra can't give a couple of local cops the slip."

"They followed him to the factory this morning; Daniele is there, also. How do you think we should handle it?" Caterina asked.

"In case he's there, I suggest we leave the Pontedera cops out of sight on the street that leads to the factory driveway."

"I understand." Caterina nodded. "If he isn't suspicious, we'll play it like we are there for the tour you requested last time we met with him. We'll get the layout of the factory, and serve him with the search warrant at the end." She slipped the warrant into an inside pocket of her black jacket.

Max took a handgun he carried in a shoulder harness out and checked it.

"You're armed?"

"Yeah, Captain DeLuca authorized it. I don't expect I'll need to use this, but I'm more comfortable being prepared." He looked sideways at her. "And you?"

"I haven't carried a gun in over a year. I've never had to fire one on the job, even when I was in the *polizia* and had to carry one."

Max returned the gun to its holster. He looked out at the countryside as they passed the exit to Empoli. "Did you see Bill Barton before he left?"

Caterina nodded. "I went to the Excelsior yesterday to say goodbye to Candy Seagraves and her husband. They were taking her son's body back to California on the late afternoon plane. Mr. Barton was there as well. I guess he left this morning so he would be in Los Angeles in time for the funeral."

Max nodded, rubbing the muscles on the back of his neck. "Yeah, I had breakfast with him. I told him we expected a break in the case soon, but didn't give him the details of today's operation. You can guess what he had to say."

Caterina didn't respond.

Max's cell phone rang. "Turner...Tell me...Not a good time. Check out the uncle with the Israelis, will you?"

Caterina lifted an enquiring eyebrow.

"That was Bob Mathews from Beirut. We know a bit more about Jamal. His family name is Majid. He's Omar's first cousin. His father is married to the sister of Omar's father. After Omar's parents died in '83, he and his brother Amin were sent to the uncle for safekeeping."

"Has he found anything about Amin?"

"No. He seems to have dropped off the map."

"You asked for info on the uncle – Majid is his name?"

"Yeah, the uncle is Abdel Majid. Mathews is going to track down Jamal's father and try once more to find Amin Jaboor."

"Maybe we'll see Jamal at Pellione Pelle," said Caterina. "We'll try to ask him a few questions before we serve the warrant. Once I call in the Pontedera police and serve the search warrant, I'm going to have to take Omar and Daniele into custody as persons of interest."

"I hope we can get Omar to stay in the office during the tour. Daniele doesn't have the same history with us. Maybe we can get him talking about their travels on Pellione business and find out if they ever split up, going different places for a day or two at a time."

"Marco is supposed to give us about thirty minutes before he goes to the apartment. That way we can let him know for a certainty that Omar is at the factory and not at home."

They met the Pontedera police and Caterina outlined the plan. She walked back to the car behind hers to talk to Marco. "I'll call you if Omar Pellione is at the factory, and then you won't have to wait. You can direct the crew that is going into Daniele's place and immediately search Omar's place."

"I'll be waiting for your call," he said. Caterina heard him instruct his driver to take them to Omar Pellione's house in the center of Pontedera.

Two cars left the freeway and took the street leading to Pellione Pelle. Leaving the Pontedera police around a curve, out of sight of the driveway or the factory, Tozzi drove Caterina and Max to the parking lot outside the office. Omar was stacking boxes with the Pellione Pelle logo on them into an *Ape* in front of the office.

"Back again, *Ispettore*? I thought Mr. Turner said he would be by himself for a tour of the factory. Or…," He turned to shake Max's hand. "…is it the appeal of Mr. Turner that makes you skip a day of work? How is your family liking Rome, Max?"

Caterina frowned, but Max smiled lazily, saying, "The family is fine. They're back in the States now visiting my parents, so I have a bit of free time and no reason to get back to Rome soon. I'm imposing on Caterina for a car and her company for one more day."

"And charming company it is," Omar said, taking her hand and kissing it. "Daniele is here today also, so he will show you the design studio, the cutting shop and the sewing rooms."

"Could I use the *toilette* before we start the tour?" asked Caterina.

"Of course. Just go into the office and Marina will show you the way," said Omar. He turned to Max, "You are with the American Embassy right, Max? I was wondering about visas to the U.S."

Caterina paused to hear Max say, "Two questions – when and for how long?"

"In June, for two weeks, I want to take my family to Disney World."

"No problem. With Italian passports, you automatically have up to three months on a tourist visa to the states. You just need to make sure your passports are up-to-date with digital photos and an informational bar code for the readers. Your daughter will need a passport, too, of course."

Caterina went into the reception area. On hearing her request, Marina wordlessly pointed toward a closed door.

Inside the small bathroom, Caterina sent a text message to Marco, telling him to begin the search of Omar's home. When she walked out of the office she saw that a short, slender man with black, curly hair had joined Max and Omar. Like Omar, he wore blue jeans and a white, long-sleeved, cotton shirt.

"*Ispettore* Falcone, let me introduce you to my brother-in-law, Daniele Pellione," called Omar.

Caterina walked over and shook Daniele's hand. "I hear you are in charge of production of the beautiful things I saw at the Persephone shop in Florence, Mr. Pellione."

His voice was soft and low, "Please call me Daniele. Max, here, says he's never been to a leather factory before. Is that also true for you, *Ispettore?*"

"Caterina, please," she said. "I have a friend in Florence who makes leather boxes by hand. He learned the craft from his father and grandfather. It takes weeks for one box to be finished. I find it fascinating. Am I right that your products can be made in days?"

"Yes, but the process is no less interesting. I learned from my father and grandfather how to design and make jackets and coats. I've added a line of shoes and purses in the past five years. Let's start in the design studio over in the factory." Daniele pointed at a two-story building made of red-orange, terra cotta bricks. Four large, square windows, two on each side of the door, were the only sources of outside light into the building. As the four walked toward the wide wooden doors, painted with the Pellione logo, Daniele asked Caterina, "Have you found Irene Paloma's killer? Omar said you had been asking about her employment papers."

"You knew Irene?"

"Of course. I know all of our employees. Omar deals more with the sales force, but I always meet them. Since she was in Pisa for a few months, I saw more of her than some of the other *commese*. I thought she was one of our more capable sales girls."

"Did she ever come to Pontedera?" Caterina could hear Max laughing at something Omar said.

"A couple of times," Daniele answered. "I sometimes ask some of the female employees to consult on our new designs. I think the last time she was here was for the *Befana* party in January. The whole company and our best customers are invited to that event every year."

"I'm sorry to say we haven't caught Irene's killer yet. Usually, if you don't find them within twenty-four hours, it takes a lot longer. But I promise you, we will find out who did this. Did you know anything about her personal life in Pisa or afterwards when she moved to Florence?"

"No, I'm sorry. I only know that Irene liked zippers instead of buttons on jackets and wasn't partial to pockets."

"Did you learn who killed Irene?" Omar spoke over Caterina's shoulder, firing questions. "Someone she owed money to? A drug connection? I meant to ask you about her immediately, but I forgot. Have you ruled me out?" He turned to his brother-in-law. "Daniele, did I tell you that the *bella ispettore* took a DNA sample from me?

Caterina wondered, *is he angry or nervous?* She stopped and turned to face him. "The lab takes a while to get DNA results back; but remember Mr. Pellione, I never said you were a suspect. I needed your sample because you were possibly the last person to see Irene alive. My boss would have been very displeased if I hadn't been thorough." She wondered if she could get a reaction from Omar or Daniele as she continued, "Especially when we found out about your relationship with Elizabeth Willingham. Tell me Omar, was Irene blackmailing you about that?"

"My relationship? Blackmail? I never said I had a relationship with Signorina Willingham. Oh, I see, you're back to the photograph found in Irene's apartment."

"You must know that we talked to Miss Willingham." Caterina said conversationally. "She told us that the two of you have been an item for the last five years. You met her in Bali. Then she moved to Italy. She says that for all intents and purposes, your marriage is a sham."

Omar's face flamed. "Your information is incorrect. I haven't seen Elizabeth Willingham for months. I don't believe she is still in Pisa."

Daniele seemed to grow pale. He put his hand on Omar's arm.

Caterina pushed on. "Your wife knows about Elizabeth, right? Elizabeth said she did."

Omar lurched at her. Daniele pulled him back. "I'm telling you there is no relationship to know about," Omar yelled. "I don't know what that woman might have imagined, but she is lying or exaggerating. I *flirt*. *All* Italian men flirt."

"And are very successful at it. I should take lessons," Max said, clapping a hand on Omar's back. "Caterina, give the man a break. We're off-duty, here to see the factory. Let's not take up their whole morning."

Omar smiled, but it didn't change the angry look in his eyes. "Daniele, why don't you take them around. I need to talk to Jamal and get him to take the *Ape* with a load of coats over to the store in Pisa. I'll catch up to you in a few minutes." He strode off toward the office.

Daniele recovered his composure and moved briskly to open a small entrance cut into a pair of massive wooden doors. "This was a granary two hundred years ago," he explained. "Big carts had to get in and out. We added the windows so we could have natural light in the design studio, but sunlight is not good for the leather, so the rest of the factory is lit from within."

Caterina wasn't worried that Omar would leave the property. In any case, the police were stationed blocking the exit road.

Inside a half-glassed wall showed off a long room with a large cutting table, one industrial-sized sewing machine, a smaller sewing machine used for cloth, and three slanted, oak sketching desks. A slender man with highlighted brown hair, wearing loose linen pants and a tight black t-shirt, was standing at one end of the room sorting through a large box containing dozens of different-sized zippers. A woman, dressed in a purple, suede, short-sleeved top and slim, lavender slacks, was sketching on a large sheet of paper pinned to one of the desks.

Daniele opened the glass door to the room. The smell of fine leather and adhesive glue was in the air. "This is, as you can see, our design studio. Franco Alberti and Letizia Parto are our designers. I also try my hand at creating some of our new looks."

From the windows in the design studio, Caterina could see Omar under the awning at the door of the office building. He was talking with his cousin, Jamal, who was loading a large box into the *Ape*. She saw Omar dig in the pocket of his blue jeans and pull out a small cell phone. *I knew he lied to Elizabeth Willingham about having a cell phone phobia*, she thought, as she watched him glance at the factory while he talked. He flipped the phone shut and went back to his discussion with Jamal.

Daniele came up behind Caterina. "I see Omar found Jamal. He'll join us now. Let's go out and wait for him."

"Yes, why don't we?" Caterina opened the door. "We have a couple of questions for Jamal. Maybe we can get him to delay his trip to Pisa for a few minutes.

As they stepped out the factory door they saw Omar glance at them and then go into the office. He was out in a minute, shrugging on a black leather jacket and carrying a shirt-sized box that he handed to Jamal. He came toward the factory, a dark frown settled on his brows.

"Now that you're here …," Daniele started.

Omar interrupted, "I'm sorry, I need to make a couple of calls. I don't want to hold you up. I'll catch up in the sewing room, or you can find me after the tour, back at the office. Sorry about this."

Max raised a hand, "No need to apologize. Daniele is doing great. We should be done soon."

"Can we have a minute of Jamal's time before he takes off?" asked Caterina.

"Sure, I'll send him over," Omar said over his shoulder as he walked off.

Max turned to Daniele, asking, "Omar travels with you when you go on buying trips, right? Does that travel have to do with sales or just with buying hides and pelts and that sort of thing?"

"He told you about our buying trips? You've got it right. The travel is mostly to find suppliers of tanned leathers and furs. Omar comes with me because he has a good eye for what will sell. Also, I think he feels a bit claustrophobic in Pontedera. He's good company for me." Daniele went back through the door into the factory. Max followed.

Caterina could hear Daniele saying to Max, "I don't know what *Ispettore* Falcone meant about Miss Willingham. She's just a client. There would be no reason for her to travel with us on our business trips."

Max asked, "Are you and Omar always together when you travel? By that I mean, does he ever go off on his…"

"Max," Caterina interrupted, still watching Omar. "He didn't go into the office." She turned back to see a red Lancia back out of the parking lot. She saw Omar look at her before he pulled around to a dirt track behind the office building and sped away. Jamal and the *Ape* were nowhere in sight.

Danielle looked out the door. "Something must have come up."

"Where does that road go?" asked Caterina.

"Oh, it goes to my parents' house, on the road to Pisa. It's the back road to the factory from the family estate. Omar will probably be back soon. Otherwise he would have told us he was leaving. I'll try to get him on his *telefonino*." He pulled out his own cell phone.

Max pulled Caterina to the side. "Call Marco. See if he's at Omar's house. Ask him if the wife made any calls."

Without a word, Caterina pulled her phone out of her purse and pushed speed dial. "Marco, what …"

Marco interrupted, "I know what you're going to say. The idiot officer from Pontedera let her use the phone. He says she was crying to her husband. You better detain him now. We haven't found anything yet. I've just started on the basement *cantina*."

"Marco, he just drove out of here like he was test-driving a Ferrari. We haven't even served the warrant."

"Follow him. I'm sure I'll find the goods on him down there. It looks like there might be a fake wall. I've just …"

"The problem is you don't have *him*." Caterina snapped her phone shut.

"Mr. Pellione, I don't have time to explain," she said to Daniele, pulling out the search warrant. "This is a search warrant for these premises. You're coming with us. Max, we have to leave." She waved Tozzi over.

Max got in the back and Caterina pushed the sputtering Daniele in between them. "Tozzi, drive out to the Pontedera police on the road," she said, as the driver slammed her door.

When they stopped beside the police car, she handed Daniele over to one of the Pontedera officers and directed him to walk Mr. Pellione back to the office and stay with him. "Tell him he is in protective custody. *No phone calls.* Don't let him out of your sight. The rest of you follow us. We're heading to Pisa."

Tozzi put the car in gear, turning on the lights and siren. The Pontedera police kept pace.

"You're thinking he's gone to Elizabeth Willingham, right?" said Max.

"I screwed up by taunting him with their relationship. She's a loose end. The only people who can tie him to the other Cobra sites are Elizabeth and Daniele; we've got Daniele, but he'll probably keep covering for Omar because of the boyfriend, at least until he sees it's hopeless to keep the secret. Omar either has to get rid of Elizabeth or take her with him. For all we know, he may really love her."

"Doubtful."

"Also, Omar won't go home and risk detention. I'll bet his wife doesn't know what they might find at the house, if anything. And if I'm wrong, and he's gone home, Marco will take care of it. If I'm really wrong, and he's not going to Elizabeth's place, then we'll need to get a bulletin out for that red Lancia."

"I'll try to call Elizabeth." Caterina pulled out her notebook, thumbing through to find the page where she had noted the number.

Tozzi said over his shoulder, "Excuse me, *Ispettore* Falcone, Mr. Pellione's man brought you a box. He said it was a present from his boss."

"Where is it?"

"Here on the seat."

She looked over to see a box about the size of a shirt box on the passenger seat. Tozzi picked it up to pass it over the seat.

Max yelled, "Don't touch it. Stop the car. Get out."

"What?" Tozzi stepped on the brakes, laying rubber on the highway.

"It could be a bomb," answered Max.

"I'll throw it out." Caterina reached over the seat.

"No, don't touch it." Max pulled her arm back

Just then a cell phone rang.

"Get out now," Max yelled, opening his own door.

Caterina flung her door wide and dove into the dusty culvert beside the road. Max hurled his body out the opposite door. Guido Tozzi opened his door just as the bomb went off. The front passenger door and windshield blew out with a roar.

Chapter Forty-Nine

MOSCOW

He called."

"Who called?" Andrei Goncharov stopped pouring a packet of granular aspirin into the crystal tumbler of water. His eyes were still glassy from the vodka he had consumed with the new girl at the bordello he frequented. He made a note to tell the management to stock her room with scotch.

"The Arab." Oleg looked surprisingly fresh and well-pressed for a Monday morning. Andrei wondered if Kiki was following through with her threat of a vegetable juice diet for her husband.

He shook his head and regretted it. "He called? He never calls us."

Oleg raised his voice. "Think about it, you idiot. Yakov is dead. Who's he supposed to call?"

Andrei tore the corner off another packet, poured the powder in and stirred the liquid with a swizzle stick. "Why didn't he call me?" He drank it down with one gulp and grimaced.

"I guess he decided you had made such a mess of this that he needed someone he could count on. I'm the one who set up the first contract with Abdel Majib back in 1991. Those jobs went like silk, never a snag."

"It's not my fault he's made things so complicated. I didn't ask for that. I didn't tell him to blow up Yakov." Andrei sat back in his desk chair. "What does he want?"

"He needs a ride."

"A ride?"

"He's got to get out of the country."

"Where to?"

"Syria, I thought would be best. He's heading to the coast. I told him that I'm sending him a chopper and will arrange the rest."

"He's a liability."

"You think so?" Oleg's sarcasm made his brother's head pound.

"Get rid of him."

"Already been done."

Chapter Fifty

As Caterina pulled herself out of the ditch, she could see Max beating the flames out of the back of Guido's coat. The Pontedera police car caught up to them within seconds, screeching to a halt, as three officers leapt out.

Caterina grabbed one man, yelling, "Call for an ambulance." She turned to the other and ordered, "Get a search going for that car – a red Lancia Ypsilon. Pisa plates. Registered to Pellione. Tell them he is armed and dangerous."

She pulled out her phone and hit redial. "Marco, don't talk. Omar's on the run. He may be heading your way. Take Paola Pellione and her daughter into protective custody. Make the home a crime scene."

"Omar Pellione is the bomber," said Marco, his voice pitched high and tight.

"No shit, Marco. He just tried to blow us up."

"No, I mean he's the *Duomo* bomber. We found a workshop in the cantina of his house. It's a reinforced room behind a wall of wine racks. There must be ten or fifteen cell phones here, some nitro, and even C-4 explosives. Enough evidence to put him away."

"We have to *catch* him first, Marco. If he's not there yet, he's going somewhere else. I'm sending the Pontedera police to Elizabeth Willingham's place in Pisa. Max and I will go with them. I'll leave two officers with Tozzi. He needs an ambulance. Call the magistrate, will you, and update him."

"I was just going to do that when you called."

"Once you're done reporting, ask him to phone me."

Caterina directed one of the Pontedera officers to call for reinforcements and to wait with Tozzi for the ambulance. She got in the Pontedera police car with Max, the driver, and another officer.

"Omar didn't go home, so I'm still betting on Elizabeth Willingham's place," Caterina said before giving the driver directions to Piazza Vittoria in Pisa.

They arrived at the building to find the front door open and the apartment empty. Caterina asked a woman passing with a baby carriage, "Did you see a woman come out of this *palazzo*?"

"Just five minutes ago. A man in a red car stopped in front and a woman ran out and got in. They headed that way." She pointed down the road.

"Did it look like the lady was being forced to go?" Caterina asked.

"No, but she looked frightened, and he was yelling at her."

Caterina got back into the police car. "Let's assume they are heading north along the coast, the fastest way to get out of the country," she told the driver. She turned to the other officer. "Call Pisa dispatch and have them send a car south, just in case."

Max asked, "How soon can you get a helicopter up?"

"I don't know. I'll call the magistrate."

They sped up the on-ramp to the northbound lanes of *Autostade A12* going toward Forte dei Marmi. Caterina dialed the magistrate's cell phone. It was busy. She dialed his office phone and Patricia Benvenuti picked up. "Patricia, is the magistrate in his office?"

"Yes, he's talking on his private phone."

"Probably with Marco. Get his attention. Omar Pellione is on the run. I need to figure out how to get a search helicopter in the air. Also, I directed the Pontedera police to put out a bulletin on Pellione's car. I need to make sure that was done. The search area has to include the whole region, now."

She was giving the information to the administrative assistant when the officer in the front seat yelled, "Look at that." He pointed at a roiling plume of black smoke far ahead.

Traffic was slowing to a stop. Their car, lights flashing and siren blaring, sped along the shoulder of the road. The driver stopped behind a red Lancia with its front end engulfed in flames. In the inside lane a van was skewed at an angle to the car. A man was using a small fire extinguisher on the flames near the windshield. Another man was beating on the hood of the car with a sodden quilt.

Caterina and Max leapt out. The police officer thumbed the radio microphone to call for help, then grabbed a large fire extinguisher from the trunk of his car.

Smells of burning fuel mixed with the smell of burned flesh. The passenger door was open. Elizabeth Willingham hung out the right side of the car. Her left arm was missing, and half of her face.

Caterina took one look and vomited on the side of the road. She turned away, rushing back to the patrol car, taking in big gulps of air.

The Pontedera police officer looked over Max's shoulder into the other side of the Lancia. The door had been blown off. "The driver must have done it," said the policeman. "He's completely decimated. A murder/suicide... or the biggest mistake that guy ever made."

Max said nothing.

Caterina, shaky, but controlled, walked up behind him and looked over his shoulder. All that was left of the driver was two jean-clad legs and a part of his left hip. There was a black leather jacket stretched across the back seat. She turned away.

"Caterina," Max said, walking back to where she stood, her arms braced on the hood of the police car, her head bowed. "Do you think it would screw up the forensics if I snag the coat from the back seat of the car?"

She didn't look up. "No, go ahead. One thing we aren't short of, is evidence."

Omar's passport and identity card were in the pocket of the jacket.

"Maybe it was just an accident," mused Max. "Maybe Omar blew himself up by mistake, but I don't think so. A bomb-maker would be more careful. If he was carrying a bomb it would have some sort of safety feature."

"Who else could it be?" Caterina asked. She thought for a few seconds. *Could Omar have backtracked and sent Daniele? No, Daniele is in custody. There's no way Omar made the switch with him.* The question crossed her mind. *Did I actually see Jamal drive off in the* Ape?

She turned to the Pontedera officer and directed, "I want a crime scene team to take DNA samples of both victims and get them to a lab immediately, even before the bodies are moved. I need a positive confirmation that this is Omar Pellione." In a lower voice she said to Max, "I wouldn't put it past him to make a switch, though God knows, he didn't have much time."

"Change the bulletin. They're not looking for the car anymore. They're looking for the man. Put out a watch for him at airports and ports." Max started to pace, while Caterina told the Pontedera police officer to get her the commanding officer in Pisa.

"What about Jamal Majid?" Caterina was pacing, too. "This cousin from Lebanon. Jamal gave the package to Guido. Could we be looking at this completely the wrong way? Maybe *Jamal* is Cobra. We never focused on him. He would fit your description – itinerant, stateless, anonymous – the perfect assassin for hire."

"Call Marco. Have him talk to Omar's wife. You want the details on Jamal, how long he's been in Italy, whether he lives with them and has access to the cantina. Everything. I still think it's got to be Omar, so ask her if there's any place Omar might run to if he isn't trying to leave the country."

Caterina made the call. After Marco learned that the Lancia had exploded, he crowed, "The bastard blew himself up. He was in a hurry and made a mistake. We had him on the ropes. His wife told him we were searching the house. He took off. Got his girlfriend. He thought he was in the wind. I bet..."

Caterina interrupted, "Marco, don't celebrate too fast. Talk to the wife about the cousin, Jamal Majid. Maybe the *cantina* workshop is his. Also, ask her if there's anywhere that Jamal or Omar would use to hide. Get all of the details you can." Still arguing against any theory of a switch, Marco reluctantly agreed to question Paola Pellione.

Caterina spoke to the magistrate next, briefing him. He was on his way with Captain DeLuca to the police helicopter pad. "We are going to the Pellione home to see the laboratory," he told her, "but we'll swing by the highway site first. We'll be at your position in thirty minutes."

Marco called back. "The bomb squad is due to arrive any minute, so I have to be brief. His wife told me that they have a beach place south, in Castiglioncello – someone should check that out. She also said that Jamal has been in the country for the past six months – I bet his visa has expired – and has been living with them. She says he's a pig and not so smart. Jamal is either a great actor or he's not the bomber."

Chapter Fifty-One

Reinforcements are being sent from Florence, Pisa and Livorno. This is a massive manhunt." Magistrate Benigni was standing on the side of the A12 freeway talking to Caterina.

She nodded. "Until the DNA samples can be compared, we can't assume that Omar blew himself up. It's not Daniele – he's being held at the factory. But we haven't found Jamal Majid, yet, so my best guess is that he's the driver here. He and Omar were dressed the same – blue jeans, white shirts. I think Omar arranged to change vehicles with him and asked him to pick up Elizabeth Willingham."

Max Turner walked across the empty highway toward them, closing his phone and putting it in his jacket pocket. "I put in a call to my contact in Beirut. Omar's uncle and Jamal's father, Abdel Majid, is one of the prime bomb-makers for the Hezbollah."

"Why didn't we have this information before?" asked the magistrate.

"Good question. Caterina and I put together a list of info we needed about Omar Pellione. But when we learned about Yakov Petrov we concentrated on him. We only started collecting information on Pellione in the last twenty-four hours. When my contact passed all the family names to the Israelis an hour ago, he got the connection to Hezbollah."

"So Omar and Jamal, both, may have learned how to build bombs from Jamal's father," said Caterina. "But none of the Cobra bombs were used for political or religious purposes."

"I've got my source looking closer at the activities and history of the uncle," said Max. "Magistrate, have all the airports been put on alert?"

"We've sent men to the Florence and Pisa International airports. A notice went out to all of the private runways."

"If you don't need Max or me, sir, I think we should take a car down to the Pellione's beach house in Castiglioncello," said Caterina. "What if Omar met up with Jamal, and exchanged the *Ape* for the Lancia? If Omar gave his cousin a rigged cell phone, he probably used some excuse like 'They're monitoring our calls. Take this *telefonino* and I'll contact you, later.' Jamal would buy it."

"That makes more sense than the bomb-maker blowing himself up," Max agreed.

Caterina continued, "Omar will have to take the back roads. He won't be traveling too fast in that *Ape*."

The magistrate nodded. "Castiglioncello is the logical destination. You should be able to get there faster than he can. Take one of our cars and a driver and head that way. I'll get the exact directions from Paola Pellione or her father. I suppose we also need to know if they have a boat in the harbor at Castiglioncello." The magistrate waved over a Florence police officer from Captain DeLuca's staff to give him instructions.

Max turned back, as he and Caterina were walking toward the assigned car. "Magistrate, is there any way to find out if the Goncharov brothers have property along the coast? I seem to remember someone saying that they were developing a resort on the west coast. Omar may contact them for help extracting him from the country."

"I'll have Signora Benvenuti run a search and call Caterina on her cell phone," Magistrate Benigni said. "I'm also going to have the Livorno police send a car to the Pellione beach house, with instruction to stay back and observe until you get there."

"Be sure to tell them not to talk to Omar," Max warned. "We don't know if he has a gun, but he's shown himself to be very versatile with small bombs."

On the thirty-minute drive to Castiglioncello, Caterina received two calls – one giving the coordinates of the beach house, which their driver, Carmine Polli, typed into his GPS unit, and the other from Patricia Benvenuti. She told Caterina that the Goncharov brothers had a house and a private jet on the Isle of Elba. "Also, AG Holdings is building a resort at Orbetello, south of Grosetto."

"Elba is off the coast, but it's closer to Castiglioncello, than Orbetello," Caterina said to Max.

"I would probably focus on someplace they live, rather than a construction site. Can planes fly off of Elba? Did you say they had a jet there?"

"There is a small airport, serving mostly private planes," Caterina responded.

"Phone the magistrate and have him notify the authorities on Elba to check for any private plane activity connected to the Goncharovs."

Caterina made the call.

They arrived at the access road to the Pellione vacation house. A rustic, but renovated, two-story stone structure was visible from the coast highway.

"It was probably a *contadini* house on a farm when they bought it. Many were bought up as holiday homes. See the pine trees behind it? About a hundred meters through the trees, is the beach."

"Would a boat be able to take off from the beach?"

"It would be difficult. There's not usually a pier, so only a rowboat, kayak, or pontoon could get off the sand. It's very shallow for about ten meters off the shore. Kind of like the Atlantic coast in the States."

"There are the local *polizia*," said Officer Polli, pointing to a beige and white police car parked sideways, blocking the access road. He stopped their car beside the Livorno police. A short officer with a weightlifter's build got out and came over to Polli's window.

"State your business."

"I have *Ispettore* Falcone, representing *Magistrato* Benigni of Florence, here," answered Officer Polli.

Caterina spoke up, reading the nametag above his pocket, "Officer Pantoliano, thank you for your assistance. Is there anyone in the house?"

"We were told not to get too close, but Gaetano, here," he said, gesturing at the other officer still sitting in the Livorno car, "went around through the field and saw a car parked in back of the house."

"Did he get the plate number?"

"Of course. It's registered to Alberto Morandi of Pontedera."

"Who's he?" ask Polli.

"Don't you listen to the police band as you go?" asked Pantoliano, shaking his head. "Ten minutes ago a bulletin came over the radio to look for his car. Morandi stopped for a guy stranded with a stalled *Ape* on a back road outside of Pontedera. The guy asked to use Morandi's cell phone and while Morandi was looking at the *Ape's* motor, the guy took off in Morandi's car and with his cell phone. Since the thief had his phone, Morandi had to walk to the nearest farm. So is this the fugitive that blew up the car on A12? We heard about *that* on the radio, too."

"Probably. Good work Officer Pantoliano. Will you go get Gaetano?" She watched as the man walked away.

She turned to Max and spoke softly in English. "I'm in over my head here. What should we do? Hold tight for reinforcements? Go in and see if we can grab him? It's got to be Omar in there."

"It could also be Jamal. If no switch was made, Jamal still had the *Ape*. We only have Marco's assertion that Jamal is stupid."

"So what do we do?"

"We have to get a view of the other side of the house into the trees and the beach. Then I think we call for help and hold tight. This guy could have the house booby-trapped or he may have already taken off through the trees."

"Polli," Caterina said to the driver, "get on the radio to Captain DeLuca and Magistrate Benigni. Tell them that we need at least ten men from Pisa or Livorno to converge on this location immediately. Captain DeLuca and Magistrate Benigni should also fly here as soon as possible from the A12 location."

She and Max got out of the car to meet the two men walking toward them. Officer Pantoliano was with a short, skinny, ferret-faced man. "This is Gaetano Bruzzi," he said.

Caterina assumed a voice that she hoped sounded assured and in-command. "Okay, you two, we're going to take positions around the perimeter and wait for reinforcements."

Bruzzi and Pantoliano looked relieved.

Caterina pointed to the north side of the house. "Pantoliano, I want you to go into that field. Stay far enough out that you can see the house, but he can't get a shot at you, if he's got a gun. Bruzzi, I want you to do the same on the south side of the house. Polli will stay in the car and cover the access road. Pantoliano, leave the keys in your car in case Polli has to move it."

She turned to Max and was relieved to get a nod from him. "This is Max Turner, an FBI agent from the American Embassy. He and I will circle the house and get into the trees to watch the access to the beach."

Caterina and Max followed Gaetano Bruzzi out into a field of high new wheat that bordered the access road. They bent low, running between the rows to a point where she and Max left Bruzzi to stand watch as they continued into the trees. They went about fifty feet into the wide strip of pine trees and then turned parallel to the back of the house.

"What is that sound?" asked Caterina. A rumble could be heard behind them in the direction of the sea.

"Sounds like helicopter to me," said Max. "Could the magistrate and DeLuca have gotten down here that fast?"

"Only if they left before Polli called to say the stolen car was here and someone was in the house. But they would have come overland, not gone out over the water."

"Could a helicopter land on the beach? Is it wide enough?"

"Absolutely. But like I said, they wouldn't have come in east from the sea. They would come south and land on the road out in front. Are you thinking they're trying not to let Cobra know they're coming?"

"No, I'm thinking that this bird is coming for the bomber. That he ordered it up to get himself out of here." Max looked around the dense woods.

They ran through the trees to the shore. The roar of the helicopter hit them full force as they came out of the trees. Caterina couldn't tell whether it was landing or taking off because of the sand storm kicked up by the rotors. Max obviously knew better. He pulled out a gun and shot at the aircraft.

A huge explosion rent the air. At first, Caterina thought the helicopter had exploded, but it was speeding into the distance.

"That was the house," said Max. "I hope neither of the other two tried to force the doors."

Caterina thumbed her phone. "Polli, what happened?"

"*Ispettore*, the ground level room on the north side blew out. The whole place is on fire."

"Are you three all right?"

"Yes, *Ispettore*."

"Call the fire services. Stay well back." She rang off, only to hit another speed dial number. While she waited for an answer, she turned to Max.

"Was Omar on the helicopter?" she asked.

"I couldn't tell. The sand was blowing too much. I'd bet money on it for sure. He blew up the house to delay us going to the beach. He probably went out the back door and into the woods when the Livorno cops drove up." Max was pacing back and forth in front of Caterina as she focused on her cell phone. "You've got to track that chopper."

"I'm already on it." Her call rang through and her boss answered. "Magistrate we think the suspect is on a helicopter that just took off from the beach west of the Pellione beach house," she reported. "Can you get someone to follow him in the air?"

The magistrate yelled over the noise of the police helicopter, "We are still too far out. I'll request a Coast Guard plane to fly out from Livorno. Do you have any idea where he is going?"

"My best guess is Elba. The Goncharov brothers have a house there. I'm guessing the helicopter is one of theirs or from a service they use. Once on Elba, he could get their private jet to anywhere."

"I've already contacted Elba to get the *polizia* and *carabinieri* out to the airport. I'll have them get a helicopter up, too. Don't worry. We've got him if he's headed to the island."

"We need a crime scene squad at the beach house. A bomb just destroyed the house. We don't know if anyone was inside. From what Polli said, I don't expect anyone lived through the explosion."

"Stay and wait for reinforcements," the magistrate ordered.

Caterina, Max, and Gaetano Bruzzi ran back through the trees to the demolished house. The sound of many sirens rent the air. When they emerged from the trees, they saw a line of five patrol cars from Livorno pull up, followed by a fire truck, a red fire department van, and a police car from Casteligoncello. Officer Polli had cleared the access road. The police pulled into the fields and the fire truck drove up to the house.

One end of the house was demolished, leaving a gaping hole, two stories high. The other end was still burning. Black smoke roiled into the air.

"Scared me shitless," exclaimed Pantoliano. "I was just about to go over and look through the back window to see if anyone was inside. It could have been me blown out into the field."

"Why did you think to approach the house?" asked Caterina.

"I thought I saw something move inside."

"Did you hear anyone? Do you think there is someone in there now?"

"I was probably imaging it," Pantoliano said shaking his head. "I never heard a thing, except the blast." He waved an arm at the firemen hosing down the smoldering rubble. "Anyone in there is dead for certain, anyway."

Twenty minutes later, the magistrate and Captain DeLuca landed, just outside the access road on the two-lane coast highway. They jumped down and ran, bent over under the blades, to meet Caterina and Max.

The Captain's phone rang. He listened for a minute; then snapped it shut, seemingly without saying anything. He turned to Magistrate Benigni. "The Coast Guard just called. They have the helicopter under observation. It's about ten minutes from landing on Elba. They haven't been able to contact the pilot and they say that they can't see a passenger."

Max was listening and said, "In that kind of chopper there is a blind space in back where you usually put luggage. I bet he's back there out of view. He must think you will take a shot at him."

"You don't think he can pilot a helicopter, do you?" asked the magistrate. "Maybe he overpowered the pilot and he's manning the craft himself. That's why no one is answering the hail."

"From what Turner told us, we have no reason to believe he's ever been in a helicopter before," Captain DeLuca snorted. "It's more likely he has a gun on the pilot. The helicopter is one from a service that is licensed to operate off of Elba. We also know that the Goncharov jet was being fueled when the Elba police arrived. They've taken the pilot into custody and cordoned off the plane."

"Are any of the Goncharovs on Elba at the moment?" asked Caterina.

"No, the pilot told the Elba police that the orders came from Moscow. He was supposed to meet the helicopter and take off for Syria."

"Not Lebanon?"

"Lebanon has an extradition treaty with Italy. Syria doesn't."

Captain DeLuca's aide ran up, carrying a cell phone, "Sir, you should hear this."

"DeLuca, *dimmi*," he barked. He listened for a minute, growing alarmingly red under his tan.

He closed the phone and said in a tight voice, "The helicopter blew up on approach to Elba."

The magistrate turned to Max and Caterina, "Are you sure you didn't see him on the beach?"

Max answered, "Sir, the beach is very narrow. The helo was taking off when we arrived. It was certainly possible for him to run up to the pilot, hand over a cell phone and tell the pilot to meet him at another time when he called. The phone could have been one of his small bombs, set to explode to distract us a second— or I should say, a *third* time, if we count both the Lancia and the house as diversions. I should have thought of that possibility. I was just so angry that we didn't catch the chopper that I didn't think of searching the beach."

Captain DeLuca was calling together his men. "Down to the beach. You three go south, you three go north. Detain anyone you find."

"Sir, stop," said the magistrate. "Tell them not to go on the sand, to stay in the trees. We need a trained investigator to follow the prints, if there are any of them."

"You're right, Benigni. Hear that, men? Stay in the woods. Move quickly. He's got a half hour head start."

Caterina put her hand on the magistrate's arm, "Sir, there is another possibility."

"What is that?"

"What if the Goncharov brothers blew up the helicopter to get rid of Cobra. He's the only one who could tie them to the bombings."

The magistrate shook his head. "Caterina, that's very unlikely. They hired *him* to make the bombs. We have no evidence that they could put something like that together in one or two hours."

"I suppose so, sir. I just think we should talk to the helicopter service and see if anything was delivered to the pilot before he left Elba. That is – if there someone to talk to – if the pilot wasn't working alone."

"We are certainly going to investigate everything having to do with today's sorry business – the helicopter, the plane, the freeway explosion, the search of Omar's house, and the search of Daniele Pellione's apartment. It seems we can't catch a break. There is going to be a lot of finger-pointing, so get ready for it."

Max turned to Caterina, "Do you think…"

Caterina's phone rang. She held up a finger to Max as she looked at the screen. She thought it would be Patricia Benvenuti or her mother calling, but the screen displayed a number she didn't recognize. "Pronto?"

"*La bella ispettore*," said Omar Pellione.

Chapter Fifty-Two

Caterina grabbed the magistrate's arm and mouthed "Omar" pointing at the phone.

"Mr. Pellione," she said as she watched her boss call to have the phone call traced. "We seem to have missed you."

Captain De Lucca paced back and forth in front of her. Max stood like a statue.

"Disappointing, I'm sure," Omar responded. "But you were close. Too close. Time to make you move back."

"What do you mean?" Caterina looked around to see what could possibly blow up next.

"I mean that I need you to stop looking for me. I'm going to have enough trouble with the Goncharovs."

Max wrote "Speaker phone?" on a business card taken from his pocket. Caterina shrugged. She had never figured out how to use that that application without hanging up on the caller. She held the phone so he could listen in.

At the same time she said, "Your employers?"

"'Clients for services rendered' would be a better way to put it," said Omar. "Past services, not future. Go after them."

"Why don't you help us with that," Caterina said, trying to drag the call out.

"No time. Sorry, *bella donna*, I can't enjoy the pleasure of a longer chat with you. I just wanted to tell you how sorry I was not to be able to personally fit you for that leather jacket we discussed. Remember?"

Jacket? Caterina shook her head to clear it. "Of course, but if you will just tell me where to meet you, I would love to see the coat."

Captain De Lucca's face went an alarming color of red as he paced in front of Caterina and Max. The Legat twirled a finger, urging Caterina to talk longer.

"Unfortunately, and I am sure the American, Mr. Turner, who must be listening, would agree; no one will ever see you in that jacket."

Max took the phone. "Why is that Omar?"

"Because in forty-five minutes exactly, the jacket — red with black trim — of the finest baby goat skin and best *Pellione* design, will be no more. Along with many others."

"What are you trying to say, Mr. Jaboor?"

There were a few seconds of silence. "You and the *bella ispettore* have a choice, Mr. Turner. Find me or find the jacket." Omar hung up.

"Find him or find the jacket," muttered Max, looking at the phone. He looked at his watch.

Captain De Lucca shouted at Caterina. "What does he mean 'find the jacket'?"

"Last week he mentioned a jacket…" Caterina's voice trailed off as she looked at Magistrate Benigni, who was still talking on his phone.

He closed the screen. "They could only pin the call to an area south of us near the coast. So why did he call you, and what did he say?"

Caterina started again. "Something about a coat. He's trying to distract us. I gave him my phone number the first day we met at the *Persephone* leather shop in Florence."

Max shook his head. "It's not just a distraction. He's giving us a choice to find him or do something else. Find the coat in forty-five minutes."

Captain De Lucca ripped the hat off his head and threw it on the ground. "Why forty-five minutes? Why a coat? Why did he call *her*?" He jabbed a finger at Caterina.

Max handed Caterina her phone. "It's a deadline. He said the coat 'and many more' would be gone in forty-five minutes." He looked back and forth between the magistrate and the captain. "When Omar Jaboor 'makes things gone' he blows them up."

Benigni picked up De Lucca's hat. "It's a bomb. There is another bomb."

"At the Pellione leather factory in Pontedera?" Caterina asked.

Max shook his head. "He also said 'and hundreds of others.' I don't remember seeing that many coats at the factory."

The magistrate asked, "Did he mean other coats or 'others'? Like *people*?"

Caterina thought of the store in Florence jammed with coats, jackets, and pants on three levels of hangers, and a cantina downstairs where more were stored. "There are hundreds in the *Persephone* store on the Lungarno. And many more people. It's only half a block from the Uffizi."

"But when would he have set that up? He didn't know we were coming for him," said the magistrate.

"He plans ahead," said Max at the same time Caterina said, "It's the cantina."

"What cantina?" asked Captain De Lucca. "The one they found in Pontedera?"

"There is a cantina under the shop on the Lungarno," explained Caterina. "He used the cantina in his home to hide his bomb-making activity. If the bomb is in the cantina in Florence, and it goes off, it might blow a hole in the brick wall that forms the side of the Arno. That area around the Uffizi is riddled with tunnels. Who knows how much force is needed for them to collapse?"

The four of them turned as one and started running for the helicopter. In less than a minute they were in the air.

"Check your phone, Caterina," Max said as he buckled his seat belt. "We should track the time from the call. I put it at forty-two minutes left from my watch."

"How long will it take to get to the center of Florence," Captain De Lucca asked the pilot.

"Thirty to thirty-five minutes if there are no head winds."

De Lucca was in the front seat yelling into his head set, instructing the bomb squad to send men to *Persephone Pelle*. His next call was to his chief of staff, to begin an evacuation of the buildings around the shop, especially the apartments above the store. He ordered the closing of the nearby Galileo Museum and the rowing club under the Uffizi.

"Thank God, the Uffizi is closed on Monday," the magistrate said.

De Lucca turned to the pilot. "Do you think you can land on the lawn of the rowing club or the boat ramp that goes down to the Arno from the Lungarno?" The pilot nodded in the affirmative.

Caterina stared at her phone. In the center of the screen, the timer app counted away the minutes.

The helicopter flew at top speed, and there was a tail wind; thirty minutes after leaving the beach house it set down on concrete slab next to the wooden dock in the Arno River. Captain De Lucca's chief of staff ran to open the door.

As they ran up the short entry road to the rowing club, Caterina could see members of the *polizia* spaced along the street named "Lungarno Generale Diaz." Traffic had been stopped all along the river front. *Vigili* were blocking pedestrians west of the Uffizi and north at the end of Via de' Castellani.

In the center of Piazza dei Giudici, in front of the Galileo Museum, a metal box with reinforced walls, the size of a municipal trash dumpster, had been placed inside a cargo container affixed to a trailer behind an armored van. A crowd of uniformed police from various services clustered at the west end of the piazza. A man in the padded protective gear and mask of the bomb squad stood outside the door of Persephone Pelle.

"Captain, we have visuals in the store," said the head of the bomb squad, dressed in a gray-blue jumpsuit, with the name "Fontana" sewn over his breast pocket. "We're going to let them look for ten more minutes, but then I have to pull them out." He led them to the side of the van where a lap top showed the video from inside the store.

"It's a mess inside. There must be at least a thousand coats, bags, purses, pants, jackets. Pockets everywhere. Impossible to check every one." said Fontana

Caterina pushed to the front of the officers and crouched down. The split screen showed both the cantina and the store. She heard Max call from the back of the crowd, "Remember, Caterina, he said it was red with black trim."

"Have them concentrate on only short jackets in red leather with a small black trim," she said. The bomb squad leader repeated the instructions.

"Also, he wouldn't have left it in the shop. It's got to be in the cantina, where no one would move the jacket to try it on or to sell it."

"Peruzzi, head down to the cantina and help Bartolini. Concentrate on the red jackets."

One side of the split screen showed the rough stone steps down to the cantina. The sound of both men breathing came through the speaker.

A voice came from the computer. "There must be twenty red jackets on this rack." Caterina could see where his lighted helmet-mounted camera pointed.

"Pat them down," said their boss. "Gently."

"Nothing here."

The other side of the screen scanned the ceiling and walls of the cantina. A flash of red high on the wall caught Caterina's eye. "Wait," she yelled. "What's that. To the right in the back. Up. On that hook. Check that."

Both screens were focused on the same spot. A red jacket with black trim hung on short rack sticking out of the wall far back in depths of the cantina. Two padded gloves grasped the patch packets.

"There's something here. Hard. Square."

"Wrap it in the coat and get out of there. Time's up," ordered Fontana.

Two figures lumbered out of the store, one carrying a roll of red leather, which he placed inside the metal box before he sealed it and then closed the back of the cargo container. Caterina and the others rushed to the edge of the piazza.

The computer screen went black and then came up green as the camera inside the box was turned on. Caterina could see the mass of crumpled leather at the bottom of the box.

Minutes went by. Captain de Lucca started to swear.

"Could we have been wr...?" Caterina turned to Max and almost missed the flash of light on the screen that destroyed the camera. The roar of the explosion emerged as the door of the cargo container blew open. The reinforced box had fractured, but held its form.

Chapter Fifty-Three

Mid-day Tuesday, less than twenty-four hours after the abortive attempt to capture Cobra, Max walked into Caterina's office, and said, "Get your coat on. The magistrate says that you can come with me."

Caterina had been reading the joint report from Captain DeLuca's team and the Livorno *polizia*. The investigation on the disappearance of the suspect, Omar Jaboor Pellione, was inconclusive. On the beach, there appeared to be footprints, most swept away by the draft of the rotors, that led to the touch down site and away. In the woods, no traces could be found of suspect's alleged escape.

On Elba, the mechanic for the helicopter service reported that a shoebox-sized package had been delivered to the pilot by one of the island delivery services. Was it money for Omar or an explosive device? The mechanic hadn't handled the box so he couldn't describe it further. The delivery service denied ever getting a commission to deliver a package to the helicopter pad.

The pilot of the Goncharovs' private jet didn't know whom he was flying to Syria. "Just someone arriving on Elba by helicopter," he told police.

In the rubble of the Pellione vacation house, the police found a box of unregistered cell phones and some loose wires, but no explosive material aside from the remnants of the bomb that had torn the building apart.

"Where are we going?" Caterina asked, grabbing her notebook and purse as well as her jacket.

"The airport," Max said, running ahead of her and down the stairs to a waiting police car.

Their driver turned on the lights and siren so Caterina had to yell, "Where are we *really* going, Max? Don't make me drag it out of you bit by bit." She buckled her seat belt as they flew around the corner onto the *vialle*.

"Remember when you said, 'I wonder if Stefanya knows who killed her fiancé?'"

"After Señor Potero called you with the info about Alberto Fernandez."

"Correct." Max nodded. "We are on our way to Barcelona to ask her that very question."

"*What?*" Caterina yelled causing the driver to swerve.

"I kept thinking about your question. Last evening, I asked Zoë Cruz, Legat at the U.S. Embassy in Madrid, to have the folks in Barcelona find Stefanya Goncharov. Turns out she is still at the university there. This morning, Eduardo Potero accompanied Agent Cruz to Stefanya's apartment. They are all waiting for us at the consulate."

"Why me?"

"Your boss demanded that Italy be represented at the questioning. I argued that Stefanya might open up to a woman closer to her age. Captain DeLuca gave you the nod."

A small, U.S. Air Force jet was waiting on the tarmac at the Florence airport. After they were airborne, Caterina turned to Max.

"A copy of the DNA analysis from Omar Jaboor's cheek swab was delivered to me this morning."

"Better late than never. Let me guess. He didn't strangle Irina."

She nodded. "I had the lab..."

Max interrupted, "Actually, the test will be invaluable in the future when he turns up again."

"I had the lab," she repeated, "compare it to the DNA sample from the driver in Omar's Lancia."

"That wasn't Omar either, right?"

"No. But we knew that already. So I had them expedite the test of the sample from the driver against the blood under Irina's nails — and got a match."

Max looked confused for a few seconds and then his brow cleared. "Cousin Jamal."

"That's what I think," Caterina responded. "Omar ordered him to kill Irina. Then Omar had Jamal pick up Elizabeth and he blew them both away on the highway. I asked the technician to coordinate with the investigators who gathered evidence from the bedroom where Jamal spent six months as Omar's guest. He said it would be a few days before the results would be available."

"Good to get confirmation."

"Once I have the proof that it was Jamal who killed Irina, I think we can safely say that Omar recruited Irina to get Bill Barton into position for the Easter bomb."

"That still doesn't get us Andrei Goncharov. Omar's statement on the phone about having 'enough trouble with the Goncharovs' isn't going to convince the powers-that-be in Moscow to act. With Omar on the run and Yakov dead, we only have Stefanya as a potential path to her brothers."

An hour later, Caterina and Max were ushered into a comfortable sitting room in the U.S. Consulate in Barcelona. Waiting for them was Señor Potero, Zoë Cruz, and a tall, young woman with long, blonde hair and gray eyes, Stefanya Goncharov. Legat Cruz made the introductions and said the interview would be conducted in English, the only language common to all of the participants.

"I've explained to Miss Goncharov that this is just an informational meeting. Mr. Turner and Ms. Falcone will be doing most of the talking. She is free to leave at any time."

It turned out that Stefanya hadn't known. She'd thought that the explosion in the museum that killed her fiancé was an ETA bomb, just like her brothers and Cobra wanted her to think. Caterina laid out the evidence for her with Eduardo Potero's input and supporting documents.

Stefanya wasn't completely convinced until Max followed up with the evidence they had collected on Yakov Petrov's travels and the bombs that followed him. Stefanya knew Yakov Petrov too well, it seemed. He had been her bodyguard.

"He tried to persuade me to have sex with him the same weekend Alberto was killed. He's an animal and an imbecile."

"A dead imbecile," Caterina said. She described how Yakov Petrov died. "He had a manual containing instructions for making a bomb."

"He said he would make himself indispensable to my brothers," Stefanya said, describing Yakov's hubris in greater detail. According to her, he couldn't keep his mouth shut. He thought it was all in the family; that she knew of her brothers' brutal business practices. Yakov wanted to impress her, so he claimed that he was in on all of the assassinations. "I didn't know whether to believe him. I couldn't tell if these were the fantasies of a sick mind, or if my brothers had really done business this way."

Max provided details of dates and locations from Yakov's travel itineraries and passport. Stefanya said that Yakov described himself as the "advance man" for the bomb-maker. He would be in place a week or so before "the Arab" arrived. He would recruit the girl who would act as the lure. He was tasked with getting any necessary equipment and scoping out the site. After each bomb did its job, Stefanya claimed that he told her he was required to report back to her brothers, claiming that they didn't trust "the Arab."

"He boasted that soon he would do it all and cut out the 'Arab,'" Stefanya finished. "That arrogant imbecile."

After consulting with Eduardo Potero, Max brought in the U.S. General Consul, who formally offered Stefanya asylum in the U.S. in exchange for providing evidence against her brothers. She accepted.

Chapter Fifty-Four

Did Yakov recruit Irina?" Caterina asked Max that evening over dinner at Osteria Guido. "I assumed Omar was in charge of everything for the actual Easter bomb, but did he bring Irina into the plot?"

Max was leaving for Rome in a few hours and then heading to the U.S. for Stefanya's full debriefing the next day.

"You are probably right," Max responded. "We don't think Yakov enlisted Irina. Either Omar or Jamal took care of that job."

"Probably Jamal, since he was able to get her up to Forte Belvedere the night he strangled her," said Caterina, taking another sip of wine. "She was expecting a payment of a lot of money. At least that is what she told Veronique."

"The payment for placing Bill Barton in front of the cathedral."

"Or for keeping her mouth shut once she survived the blast."

"It's too bad Yakov kept calling the bomb-maker 'the Arab' and never actually identified Omar Jaboor by name to Stefanya."

"It seems there may have been two Cobras," Max said, finishing off the last of the fried artichokes from a small plate on the table.

"*What?*" Caterina asked. "*Mio Dio,* why would you think there are *two?*"

"After we left, Stefanya told Zoë that Yakov described an older man who was injured by one of his own bombs after he had worked for the Oleg Goncharov for a few years. We think it was Abdel Majid, Omar's uncle."

"Jamal's father?"

"Right. He probably worked for Oleg prior to his rise in the oil industry, during his arms-dealing days."

"Where does Omar fit in this scenario?"

"Majid was injured about six years ago, just before the Jakarta incident. He most likely groomed Omar to take his place in the Goncharov enforcement business."

Caterina nodded. "Omar left Lebanon. His mother's Italian citizenship would get him a visa to Italy easily. And once he married Paola Pellione and changed his name and got citizenship, he could travel from here to almost any country." She took a sip of wine. "So why was Yakov killed at the Duomo?"

"Remember, he bragged to Stefanya that he was going to take over the whole strong-arm operation, make and set the bombs, and become indispensable to her brothers?"

"Do you think Omar meant to kill him?"

"I wouldn't be surprised. Remember this was a much bigger bomb than any of the previous ones. Yakov was tasked with the job of confirming the kill, so he placed himself close enough to see Bill Barton."

"And Omar didn't warn him about the power of this blast."

Max nodded. "With both Yakov and Irina out of the way, he probably thought there was no way to tie him to the bomb. But whether it was because she was smart or just lucky, Irina didn't die in the explosion." He gave a silent salute with his wine glass. "When you started asking questions about Irina, how was Omar to know that you were just looking for a way to contact Bill Barton's parents, and that led you to him?"

"So Omar and Jamal agreed Irina had to go. Jamal got the job. Omar doesn't kill up close." Caterina took a sip of her wine.

Max nodded. "Once you started investigating Irina's murder and talking to Elizabeth Willingham, Omar knew he had to get rid of Jamal and Elizabeth as well. With them dead, he really didn't have any witnesses, except the Goncharov brothers, and they are as deep in this as he is."

"Are the Goncharov brothers going to prison?" Caterina picked up the last of the *crostini*, popping it into her mouth.

"Perhaps. Bringing the powerful to justice in Russia can be tricky. But both the Italian and American governments are motivated to take this to the highest level; therefore, there is some hope for a satisfactory resolution. However, I'm willing to bet the Goncharovs will never use Cobra to facilitate their business deals again. And they have a strong incentive to get rid of him permanently. There may not be much satisfaction in that for us, but it's something."

"So you think he's still out there?"

"Probably, but I think he's long-gone from Italy. He's not going to be your worry." Max leaned over and touched his wine glass to her glass. "You uncovered the killer, now it's our job to take it from here."

"*Attenzione tutte due!* Make room for my *spaghetti con vongole e cozze incredibile.*" Caterina's father placed two huge steaming bowls, redolent of clams, mussels and garlic, in front of them.

THE AUTHOR

Five years used to be Ann Reavis' attention span for any career. She's been a lawyer, a nurse, a presidential appointee in a federal agency, a tour guide and a freelance writer. She's lived in New Mexico, Texas, California (San Francisco Bay Area), Michigan and Washington, DC. Then she broke the pattern when she spent fifteen years in Florence, Italy, learning to be Italian. She published *Italian Food Rules* and *Italian Life Rules* to celebrate the experience. For now, she has settled back into life in Washington, DC, where she has turned her hand to mysteries and thrillers set in Florence and Tuscany.

Made in United States
Troutdale, OR
08/13/2023

12063668R00300